INVISIBLE SON

ALSO BY KIM JOHNSON

This Is My America

INVISIBLE SON

KIM JOHNSON

Random House 🏠 New York

Text copyright © 2023 by Kim Johnson
Jacket art copyright © 2023 by Chuck Styles
Interior art used under license from Shutterstock.com

Visit us on the Web! GetUnderlined.com

Educators and librarians, for a variety of teaching tools, visit us at RHTeachersLibrarians.com

Library of Congress Cataloging-in-Publication Data
Names: Johnson, Kim, author.
Title: Invisible son / Kim Johnson.
Description: First edition. | New York: Random House, 2023. | Audience: Ages 14 and up | Summary: After spending two months in a juvenile detention center for a crime he did not commit, seventeen-year-old Andre Jackson returns home and tries to adapt to a Covid-19 world and find his missing best friend.
Identifiers: LCCN 2022026158 (print) | LCCN 2022026159 (ebook) | ISBN 978-0-593-48210-0 (trade) | ISBN 978-0-593-48211-7 (lib. bdg.) | ISBN 978-0-593-48212-4 (ebook)
Subjects: CYAC: Missing persons—Fiction. | Race relations—Fiction. | African Americans—Fiction. | LCGFT: Novels.
Classification: LCC PZ7.1.J623 In 2023 (print) | LCC PZ7.1.J623 (ebook) | DDC [Fic]—dc23

The text of this book is set in 11.25-point Adobe Garamond Pro.
Interior design by Michelle Crowe

Printed in the United States of America
10 9 8 7 6 5 4 3 2 1
First Edition

To those who lost loved ones and missed milestones
To those who bring beauty, love, and joy to others
To those fighting for justice
To Dad, 1930–2021

Contents

DON'T SPEAK

February 27, 2020

I live in the whitest big city on the Blackest block. Simultaneously seen and unseen. I used to hate the erasure. But now, well, now I don't mind if I stay hidden. Especially since MacLaren Youth Correctional Facility is in my literal rearview. But the longer we idle in Portland traffic, the more reality sinks in that that's not how any of this works.

Marcus tries to bury this truth with conversations on moving forward. On possibilities. But it will be as hard to shake the strike against me as it is for the windshield wipers to win their battle against this torrential downpour.

Marcus's and my coexistence in this car proves that fact. There will always be somebody to check me. To explain myself to. To keep at a distance. Which makes *who* I roll with matter more than ever. And I don't mean my boy Boogie, who knows I'm more likely to be up late reading Octavia Butler or scouring through my collection of Black Panther comics than be hanging out. I mean my other so-called friends. Correction, white friends who've been known to mouth off to an officer without fear. Who don't think twice about trying to be anything they want.

Meanwhile, I'm not trying to be nothing at all.

Marcus hands me coffee he picked up from the first drive-thru after we left the facility. Coffee is nasty. My stomach can't take it, but I also can't say no to him. I'm so close to semi-freedom—I'm not taking any chances. Not today.

"Dre, how you really feeling about all this?" Marcus adjusts his mirror like he'll see better.

"All right." What am I supposed to say? Living the dream riding with my probation officer? Can't wait to get home . . . so I can still be under surveillance? I know I'm wallowing in my situation, which isn't like me. I'm the type to kick my feet and claw my way above water—even if it's only with words. But staying silent seems like the best way to just get home.

Besides, he's asked this *same* question fifty-eleven times. He wants something deeper 'cause he takes my silence as not caring. But he's wrong. I do care. My life felt like it was about to be over until I got community monitoring. But even without more juvie time, I'm still twisted inside with all types of feelings. Like how I got caught up in the first place. And how bad I wanna roll down the window and let the rain drench me as I yell out, *I'm free. It's a wrap. Dunzo.* Then swipe my hand below my chin with a cocky grin. But that's not the kind of care Marcus wants.

"That's all I get? All right?" Marcus sighs, giving me a once-over.

"You hit the jackpot, Dre. The sooner you realize it, the better. Use your mind." Marcus taps his temple like he just dropped some knowledge.

"Yeah, okay." I bounce my right foot, fighting the urge to scratch at my ankle.

Don't get me wrong, Marcus is supposedly one of the *good ones*. And I came up having a Black juvenile counselor who is more likely to see me as a person than a problem. That's not how it always goes. Inside, the guys talked about all the power trips from probation counselors who were just waiting for you to fail. The fact mine's Black *and* used to be a teacher, I hit the lottery. No question. But this doesn't change that I have no choice in our situation. He says jump and I gotta say how high.

"You're close to putting this all behind you now," Marcus says. "Just lay low. Focus on school."

I chew on the corner of my lip, holding back a response. Holding back anger to stay numb.

"Come on." He nudges me. "I know you're excited to be going home."

I give a weak nod.

His gaze studies me before he speaks. "Not feeling moving in with your grandparents?"

"I'm fine with it." I've practically lived with my grandparents my whole life back and forth between their house and apartments in the 100s blocks. So, when I think about home, it's always the people, not the place. But this time I have to face them knowing they'll look at me different. And I'm afraid of what they'll see. There's no way to go back to what was. I'm Dre now—the Andre they knew is gone.

"I need details if this is gonna work, son. Think of me like family. You can even call me Uncle Marcus. Some kids I work with do."

"I'll stick with Marcus," I deadpan, all business between us.

He's saying this because I treat him like the probation officer he is, and he's offended at any insinuation of law enforcement. He's more *police-adjacent,* he likes to say. But his actual title is juvenile court counselor, and let's be real, it's the same thing.

As much as everybody who works for Multnomah County Juvenile Justice been calling me son. Kid. Young man. Like we're kin. I know the truth: it's their J.O.B. They're following some guidebook on how to make connections. Before I was assigned to Marcus, calling me son sure didn't stop the first juvenile court counselor from recommending I get an ankle monitor even though the judge wasn't pushing for that during sentencing.

Here's the thing, I appreciate that Marcus cares, but we're not family. Dad wouldn't like it anyway. Not when Marcus is part of the system designed to lock me up in the first place.

Marcus stares, again. I avoid his inspection by sipping the nasty coffee 'cause I don't wanna be in my feelings. Things have changed. I need to let the night that led me here go, as hard as that may be.

Once I catch sight of the Coliseum and Lloyd Center, my body loosens up. We're getting closer to home.

GPS gives directions, but Marcus navigates the streets like he knows them well. I hold back from asking if he's from my neighborhood. I'd rather believe Marcus was just an old-school dude from Black Portland watching out for me. Not somebody who's just got a lot of Black and brown kids he calls son.

Marcus veers off route, cutting through the good Popeyes parking lot. *Damn I'd love me some Popeyes right about now.* I sip more coffee to smack the flavor of butter biscuits and spicy chicken sandwiches out my mouth.

"I'll go over everything with your family, then follow up with your parents. The paperwork said your mom's a nurse at a hospital?"

"At Legacy Emanuel." He knows this, but I play along. "Won't be home until five a.m., though."

We get closer to the edge of my grandparents' neighborhood down Martin Luther King Jr. Boulevard, near my dad's bookstore. Malcolm's Bookshop is tucked between a coffee shop and Salt and Straw ice cream, which has a line down the street that blocks the bookstore's entrance.

I sit up to catch a glimpse of my dad as the open sign flashes in the window, but all I see is the faded Black History Month sign he drags out every year. Books on Martin Luther King Jr. and Rosa Parks are front and center to catch people's attention. The rest of the display is filled with writers I've known my whole life—Amiri Baraka, Gwendolyn Brooks, Ralph Ellison, and Nikki Giovanni—and new releases.

Dad's gotta be on cloud nine because it's a leap year, which gives him one extra day for his best sales month. The month he always reminds me is still the shortest of the year.

I can't say for sure it's him when someone passes the window. The truth is, I don't know if I want it to be him. Because if it is, that means he's not waiting at home for me. If it isn't, then I'll have to pretend not to see the disappointment behind his smile when Marcus goes over the program rules.

When the light turns green, I distract my brain with sights of the old and new.

"Things keep changing," I say, to no one.

I've been gone two months, but it feels like a lifetime. The vibe's all different. Like it's a dream and I only got part of the details right. And even though I know this view, the colors seem wrong. Red doors and trims. Stakes lodged in grass with security signs. Little things I want to remember from the past to anchor me, to let me know I still belong, but it's all just out of reach.

"Yeah. Blink of an eye. But it ain't so bad," Marcus says. "I mean . . . I'm lucky, I guess. My parents passed their place down to me. My family, though, they tried to get me to cash out, but that won't ever be me. We gotta keep ours. Get that generational wealth."

I take stock of Marcus, ready to connect to him on some other level. Because I feel all that, the way my grandparents are trying to hold on here. Not let a white rich family push them to cash out on the only place they were allowed to make a home in the first place. But the tightness of plastic around my ankle stops me from responding.

Marcus turns down my grandparents' block—filled with manicured lawns and renovated solar roofs. Stoops fixed up, but empty of people on the porch.

"Yeah, this is nice, but . . ."

"Too manufactured."

"Something like that," I mumble.

Marcus points. "That their house?"

"Yeah, that's it."

Relief washes over me that my grandparents' house looks the same, even with fresh paint. Mom said Dad took a whole month to do it. And it looked good, but she wasn't going to tell him because he complained about his back the entire time. I laughed, but inside couldn't help but worry these changes meant my grandparents were next to leave the neighborhood.

Two lanky white kids dash across the street and Marcus slams his brakes, causing a puddle to splash around us. Marcus honks his horn before pulling into my grandparents' driveway. Brian Whitaker flashes an apologetic grin before swiping his blond hair out of his eyes. Like always, he's unfazed even though he was milliseconds away from catastrophe. Lockstep, Gavin Davis smiles and waves. Then he takes off down the street. Seeing me is no big deal, it's as if I never left. Nothing bad ever happens to Gavin, no matter what he does.

"Damn. That was close," Marcus says.

I do a double take when I see Grandma Jackson waiting on the porch. She clasps her hands together when she sees me and I let out a loose smile, one I've been holding on tight to since New Year's Day. Grandpa waits in the doorway wearing his faded green Vietnam Vet hat, patient as usual.

I grab my crumpled-up duffel bag and step out the car with my hood on to block the rain.

Grandma Jackson wastes no time coming down the porch steps. She throws her arms around me and I melt into her soft skin. Not letting go until I take everything in. From her feeling like she shrunk, to the rose scent coming from her shirt she must've line-dried before the rain.

I step back to survey her again. "What's with the plastic gloves?"

"Oregon's got its first coronavirus case. Church been talking about keeping safe. This virus is coming whether we believe it or not."

I wonder which one of these old church ladies filled her head with paranoia that probably also includes slathering Vicks on their top lip to kill whatever's going around.

In detention, *Jeopardy!* and the news were all we could watch. I know there were a few cases in the US, but I heard the only place it spread was isolated at a nursing home and I guess it was only a matter of time before it came to Portland. But I didn't want to believe it could touch us. Not now. Not when I'm just getting my life back.

"All right, Grandma J, you can let go now." I pull out of her hug. Marcus grins at us like he's part of this reunion.

"This is Marcus Smith," I say. "My juvenile court counselor."

Marcus sighs, acting butt-hurt I was all official-like.

"Nice to meet you." Grandma J eyeballs her gloves before taking them off and wrapping her hand around Marcus's.

My mom says the aging hands of an older Black woman are filled with more knowledge than the world can contain. I think back to when I had a temp fade with zigzag braids done right on this porch. Mom wouldn't do it, but Grandma J took her time, telling me stories as she pulled and tugged at my head. When I went to school I swatted away the hands of anyone trying to touch my braids just in case my scalp was truly anointed. I haven't thought about that in years. I lean in closer to her, reminding the ancestors that I'm still here. That I wouldn't mind them watching over me every once in a while.

Marcus clings to her hands like he also knows their power.

"Andre will be fine." Grandma J taps Marcus's hands before letting go. "You don't have to worry about a thing."

"I'm sure that's true." Marcus clears his throat. "But I'll need to do a walk-through of the house. Go over the rules before I sign him out."

Grandma J leads him inside.

"Hey, it'll be all right." I nudge Grandpa, hoping to ease the strain in his eyes. He tugs at his hat. I glance past his shoulder, expecting to see Dad. I blink back the disappointment when no one's there.

"Good to see you, son." Grandpa gives me a knowing hug that envelops me in coffee and Old Spice. That combination should make me turn up my nose. Instead, I feel safe again.

After Marcus tours the house, we end up at the kitchen table, where Grandma J serves a plate of warm pound cake. I don't hesitate to get mine.

Marcus balances his cake on his clipboard. He's already got that look in his eye like he can't wait to be invited to Sunday dinners. Him being *family* and all. I gotta give it to him, he practices what he preaches. That is, until he stacks his papers on the table. My appetite shrivels right on up.

"Dre will be part of our Community Monitoring Program for Multnomah County Juvenile Justice."

"Andre," Grandma J corrects.

"I'm sorry?" Marcus says.

"He's Andre. Been Andre Jackson his whole life." She sits up with her shoulders back, letting him know who I am, for real. I lift my head higher, begging for the old me to stay in her eyes.

"Yes, that's right. Andre." Marcus hands over the materials.

"The program helps keep Andre in the community with a restorative justice plan we've developed together. You all are an important part of his success."

Grandpa slides his glasses on, cross-examining the fine print. Distrust written all over his face. Shame strikes me with every restriction as it's shared with my grandparents, like I'm being kicked in the chest.

"He'll have his monitor on for GPS tracking." Marcus points to my ankle.

I reluctantly lift my right pant leg. The black monitor's on snug like an extension of my limb.

"The judge approved community service for his detention with a required electronic monitor. He has to charge it every day for two hours." He hands over a long extension cord to go with the charger.

And here's the thing, the look my grandpa gives me, it verifies my situation more than when the judge made her decision.

All I wanted was to come home, so I had no problem with having community monitoring instead of a longer detention sentence. Even the guys inside gassed me up after court, making me feel like I won.

I didn't win.

Yeah, I left detention, but the guilt still clings to me. Now literally to my ankle. I flash back to Gavin running with Brian next door. Probably hanging out with my boy Eric. The guilt sure didn't stick with Eric and Gavin, that just bounced right off and onto me.

"He'll need to keep within these designated areas." Marcus

highlights my limitations on a printed map of Portland. It's the same, but somehow seems more restricted than the first time he showed me.

"Is this really necessary?" Grandma J says.

"Unfortunately." Marcus shows the paragraph where it details the boundaries.

"He can work, or is it only free labor at the pool house?" Grandpa doesn't break eye contact with Marcus after practically calling my service requirement slavery.

"Five hours a week is the agreement, plus restitution."

"Can he get it wet?" Grandpa asks.

I tap my foot waiting for the answer. The only reason I didn't ask myself is because I want it so bad.

"He can. It's waterproof. Sometimes it acts up if it's submerged for too long."

I release a relieved breath that doesn't last. There's no guarantee Terry will even let me use the pool. I haven't spoken to him since my fate was sealed with the backpack full of stolen goods found in my Parks & Rec locker. And even if he does let me, there's a little part of me that fears the pool would empty at the sight of me doing laps with an ankle monitor. Liberal whites' façade be damned.

"He'll be monitored for strange patterns. Curfew is nine p.m. within one hundred feet of home." Marcus takes an exaggerated pause. "And no parties."

Marcus expects me to react, but that's the least of my worries.

"What about school?" Grandma J says. "He's a senior, why wait to get started in spring?"

"The school preferred he begins after spring break."

"Seems like y'all want him to fail. What's he supposed to do with all his free time then?" Grandpa's glasses slip down his nose as he locks eyes with Marcus, then Grandma J—something between them goes unspoken. But I can read between the lines, they don't trust I'll stay outta trouble. Grandpa's words of warning, *Don't ever give them reason,* repeat in my head.

"He still has assignments to finish from MacLaren," Marcus says. "Grant High School has agreed to provide credit. They are a restorative justice school, so this should be a good transition place for your grandson."

"Well, the rule in this house is we go to church to restore our souls," Grandma J says.

"I can't make it." I wince. "I have to report to the Parks and Rec."

"On a Sunday?" Grandpa shakes his head. "You need Jesus, not manual labor. That's the problem, they always thinking labor gonna solve things. Seems to me, free labor caused all the problems, but you probably don't understand all that." He sneers at Marcus, and I'm sensing he's got the same view as Dad—Marcus is a sellout. I almost feel bad for Marcus. *Almost.*

"While Terry Jones is disappointed about what happened, he also believes in your grandson. I'm sure they'll work something out. We all want him to succeed. . . . That's also why I need to be in contact with Dr—Andre twice a day. There will be at least one surprise home visit a week."

I jump up. "Twice a day?" They told me he'd be in touch. They didn't say *that* in touch.

"Mostly quick calls." Marcus pats my shoulder. "But I expect you to answer right away, son."

"How long is this for?" The bass in Grandpa's voice picks up, claiming Alpha. I'm *his* son as far as he's concerned. And he doesn't like anybody monitoring me but him. Even my dad defers to Grandpa. Grandpa breaks his gaze and takes his glasses off, letting them dangle at his fingertips.

"Six months. Until he turns eighteen. If he completes the program, he's done."

This'll never be done.

"He's a good boy." Grandma squeezes my hand. I want to cling to that side of innocence, not let the world turn me into . . . a man. A monster.

Marcus nods before going over more rules. I pretend I'm not fazed. Pretend that somehow, I'll get back to the way things used to be, like playing ball at the courts with Eric and our friend Boogie, being a lifeguard, teaching kids how to be guppies who will grow into dolphins. But inside, I'm a raging storm filled with anger and humiliation that everything I was before is gone. Because the world sure don't look at me like I'm still Andre. It's Dre now. No matter what Grandma J tries to tell them.

I CAN'T GO FOR THAT

February 27, 2020

The second Marcus leaves, Grandma's on her tippy-toes covering my cheeks with kisses. It's as if she's playing catch-up to everything that's changed about me. I've been so starved for positive attention I soak it all up.

I sling my arm around her. And for a moment, I let myself believe that everything's fine. That this was only a blemish on my life. And the people I love, well, they won't let the outside world dictate who I am.

When it's clear I slow down her cooking, she kicks me out the kitchen.

For a split second I think Grandpa will let me sit in *his* chair, but nope. He directs me right on back to the couch instead. The way he's inspecting me, he's probably been making a to-do list since he heard I was being released.

Grandpa turns on the news. The president, who I refuse to acknowledge, speaks at some rally in South Carolina:

So a number that nobody heard of, that I heard of recently and I was shocked to hear it, thirty-five thousand people on average die each year from the flu. Did anyone know that? Thirty-five thousand, that's a lot of people. It could go to a hundred thousand, it could be twenty-seven thousand. . . . You hear thirty-five and forty thousand people and we've lost nobody and you wonder if the press is in hysteria mode. CNN fake news and the camera just went off, the camera. The camera just went off. Turn it back on. Hey, by the way, hold it. Look at this, and honestly, all events are like this. It's about us. It's all about us. I wish they'd take the camera, show the arena, please. They never do. They never do.

Grandpa lowers the sound and falls asleep within minutes. The continued lunacy the so-called president spews is mind-boggling. I don't know what's worse, that he gets away with saying this stuff out loud or that people travel in droves to listen to him. I think he'll say anything as long as the cameras keep rolling. And if it brings viewers, well, the media will keep the spotlight on him. Both right and left.

I focus on the news ticker at the bottom but it's all doom, way too depressing. I thought in the new year the chaos of politics would be settled, but things aren't better. In fact, they're worse.

I scroll through my social media, recalling old passwords.

Then go down my feed for what I've missed. It doesn't take too long to realize the world kept spinning and I don't have the energy to catch up.

Grandpa snores. Taking a nap right now is tempting, but I don't dare go to my room here because I know Grandpa will rise up like he caught the Holy Ghost and give me something to do to stay outta trouble. So instead, I get up and wait for my dad by the window, stomach twisting with nerves.

The neighborhood is quiet as rain pours. I'm strangely alert, standing in the same spot Grandma J was when the whole block lit up with red and blue flashing lights. Prickles run up my neck. I feel like I've been transported, replaying that day over and over again.

I wish I took my Black ass home early New Year's Eve. Wish I went to Boogie's house instead of the Whitakers'. Wish I did so many other things. My list of what-ifs just keeps growing.

What if I hadn't let my guard down when Mr. Whitaker pressed his pointer finger to his lips and handed me a glass of champagne as soon as I walked in. I let how chill that night was fool me into thinking I could just kick it like my *other* friends. When Mr. Whitaker's adopted daughter, Sierra, begged me to go with her and her biological brother, Eric, it was because she didn't trust he would keep out of trouble at Paul Chase's New Year's blowout. Being a sucker for Sierra, I agreed, even though I knew good and well that Eric *did* whatever Eric wanted.

Eric never understood *we* can't get away with things our white friends do. He never liked hearing it, but it's the truth. Even

Mr. Whitaker knew that. As a white dad, he knew he failed to expose his Black adopted kids to their own culture. Sierra and Eric needed a guide to navigating Blackness in Portland. Insert me. Mr. Whitaker trusted me with that role.

Except on New Year's Eve I didn't want to be a guide. I wanted a day off from being cautious. From being perfect. That's why I ignored what's been drilled into me since I was ten years old, when Dad couldn't fool me with innocent reasons we were pulled over too often. When it was time to have the other talk—we were suspects before we were citizens.

But all that blanked from my mind. Sierra was by my side and it felt like the kind of night memories were made of. That is, until the party busted up early because Eric got into it with his best friend, Gavin. By then, the moment was over and we were headed home.

I shiver at my next memory. The one that makes it hard to look my grandparents in the eye. How the very next day, I was in my room recording my YouTube videos, and bam—my life changed just like that. I've been fighting my way back from all the lies I told since. Fighting a series of what-ifs. I should've just admitted the truth from the start:

I went to Paul Chase's New Year's party.

I rode with Gavin and Eric sometimes.

I knew what they were up to. But it wasn't like I was involved.

While everyone was living their best life, too drunk to care, they would hit backpacks and purses. Grab anything they could sell, knowing the kids wouldn't admit their things were stolen at a party they shouldn't have been at in the first place.

I kept my mouth shut while it was happening because the rules growing up were never ever rat. Besides, I figured eventually a classmate would catch them in the act.

So when I got picked up and was questioned by officers, instead of telling the truth, I repeated, "I don't know nothing." I didn't think I was the target. I thought they were just trying to get me to break down and snitch on Eric and Gavin.

Then while I was waiting for things to pass, Gavin lawyered up, got his story straight while I played dumb. So dumb, the stories lined up straight to me.

The first lie was busted the same day I told it. *I wasn't even there, Officer.* I mean, who wouldn't have noticed *us* at Paul's New Year's party? Eric, Sierra, and I didn't stay long, but we were the only Black folks there. We wouldn't go unnoticed.

When I got caught in that lie, I made another. Things spiraled so much, all they saw were lies. Then a backpack of stolen goods was anonymously reported, which officers found in my locker that Thursday. I still remember the canary smile on the officer's face as he came into the holding room with a backpack in hand. For a second, I thought it meant I was being released. Until I caught on that he wasn't on my side. He was saying, "Gotcha."

That's when I gave up trying to explain things away.

Mr. Whitaker showed up the following Monday. I thought he knew Eric was involved, but he came to hook me up with a big-time lawyer who finally laid out the situation for me—I was the only suspect. That's when I made the decision between worse and worser. Even if I ratted on Eric and Gavin, I was still going down as an accomplice.

As irrational as it sounds, it was safer taking a no contest plea than telling the truth. Because the police had no evidence on the other robberies, so there was no guarantee they'd be charged. And if I let the case blow up bigger, it could move me to Measure 11 territory, a guaranteed ten-year minimum sentence. That'd mean MacLaren until age twenty-five, then adult prison. There was no way I was going to take a chance of prison. So I took the deal. Grandma J would say it's karma for keeping quiet, but I don't agree. 'Cause why'd karma come for me and not them?

When my sentencing was done, Dad asked one more time how the backpack ended up in my locker. I looked him in the eye and told him the truth—it wasn't me. Dad tapped my hand and said, "All right, Andre." But he never looked at me when he said it.

I step away from the door, glancing out the window to the Whitakers' house, which shadows ours.

Grandpa is awake now. And Grandma J checks on her roast. Again. It's been done. But if she admits that, she admits Dad's late. Two hours late.

She acts like she's fine. She's not.

Neither am I.

"Dad stay late working often?" I say.

Grandma J hesitates. She restacks the plates before speaking. "It ebbs and flows. You know how he is, getting lost in work."

She says it and it makes me feel like nothing. Confirms my return wasn't enough to get my dad to change up his schedule. To get my mom to switch a shift.

My eyes blur. "We can eat without him," I say.

"We'll wait." Grandma J stirs the mashed potatoes so the top doesn't harden. "He'll be here soon."

Grandpa ignores her, taking a seat at the table before buttering his bread. Nobody messes with Grandpa's food when he's hungry.

I take the cue and sit next to him, not making eye contact.

The phone rings, and Grandma J hustles over to answer it.

"I'll get it," Grandpa gruffly says.

Grandma J stops in her tracks. I can't help but stare.

When I hear Dad's voice through the phone, I ear hustle. Grandpa paces back into the kitchen, and my shoulders slump because the kitchen fan's too loud to hear Dad.

"Hmm. That so," Grandpa grumbles. "I'll tell the boy."

Click.

Grandpa takes his seat at the dinner table.

"Let's get started."

"What he say?" Grandma J waves a spoon at Grandpa.

I sit up straight.

"He had to let Tom go temporarily since the store's slowing down. He's behind doing inventory. He'll be home late."

Grandma J reaches for the phone.

"Let him be." Grandpa waves her away. "Let's eat. We got a young man to celebrate."

Grandpa covers my hand with his, and his grip warms me. I wanna tell him it's no big deal, but my throat closes in on me.

The past two months all I could think about was the day I'd come home. Where my life would return to before. Mom always being by my side, Dad believing I could do anything, and my grandparents thinking the world of me. All that would be enough to erase what I've been through. How I had to fight for the world to see me for me. Maybe I couldn't erase the lies I told, but they'd believe in me enough to know that I had good reason to lie in the first place. That my deceit wasn't to save myself but to save Eric. But when you let yourself fall in a place that too easily thinks you're guilty anyway, well, it's quicksand. The harder you fight, the faster you sink.

EVERY TIME I SEE YOUR FACE

February 27, 2020

After dinner, I wander to the front door windows again. Except this time, I'm hawking the Whitakers' house for a sign that Eric's home. I need confirmation he was smart enough to get rid of whatever else he jacked. That there won't be more charges. I need him to convince me that he's straightened up his life.

When lights flash as a car turns down the street, I hold my breath expecting to see Dad, feeling both wrecked and relieved. But it's Brian again. This time he's not dodging traffic but pulling up with a full car.

The Whitaker kids could be the cast of a Disney special. Brian, the oldest, just started at Reed College but lives at home. He hops out of the driver's seat as his sister Kate pushes open the passenger door. She's a senior like me and Sierra. Kate's eyes are bright blue, like Brian's, but her hair's bleach blond. Those eyes are about the only thing she has in common with him, though. She's direct and always on the lookout. You can't get anything past her. She's relentless at getting her way. She only seems to shrivel under the weight of her parents' expectations. Then Luis jumps out, a freshman with black hair slicked back in a ponytail. He's adopted, just like Eric and Sierra, but his bio parents are from Mexico. Sierra and Eric are only a year apart, and true biological siblings. I'm waiting on them.

I bite on my lip until I see her: *Sierra.* My heart jumps, an unavoidable response. At MacLaren what kept me going was escaping into thoughts of us being together. Now, I'll have to contend with reality. What made me whole in detention was actually a mirage—we never got together. She never wrote. She never even said goodbye.

Sierra steps out the car like she's in slow motion, a spotlight beaming down on her.

Back in the day I'd have hid behind closed blinds, flicking one open with my finger to monitor. Not checking for her. But not *not* checking for her.

Sierra's eyes widen when she catches me gawking through the window. Her lips perk up as she and her siblings file into their house. I search for Eric, but he's not with them.

Sierra is the last to enter. She leaves the door wide open for me like old times.

Everything I've been through should stop me, but I reach for my gray hoodie and pull my sock up over my monitor. Grandma J follows me from the kitchen to the porch like she smells fire. To my surprise, she doesn't say anything, but she's got her eyes locked on me as I pass Grandpa, who's out cold in his chair in a food coma.

I run across the lawn, then knock on their open door. The sound of my knuckles on the wood is silenced under their arguing over dinner. I'm frozen. I wanna stroll in like nothing has changed, but so much has.

"You gonna stand there all day?" Sierra smirks, walking into the hall from the kitchen. Her dark brown hair is straightened, a soft big curl around her ears with brown skin that matches mine. She's wearing large gold hoop earrings, and her lips are glossy, kissable.

"Been a while," I say. "Didn't know how y'all feel about me coming in like old times."

Sierra makes her way toward me. Everything inside me shouts to stop studying her like I'm fifteen again, but my heart is leaping out my chest.

I take in a breath before pulling her close, then I go all-out corny and lift her in a halfway spin. The hardwood floors steady under my feet as the echo of my arrival bounces up the staircase. The Whitakers kept the architecture of the neighborhood, but inside, the entire house was stripped to the bones, redone and expanded.

"Andre," Mrs. Whitaker says as she comes down the stairs. Her mouth purses a bit. I study her for a clue to how she really feels about me being back.

Crashing back to earth, I put Sierra down, still unable to wipe the grin off my face.

"Mrs. Whitaker." I brace myself.

"I told you, call me Mary." She puts her arm around Sierra.

"Are you staying for dinner?" Sierra says.

"Yes, please do," Mrs. Whitaker says. "Eat whatever you want."

I turn away from Mrs. Whitaker's gaze so I don't overthink if she's just being polite. She's always been wound up tight. I just hope my friendship with her adopted kids will make her sympathetic, or at least stop her from banning the Whitaker clan from seeing me. Banning *Sierra* from seeing me.

I clear my throat. "I ate already, but thanks."

"Come on anyway." Sierra waves at me to follow, and I'm now seasick with all her curves.

We pass Mr. Whitaker's study. He's hunched over his desk. I pause before lifting my finger up, signaling I need a minute.

My chest thumps hard as I tap on the door.

I've been thinking about what I'd say to Mr. Whitaker. There aren't words that cover how I feel. I'm home because of him.

"That's not the deal." Mr. Whitaker's voice rises. "I make the decisions." I step back so I'm not in the chamber—what Eric calls his dad's office. I second-guess whether to talk to him after he hung up with such a harsh tone, but it's too late.

"Andre!" Mr. Whitaker stands. I watch, frozen, as he runs his hands through his dark hair. "Mary told me to be patient and give you a chance to visit with your family. I was ready to pick you up myself!"

He grips me in a firm shake.

"I came home earlier today."

"Of course. I'm surprised I didn't see a carful of people at your house to celebrate! Your parents are overjoyed, I'm sure."

I wouldn't know.

"Yes, sir." I can feel his piercing blue eyes on me. I hold a fake smile, surveying his office corner, which now stores campaign posters and yard signs.

After Mr. Whitaker got involved with my case, it inspired him to run for a city commissioner seat. His platform pushes for changes in the justice system. From all he did to help me, he saw me beyond my situation; he never doubted that I was telling the truth. Now that fire is fueling his campaign.

I run my hands across a yard sign to distract my nerves. I shouldn't be jumpy, but I want to prove my worth. Even when what I did was shield the truth from the things Eric did.

"Ah. Don't judge," Mr. Whitaker says. "It's obnoxious, right? My name on a big sign. Mary keeps telling me to display them out front, but I don't want to make the neighborhood a spectacle. I'd rather people showed support with no pressure. I got your family's vote, though, right?"

"Of course."

"I'll leave one for you if you want." He tentatively touches the sign. "No obligation."

"I wish I could vote."

"Ahh, soon enough."

Mrs. Whitaker yells from the hallway, "Don't keep him all day!"

"Who am I kidding, you don't want to talk politics. Hang out with the kids."

I nod, stepping back. "Thanks, Mr. Whitaker. I don't know how to repay you."

"You're practically family. Don't even think about it." He

pauses. "Downtown I have a political office, voter drive calling campaigns, stuffing envelopes. . . ."

"You don't even have to ask," I say, leaving.

Back in the hallway, the stairs call me. I'm ready to corner Eric so we can finally talk. Us keeping our distance during the investigation was an unsaid thing. But I've kept silent way too long. The only thing holding me back is his parents knowing I've broken their sacred no guests upstairs rule.

I drum my fingers on the banister, lay eyes on the life-size portraits of the Whitakers. The portrait in the middle is when it was just the four of them, before adoptions.

From afar there's nothing that distinguishes one photo from the next, but if you know their personalities, it's striking. Brian's changing hairstyles, long to short, spiky to buzzed, but in every shot his eyes are wide and his mouth perks up like he was caught by surprise. Kate's smile, blond hair sleek and cut bluntly past her shoulders, is interchangeable with any year, always the image of perfection like her mom. Luis's outfits are varying-colored polos and khakis, although in real life you'd never catch him in either. And Sierra, who must be allergic to professional photos because the directness of her stare, her tight smile, like she's muttering something under her breath about hurrying up, don't look like any of her photos online. Then there's Eric, doing his hair 364 days of the year, but never for family photos. Always daring his parents to say something about his halfway-combed Afro or fuzzy braids.

All I want to do is give Eric one big sucker punch, just to get it out of the way. Then we can be cool again. I shake my head—I'll get to Eric soon enough.

When I turn away from the stairs and walk into the kitchen, the waft of a dozen lemons in a bowl reminds me of one of our apartments in the 100s where we'd try to hide the smell from the restaurant next door. The next time my parents moved us, we got lucky and the laundromat exhaust made our place smell like clean linen.

The chaos in the kitchen is refreshing. I take in all their sibling banter as they float around the spacious kitchen. Unlike my grandparents' place, where things are shoved in every crevice to make room for mismatched dishware, there's a spot for everyone, including me, here.

"Damn." Brian balances snacks and plates with expert hands. "I couldn't believe it when I saw you pull up."

His voice has a forced swag.

"Yeah, I'm back."

"You staying for good at your grandparents', or what?" Sierra passes me a bowl of chips.

I pause before answering. "Not for long . . . just to help them out while my parents work." I cringe at the lie.

"Is that part of your release?" Mrs. Whitaker asks.

My smile falters. I hide behind designer pans that hang on metal hooks above me. "No, ma'am. Just looking out for them."

My cheeks are flaming hot. Mrs. Whitaker sees me now as the neighborhood kid who got in trouble. I'm ashamed I lied about my grandparents needing me, even though the truth is, it's the other way around. I don't need pity. Especially from someone who already expects less of me.

"Andre!" Luis comes up from the basement with his skateboard slung behind him. "I thought Brian was lying."

I give him a side hug and the kitchen goes back to chaos. Luis hangs back, waiting his turn, the curse of the younger sibling. He's not that much younger than us, but he can't shake being the baby of the group.

Platters filled with cut cheese, nuts, and crackers that has some fancy name for it I can't recall. Food has been so constant today, I have to force myself not to gorge, remembering I won't be rationed and on a clock anymore.

"You want some?" Kate offers me her plate.

I shake my head.

"You sure?" she whispers too close to my ear, and I flinch a step back, my eyes automatically searching for Sierra, before leaning on the counter next to Luis.

"Kate's going to Brown!" Mrs. Whitaker chirps. "Premed. She's going to be a doctor."

Mrs. Whitaker's been talking about Kate becoming a doctor since, well, forever. I've yet to hear Kate confirm that she wants to be one.

I slow my response as I hesitantly look in Kate's direction.

"Congratulations."

"Andre, you hanging downstairs?" Luis changes the subject, eager.

I glance at Sierra to make sure it's still cool. "Yeah, I'll stay for a little bit."

The basement is our permanent hangout spot, and it feels good to get back to something normal. Downstairs things are the same: the oversized tan sectional covered with plush bright pillows, the paint a light blue-gray color so it doesn't feel like a dungeon, and a wall-mounted television. This is the only space that's allowed to be messy, but somehow their messy only means pillows not straightened and crumbs on the table.

Luis parks on a footstool, balancing his plate in one hand as he navigates the controller to play *2K* on the Xbox.

"Luis," Sierra groans. "Seriously. Kate and I live here too. I don't get why we can't watch an actual basketball game."

"Oh, you're a sports fan now that you get box seats?" Brian snickers. Sierra flashes him a dirty glare. It's a reminder I've been gone too long because I'm not sure what that's about.

"Just a few rounds," Luis says. "Be done in an hour and it's all yours."

"Yeah, just an hour." Brian grabs the other controller and slumps back on the L-shaped couch, his plate floating on his lap.

Their bickering is so natural, it helps me settle, knowing that some things haven't changed.

"We need a bigger space," Kate says.

My brow furrows. All their space is the reason I come over here. I'm also hard-pressed to think of a time they all came over to my grandparents' house. And Eric's the only one who's actually been to my apartment.

"Wanna play?" Luis offers his controller.

The last thing I need is for Sierra to see me get sucked into a game for hours. Although I'm not gonna lie, I'd love to work out my players to get back on top.

I resist from sheer will and sit back to watch. I should get a medal.

"So, Kate," Brian says, "when you gonna tell Mom you didn't get into Brown."

I raise my eyebrow. "Word?"

"Shut it." Kate bites her nails, flitting her eyes to me. "I didn't make early decision. Doesn't mean I won't get in." She tosses a pillow at Brian, who ducks just in time.

"What are you gonna do if you *are* admitted?" Brian says. "Show her your photoshopped early decision letter and say just kidding?"

"You should just tell Mom," Luis says. "It's still early, and you'll get into a lot of other good schools."

"I just wanted her to stop talking about Brown, okay? Anyway, why upset her?" Kate flicks her hair. "Might as well make her feel like she did *something* right a little while longer."

There's an undertone in Kate's voice that hits a nerve everyone seems to know about. That is, everyone but me. Being around the Whitakers, I've gotten used to things that go unsaid. The land mines they try to avoid. The jokes that turn to fights too easily. Today I can feel an elephant in the room. And it's not me.

"When's Eric coming home?" I say. "I wanna see him."

The room goes quiet.

Sierra rushes upstairs before anyone can speak.

I stand up, tugging at my sweats so my monitor doesn't show. Unsure if I should follow her to make sure she's okay or stay to find out why everyone is dead silent.

"What'd I say?"

Crickets.

Luis finally replies, "He's gone."

"Gone? What do you mean, gone?"

"He split." Brian swipes his hand below his chin. "That same week you got picked up."

"You're kidding. But I saw Gavin here earlier?"

Portland's known for runaways. Whether by choice or by force. But Eric? After all he's been through to get a place to call home . . . No way he just left.

"Gavin still comes by every once in a while. You know our dads are close. Think he's lonely." Brian shoves food in his mouth between talking and setting up his player stats. "But yeah, Eric left, packed up all his things when we weren't home. He called my parents and said he wouldn't be back."

"What'd he say to Sierra?" I focus on the door.

"He hasn't called any of us." Kate snorts. "Freak. What kind of asshole does that to his family? He had everything. So ungrateful."

Luis has a dark look in his eye before he chucks a pillow at Kate, nicking her shoulder.

The Whitaker kids are tight, until they have to choose a side. That's when they go by blood. Brian always chooses Kate. Eric always chooses Sierra. And Luis is in the middle of them all, so he flops between the two sets of siblings. The mediator. Unless it's about being adopted. About the things that Brian and Kate will never understand.

The tension is saved by my phone buzzing. I slide it out my pocket, answering Grandma's call. "I'm coming," I say before she gets a chance to speak.

"I don't want you cutting it close on your first night home," she says.

I should be good here even after curfew, but it's too early to test my theory about the hundred-foot radius. And Mom wouldn't like me here regardless. I'm finally back at home, safe, and already heading over to the Whitakers'—the family Mom secretly can't stand, though she's too Christian to admit it. She begrudgingly let me join them on family trips. Skiing at Mount Hood. Surfing on the coast. Camping at Crater Lake National Park. With the Whitakers, I did things that couldn't happen in our household, the things we pushed off for some time in the future that never came.

"I got it, Grandma J. I'm leaving now." I hang up.

"Stay." Kate steps closer.

"Nah. I gotta go. I'll see y'all around."

"A'ight," Brian says.

I chuckle 'cause he's such a try-hard.

"A'ight," I mimic.

I climb the stairs, eager to spot Sierra and find out what really happened. She and her brother were tight, there's nothing they'd hide from each other. So if Eric left, there was a good reason. And my worry is it might be a sign this isn't over for me. Because if more charges come, he could be headed to juvie himself, with charges that would add to my time too. That might be why Gavin still comes by, just to see if they've heard from Eric.

A smile rides up my face when Sierra's helium-filled laugh rings out from the living room. I stride down the hall, grinning 'cause she must be waiting for me. Maybe we can erase the lost time and start where we left off—on the verge of something more.

My stomach drops as I walk in on her. She isn't alone.

"Hey, Dre!" Paul Chase points at me. "You're out."

I jerk my head back at him like, we're cool? It was his party that got me busted. A rich white boy calling about a robbery only sealed my fate.

But to be honest, I *really* want to punch him in the throat because he's got his hands wrapped around Sierra, and it's not reading they just friends.

"Paul just stopped by," Sierra says.

Paul looks at her funny. He doesn't have to say this is a regular thing now. It's written all over his face.

"You leaving?" Sierra pushes Paul's arm away, like she's clueing him this shit ain't cool. All right, maybe *she* wasn't thinking all that. But damn. This shit ain't cool *to me*.

"Yeah." I cough, nervously trying to pull myself together, but I can't even focus on anything else but this dude's hands on a scavenger hunt over Sierra's body.

I'm about to say more, but Paul makes a G move and kisses Sierra on the cheek like I'm not standing right here.

I'm done.

This is too much. Eric is gone, out the blue. No one's heard from him and no one thinks that's strange? Sierra is fooling around with this clown who's so tied to my situation. My brain can't handle these puzzle pieces not fitting like they're supposed to. It's like Eric and me leaving tipped everything out of sorts. Since getting out, I've thought there must be something wrong with the world itself . . . but when I lay eyes on Sierra, I know it's me who doesn't fit around here.

I wave my hand up giving deuces, then pull the hood of my sweatshirt over my head and make a beeline for the door, but not before hearing Sierra say, "Not funny. You didn't have to rub it in."

Yeah, Paul, you didn't have to rub that shit in.

SWEET DREAMS

February 28, 2020

I thrash around in my sweat-soaked bed, fighting sleep to avoid flashbacks of being jammed up at the police station. The accusations being hurled, questions on top of questions. My nights in juvie.

As much as I run my fingers along the hem of the covers, breathe in the smell of fresh sheets, my brain tells me being released was a lie. The shadows of my room keep fooling me into thinking I'm in detention. I keep expecting Bobby to be at my left, with his mouth drooling and funk wafting my way. And to my right, Dave's long ashy legs hanging at the edge of the bed with one sock on.

I stare at the ceiling, letting the blanket of darkness hide the welling in my eyes until I can't keep them open any longer.

In the morning, something touches my face and jolts me

awake. I throw my arms up—ready to fight until the soft humming confirms it's Mom. I breathe out, relieved that last night was a dream. That I'm here now, and not waking up . . . away.

"Shhhh. It's okay." Her warm hands put my arms down.

"I'm sorry. I—"

"Sleep." She cradles me in her arms. That's the thing about Mom, she knows just what to do. I feel my tense body trust that I'm safe.

"What time is it?" I rub my eyes, releasing an embarrassed smile. The last thing I remember is hearing my dad's car pull up and heading straight to bed.

"Way too early." She shushes me. "Sorry I startled you. I'll be more careful next time."

"I had a bad dream is all." This is the first time I've let myself falter in front of her. During detention visits I didn't want to add to the worry already laced in her eyes. So I never spoke to her about sleep quarters in detention, how I got jumped the first night. Nothing to hurt me, but everything to remind me where I was and my situation. Since that first night I've woken up on alert. Mostly terrified. When I knew I was coming home, I didn't even tell anyone at MacLaren the exact date. I didn't want the way I came in to be the way I came out. But how Mom looks at me, with her eyes crinkled, she already knows all this. With her by my side now I'm ready to let go. Ready for the anxiety and depression that have wormed their way inside me to release. I search her eyes for confirmation that the walls I've built can tumble down.

"I couldn't wait to see you. I knew if I went to bed, I'd be out like a light until shift." Mom's baggy eyes tell me all about her long nights.

I sit up, against her protests.

"I'm so glad you're home," I say.

"You doing okay?"

My throat aches as I sift to the bottom of what I've buried deep inside. Each memory unlatching from secret places. All the times during MacLaren visits when she asked me how I was doing and I told her I was fine, when I was everything but. All the times I swallowed the fear because there were too many eyes already waiting to hold something against me. But here, now, in my grandparents' home being held by my mom, waves of these moments take me over.

I try to fight the tears by coughing them away, but they've been dancing on my lids since last night. That's the thing, choking down the pain only lasts for so long. Seeing Mom brings what I've been holding to the surface. All that was on the line. Still on the line.

As soon as Mom wraps her arms around me, a heavy sob erupts. My chest convulses, heaving in and out between bursts of saying how I'm happy to see her. I melt into her hug and finally release my secrets.

The truth comes out in spurts. Stories about my first night in detention. How nothing happened in the showers but I was still paralyzed by fear of things I'd heard and how they use that against you. How night after night I fought sleep to stay alert. How I never thought I'd come home.

With the close of each jumbled story, Mom pulls another out. When she rubs my back the weight doesn't feel as heavy. And even though she knows only part of what I've been through, it's enough.

After a long pause, Mom speaks. "How was dinner?"

I take a breath before answering. "Dad didn't show." The scars from last night rip open.

"You know how he gets about the bookshop."

I know this. But that doesn't change how I feel. There's more, though. I can tell their relationship is strained with finances. Their visits in detention felt like they were weaving their stories together with unpracticed lines of reasons we were moving again.

"I can get a job to help." I have to do something to make it all right.

Mom peers at the ceiling, probably making up what she says next. "We'll be fine. Besides, staying here is stable for you while you finish your program and focus on school. I don't want anything to threaten that."

I nod, even though I don't agree.

"Dad is happy you're home." She squeezes my arm. "Just talk to him, you'll see."

"I'll catch him before he goes in."

Mom gives me a look.

"What?"

"He's gone already." She takes my hand and taps it. "But tonight, after work . . ."

I swallow the growing lump that sits in my throat.

We change subjects, talking like old times, catching up. Although she swears juggling work and home hasn't been so bad, I know she's exhausted. It doesn't bother me when her eyes drift. She quietly mumbles to show she's still listening, until she's knocked out.

I slide out of the bed and cover her with my blanket before going down the hall to the kitchen.

"Hey, Grandma J." I kiss her cheek before taking a seat at the table.

Grandpa sips his coffee, scooping eggs on his toast like I've seen a thousand times. I do a silent prayer of thanks when Grandma J hands me a matching plate. The first bite erases the rubber eggs at MacLaren from my taste buds. No more trays of bland food with white bread on the side for every meal.

"You see Dad before he left?" I keep my eyes down, haphazardly moving my eggs around with my fork as I wait for his answer.

"Nope," Grandpa says before popping his newspaper open. Now I'm facing headlines.

I scan the front page. My mouth drops at all the news on the coronavirus.

WASHINGTON STATE MAN BECOMES FIRST US DEATH FROM CORONAVIRUS

800 NEW CASES CONFIRMED IN SOUTH KOREA

ALMOST 3,000 DEATHS FROM NOVEL CORONAVIRUS WORLDWIDE

TRUMP HOLDS RALLY IN MIDST OF LOOMING PANDEMIC

"You see this?" I point to the paper, then up at Grandma J. She's locked into Trump speaking on the news:

We've taken the most aggressive actions to confront the coronavirus. They are the most aggressive taken by any country.

"I can't take this foolishness before I've had all my coffee," Grandpa says.

I bust out a chuckle. "You think it's true, we have it handled?"

"Son, you haven't been gone that long. You think he does?"

"He ain't like President Obama." Grandma J admires a framed family picture of the Obamas on the wall. "There's probably some confidential national report being used as a coaster for his Diet Coke right now."

"One day it's a hoax, the next day we have the most aggressive plan to stop it," Grandpa adds. "Just make sure you don't touch anybody, wash your hands, and you'll be fine. Can't trust any of these politicians. Especially Trump. He's probably already thinking about how he can profit off this."

"You changed your affiliation so you could vote for him in the primaries," Grandma J says.

My mouth drops open. *He what?*

"It was the primaries." Grandpa clears his throat. "The Democrats don't automatically get my vote because I'm Black."

Grandma J and I share glances.

"I voted for Clinton in the general election," Grandpa continues. "Besides, every politician is the same whether they're blue or red. I liked Trump's plain-speak, business background . . . until he started talking all that hate and making no sense, in over his head."

Grandma J gives him the side eye like she still doesn't believe he changed his vote in the presidential election. I, however, refuse to believe anything different.

"That's why we need to take care of ourselves," Grandma J says, turning to me. "Let's stock up on food and supplies for the house. You go do some errands for me?"

I rub my hands together, already making plans to turn it into hanging out with my best friend.

"Abraham Tewolde can give me a ride after school." I make sure to say his *full* government name.

"That one of them boys hanging out at all those parties?" Grandpa lowers his paper to study me.

"No, sir." I pause. "You know he's focused on school and his parents are stricter than you." I drop that info 'cause things like that matter to Grandpa. Good grades. No, *great* grades.

"That so." Grandpa sips his coffee. "Well, glad he stays outta trouble." He believes if we're perfect, then we're untouchable. But deep down even he knows that's not true.

The way you speak, dress, things that can give a false sense of control you won't get in trouble. I used to think that was true too.

Oregon has a way of doing that—promoting Black unicorns. But code-switching and dressing a certain way don't really keep you safe. Good grades and joining Jack and Jill don't stop you from being judged. I learned the hard way that acceptance gained by pretzeling yourself into other people's visions of you never lasts.

I occupy my time catching up on music and reading ahead. That is, when I'm not Grandpa's personal assistant. He yells from his leather recliner for me to get something in the same room as him. Acting like he doesn't know where it is. The last time, it was the "clicker"—which is what he calls the remote. I handed it to him, even though it was smack-dab on the table next to him. I swear I saw his eyes crinkle in amusement.

Outside, I drag the garbage bins down the driveway. I'm rushing at the sound of the garbage truck coming closer to our neighborhood. I almost catch the foot of a dog popping a squat near Grandma J's flower bushes.

"Watch yourself!" Mrs. Glendale snaps at me. She's an older white lady that lives across the street.

"I'm sorry," I say, because I wasn't raised an animal—even though she's the one on our property letting her dog do his business on some azaleas.

"This is a peaceful neighborhood," Mrs. Glendale says. "We don't like people going through our garbage."

"I . . . What? Mrs. Glendale. I'm Andre Jackson." I touch my chest to make her see me. "We've met, like, a lot of times."

She gives me a once-over before snapping her dog's leash and briskly walking across the street.

"Have a nice day." I wave at her sarcastically, then assess the damage.

I run my hand across my neck. Grandpa's eventually gonna make me clean this up, but I take my chances it's not today and suck my teeth in, still disgusted as I jog inside.

Around four, Boogie taps on my bedroom window. That's Abraham's nickname, not that I'd call him that in front of Grandpa or Grandma J—they'd take it the wrong way. They'd take *him* the wrong way.

I signal him to meet me at the front door, rushing to beat Grandpa there, but I'm too late. This has to be the first time Grandpa's left his chair all day.

"Don't run up in this house without your manners. Shoes. Hat." Grandpa points out the rules like Boogie didn't already know.

"Mr. Jackson, good to see you," Boogie says, fixing his shirt and pulling his pants up before Grandpa says something else.

"That a new look, Abraham?" Grandpa clucks his teeth, studying Boogie.

"What, sir?" Boogie examines himself.

"These tight jeans that just hang off your backside. Don't even make no sense. Either baggy or tight, not both, son."

"All right, Mr. Jackson." Boogie hugs him. "I'll take that as a tip."

"Andre's on a tight rope, now. Errands and back. Then he ain't going anywhere, y'all staying inside," Grandpa says.

"Yes, sir." Boogie salutes.

"Make sure you go to the pharmacy by Mississippi highway," Grandma J says.

"Where's that?" Boogie says on our way out.

"She mean I-5."

Boogie's mouth turns into an O. Nothing else needs to be said. The old folks who used to live out here remember when the city placed the highway smack-dab in the middle of Northeast, displacing three hundred Black-owned homes.

"And clean up that dog mess out there." Grandpa points toward the front of the house.

I shake my head—never fails.

We get in Boogie's car and it's the first time being back I feel normal. I don't have to act or even guess about what he's thinking.

"Hey," I say.

"Hey."

"It's been so long I don't even know what to talk about," I admit.

"You already forgot?" Boogie raises his eyebrow. "We don't have to talk."

I relax 'cause it's true. Nothing about us was ever forced.

Boogie chuckles back before covering a cough.

I flinch, adjusting my seat.

"You bugging on this thing too." Boogie squirts sanitizer. "My mom's been spraying me down with Lysol, which is only making my chest hurt."

"Grandma J handed me these." I flap the plastic gloves on the dash and Boogie hollers.

"I'm surprised your grandparents let you out the house." Boogie inspects my monitor. I tug the hem of my jeans down and the tone shifts.

"They were just feeling bad. Dad didn't show up for dinner last night and skirted out early before I could see him," I say low, fixing my eyes on the tapestry of my neighborhood I need to memorize again. I study the changes to note if any new people moved in, but I remember it hasn't been that long. What I want to see, though, are my old hangout spots. The ones that have been gone since before I left. I want them still there. I need them there.

"That's messed up. Sorry, man. We can swing by the store and see him."

"Forget it."

As we back up, the Whitakers pull in. Paul rides in what would normally be Eric's seat.

Brian waves, but Sierra doesn't move. When they step out,

Paul snatches Sierra's hand, pulling her close. They share words back and forth before they head inside. From the look she gives him, she didn't see us. She was laser-focused, throwing her wall up so high it's impossible for most people to climb. I'm not most people.

I swallow hard, wondering if Paul got past her wall.

"You talk to her?" Boogie breaks me from staring.

"Yeah. I was over there yesterday, only talked a couple of minutes. Been giving it space."

"Space, huh." Boogie smirks.

"What?" I shrug.

"Go ahead, ask."

"Ask what?" I wrench my neck back, throwing up innocent hands.

"Bruh."

Boogie loves to see me squirm. Until I explicitly ask, beg, or plead, he'll keep all the juicy details to himself. While I don't feel like begging, I'm not beneath asking.

"Fine," I say, "Paul Chase. How'd you let that happen?"

"How'd *I*?" Boogie leans back in his seat all exaggerated-like. He knows the rules. I don't know why he's acting innocent.

"I said to keep an eye on her."

"What am I supposed to do? Follow her everywhere she go? Be her babysitter? She grown. Besides, y'all wasn't even together."

"First off, yes on all counts. You're supposed to be my boy and make sure something like Paul Chase never happened. And we wasn't *not* together." I slap at the hat he's cocked to the side.

"What does that even mean?" He mimics my voice. "We wasn't *not* together?"

"I mean, Paul 'No Personality' Chase?" Paul is vanilla plain. There's not one distinguishable thing about him or his whole crew, including his sidekick Gavin. "What she even see in him?"

"I guess what everybody see in him—dollar bills, y'all."

"Okay, there's that, but what else?" Paul's parents could've sent him to a Portland private school like Gavin's did to Jesuit so he could play on their basketball team, but they wanted to support public schools. Both of them are still on top of the world, which to me means they also have a lot to lose.

"The whole mansion thing. Brand-new car." Boogie counts off all the things Sierra might like about Paul.

"Please, surface things."

"A pool."

"It rains nine months out of the year."

"Season tickets to the Timbers and the Blazers."

Check. Check. Damn, now he's even got me counting.

"Plays every sport, and then volunteers *after* practice."

Enough!

"Like, who does that?" I say. "There's something fishy, right? Next you'll say he probably walks grannies across the street."

"Not to rub it in, but didn't he LIT-ER-AL-LY help Grandma J cross the street on her way to pick you up from swim practice?"

"What? No." I scrunch my face. But yes. Paul did that. Once, though. Once!

"Anyway, I figured better him than somebody else," Boogie says. "Won't last. I'm sure she'll recognize your humble ways as charming when you start pining after her again. This time, can you at least shoot your shot?"

"Pine? Who's pining?" If I hadn't been arrested, we'd be

together by now. Even if I'd shot my shot with her and missed beforehand . . .

"You, Andre. Mouth stuck, drooling. Look at you—a whole-ass embarrassment." Boogie shakes his head. Then he takes a turn down the street, passing Grandma J's first stop on her list. I give him a look he ignores, then I let it go because it doesn't really matter. It just feels good to be out.

"Northeast is totally gone." I'm King of Distractions, so I switch up our conversation by pointing out the organic dog food store sandwiched between two different vegan-related shops.

"Don't forget these popping up everywhere." Boogie points to a dispensary. "They're all over Portland now."

"I don't get it," I say. "Northeast used to have a bad rep. Then they come in to clean it up, and a decade later actual brick-and-mortar weed shops are on every block, and that's fine?"

"Simple. Bougie white folks say it's okay, so now they grab their edibles to top their ice cream and mocha chocolattes."

"It's a damn shame."

Boogie navigates the streets, passing another stop, and my eyes narrow at a store under construction in what used to be a zoned neighborhood where they didn't allow business development. I know because Dad was denied a business loan once the city stepped in. It would've been the perfect location for the bookshop, but I don't say anything.

"How's school? I mean, other than you not doing your job for me."

"Man. Whatever," Boogie says. "There's rumors school's closing down a few weeks. They think a school employee in Lake Oswego's got that virus."

"Dang. I'm supposed to start after spring break; I hope they don't close." As nerdy as it sounds, I was looking forward to going back to normal at school, like dropping by Mrs. Peters's after biology to help clean her lab while she shows me her experiments.

"Either way, Principal Collins is gonna try to push you out. Watch," Boogie says.

I swallow my words because I know it's true. They just haven't figured out how to do it yet. When Mom was asking people to act as character witnesses ahead of the trial, Principal Collins said it was against regulations. He wouldn't even stick his neck out for me. We're still waiting for him to show us exactly where that's against the rules. When my community monitoring was put in place, the school administrators originally refused my return. The only reason I'm coming back spring term is Marcus convinced them it would be more disruptive for me not to end my senior year there. My perfect attendance meant nothing to them.

"Hmm . . . you know what happened with Eric?" I ask. "Luis said he left and hasn't even been in touch with Sierra."

"Dang, I thought you already knew. Went ghost, right around the time you were dealing with your case."

I do a double take. The way Boogie says it feels like an accusation.

"You think Eric had something to do with it?"

"Don't you think that's weird? And who else would get in your locker, Sherlock? I bet he took off to stay with his birth mom."

"No way. He'd never do that. And definitely not without Sierra."

Thoughts I've been holding in begin to unravel inside me—suspicions I long buried about the only other person who had my locker combination when those stolen items were found in it. The one who's gone. But I swallow them back. Eric has always been my boy, here or not. The stealing and reselling were all Gavin. He did it for the thrill, not because he needed money. Eric just went along with everything he did because he's naive. But Gavin isn't.

Boogie has officially passed all Grandma J's stops. I know where he's headed but don't say anything. Wouldn't be Boogie if he didn't force me to face things head-on.

He pulls up and reverse-parks into a space, unbuckling his belt and acting like seeing my dad was at the top of our list.

"For real?" I say.

"You know you wanna see him. And he's just as stubborn as you, and almost as stubborn as your grandpa."

I take in Malcolm's Bookshop. Lights blinking "open." Through the store window I see my dad walking around with no customers. He's poured everything into something nobody here wants anymore: the last relic of an old Black neighborhood.

Everything I was mad about before shrivels up.

Boogie knew exactly what he was doing taking me on errands.

Maybe that's why I called him. To help me face my dad, so I wouldn't have to do it alone.

5

JUICY (DON'T LET 'EM HOLD YOU DOWN)

February 28, 2020

A small crowd is lined up at the new coffee shop next door to the bookshop. This one, according to the chalkboard sign, also features homemade kombucha in thirty-one flavors like Baskin-Robbins.

I turn back to the bookshop, staring at the mural to avoid going in to see my dad. The art keeps our history of how shipyards and flood lines moved Black families from here to the overcrowded northeast part of the city.

"History is a study of the past," Dad likes to say. "But who keeps the record, Andre? If you're not in the books, you never existed. Never forget that."

I just wonder if he's marked my history somewhere out of reach. Then I'll never be able to earn his trust again because my arrest is where my record now begins.

With blurry eyes, I study the sweeping strokes of black, blue, and gray that frame the edges of the mural; in the center are Vanport's temporary homes. These were made of wooden blocks and fiberboard walls that were protected from flooding by dikes—until they weren't. The mural documents the history. Water rising, encroaching on homes and washing them all away. On the right side of the building, facing traffic, are words from the housing authority flyer distributed to eighteen thousand residents.

On May 30—Memorial Day, 1948—
REMEMBER.
DIKES ARE SAFE AT PRESENT.
YOU WILL BE WARNED IF NECESSARY.
YOU WILL HAVE TIME TO LEAVE.
DON'T GET EXCITED.

"I still can't get over they didn't warn anyone the dikes gave way," Boogie says. "That same day, too! They don't teach that anywhere."

Ten thousand homes washed away and it's like nobody cares. Like it never happened. I don't completely agree with what my dad says about history. He asks who keeps the records, but it's not us. . . . History books are written like the past don't affect the present. I got family who lived through the flood. Died in the flood. That's why Dad's got the names of lost residents lining the walls like tattoos. Except with this history, the official numbers have yet to be recorded.

Boogie taps my shoulder. "You ready?"

I step back, admiring my favorite part, how the mural's waves

51

transform into a part-slave-ship part-Noah's-Ark that carries Black Vanport residents to safety. In real life, refuge was found in the redlined Albina district in Northeast Portland, but for the mural's sake, it's the entrance to Malcolm's Bookshop.

I finally take a deep breath, ready to be greeted by hand-carved African wooden doors with the engraved word *Karibuni*. A yellow flyer taped to the door mars the aesthetics.

"Look"—I point—"an offer to paint the exterior of my dad's shop. For F.R.E.E." I pluck it from the door, crunch it up, and toss the flyer in the trash can.

Dad's shop is the last one left of old Black Portland still hanging on on this side. Notices like these have showed up over the years like flies swarming businesses.

"What?" Boogie says. "The visuals of Portland flooding Black residents don't appeal to white liberal guilt buying property in Northeast?"

A couple takes a photo of the mural, then passes Dad's shop. Boogie drops in an exaggerated bow, widening his hands like he's directing royalty to the coffee shop next door.

They tap on their phones, walking right past him like he doesn't even exist.

"Let's go, Your Majesty." I flick his hat.

The familiar ring of the bell is quickly followed by a cheerful "Karibuni." Dad welcomes us with the one Swahili word he knows. His eager smile turns down slightly when he sees it's us.

His reaction isn't about me, though. Dad needs customers. The stillness of the store bleeds this fact.

Malcolm's Bookshop is the kind of place people go to as a tourist stop or for directions. Maybe to get a cup of cheap, refillable coffee, or to waste my dad's time as he identifies hard-to-find books for customers who leave speaking empty promises of return. We all know that these same people turn around and order online for a cheaper price.

"You came." Dad acts guilty for ditching me. "I promise I planned to be home early tonight. You didn't have to make a trip."

"Wanted to see the bookshop," I say.

"Should I be worried?" Dad stops lining up the books and makes his way to me.

"Things are good," I say. "Seriously, just dropping by to say what's up."

Dad's smile warms and he wraps his arms around me. "It's good to have you home."

I swear to God I feel like I'm ten years old again. The guilt I've been carrying releases while I'm in that hug. Dad's always been there for me. From chess, to debate, to football, basketball, soccer, the works . . . even hockey. He got me whatever I needed. He didn't show disappointment when I left a closetful of equipment and moved on to swimming, even though he didn't get why I loved the solitude of the pool more than team sports. How I could so easily wake up at five a.m. for laps, but barely take the garbage out on Friday.

When I was arrested, Dad didn't find out until he was off work. But after that he was right there, fighting for me. Just like he did when teachers graded me unfairly, or placed me in lower-level classes instead of AP. He was even there when they blamed me for fights at school. I was always silent while he reasoned with the powers that be. And what I don't like to admit: he taught me how to apologize for things I didn't do, just like Grandpa taught him.

I never understood why it was my fault that teachers treated me unfairly, underestimated me, or blamed me for some asshat calling *me* the N-word. Sticks and stones, I guess. Whatever. Staying silent is what I've always done and probably the reason things were dumped in my locker in the first place. Gavin figured I'd take it lying down and not say anything. I guess he was right.

As Dad releases me, he eyes Boogie, then points a finger at me. "I hope you're not giving your grandparents too much trouble."

"I'm not," I say. "We're just doing errands for Grandma J. She gave me two hours."

"Oh yeah?" Dad observes me. "How long you been gone?"

"Not long," I say.

"Hmm," Dad says. Then we kind of just stare at each other until Boogie speaks.

"I thought that since I'm taking him around we'd swing by the store since you left early." Boogie didn't mean to give shade, but shame crosses my dad's face anyway.

"I'll be back by dinner." Dad looks away.

"I can help around here."

"Hey, as long as kombucha is in the deal." Boogie jumps in. "I can pick him up and take him to work."

I throw a look at Boogie, but Dad doesn't pay him any mind.

"You can start by grabbing that box over there," Dad says.

I hesitate. "Let me call Grandma J and let her know I'll be home late."

"You know what . . ." The light in his eyes dims. "Let's figure out a schedule. I'll let you know when you can come in."

I was supposed to fulfill *all* of my family's dreams, and cash in on the ones deferred. The way Dad poured everything into me was his way of investing in the future. All leading up to college, hopefully Morehouse. Now he doesn't know if he can rely on me to stock the shelves.

"Yeah. Okay." I force the tornado that's stirring inside me to stop letting these reminders affect me.

"Good to see you, son."

He says goodbye like I'm not coming back. Like the flick of a switch, things changed with my dad, and we might never get back to the way we were. I realize, leaving the store, that he didn't look me in the eyes the whole time I was there. It's like he's done dreaming of my possibilities. Now he's just waiting for me to leave.

6

IT WAS A GOOD DAY

February 29, 2020

We zip across town—Boogie's unbothered by how long it's taking
even though almost every store is out of stock of what we need.
To him, my list is a breeze. His errands for his family are usually a minimum six stops, guaranteed to include Merkato's Ethio-
pian Music & Food Store and at least two Eritrean relatives. I'm
now an expert on where to get the best berbere spices, coriander,
cumin, and fenugreek.

His East African community runs deep in Portland. Boogie
doesn't complain about driving me around because he owes me
for all the times I tagged along for cultural events where he needed
a wingman—Habesha weddings, funerals, and baby showers. I
don't count last summer's trip to California with his brother,
Kidane, for the Eritrean Festival North America. That trip was
off the chain.

Boogie pulls up to my grandparents' house and pops the trunk. But my eyes are on Marcus's car parked in front.

"He the one that's gonna be riding you the next six months?" Boogie checks out Marcus with Grandpa Jackson.

"Yeah." I suck my teeth in.

"I hope he's not one of them brothas out to prove he'll be twice as hard on you."

I gulp at the thought.

Marcus meets us, grabbing bags without asking.

"Everything good?" I say, following him into the house, legs shaking at my first check-in.

"You been active today." Marcus places the bags on the kitchen table.

"Stores busy?" Grandma J says.

"Yeah," I say. "Shelves were empty. It felt like last-minute shopping before Christmas and a storm coming all at the same night."

"I've never seen anything like it," Boogie says. "The lines went all the way down the aisles, people fighting over toilet paper and soap. They were fresh out, but we got lucky at the pharmacy."

We tap fists because it was Boogie's genius idea to check there. We also keep where we got the spaghetti sauce a secret because Grandma J would turn up her nose at that, overpriced and dusty bottles.

"Let's talk outside," Marcus says.

Boogie follows me to the front door. We throw glances back and forth, speaking our own language.

"Alone." Marcus blocks Boogie before stepping outside.

"My grandma told you I was doing errands, right?" I shove my hands into my pockets.

"This is the kind of thing you might wanna give me a heads-up on." His voice is stern. "You got my card, right?"

I should've known he'd be hard on me regardless of what he said about calling him Uncle Marcus. Now I'm getting whiplash thinking of him being both types of dudes.

"What's the point of having an ankle monitor, then?" I wish I was bold enough to tell him what I really think. That it's a joke to be this excessively monitored. How am I supposed to get my life back living like this?

"You've only been back one day. Your every move is going to be scrutinized."

"Going to Fred Meyer's and the pharmacy counts as breaking rules?"

"Your trip was flagged as risky activity."

"How so? It's hardly six o'clock. Check my bags if you're concerned."

Marcus rubs his chin, giving me the *I'm not tryna be hard* look. "I'm not the enemy, son."

There he goes calling me son again.

"Listen. I'm sorry. . . . I'm not saying this to scare you, but it's not just about you following the program." Marcus walks to the edge of the porch, a serious pinched face. "You got community monitoring because what you did was considered a low-level crime."

"I know." I shake my head, confused what he's getting at.

"Before I took your case from—"

"Cowboy Jim?"

"Jim Adkins." Marcus glares.

Jim was my first juvenile counselor, an old white guy who had a reputation for pushing more Black and brown kids to detention than alternatives. He's the one who got the ankle monitor added by telling the judge I was a chiseler. Which I had to look up to learn it was old Western slang for a swindler not to be trusted. That's when I finally understood how he got his nickname from the guys inside.

"He's keeping an eye on you. He hasn't let your case go. I hear he's still in touch with your arresting officer investigating more charges."

"No. He can't do that, can he?"

"Will he find out there were more robberies?"

"No way. I had nothing to do with those!" I bark back at him, then relax. "No. This was never on me—bad luck got me. I'm not taking the blame for whatever he finds next." I throw my arm around like I can fling the accusations away.

But Marcus doesn't want to hear me claim innocence. That's not part of embracing the *rehabilitation* process. My mind races.

"Look, I'm not trying to be hard on you," Marcus says. "I shouldn't have brought it up. . . . I know you're a good kid. I did dumber things growing up, I'm just lucky I had the right people watching out for me." He places his hand on my shoulder and I fight the urge to dip out of his grip. "If you get out of this clean, you've got another chance. But if you keep going the way you were headed with all you associated with, got blamed for, whatever . . . That's the wrong path, son."

I nod like a good boy. And that's when I catch sight of Sierra looking across from her bedroom window.

Watching us.

Watching *me.*

I give her two fingers to let her know I'm *good.* She hesitates but steps away from the window.

When I turn back to Marcus, he's wearing a big old goofy grin on his face.

Damn.

"Now I see why you were all into staying at your grandparents' house. 'It's all right. . . .' Huh, so this a crush situation next door."

"It's not like that." I look away.

"Right. You wide open, Dre. I see you, heart jumping out of your chest."

I turn my head, mouth pursed. I know he's not giving me a lecture and love advice at the same damn time. Who does he think he is?

"Listen," Marcus says. "If you really want to catch her attention, having your counselor check on you won't help."

There's no point in arguing, so I let him go off.

"And just in case Jim is really on you, I suggest you keep me up-to-date on all your whereabouts."

"So should I text you when I'm taking a—"

"Just give me a call if you're gonna to be out long." Marcus gestures toward Boogie, who is hemmed up with Grandma J. "What's his story, he got a record?"

"Highest GPA."

"Don't be smart. Just answer the question."

"No. He doesn't have a record."

"Good. Let's keep your circle tight, okay? And hey, bet you didn't find this at the store." Marcus pulls out a bottle of Purell from his back pocket, his eyes shining. He must expect some big thanks.

"How'd you know?" That's the only thing I couldn't get off Grandma J's list.

"Everybody's looking for this stuff. Take care of yourself, son." Marcus shakes my hand before giving me the Purell and making his exit.

I squeeze a drop on my palm for good measure before going inside. Boogie sits at the table with my grandparents, throwing down on leftovers.

"What'd he say?" Grandpa Jackson asks.

"He said to call if I'm going around town."

"You lucky that's all he said," Grandpa grumbles at me.

Of course he'd say it like that. Like I must've messed up. My heart thuds from the constant nitpicking I have to deal with now, from Marcus to my own family.

"Eat, honey." Grandma J puts a plate of food on the table.

I choke my anger down, shoveling food so I don't have to speak. Not taking a chance I'll mess that up too.

—

I FLOP ON my bed as Boogie opens my computer.

"You touch your YouTube channel?" he says. "Let the fans know you back?"

"Nah. All my followers are probably gone."

"Log me in."

"For what?" I do it anyway.

Boogie makes a few keystrokes.

My stomach turns when he opens up my YouTube channel. He scrolls, then rubs his chin before turning to me.

"You watch this?" Boogie points out the last live video I made—it was filmed at the same time police knocked on my grandparents' door.

That day, I was all juiced to plot out my top ten favorite song reaction videos of 2019. Still queasy as hell from the night before, I propped myself by the window to get fresh air and work on my live recordings. I don't even remember having left the laptop recording when I jumped out of my seat to get to the door.

Boogie plays the video, but I don't need to know how bad it was. I was there. Now that moment is not only seared in my mind, but recorded live, watched, then shared exactly 1,369 times. Heat flashes to my cheeks as I think about all the people who've not only heard about my arrest but shared the worst night of my life. Boogie never said it, but I know the entire school was talking about me and filling in all the gaps for the drama.

I wince at the video—hearing cops knocking on my door, and next thing you know, Grandma's screaming. Everything moved so fast I was scared to death that something happened to my parents.

I wish I didn't stay over, then my grandparents wouldn't have witnessed me go down like that. All I could do that night was repeat, "I'll be fine. It's a misunderstanding."

The last thing I remember seeing before I was taken in was Eric standing near the Whitakers' front porch. That image is still fixed in my mind.

I glance out the window now, still expecting Eric to be waiting for me. That night, I swear fear was dancing back and forth between us because we didn't know if he'd be next. I tried to not act freaked, so he wouldn't worry, when I should've been thinking about myself.

I thought I was better off staying silent at the station that first night. I told myself Eric had more to lose than me, the way he had to bounce from foster home to foster home before being adopted.

"I should've been there with you at that party," Boogie says. "I didn't go because I could feel trouble coming on. I keep thinking about what if I would've gone with you. Or made you and Eric come to my family party instead."

"Who knows how things would've went down. Trust me, I've thought all the same things about what I could've changed. Forget about it."

"What are you gonna do about Gavin for letting you take the fall?" Boogie asks. "Payback? Just let me know."

Thoughts of revenge have turned in my head a thousand times. A beatdown. Takeover of a school assembly to call him out. Anything that'd let me watch his Ivy League dreams vanish into the ether. But from every angle I look, I end up losing. Nothing helps. Gavin should've been the one who got arrested, not me. He got off because he had a good lawyer that came the same night we were arrested. I was just the last one left, lawyerless, with no clue what to do, while everyone else was cozied up in bed counting sheep. Except, of course, whoever stashed the stolen goods in my locker at the Parks & Rec.

The thing about going through something like this is that everybody turns against you without bothering to hear your side.

There's no such thing as innocent until proven guilty—it's just guilty until proven innocent. No one *really* wants the truth. They just want it to be done with.

Boogie waits on me to say go. To name a time and place.

"He'll just get me in trouble again." I turn away. "It's whatever."

"It's whatever? You can't let Gavin get away with that. And Eric ain't so innocent either."

"They already got away with it, Boogie. I gotta leave that stuff behind. Keep out of trouble. They'll get theirs. I just won't be the one to do it."

"I hear you."

He doesn't, but he lets it go.

Marcus has been getting me ready for this. He told me to take my time—think. Don't get caught up in trying to get back at the world. After hearing his warnings earlier today, I gotta be extra careful. So even though Boogie is itching to help me give a beatdown, I'm not sure it's what I want.

"You see these comments." Boogie scans my YouTube channel.

I lean over his shoulder, stunned at all the comments I see.

This is messed up!

Yo @dog99$ you see this video yet?

You okay? Haven't updated your channel in a long time.

Where can we send bail money?

This a hoax?

Then I rewind the video and squint as I look at the blurry figure of Eric caught in view when my laptop was left on recording. Eric watches from across the lawn just like I remembered, except this time I finally accept he did me like this.

"You gonna look for him?" Boogie says. "He can't stay gone forever."

"I'm stuck for a while." I point to my ankle. "But I need to talk to him. Make sure this is really all over. Can you go by his old spots for me?"

"Yeah," Boogie says. "I got you." We clasp hands and do our handshake. "I'll ask around school, too."

I think I'm still in shock at reliving my arrest from outside my body. It felt like a movie when it happened, but reading the comments, seeing how terrified I look, makes me sink deeper in my seat. Sharp pain shoots in my chest, I'm experiencing it again so vividly.

"Hey." Boogie nudges me. "Forget about this stuff for a while. Let's do some live reaction videos?"

"Not feeling it tonight."

"No rest if you're trying to make the top five greatest YouTube reaction channels."

"Yeah, with all my hundreds of followers."

"Check again." Boogie logs back on, tapping at the screen. "Over ten thousand followers."

"Stop playing. . . ." I scan through more comments, checking my exponential growth, sparked like a match by my arrest. "Definitely wasn't on my marketing plan."

"The people love DJ Andre." Boogie hits my side. "Give them what they want."

"Scoot over." I shove Boogie aside, shamefaced but unwilling to let my channel's legacy be left with the tremble in my voice and the wail of Grandma J.

My shoulders relax once I focus on the music. I don't bother deleting the video because it's already been viewed and rerecorded so many times, I might as well be a man about it. I try to keep perspective as it could've been hella worse.

I wasn't naked.

Didn't cry.

And didn't take no beatdown.

My channel is all about first-time reaction videos to the early 1980s and '90s music I never heard before. I pick a song and nudge Boogie. "You ready?"

He reaches for a cough drop in his pocket, then we do a count-down so we can pose at the same time.

"I'm back." I cross my arms.

"We back." Boogie leans in next to me, hanging his arm over my shoulder.

"We're back." I throw a smile. "Coming to you from the five-oh-three with another so-called hit. I'm a little rusty, but fortunately for you"—I hit my chest twice—"I'm searching for the greatest, not the latest."

"Ya feel me," we say in unison, throwing our hands in the air and dancing as my intro video plays.

"We got Kurtis Blow for you. All about 'The Breaks.' And Lord knows I've needed a few."

When I don't know what to pick I usually search for titles that match my mood. I hope Kurtis Blow is talking about catching a break and not break dancing.

As soon as the song begins, Boogie lets out a laugh and makes a face, imitating Kurtis Blow. He pauses, then smiles wide. I mimic Blow's reaction as the beat drops. *These.* Pause. *Are.* Pause. *The breaks.* Smile. I let him get in a few bars before pausing the video and speaking directly to Boogie and the screen.

"He lists all kinda breaks." We're still live but I pause the music video as I count off my fingers. "Brakes on the bus. Brakes on your car. Being a superstar."

"When your girls run out on you," Boogie says. "The IRS calls." Then he points to me but keeps his gaze on the camera. "This is definitely your song, man."

"Shut up, man," I chuckle. "All right, let's see what else they got, other than all your families' jewelry on his neck. Look at all that gold." I slip that in before Boogie gets time to respond while the video plays.

We let the song ride out, mimicking Kurtis Blow. Drums are going off in percussions and we follow Blow's head bouncing up and down at each escalation. Getting back to something normal releases all the stress I've been holding on to. Listening to a new song is like swimming to the bottom of the ocean, never knowing what each trip will bring. I let the music lift me up and carry my thoughts away.

7

LOST IN EMOTION, SIERRA SIERRA

February 29, 2020

A tap at my window draws my attention. My gaze lands on brown eyes that instantly hold me hostage, my trance only broken when Boogie speaks.

"You gonna let her in, or just keep looking goofy?"

I rush to the window before Boogie says something else she can hear through the glass.

"Sierra." I stare at her, knowing my smile is too wide.

"Open." She hoists herself up to my window from a large rock we planted there years ago. The sweet scent of her cinnamon gum floats to me.

"Kurtis Blow!" Sierra plops on the bed, kicking off her shoes. She has a way of making the world spin around her and it's hard not to be pulled in.

"How'd—"

"Got a notification." She shows her phone. "You really started without me?"

I replay the music video without our commentary. For YouTube, we have to pause the song we listen to on air to avoid getting fined or shut down because of rights, so we fill the time with our reactions. After hearing a song, Sierra always likes to play it again, uninterrupted.

But Boogie's ready to move on, so he gives her a look.

"What? It's always better the second time." Her laugh tinkles as she watches the video.

I'm trapped in her presence.

"What else you got?" Boogie says, before a round of coughs bursts from him.

"Here." I pull out my phone for my song list tracked in Notes.

Sierra snatches it before Boogie can take control.

Today we were live, but we usually record each play and only upload the songs we're feeling.

I prefer songs with actual videos, although sometimes there aren't any. If the song's wack, it doesn't get loaded on my channel. Good vibes are what I go for, exposing people to all kinds of music. Before I started my channel, I used to be rigid about what I was into—heavy about Christian rap because Grandma J didn't like me listening to secular music. It was my way of still playing rap, until I got caught up into it and began feeling the messages like with Lecrae or KB. Every once in a while, she freaks out when she thinks she heard something bad, but I'd come at her like, "Nah, Grandma J, he said forget it. Jee-zus as in savior. Son of God." But when I opened up the type of music I listened to, I realized there's so much out there I hadn't even given a chance. I got tired of people assuming what I liked and didn't like. Being back home, doing the thing I love, well . . . it's got me sentimental. I'm ready to play all night.

"We just got lucky with back-to-back hits," I say as the viewer count slowly grows. "It's been a long time, so get ready for a night of the greatest, not the latest."

We play an old-school early-'90s R&B classic and I can't help but watch Sierra as she nods to the beat.

Boogie moves off-camera and starts ogling me from behind Sierra's back, calling me out for studying her so hard. I can barely focus when he starts making kissing faces at me. He's a man-child.

When it's done, we stop going live to sort through songs that followers want us to play.

"How about this one?" Sierra picks Mary J. Blige's "I Can Love You," which is late '90s but I let it slide since it's technically in the decade even though I usually stick with early '90s.

"Yeah, let's do that one," I say, too eager.

"Yeah, Sierra, whatever you want," Boogie mimics me but all exaggerated-like.

We pause the song and repeat the lyrics, which are dope. Then press play again. I flick my eyes at her, then nod to the beat.

"Who's gone love you like I do? Huh? Wha?" Boogie repeats Lil' Kim's verse now that he has it down, then he dances in his seat, mean mugging and moving his pointer fingers back and forth at us like he's calling us out.

I sock him in the leg so he'll stop. Sierra makes a quick turn to catch what's going on. That's when I run my finger across my neck, glaring at Boogie. He lets out a laugh but chokes from a coughing fit.

"You sick, man?" I say.

"Just a cold I'm getting over. My cough medicine must be wearing off."

"Don't be passing us the plague," I joke.

Boogie rolls his eyes, then nurses his growing cough by guzzling water.

The music is easy to get lost in. Well, more like Sierra's easy to lose myself in watching her. That's why it takes me a minute to notice Boogie packing up.

"I gotta go." Boogie hits his elbow with mine. "This cough's killing me. I need to crash so I can be good for school on Monday."

"Yeah, all right. Thanks for rolling with me today."

"I got you. Good to see you, Sierra." Boogie gives her a hug, then he eyeballs me to see if I'll react. I shake my head instead.

At the door Boogie stops. "If I find anything out, I'll let you know. . . ."

I nod thanks.

"A few more songs?" I say, hoping she'll stay.

"Yeah. Okay." She sits next to me at the computer. "What's next?"

We hardly miss a beat. Cracking jokes, or dead silence when there's a song we're both taken by. I play "Nothing Compares 2 U" by Sinead O'Connor, not Prince's version. Sierra closes her eyes, nodding to the music and mouthing the words. When it's done, I wait for her response.

"I like her version better, I think."

"No way. It's good, but *Prince*. Come on. He wrote that, you know." I load up Prince and play his version.

"It's close," Sierra says when it's over. "They're both good. Depends on what kind of mood you're in."

"Yeah, I can see that. Like right now you're in that emo zone, where you don't need much soul and vibrato, just all the angst."

"Stop," she laughs. "That's not even it."

"Okay. Whatever."

The music puts me in a Prince mood so I search through different versions of his covers and songs. The last I choose is his live performance at Paisley Park. From the way Sierra is getting lost in the song, I can tell I've converted her with this take but she won't admit it. So, I play the next live at the Park with "Purple Rain." Eleven minutes of perfection. When it's over, Sierra's misty eyes make me smile.

"I missed you," she says. "You know that, right?"

My chest rips open. A million questions float to the top of my mind. Why didn't she go to my pretrial or answer my calls or respond to the dozens of letters I wrote? But I'm afraid the answer is Paul, or that it's got to do with Eric. Or worse, my mark in juvie has forever changed the way she feels about me. The same way it's changed the way Grandpa and my dad look at me now. They might act like time in juvie didn't matter, but deep down we all know it does.

We lock eyes before I speak. "I didn't know if you wanted to see me."

"Course I wanted to see you. Why would you think that?"

I shrug because it's hard to answer. Dredging up the past is too heavy.

"I . . ." Sierra dances around her words. "You just reminded me of my family, before we went through the foster system. I used to feel so let down, hoping things would change if my mom got her act together. I couldn't do it, couldn't see you like that, where I'm helpless and can't get you out."

"I didn't need you to try to get me out," I say in a parched voice. "I needed help getting through it."

Sierra reaches for my hand. A tear escapes and she lets it slide. I wanna reach for it, but also don't want to let go.

"Did you even read any of my letters?" I scrunch my eyes, holding back those memories ready to explode like the Vanport dike. It'll pour out eventually, but right now I just want to swallow all the bad. How I wanted my family and friends there for me so I wouldn't have to rely on the people inside. Some of them were cool, but most of them I couldn't trust so easily.

In juvie, everyone fights for their own existence. Especially the ones headed to adult prison after twenty-five.

Every day, I searched for things to remind me of the Andre I knew myself to be, not the Dre the officers and guards kept telling me I was. They didn't lead with second chances, they led with threats and consequences. They pushed most people until their backs were against the wall. Until all anyone could do was fulfill their expectations.

I tap my chest with a fist to remind myself I'm not there anymore. I'm here. I'm me.

"I read them." Sierra takes my hand from my chest. "At first, my parents kept them from me. I found a stack of letters in my father's desk drawer."

"What?" It hadn't occurred to me that Mr. Whitaker would

ever do something like that. Anger filled with betrayal spins me inside. I was good enough to help, but not good enough for their daughter?

"He said he was waiting for the right time," Sierra says.

I scroll back and forth on the computer screen, mindlessly distracting myself from looking at her.

"When I found the letters, they let me keep them, but I was worried he'd do better at hiding the ones that followed if he knew I was writing you."

Or read them, but we didn't have to say that part out loud.

"It's been a lot since Eric disappeared, not hearing from him." Sierra takes my hand from the computer mouse. We intertwine our fingers. "I didn't know what to say after finding all those letters, after not answering. . . . I didn't know if you'd be mad at me. And I didn't want to write back blaming my parents, in case they saw it."

"I told you. We're family. Forever. I'd never let anything happen to you. I'd have your back, just like I had Eric's." I pause. "You think Eric went to find your birth mom?"

"Never." Sierra pulls her hand away, trailing her fingers on her leg.

We both know Eric could've been caught up with the police just as quickly as me, worse even. I watch her, wondering if she knows more than she's letting on, but the sadness in her eyes tells me not to ask.

Does she think Eric will return because he's safe now that the case is closed? And is that only because I didn't rat him out? I sneak a glance at Sierra to see if she's wondering the same thing.

"I'm back," I say, despite my thoughts. "Not going anywhere."

Sierra reaches down for my monitor, tracing my ankle line. She tugs at it, and I cringe a little. I didn't want her to see it, much less touch it.

"I'm not gonna get caught up," I say.

"That's not what I'm worried about."

"Then what?"

"People judging you. I'm sorry I wasn't a better friend."

"Well, it looks like you're just gonna have to make it up to me." I force a laugh, choking on my achy throat because maybe Sierra will be different than my dad. "I don't wanna talk about this anymore. I just wanna know we're still cool."

She releases a smile. I almost tell her how much I really missed her but Sierra's already scrolling through her phone's reminder list for songs. She hands over the ranked list, and I can't help but let my heart reach for her even more.

"Let's record this one live," she says.

I don't say anything. I just do what she tells me and start a new session.

"Coming to you from the five-oh-three with another so-called hit. Not the latest, but the greatest. And I've got my special guest, yours and my favorite, Sierra Sierra."

Sierra chuckles when she hears my old channel nickname for her.

"Tell them what's new, Sierra Sierra," I say.

"Things that are new . . ." She pokes her lips out and taps at her chin before pointing. "A new haircut, lipstick, earrings, and of course, new cuts to play."

"Ya feel me," we say in unison with our signature hands raising above our head. "Let's go."

"Here's a ballad for this beauty." I point to Sierra. "'Take My Breath Away' by Berlin."

I'm cheating because I know this song, from *Top Gun*. Another one of my quirks is watching old movies.

Beneath the table Sierra and I hold hands, earbuds in, music blasting. I almost forget to pause for commentary because the song has my feelings all tangled up. When it ends, we're still locked by our fingers. I don't even think about moving because I don't want to disrupt this vibe. But then I feel Sierra's finger twitch and it's like we're both released.

"All right," I say to my audience. "I'll catch you next time. You like what you see, click that subscribe button. Add those comments below on what we should play next time."

When I log off, Sierra has a smirk on her face. "You knew that song already."

"What, no?" I wink.

"You totally did. You were that air force guy for Halloween in eighth grade."

"And?"

"And . . . I watched the movie after. That song is totally in there."

"Oh, so, you watched then?" I grin. "Couldn't stop thinking about me, had to see the inspiration."

"Stop," she laughs, then grabs my phone to check my song list.

I reach for her, catching her between me and the computer. The replay button hits on the computer and the song plays again. She shrugs her jacket off, and I don't know what takes me over, but I cup her face in my hands, running my finger along her cheek and then her lips. She leans, and I start to close the gap between us as she reaches for me.

The sight of bruises on her wrist stops me.

"What happened?" I try to take a closer look, but she snatches her hand back like she's touched a flame.

"Nothing." Her tone grows distant. "Wow. What are we . . ." Her body has now turned rigid. I've been gone awhile, but I still know her. Her wall is building up before my eyes. Maybe she's realizing this is a mistake, remembering that she's with Paul and feeling like what we had can't be rekindled. I grasp at what to say to bring her back to that moment, but it's totally shot. She's already pulled on her jacket, dipping under my arm and grabbing her things.

"It's late," she says.

"Yeah, okay." I search my mind for some way to fix this moment, but she is practically flying out the window.

She trips on the ground, then waves back at me to say she's fine. I watch her run across the lawn, past the rosebushes, to her front door.

Next time just kiss the girl, Andre.

POISON

February 29, 2020

Before I get a chance to see if Sierra's changed her mind and is looking at me from her bedroom window, Grandma J barges into my room. I'm surprised she controlled herself for as long as she did.

"Uh, do I get some privacy here?"

"Privacy?" Grandma J searches for Sierra. "She don't know how to use the front door?"

"The window's faster," I say.

Grandma J's got two slices of pie on a plate in one hand and the other on her hip, so I know that all must be forgiven anyway. Her gaze searches for Sierra, who is long gone.

"I know you got some feelings for her, but she can't distract you from what you're supposed to be doing."

"Which is?"

"Focusing on yourself."

"You sound like Grandpa." I take a bite of her pie. She thinks she's nothing like Grandpa, but she's just as nosy. Grandpa at least gives me the dignity of eavesdropping from the family room.

"Sometimes pretty girls are more trouble than they're worth."

"Her parents are probably saying the same exact thing about me," I say. "Anyway, we were just playing music. Do you know what kids these days be doing?" I point out the window like there's people acting a fool, running the streets.

"I know exactly what everyone's up to. Just because me and Grandpa are older doesn't mean we don't know what's what."

I chuckle, then shake my head.

Grandma's soft eyes tear up and I'm immediately back to the moment I was dragged away. The fear that shook from her body haunts me.

"I promise on everything. No trouble from me. I swear." I lift my Boy Scout hand, the only thing I remember from the two meetings I went to before learning I had no interest in mastering the art of camping, tying knots, and wilderness things.

"I'm not worried about you getting into trouble. I'm worried about you getting your heart broken."

She points at the window, and I follow her gaze. My stomach drops when I see Paul pull up, hovering between our houses.

Sierra opens her window and climbs out, a longer drop to the ground than mine. She brushes herself off, then runs to Paul's car.

I feel hella played.

All my hopes crash to the ground. Sierra wasn't thinking about me the same way.

"She's been different since Eric left," Grandma J says. "Hanging out late, getting picked up . . . arguments."

I'm silent. It's one thing for Boogie to be giving me a hard time about Sierra, but knowing even Grandma J's got neighborhood watch on lock for Sierra—and she's witnessed Sierra falling for some other dude . . . That breaks my heart more.

My thoughts pause on Grandma J's comment, *arguments*.

I remember the bruises on Sierra's wrist. I've never seen anything like those on her before. I wanna believe they're exactly what she said they were. I should've stopped her from leaving, but I was too busy thinking about her lips on mine.

Paul's car drives away with Sierra. My stomach turns. If he hurt her . . .

"You want ice cream with that?" Grandma J cuts into my thoughts.

I follow her down to the kitchen, catching Grandpa all up in the front window.

She spoons ice cream onto my plate, then adds another slice to the one that was for Sierra. I cock an eyebrow, confused, but don't question her. Maybe she knows it's one of those days.

We sit on the porch. It's an old ritual of ours. Usually after I've gotten into it with my dad, or fallen off my bike, or gotten a bad grade . . . Sitting on the porch with Grandma J is no match for whatever is keeping me down.

Outside, with the sky darkening, all you can hear are crickets, and there is the smell of fresh rain, earthy and moist. No matter how bad I feel, those smells always make things better. As I take each bite, I think of all the pies I missed being stuck in juvie with nowhere for my feelings to go.

I choke down food as my throat swells.

"I'll never forget the first day she broke your heart," Grandma J says. "You were riding your bike right out here. That summer they'd just moved in, you spent hours outside with her and the Whitaker kids."

We were twelve. That was the best summer of my life, until her last foster mom came to take her, the one before the Whitakers finally adopted them.

"Her face lit up so bright when that car pulled up. You just burst into tears, the saddest kid on the block."

Sierra and Eric packed up without saying goodbye. Gone three weeks.

"You worry me because you give yourself to the world. I saw how heartbroken you were. When she came back, for good, you were brought to life. I thought, *Andre is gonna love some girl so hard one day and she's just gonna break him.*" Grandma J squeezes my knee.

I look away, tears forming.

"Look at me." She grips my chin and makes me focus on her. "You can't heal somebody else, Andre. All you can do is be the best person you can and hope they do the same. Then somehow you find each other and make each other even better because you worked on you first. Money can't buy that kind of love. It only makes it easier. She's looking for somebody to love her and not leave her. And you scare her because you left."

I nod because I get what she's saying.

"When Eric disappeared after your arrest, we were all expecting the police to be picking him up just like they did with you. When he came back and didn't even stick around to say goodbye to Sierra, I knew it was gonna be bad for her."

"You talk to him?"

"No. He came home with his dad. I thought he was back for good, but he must've been getting the last of his things because the next day, they were still all talking about Eric being gone."

I gape up at Grandma J, ready to ask her if she knew all along I was covering for Eric. But I swallow the truth. It doesn't matter anymore.

"Well, that's enough advice from an old woman for one day," Grandma J says. "Now, this isn't for you." The pie is wrapped in Saran Wrap, marked *L & S,* for Luis and Sierra. "And don't take one step beyond my porch after you drop this off." Grandma J tugs my chin before planting a kiss on my cheek.

"I heard you, Grandma. I heard you."

Grandma J shuffles inside to the house. Grandpa waits on the other side of the door.

Movement on the roof of the Whitakers' catches my eye.

Luis sits with his feet slung over the edge, scanning the neighborhood, lit cigarette in hand. He's always been a night owl, but this is the first time I've seen him smoke. If Eric was here, he wouldn't stand for this. I'm reminded how much they need Eric. If he was here right now, he'd either play like he's gonna throw Luis off the roof or smoke a whole pack until he throws up, making Luis sick just watching him. Eric always takes things to the next level, and it somehow just works. But he's not here, so I step up, lifting the pie in my hand toward Luis, putting it in view as I walk to the edge of our lawn. "This is for you."

The light on Luis's cigarette goes out. Then he climbs back inside his window, and a few minutes later he steps out the front door with a fork in his hand.

"Thanks." Luis takes the back of his fork and separates the pie in half before eating his side. Then we walk across the grass to my grandparents' porch swing.

We've always been cool. Eric was a friend, but Luis was like my little brother. His eyes lit up when I'd give him a little bit of attention. It made me feel what it would be like if I had a sibling. I don't mind being an only child, just sometimes it'd be nice to have someone who gets what it's like to not have what everyone else did. What it was like moving all the time, taking care of my things so they'd last longer. Boogie is the closest thing to me, but there are still things I don't like to share. I wouldn't have to explain it to a sibling.

"School going okay?" I say.

"Yeah, it's fine."

"Didn't sound like it from Kate."

"Since when do you listen to Kate?"

"Good point." I force a chuckle. "It's just not like you is all." I pinch my fingers and draw them up to my lips to imitate his smoking.

"Don't get on me too. I'm not addicted, all right?"

"Not yet," I joke, but I'm still bothered, wishing Eric was here to stop him.

We sit, quiet again. Luis was always a thinker, but if you wait it out long enough, he usually opens up.

"I'm not acting out, okay? And besides, I know how to not go too far. Don't want to be shipped off to some military boarding school."

I study him before saying, "Well, that would never happen."

"Okay." Luis raises his eyebrows when he says it.

"It wouldn't. Look at how your parents helped me."

"Right," Luis says.

"If you're trying to get away, flunking school might make that harder."

Luis clucks his tongue. "My parents would totally ship me off if I pushed them. And I don't have to stay here, I can go anytime. Except there's nothing out there for me to run to."

"Is that what happened to Eric?"

"Military school or running away?" Luis says with an irritated tone. "What's the real reason you're asking? Because you care or because you want revenge?"

I blink fast. I didn't think Luis knew the truth about my arrest.

"I care . . . and I want to know if I should be worried still."

Luis stands. "I'm sorry about what happened, but Eric had no choice. He never did."

I linger at his words, wondering what he means.

"Eric's my boy. You think he ran because he was worried what I'd do? What the police would do?"

"I think Eric was scared. I'm sure he got rid of any evidence before he left."

My eyes widen, hoping that's true. "And Gavin?"

"You tell me. Don't you know him better than I do?"

After one of my shifts at the Parks & Rec there was this mousy-looking kid at the park who'd sometimes get picked on. This one time I saw Gavin getting on him, Eric began to rag on him too. I called Eric out because it wasn't like him to join in on that kind of thing. The next day, Eric bumped into him, half as hard as the guys earlier. But guess who the kid ended up reporting to Terry at the Parks & Rec?

Eric was easy to point out—a skinny Black kid. See, even

when you're bullied, you know better than to go for the top dog. Gavin didn't say nothing, and neither did Eric. It's always been like that with them. So to Gavin, I was an easy target to save his friend. With me gone, Eric must've known he was next.

"Yeah, I know Gavin," I say.

Luis stares at his house, then back at me. "Tell your grandma I said thanks."

He hands me the plate but I push it back to him.

"Leave it in her room . . . for when she gets back." We lock eyes for a second too long and I feel exposed. "She all right?" I shove my hands in my pockets and break eye contact.

"She's . . . Sierra." Luis shrugs, then walks back home.

"Hey, Luis," I call after him. "I'm here, man. If you ever need me, a'ight?"

Luis gives a half smile, then keeps on walking.

Inside the house I replay our conversation. He seems grown, too grown. As I try to make sense of it, thoughts of Sierra snake into my mind. I feel betrayed by her being with Paul. I shouldn't, but I do. I distract myself by focusing on what's important— finding Eric so I know for sure there won't be another charge of robbery looming over me.

I search on social media for any presence of Eric that can lead me to where he is. Then follow all the people who used to be cool with him. I scroll through Eric's photos, searching for people, re- calling anyone from the New Year's party he might have talked to. Then I send a DM to Eric:

I'm back. Case is settled. Hit me up.

I'm not naive. Eric bouncing and letting me take the fall was a bad move. But I know him. I also know I chose to take the fall.

Eric didn't know what I was gonna do. It was unspoken. But now that I'm out, I need to know if he was as loyal to me as I was to him. I need to know he won't screw me again.

When I reach for my lamp, a piece of paper flutters to the ground. Sierra's curly handwriting. It's every song that we've ever made a reaction video to written in small cursive, *been watching these since you've been gone.* A sly smile sneaks across my face. Maybe not everything is lost.

STILL D.R.E.

March 1, 2020

Early Sunday morning, I eat breakfast with Mom before she goes into work. Then, on my way to Albina Parks & Rec, I swing by Eric's old hangout spots. Even though I'm on a mission to get to work, I can't help but look for him as I take in the rush of being out in the open. From the air on my skin to the boundless thrills with each bump beneath my tires, swerve on the road, and hill I climb, freedom spins inside me. I'm out and don't have to look behind my shoulder.

I take my time searching various spots for Eric. A growing sense of dread builds from his absence. In alleys, I stop to talk with kids my age living on the street. Usually I'd ignore them, but today I approach, flashing them photos of Eric. I get nothing but empty stares back.

Ready to give up, I ride another block past a corner market where Eric used to get sodas. I pop in, grabbing a drink before heading to the cashier.

After I pay, I hold up my phone. "You seen a guy like this around here?"

The lady puts her glasses on and squints.

"I think so."

My eyes widen until she shakes her head.

"A few months ago. Short kid, got a sister named Sarah or Serena?"

"Sierra," I say. "A few months then?"

"Hmm, yeah, like December maybe? His sister asked the same thing last month. Sorry, kid."

My shoulders slump. I place my phone back in my pocket and exit, riding faster so I make it on time to Albina Parks & Rec.

Eric used to tag along with me when Gavin was at baseball practice. He'd help me clear the pool, locker room, even storage. And when Terry gave him a hard time because he wasn't on the payroll, Eric would play ball outside. Mind you, he couldn't ball for the life of him, throwing bricks, double dribbling, but his big smile and easy laugh kept him around. I knew what was behind that laugh—a mask to fit in at all costs.

I pull up to the park, locking my bike as nerves take over. Two summers ago, you couldn't tear me away from this place. I practically grew up here. Raised by the basketball courts, playing in the sandboxes as a kid, even had my first kiss in the park's tire tunnel. What cemented it as home for me was the summer program for Black kids to learn how to swim.

It was a program meant to dissolve fears passed down from generations, back when pools used to be segregated. Growing up, I heard all kind of excuses why I shouldn't swim. That water was our enemy, haunted by ancestors left on ships and those who jumped in the ocean to choose their destiny. Stories about bleach being poured into the water because white folks didn't like us swimming in their pools. Avoiding pools so your hair wouldn't go brittle or skin wouldn't dry out crackly, like an alligator. I shudder at ashy skin.

When I defeated those fears, swimming silenced the world. It shut down everything coming at me, the things telling me who I am and what I ought to be. There was peace in a way I didn't know I needed.

While *away,* I missed holding my breath underwater until my lungs felt like they'd explode. I'd chase that feeling by practicing in the shower, letting the water splash over me while I held my breath so long I felt like passing out.

Now I don't know if I'll be able to swim here. I can taste ammonia in the back of my throat just pulling up. My eyes burn like chlorine. *I swear that's why my eyes are watering.*

Before I enter, I swallow hard, then slump in the lobby seats waiting for Terry, the director.

Terry Jones gave me my first job working summer camps. Once I joined the city swim team, I'd found my way in. He's the type of dude that's been in the neighborhood a long time. And as he likes to remind everyone, he done seen some things. Terry's a Black Mr. Miyagi, making you do stuff that makes no sense. But once you hook him by not giving up—he invests in you.

My phone buzzes with a text from Boogie:

Boogie: Mean ass Terry chew you out yet?

Andre: Still waiting in the lobby.

Boogie: He's making you wait? Anyone in there?

Andre: Nope. Not even on the phone. I'm in the doghouse, bruh.

Boogie: Hope you brought lunch, bruh! Hit me up after.

Andre: 👍

With each passing minute I wish I wasn't here. At first, I thought having to do my restitutions service at my favorite place would make things easier. Now there's dread burrowed inside me because it only makes it worse. Anywhere else I could punch in, do what I had to do, and move on. But here, everything is a reminder of the trust I'd earned and have now lost. I work up the nerve to text Marcus that this was a mistake and I want another assignment, but then Terry calls me in.

"Hey, Terry." I stand up straight.

"Andre." He gives a firm handshake.

I make sure to look him in the eye. I don't want him thinking I've got anything to be ashamed of. Even though I'm sure he has all types of thoughts about being served a search warrant for my work locker. I could feel his hard stare all the way from the precinct.

"I only agreed to service hours because it's important for you to face what you did."

"I . . ." I stop. There's no point in explaining what really happened.

He hands me a schedule, then I follow him to storage even though I want to break away and make that call to Marcus.

I groan as soon as we enter the storage room, but cough to play it off when Terry gives me a look. This is the absolute worst job. I know, because it was my first. I suck it up and don't ask any questions, just pick up the checklist and read it over. This will be about a week's worth of hours, and based on my name being the only one that's on the schedule as "storage," I'll be doing it for a while.

By the time I turn around, Terry's already gone. I pop in my earbuds and listen to music. For the first hour, I sulk, but after a while, my feelings settle. There's something relaxing about mindless work, checking off equipment, deciding what's salvageable and what should be tossed. If I keep my head down, I might be able to keep my dignity.

Marcus and Terry both think this is a chance for me to prove myself. Change my story. Funny thing is, that's what they said MacLaren does too, but I didn't see how that worked there for most people?

In juvie, there was this big white kid named Bobby, who at fourteen got into a fight with someone who'd been bullying him for years. Bobby killed the other kid by accident, but he still got the name Lil Killa. He didn't speak much, but his bed was next to mine. Each night I heard him sniffling, covering up his cries. I couldn't see him as Lil Killa after that. He could've been my baby cousin or something.

In group therapy, he wormed himself inside me each time he spoke about all the stuff he'd been through. He never had visitors. No mom, no dad. So before he ever got into a fight, or came to MacLaren, his story was already written. But that didn't matter to the therapist who kept pushing on him about his choices, how the things *he did* led to that deadly fight. And all I kept thinking about was how come nobody was there for him before?

We each came in with a story, but we were mostly treated the way they thought we needed to be. Nobody in charge bothered to ask what I needed, so I kept questioning myself. What was *my* story? How could I still be me and not leave MacLaren somebody else?

In the hours spent cleaning the storage room, I try to make sense of why doing this helps change how the world thinks of me. And every time, I end up with no good answers, so my anger turns back to Gavin. He's the reason I got in trouble. Maybe why Eric ran. Or worse—why he's still missing.

When I'm all done at the Parks & Rec, I hop on my bike. Inside, my chest is rattling, ready to explode at the thought of Gavin getting off and leaving me to pay the price and Eric to run. This time I want Gavin to know I'm not somebody he can mess with again. I kept quiet for Eric, not him.

I should turn left on Hawthorne to go home, but I cut through a path to Gavin's. My phone rings, and I stop dead in my tracks.

"Marcus," I force out calmly, but my body is shaking as the invisible barriers to freedom close in around me and clamp down on my ankle monitor.

"Where you headed?"

I whip my head back and forth, looking for him. All I see, though, are bushes on the path and cars flashing by that shouldn't be able to see me from the road.

"Home."

"You sure about that?"

"I—" He followed me to the Parks & Rec?

"Terry said you were in the parking lot awhile after shift, so I checked the GPS. Seems like you're headed in the wrong direction."

"I'm h-headed home," I stutter out. "Trying a path to be away from people, that's all."

"For good measure, why don't you keep shortcuts out of the equation."

"All right. Yeah, cool." I linger, still thinking about asking for a new community service option, but what I already know about Terry outweighs working with somebody who doesn't know me from before, just the aftermath of my sentence. I hang up, taking a long breath before heading home for real.

When I reach my grandparents' driveway, I lock up my bike. The urge to talk to Gavin is still heavy on my mind. If I see him in person, things could escalate. But I'm the one that's on the hook. I whip my cell out and call him instead, full-on expecting to be sent to voice mail.

Gavin picks up on the third ring.

"Andre. That really you?"

My mouth tangles up thinking about how risky this is.

"Andre?"

"Yeah," I say. "What's good?"

"Nothing. I . . . You home?"

I pace, wishing I'd thought more about what to say.

Gavin breaks my silence. "I really appreciate what you did. You could've ratted on me but you didn't. I owe you."

Is he really saying this right now?

"I . . . What happened to Eric?" I'm not ready to blast him yet.

"He left."

"So you spoke to him? You still in touch?"

"No. I mean, yeah I spoke to him—after I left the police station, he came by."

My heart is thrumming in my ears, waiting for Gavin to admit he set me up on purpose.

"Eric said he was turning himself in. I was really freaking out for a while there. I guess he changed his mind."

"You were gonna let him turn himself in and hope you wouldn't be mentioned?" There's a rush of relief that Eric wasn't going to let me rot, but what happened? And even though Gavin is acting cool about Eric going to the police, he'd never just sit back and wait to see what happens. Him and Eric were the definition of thick as thieves. An arrest for Eric would guarantee Gavin as his obvious accomplice.

"He said he would leave my name out of it all, help clear yours," Gavin says.

"But then things changed?" I want to yell, but I don't want to lose him. ". . . I get it, you're boys and all. So it was you or me."

"No. It's not like that."

"Isn't it? Because how I see it, I called you to find out what happened. Not the other way around."

"If I talked to you, we'd be connected. My dad said it was better to stay away because things could blow up on more of the robberies they didn't know about."

"Your robberies, not mine."

"Listen, it could've been so much worse. I tried to tell Eric that, but he didn't listen. He never did."

I think back to the New Year's Eve party. Sierra, Eric, and I were there less than ten minutes. I never learned what caused Eric and Gavin to get into it, but it had to be serious for Eric to want to leave the party. Now Gavin's talking about being cool waiting to see what Eric was gonna do? I'm not believing this all-too-cozy picture.

"What happened between you two on New Year's Eve?"

Gavin takes a long breath. "Eric was mad because I wanted to stop the party-jacking. My dad found out. He was gonna, like, legit turn me in if I didn't stop. I told Eric to get rid of our stash but he disagreed. Then the next day things fell apart when Paul's dad reported a robbery. I'm sorry about what happened to you, but I couldn't turn myself in. It would've made it worse."

"It *was* worse—for me." I'm still pacing, anger bubbling over. "Do you even care that Eric's gone?"

"Of course I care. I want him back just as bad as you."

"Where is he?" I yell, frustrated at all Gavin's excuses. I'm done with him. I need to talk to Eric.

"I don't know."

"You've gotta have some idea."

"I mean . . . He's always talked about getting enough money to run away. He wanted to take the money and live off the land or something weird like that. I just never thought he had the balls to do it."

"What do you mean—take all the money? Live off the land?" I shake my head.

Eric never said anything remotely like that to me. He only ever talked about following Sierra to wherever she was going to college. Skipping town alone? Never.

"We were stashing everything we got in his Parks and Rec locker because he couldn't hide it in his house."

"You mean *my* locker?" I'm stunned. But I also don't believe Gavin. He's had plenty of time to tell his side of the story. With Eric gone, he can say whatever. Just like when I was at the station it didn't matter what I said once fingers started pointing at me.

"No. Eric wouldn't do that. If anything, he was holding it for later because he thought the police would eventually come for him, so he left all the money and jewelry there. He was scared. We were scared. We had like over five grand worth of stuff and money in there."

"You're lying." My mouth hangs open because I don't know what else to say.

"You should know. They found the backpack in your locker."

"That's the thing, Gavin. Dumped in my locker was some fake jewelry and an old laptop, not cash."

"Now *you're* lying," Gavin says.

"Why you think I'm in the community monitoring program and not still at juvie? More in stolen goods would've been Measure Eleven time."

"You don't think Eric would've . . ."

Gavin stops short. He sounds hurt that Eric is gone, and it doesn't sound like it's about the cash for him. But I also know he can miss his friend *and* want to survive. . . . If Eric didn't tell Gavin or Sierra where he went and Gavin is telling the truth, then where is Eric and why did he run?

10

WITH OR WITHOUT YOU

March 1, 2020

Boogie leans on the porch swing, ready for the play-by-play. "I can't believe you talked to Gavin without me. Please tell me you messed him up."

"Nah." For a second, I think about playing it off like I planned to, but Boogie knows me too well. "I was headed there in person, but Marcus got to me first, so I called him."

"You tell him he better watch his back?"

"In so many words—"

"In so many words? Bruh." Boogie grunts, mirroring the disappointment.

And then we just bust out laughing. None of this is funny. But sometimes you gotta laugh so you don't cry.

"But seriously, though." My voice lowers. "I asked him about

Eric. He thinks he ran off with enough cash to live on his own for a while."

"For real?" Boogie leans forward and whispers back when Grandpa passes by the front window. "How does he know this?"

"I don't know." I chew on the inside of my cheek. So many times, I thought about what it would be like if I'd worked harder to convince Eric to stop or told the police everything. And what I hate to think about more, is if the roles were reversed, would Eric do the same for me?

"He knows he let you take the fall."

"True." I probe the door to see if Grandpa's still there.

"What am I missing then?"

"Eric splitting I get. Eric splitting without letting Sierra know?"

"Impossible," Boogie confirms.

"Exactly. I mean, he's still gotta be close, right?" I run my fingers across my chain. "I think he's scared that when it comes down to it, Gavin'll throw him under the bus too."

"Maybe," Boogie mutters.

I know what he's thinking, but he's wrong. Eric's my boy. He wouldn't intentionally set me up. He was caught up, just like me.

"Still think you made the right decision?" Boogie says.

"I can't deny I wish I played it different. Maybe even claim my stuff was taken. Then maybe they wouldn't have stuck it on me." Although as I say it, I don't believe it would've made a difference. The police came to my house and brought me in. They weren't looking for an interview, they already had their suspect.

"You believe Gavin?"

"I don't know what to believe."

"You're not gonna get the truth from him." Boogie sighs, then pauses a few seconds as he watches the Whitaker crew pull up. "But I bet they know way more than they're letting on."

We walk across the grass. I keep an eye out for Paul, ready to retreat if necessary. Boogie pushes me on.

"Hey," I say as they crowd by their door.

"Can you hang?" Luis is the first to speak.

Kate puts her phone down and flashes me a smile I don't match, then throws another at Boogie. I swing my gaze to Sierra. She lifts her head up and just her look cuts me into vulnerable pieces. I bite my lip to fight a smile.

"Yeah, for a little bit." I elbow Boogie, who mostly avoids the Whitakers' house.

Sierra slows so we can catch up to her.

Boogie shoves his hands in his pockets, checking things out as we enter. His eyes travel upstairs to the forbidden zone.

"Quit being weird," I say under my breath.

"I'm not the weird one here."

"Then chill." I stick a hand out. "For me."

"I am." He pulls at my shirt so I can lean in. "No family dinners and I promise I'll be good."

Boogie's heard all about the formal Whitaker dinners I try to avoid. It's always too much: remembering what fork to use, watching Kate smile at her parents to make them feel like she agrees, holding back when Eric inserts himself if Sierra does something to break dinner etiquette, noticing how Luis stays under the radar, and cringing at Brian constantly putting his foot in his mouth. It's a lot going on in one big family. I know it sounds worse when I say it out loud. It all just feels like a show for family time that I'm not sure makes them tighter. Today, I'm grateful it's another low-key day at the Whitakers'.

"You can't take the last of everything." Kate eyes Brian in the kitchen pantry. "Shouldn't you be living in a dorm or something?"

"My bedroom is bigger and the food here is way better. So why live elsewhere?"

"Because you're in college. You don't even go here anymore," Sierra chuckles out.

"That doesn't even make sense." Brian munches on some chips.

"I still don't get why you stayed in Portland," Luis says.

"Like I had a choice," Brian spits out. "If I moved out, I'd have to work twice as many shifts. Dad's on some 'earn your way' trip. Besides, I'd miss my baby brother growing up." Brian tackles Luis to the ground. A flop of black hair is all I see, until Luis taps his hand for release and Brian lets him go.

"Wait," Boogie says. "They're *making* you stay home? They can afford sending you anywhere for school—you believed them too easy. They would've caved and paid for you."

"Is that what you'd do, huh? Where you headed?" Brian's voice turns firm, defensive.

I smile hard, like I do every time Boogie has a chance to brag.

"Another small school . . . maybe you've heard of it . . . MIT," Boogie says, unflinching.

"MIT. Like in Boston." Brian's face contorts as he inspects Boogie up and down. "Oh, I get it. Yeah, makes sense. Good for you. Diversity scholarship, right?"

A shared groan rings from Kate, Sierra, and Luis. My mouth opens because sometimes Brian be saying ignorant stuff without realizing it. I study him, and he honestly looks like he believes he didn't just say something offensive.

I check to see if Boogie's gonna drop Brian in his own house. The kitchen is completely silent. Brian diverts his eyes to each sibling, waiting to be clued in.

"Yeah." Boogie drags it out. "Presidential scholarship. Four-point-five GPA and an almost-perfect SAT score. But go off, Brian. Affirmative action, right? Took your spot?"

"I wasn't . . ." Brian trips on his words, his eyes going bigger once it clicks for him.

"Of course not," Boogie says. "That would be racist. And how could you be racist, having Black and brown siblings and all."

"All right. I think that's enough." Kate's cheeks are flaming red. "Badass getting into MIT, Boogie."

"Thanks." Boogie doesn't break eye contact with Brian.

"I didn't—" Brian mumbles, but is interrupted by Kate.

"Hurry up before Mom changes her mind and makes us do family dinner." Kate shoves a bowl of chips in Brian's chest and he retreats to the basement before I can blink.

Boogie gives me a look like he'll bounce if dinner's involved.

"Come on." Luis follows after him.

"You can't hog the TV!" Kate follows and I'm annoyed they're just gonna let this pass and not make Brian grovel.

"Can you believe that fool," Boogie says.

"Work in progress." Sierra's voice hangs sharp, then she flashes a smile and leans over the table, flicking a carrot my way.

"What have you been up to?"

"Staying low-key." I make my way to Sierra, bumping her shoulder. She doesn't pull away, so I turn to face her.

"What?"

"Nothing." I throw innocent hands.

"You're thinking about something. I know you, Andre. Spill it."

My voice is stuck in my throat.

"We were just going over what might've happened at the New Year's party," Boogie cuts in.

I narrow my eyes at him being too direct.

"Who knows," Sierra says.

"Eric didn't say what happened between him and Gavin?"

"Not really. You know how he gets, all about the bros." She pops the carrot in her mouth, chewing slowly.

"I called Gavin, didn't get much from him, either," I say.

Sierra raises an eyebrow. "What are you two getting at?"

I can see Boogie fighting the urge to take over with a flood of questions. I give him a look so he knows I got this.

"I don't get why Paul's party was the one to get the cops involved. We even left early."

"This about Paul, or . . . ?" She places her hands on her hips.

"About all of it," I say.

"Andre should know what really happened to him," Boogie says. "Eric needs to set things straight."

Sierra steps back, focusing on me and not Boogie. "What are you going to do to him?"

"Who, Eric?" I shake my head. "I just wanna talk to him. Find out what happened."

Boogie picks up his phone, giving me a nod as he goes toward the door.

"Catch up with me later," I say to Boogie, thankful he's giving me space to talk alone. But then I note his face is clammy, like something's off. I raise my eyebrows at him to see if he's cool but he ignores me.

"Yeah. All right." Then he gives Sierra a nod.

I wait for Boogie to shut the door before speaking. "What do you think happened with my case?"

Sierra scrunches her mouth, searching for words. "Your arrest? I . . . Listen, I get you got caught up in something with Eric. I know that's not who you are."

My mouth drops. All this time Sierra thought I was involved?

"You think I really did this?" I touch my chest. "Does your dad?" I pace in the kitchen, reeling in this truth coming out. All this time I thought they believed I was innocent, but they just felt bad for me. I gape at Sierra, not wanting to believe our relationship is based on her pitying me.

"What exactly did you think happened? I was with you the whole time. We were there less than ten minutes. I had nothing to do with any of it."

"Wait, what?" Her lips quiver as she reaches for my arm. "How would I know? I just assumed you made a mistake. I never ever judged you for that."

"Never judged me?" My voice breaks. "You didn't believe me. That's really why you never wrote, isn't it?" My eyes blur at this betrayal.

"That's not why. I told you." She touches my arm. Her eyes get wide before she whispers, "Eric. That's why he's really gone, isn't it? That's what this is about."

I thought having to say I'm innocent was unsaid between us,

but I'm realizing it needed to be stated. I wasn't just saying I was innocent because I feared getting in trouble, it was the truth. Sierra covers her mouth in shock as I rush to tell her everything. Seeing her disappointment in Eric helps me let go that she and her dad acted just like my family. Being there to fight for me, but not because they thought I was innocent.

"You seriously haven't heard from him?" I ask.

"Seriously. He just . . . vanished." Her voice shakes. She snaps the tab of her drink open and sips. "I can't believe Eric did that. Why didn't you say anything?" She doesn't break eye contact.

"What could I have said? Besides, by the time your dad got me a lawyer, I was better off keeping the focus to my locker than on all the other things they stole."

"You must've felt so . . . alone." She leans in to give me a hug.

"Hey." It's good to have her close. I touch her back gently. "He'll be back. He's probably scared I was gonna kick his ass," I say to lighten up how I'm feeling as well. "I mean, I'm *definitely* gonna kick his ass. But on some front yard shit, you know? Get Grandma J screaming and your mom all worked up."

"Oh my God! I would die! Your grandma would be so pissed." She lets out a real laugh choked behind tears, the tension breaking. "Normally I'd be talking you out of it, but yeah, you have my permission."

We laugh but it fades into more silence.

She tangles her fingers through mine, and I can feel the weight of her still thinking about Eric.

I want to be there for Sierra, but I also can't help thinking about myself. The more I think about my situation, the angrier I become. I was good to Eric. Always. And when I needed him most, he was gone.

I touch her hand softly. "Help me find Eric. He'll know if I should be worried about Gavin. The least he could do is make sure this is over." I pause, watching a conflicted Sierra be tormented by this truth and his absence. "He owes you an explanation too."

"I searched for him." She sniffles. "Everywhere I could think. Called his phone, which always goes to voice mail. I visited anyone who knew him. But he must've known I would. That's why he just ran off without a trace. He doesn't want to be found."

"I'm gonna find him. Hell, I've got nothing else to do, right? I'll bring him back home."

Sierra sticks her hand out for a shake. "And if you do that, I'll help you kick his ass."

"Watch your language." Mr. Whitaker steps in and we immediately stand up straight. "Andre. Good to see you."

"Good to see you, too." I clear my throat. "I was egging her on. No violence here." I lift up more innocent hands, my new trademark.

"Was that your friend leaving?" Mr. Whitaker's voice is filled with concern.

"Yeah, Boogie. My best friend. You've met him before." Many times.

"Oh. Okay. Thought so." Mr. Whitaker softens, turning to Sierra. "Mom home?"

"She's in the back getting her gardening on." Sierra gestures in the direction of the yard. I hadn't noticed but Mrs. Whitaker is out on the deck with a glass of wine in one hand and a small gardening shovel, caring for her rosebushes.

"Since when has your mom gardened?" I say.

"She has quite a green thumb; I thought it was just used for swiping cards," Mr. Whitaker laughs. I join him awkwardly and Sierra rolls her eyes.

"She wants to plant an entire rose garden. They're growing all over our front yard now and she started one down the street at the community garden."

"Roses? The revitalization?"

"Yup. She has it all planned out," Sierra says dryly. "She thinks *roses* are a more attractive aesthetic for the neighborhood."

"What about the people who used the garden for food?" I think of the last old Black couple left in the neighborhood besides my grandparents.

"We have grocery stores close to the neighborhood now," Mr. Whitaker says. "It's no longer a food desert. Roses make it feel more Portland-like, don't you think?"

I don't agree, but I guess when you can afford to shop at organic markets, that's not something you care about. The Whitakers don't get it. It's about community. About growing something, together.

"Coming?" Sierra waves me to the basement.

"Nah." I shake my head. "I gotta go home. Stay close, you know."

"Yeah, okay," she says.

She follows me to the door. "Hey, thanks for the talk. You're right. I'm not gonna give up that easy."

My face brightens as I watch her go down the hall.

Mr. Whitaker furrows his brow and watches me. I ignore his gaze, but I feel his eyes on the back of my head as I make my way home.

11

WHEN DOVES CRY

March 3, 2020

I wasn't eavesdropping, my parents' raised voices just trickled down the hallway. That's what I keep telling myself as I edge closer.

"It's for the best," Mom says. "I'll stay there a few weeks and we'll see what happens. He won't even notice I'm gone with my hours."

"But we agreed moving in was the best thing," Dad sighs. "He just got home."

My throat tightens. I brace myself against the wall. This is all my fault.

"We don't even know if this virus will spread," Mom says. "Let's just wait and see."

As soon as I'm about to leave, their bedroom door opens.

"Andre." Mom jumps back with her hand on her chest.

"I was headed to the family room. . . . I . . . Are you really moving out?"

"No big deal." Dad places a hand on Mom's shoulder. "Just for a little bit to take precautions."

Mom glances at Dad. "I'll be at another nurse's place. She lives alone, our shifts are different. It's just . . ."

"Safer," they say in unison.

Even though I know they're not on the same page, their united front makes me feel better.

"Should we be worried?" I say.

"No, honey. It's just to be cautious. There's lots of talk at the hospital, getting prepared. Just in case."

I study them for any clue I'm part of the reason for this temporary separation.

———

AFTER DINNER, GRANDPA leans back in his recliner, getting real comfortable before he speaks. "You take the garbage out?"

"Yes, sir."

"Put them like you s'posed to?"

"I lined them up the way you like." I've cleaned the bathrooms, mowed the lawn, done all the laundry, folded the towels.

"Grab me that." Grandpa points to the TV remote, which is now out of reach since he reclined in his chair.

I shut my eyes for a second and breathe heavy, crossing half the distance of the family room to hand it to him. I see a crinkle in Dad's eye. Half pity, half amusement.

"You keeping up with your studies? Only one more term until you graduate," Dad says.

"Homework's pretty easy. I've been catching up on readings for Grant High, so I'll be ready for spring."

"You been keeping up with your counselor?"

Dad calls Marcus my counselor. Grandpa says overseer. Grandma says friend. Mom says Marcus. They each have their own way of explaining his presence in my life now. Whatever he's called, Marcus is weaved into every conversation. That's why half the time I retreat to my room, except when it's late and I want to avoid going to bed, where my nightmares about detention await. Last night I stayed up until sunrise scouring Gavin's social media, sorting through comments and posts. But there's two months of group chats I'm no longer in.

"Andre." Dad repeats himself.

"Yeah, he calls twice a day."

"You been staying out of trouble?"

"All I've been doing is working and being around the house."

"That's good," Mom says. "I don't want to worry about you when I'm not here."

Grandma J raises an eyebrow while Dad explains.

"I don't think that's necessary," Grandpa says. "This'll blow over. They're making a big fuss to scare us on the news."

"We should all be staying close," Grandma J says. "I don't trust they'll do the right thing. You think the president's reading briefings on this, ha! He probably has one of his kids running the CDC now."

"I think this thing's man-made." Dad leans back in a chair.

"Some reason to get us in another war so we'll have a two-term president."

"Well, whatever it is," Mom says, "I need to make sure I stay away from you all until we know more."

They go back and forth, Grandpa giving us the blow-by-blow on news stories while Dad throws out conspiracy theories. And Grandma J, well, she's just trying to convince Mom to stay. I sit up awkward 'cause her concern is really about me. Grandma J always thought I could do no wrong. That image has cracked. And no matter what I do or say, she'll forever have doubts. What hurts the most is, I can't even blame her. I catch Grandma J's eyes on me and I must've telegraphed all my thoughts.

"Why don't you visit with Abraham," Grandma J says from the kitchen.

I shoot up in my seat, making sure I heard her right. Grandpa and Dad trip over each other trying to get the first word out, but Grandma J talks over them, stopping any objections.

"Just get back before nine, no cutting it close, okay?" she says.

I'm cheesing hard as I get up, texting while I walk.

Andre: You better be home, Boogie. Got my out of jail card to see you.

I don't waste time waiting for him to respond, just grab a sweatshirt by the coatrack and wrap my arms around Grandma J before exiting.

Out the door, I hear Grandma J lecturing Grandpa and Dad: "If you hover over that boy, he'll really be running to the streets."

I smile as she ignores their protests and keeps going hard for me. Before I ride, I call Marcus.

"To what do I owe the pleasure, son?"

There he goes again. I take a long breath.

"I was just checking in. I'm about to visit my friend you met, Abraham. He's within the boundaries. . . ."

"How's the work going?"

I pace in front of my bike, annoyed.

"It was good to be out. Back-to-normal kinda thing. Terry was . . . well, Terry, I guess."

"Terry's good people."

"Yeah . . . so it cool to see my friend, or . . . ?"

"I'm gonna give you a call in an hour so you can head home. Make sure you pick up right away."

I lift my head, holding back the burn in my throat and letting my stinging eyes calm. I hate this. Hate this chain on my ankle. All for something I didn't even do. But it has me feeling guilty all the time. So I have to think like I did something, so I don't get treated like I'm still doing it.

"You there?" Marcus says.

"Yeah. I heard you."

Marcus hangs up, but the tightness in my chest lingers.

I take my bike up to Boogie's porch so I don't have to worry about locking it up. I jam it in between an old radiator and a TV his dad's probably thinking he can sell.

Boogie's house is an extension of mine. Like old times, I tap on the screen door before opening it, knowing his mom's watching her *stories* on the television. I expect her to be alone, but his grandma's wrapped in a blanket on the couch.

"Hey, Mrs. Tewolde. Ma Ma."

"Andre. Good to see you, my boy," Boogie's mom says. His grandma lifts her head up and smiles but doesn't have the same welcoming energy. I hesitate, wondering if this was a good decision, before taking off my shoes to greet them.

"No. No," Boogie's mom says. "We sick, don't come close."

"Oh, I'm sorry. Want me to get you something?" I bite my tongue because this could result in a multihour shopping trip.

"Kidane picked us up some things. It's nothing my special tea tinctures can't fix."

I sniff, realizing his moms boiled up her own natural concoction of garlic, pepper, lemon, and honey, which is humming out the kitchen. My eyes water instantly.

"All right, I'm just gonna head to Abraham's room."

"Yes. Yes. Tell your mother I say hello, okay?"

"I will."

As soon as I open Boogie's door I know it's a mistake. He got a diffuser on and a pile of snotty Kleenex piling out his room, coughing loud as hell. The smells from the kitchen still hit his room.

"You *sick* sick, bruh," I say, stepping in.

"I'm not contagious, I swear." He coughs into his arm. I open up his window to catch some fresh air, then toss the clothes piling on his chair to the side.

"You good?" Boogie says.

"Yeah. Just needed to get out. You get my text?"

Boogie reaches for his phone.

"Missed it." He sips his mom's healing tea, then downs some coconut water.

I pick up his basketball, tossing it up as I check my form. I can feel Boogie's eyes digging into me.

"You still cold on Sierra?" Boogie says.

"I'm not cold on her." I look away so he doesn't see how much it hurt to find out Luis was the only one that knew I was innocent all this time. "I just don't think she thinks about me the same. She moved on. Hell, she's with Paul."

"Do you really want me to do this?"

"Do what?"

"Listen to your BS and not call you out?"

"Call me out." I shrug.

"Sierra likes you. Has always liked you. You've just been too chicken to go do something about it, waiting on her to make a move. You were gone, her brother missing, it's not her job to be sitting around crying when you weren't even honest with her. Her hanging out with Paul Chase has nothing to do with you. You out of the way, Paul just had an easier time asking her out. You should be mad at Gavin and Eric. And for God sakes, fight for Sierra if you really like her."

My mouth is all dry, stuck on a response. I want to tell him he's the worst friend and should have my back, but all I can do is pause before saying, "You right."

"I know I'm right. Feels good to get that off my chest. I should do that more." Boogie coughs again.

"Look at you, all out of breath trying to tell me about myself."

"Shut up." Boogie smirks. "What're you gonna do about Eric?"

"Sierra has no idea where Eric is, neither does Gavin. I *need* to get more eyes on the street looking for him. You think you can go some places for me, ask around?"

"Yeah." Boogie covers his cough.

"When you're better, that is."

"I can check in with Te'vonte downtown. He's been out hanging on the streets for a while."

"For real?"

"He dyed his hair green, pierced his septum, and got some straggly-looking dog. Just know, you owe me big-time for walking around with him." Boogie grimaces as drinks his tea.

I searched for Eric closer to my ride to the Parks & Rec, but downtown is where you find most runaways, hanging on the corners, under the bridge, up and down the shops, asking for money. If Eric was out on the street, he'd have found a crew to roll with easily.

"You could go by his other old spots," Boogie says. "See if anybody seen him."

I've been through a few, but not enough. I'm ready to jump up, look for Eric and pass through places he used to eat at, like Burgerville, but my phone rings. Marcus's name flashes.

"It hasn't even been an hour," I say, answering on the second ring.

Boogie gives me a knowing look. I won't be riding around searching for Eric tonight.

"I know," Marcus says. "Making sure you don't get too caught up making plans for your big return."

I suck my teeth before speaking. "I'm not out there like that. Just checking on my boy, he's been sick."

"It's not easy coming back, getting used to these rules."

"I get it." I don't. "I'm headed home, a'ight." I hang up.

"You should go," Boogie says. "I'm sick anyway. Save your freedom for something else."

"Take care of yourself."

Boogie nods, closing his eyes as I exit.

Outside, I half expect Marcus to call me back, but he doesn't. I ride on MLK. The K always used to signal I was home, but the air I'm breathing feels borrowed.

I veer, taking the streets so I stay within these invisible walls that define my existence. Borders that, if I'm honest, I've always felt like I had to live within. From keeping up how I look or act in white spaces, to holding fake smiles and code-switching. Anything else—being myself, no filter—is too *threatening*.

Before, when my lawyer brought up the community program option, I was down for anything that would get me out of juvie. Somehow, this feels worse. At least inside I knew what I was getting. But out here, things look free, but they're not.

I turn on my grandparents' street, rushing like the sky was opening up following me with satellites. Almost to their driveway I pass a sedan parked in front. I jump when the window rolls down.

Smoke trickles out. At the end of a cigarette is Cowboy Jim. What's he doing here?

I blink hard, making sure I'm seeing things right. But I could never forget the posture of my first assigned juvenile counselor, not when he looks at me like I'm nothing. A cold chill runs through my body and my bike wobbles beneath me. I can't move.

"Cutting it close," he says.

"Ex-excuse me?" I stutter out, throat closing.

Cowboy Jim taps at his watch, then points at me. "This isn't over. You're gonna slip up, and I'll be there to make sure you serve the rest of your stolen time."

"I'm following the rules." I squint hard, confused. He was the one who recommended firmly to the judge that I needed an ankle monitor as part of my release. Was him checking up on me part of the deal? "Marcus knows where I was. I just got off the phone with him."

"Mr. Smith's style's a little loose for my liking. He's new. He'll learn that these new methods will only get you burned. I've seen it a thousand times. Kids like you, they grow up and do major time because someone was too easy on you. It doesn't seem like it, but I'm the one doing you a favor."

The engine runs as he moves the car into drive and swings around. I don't know what to do, so I pull out my phone with shaky hands, ready to beg Marcus to come.

Jim stops across the street from me. "Let's keep this between us."

I tuck my phone in my pocket and stumble, light-headed, on my way to the house. When I enter, I can feel a big sigh of relief from my parents that I made it home.

"What's wrong?" Mom rushes to me.

Dad steps closer, joining her as he runs his hand over my hair.

My eyes tear, and I drop my head onto my dad's shoulder, grinding my jaw to stop myself from falling apart.

After a few minutes, Dad pulls back and says, "What happened?"

I tell them everything.

"Listen to me." Dad tugs at the back of my neck. "This is what the system does. These people with authority think they run things, no one guides their behavior, they get away with this stuff. But you control your destiny."

"We should call Marcus," Mom says. "Or the director of Multnomah County Juvenile Justice. They can't do this to you."

"No," Dad says. "His counselor still works with this man. If he has to choose between you and that guy, with his job on the line, you will always lose. You can't trust him, either."

"Malcolm," Mom pleads. "We can't have him following Andre. He could make anything up."

"Let me think about what to do." Dad looks at me. "What you know about your counselor?"

"Marcus warned me about him."

Dad's eyes widen.

"He heard Cowboy Jim was still working to get me more time, following a hunch about more robberies. Marcus don't trust him either."

Dad steps back, pacing. "Let me talk to Mr. Whitaker, see if we can still use the lawyer."

Mom's mouth tightens, clearly uncomfortable with the number of favors from next door stacking up. Even though she's against asking the Whitakers for help, she keeps quiet.

"Think he'll find something?" Dad stares into my eyes, and this time I don't talk around things. Even though I've claimed my innocence before, I've kept secrets that make it harder to believe me now.

"I didn't steal anything at that party, I was barely there. I told you that. . . . But I didn't tell you I know who did, I just didn't want to make it worse. That's why I kept quiet."

"You should've said something." Dad's voice booms. He shakes his head vigorously. "Unbelievable." Dad looks to Mom. Her mouth flinches, but she stays silent.

"Who's involved?" Dad says.

"Gavin . . ." There's freedom in speaking truth, at least part of it, even if I don't know what'll happen next. "At the station I was scared. I thought the charges would go away when there was no evidence. But then when they found the backpack I knew if I changed my story you wouldn't believe me."

"You're not making sense, Andre. There's nothing you can't come to us with." Dad grips my shoulder and the guilt just washes over me.

"If I said something, the police could've found out about the other parties, and with my locker having the backpack—"

"They'd blame you for an even bigger crime," Mom finishes.

"Dammit. Andre. You should've said something. So if Gavin was the one behind this, then that means Eric was involved too?"

I swallow the lump growing in my throat.

"That why Eric is gone?" Mom says, then raises her voice. "Is this why Mr. Whitaker helped you?"

Dad and Mom meet eyes, then wait for me to answer.

"When I got back, I heard Eric was gone. I'm assuming all this is why. I don't think Mr. Whitaker knew he was involved, though."

"You sure?" Dad says.

I nod. "I don't think he would've helped me get a lawyer if he thought I could rat on Eric to defend myself."

Dad lets out a long breath and runs his hands over his face. "I'll call the lawyer, see what advice they have."

"Don't say anything about Eric to Mr. Whitaker," Mom says. "Let's just keep that to ourselves."

"Nothing about Eric," Dad agrees. "Okay, get to bed. We'll figure this out in the morning."

"Come here and give me a hug," Mom says. "I'll be leaving for work and staying away until things with the virus get better, but I want you to be in touch. A lot. And please stay close to home."

"I will." I hold on to her tight. My throat aches at everything falling apart.

I head down the hallway before Dad follows me. "I know Eric's your friend. But if you know more, it's time to protect yourself. I don't want to hear about this ratting stuff. That don't apply to you anymore. You don't owe anyone your life."

I throw myself on my bed, relieved my parents finally know the truth, but terrified of what comes next. When I was at MacLaren, I spent my nights looking up at the ceiling, squinting through the sliver of a window to the sky, waiting for the truth to come out. It never did. Now that my parents know the truth, the weight I've been carrying is a little bit lighter. And I'm realizing how everything Dad said is true, I can't sit back and wait for things to happen to me again.

I check Eric's social media again. January first was the last post, a photo dump in the morning. I swipe left, memories rushing back to me—the feeling of that night versus twenty-four hours later. A photo with Sierra, her eyes glaring but she flashes a crooked smile so she still looks cute. The last photo is Eric on New Year's. I scroll down, reading comment after comment:

Bro3478: Happy NYE

LisaG00: Why you leave early?

Trouble03: We made it to 2020! This is gonna be the best year!

BigDeezy4Life: One more year until $rump is out! Fuck yeah!

Then I scroll down, reading more post comments that dip into January.

> **Gavin23:** Miss you bro! Where you at?
> **SierraW04:** Call me.
> **SierraW04:** Call Me.
> **SierraW04:** CALL ME!

Is this how they communicate? Instagram comments? Maybe Sierra can reach Eric through his DMs. But then I shake the thought at how she keeps commenting publicly all through February, knowing how much Eric would hate that.

> **SierraW04:** Quit playing around. This isn't funny! Where are you?
> **SierraW04:** I hate you for this, Eric!

I rub my head, still reeling from telling my parents everything and the surprise shady visit by my old juvenile counselor before Marcus. Then I scroll through every photo of Eric's, searching for clues. I stop on a video he made on Sierra's last birthday.

"This is Sierra. Say hi, Sierra," Eric says. A wide smile is planted on his face.

"Hi, Sierra," Sierra says.

"No, say hi to the camera."

"Hi, camera," Sierra chuckles.

"Okay, well, clearly she hasn't gotten smarter with age." Eric dodges a punch from Sierra. "But she's the best thing about me. And I love her more than anything."

A crowd circles around them and I see my head pop up in

the back, moving closer with a crystal glass filled with sparkling water. Mr. Whitaker shakes his head at Mrs. Whitaker. Eric's cup is suspiciously something else. Proven by the way he slurs his words. Everyone is laughing and enjoying Eric gushing over Sierra, except for Mr. Whitaker. So unlike the night he handed me champagne with no problem.

"You saved me so many times," Eric says, the camera going crooked as he points to Sierra. "We've been through some hard things together. Things we don't even talk about anymore. But we never gave up on each other, so here's to you, sis! Together we can do anything."

"Cheers" is repeated from the crowd.

Eric opens his mouth to speak, but not before Mrs. Whitaker grabs the phone and in a hushed tone says, "That's enough of you making a fool of this family."

The video ends.

12

A CHANGE IS GONNA COME

March 6, 2020

The smell of a hot breakfast wakes me up. At first, I'm disoriented as I stretch in bed. I used to think all the rotating bedrooms I've had were small, but after staying in one big claustrophobic room with rows of cots, this feels like a palace.

Out of habit, I make my bed military style, tossing a coin to see if it'll bounce. I'm almost satisfied at the fact that it only plops on my plush bed because then I don't have to keep pinching myself. This isn't a dream. I'm home.

Down the hall the sound of a chronic cough grows. Normally I'd assume it's allergies. But Grandpa's cough hits different.

Grandma J is in the kitchen with her robe and curlers still on. She warms up a pot of oatmeal on the stove. No toast and eggs on Grandpa's plate.

"Everything okay?" I hug Grandma and give her a kiss on her

cheek. Then I hear it again, a low cough coming from Grandpa at the table.

"How long's he been like that?" I whisper to Grandma J.

"All night." She leans in. "He just kept burning up next to me like a heater was on."

"Should we take him to the doctor?"

"Your mom will check on him when she gets off work." Grandma J puts breakfast on the table.

"You don't think it's—"

"No," Grandma says firm, and I shake off the thought it's coronavirus. Only a few people in the entire state have caught the virus. It can't be as bad as they say. But it creeps into my mind like whispers in the night I can't ignore.

When I join Grandpa, I notice his paper is missing from the table. There's only the sound of him eating slowly, trying to hide a sneaky cough underneath a wheeze. I never thought I'd miss the loud snap of his newspaper as he reads the headlines.

I bite at my lip between glances to Grandma J.

"You stay here while I pick up his prescriptions." Grandma J watches me close.

"I can do it before I start my assignments."

Grandma J smiles. "We need something for the cough and the fever. I already called in a refill for his steroid inhalers at the pharmacy." Grandma gets paper to make a list and hands it to me.

"I'll be back soon, Grandpa."

He saves his breath, nodding before taking a sip of his black coffee.

I hate seeing him like this. He's always said so much, without saying so much. Now his body is so exhausted even it's got nothing to say.

I get in Grandpa's car and head down the street.

On the road, I notice a car trailing me, following each turn, and edging in closer when I get on MLK. I don't wanna act paranoid, but there's something about the way this car ebbs and flows, following me on these random streets I now find myself taking. My hands tightly grip the steering wheel as I push away the memory of Cowboy Jim's late-night visit.

At the pharmacy, I park, waiting to see if the car pulls in behind me. I take a breath and shake off the feeling of being followed.

Then drop a text to Marcus.

Andre: My grandpa's sick. Picking up medicine.

Marcus: . . .

Marcus: Keep me posted on how he's doing.

I give a thumbs-up emoji.

IN LINE AT the pharmacy someone tugs at my arm. I full-on expect it to be Jim with a menacing hiss: *I'll always be close.*

"Mr. Whitaker." I jump a little. "You scared me."

"Sorry, Andre. I saw you come in."

He joins the line with me. I want to ask what he wants, but I owe him in a way I can't ever repay.

"We're all glad you're home safe." He takes a long pause. "Sierra seems to be in a better mood spending time with you. I want you to know we're here to support you, but we also want to give you the space you need. With Eric being gone I wouldn't want you to feel . . . obligated . . ."

My cheeks go hot, but then my jaw tenses when I get what he's really saying. It's about Sierra.

And that he doesn't want me around her.

Like I'm a bad influence.

Like I don't care about her.

Like I wouldn't do and haven't always done everything I could to make her happy.

We both stand, awkwardly watching the line move like molasses. I don't want to add to him not thinking I'm good enough by not even knowing I've got enough cash to cover this. I don't want to be his charity case, not this time.

Before I can pay for my items, Mr. Whitaker throws down his platinum card and covers my bill, including prescriptions that Grandma was already worried about because insurance wasn't covering Grandpa's regular meds. Things we'd have to scrounge to pay for—he took care of them with the swipe of his card.

"You didn't have to—"

"Don't even mention it, Andre." He pats my shoulder as we walk out together. In the parking lot, Mr. Whitaker scans like he's waiting on somebody to notice who he is and isn't sure how he feels about that. Something tells me he wants to say more or he would've left, but now I've got something to say.

"It's really too bad about Eric," I say. "Real hard on Sierra."

"Has she talked much about Eric?" Mr. Whitaker's voice softens.

"I mean they've been through a lot, so I know she's hurt that he left without saying a word and hasn't even reached out."

I don't actually know what Sierra's been going through, but I know she wouldn't lie to me about not seeing him.

With all Mr. Whitaker's connections, I now realize it's hard to believe he can't find Eric on his own.

"He really left without saying goodbye?"

"None of us understand. Sometimes you don't know what people are going through, especially someone with Eric's . . . background. Did he speak to you, before . . . you know . . . ?" Mr. Whitaker narrows his eyes at me.

"I haven't talked to him. I found out he was gone when I got back." A little part of me wants to tell Mr. Whitaker the truth, but I remember my mom's warnings. He was the one, after all, who intercepted my letters to Sierra.

"Of course you haven't spoken to Eric. Sorry if it seemed like I was accusing you. I guess I just get so worried . . . with all the trouble Sierra's been in lately."

I glance up at him, concerned.

"She isn't as open, even with the kids. I thought . . . maybe if she mentioned anything yesterday you might—"

"Of course. And if I knew where Eric was I'd say something."

"I know you care a lot about her." Mr. Whitaker pauses, then speaks so low my heart beats faster. "There's something you should know about Eric. Things my kids don't know about. Can I trust you with this?"

I nod firmly, then scan to see if anyone can hear our conversation. There's something about the way he says it. Forcing an agreement that I'll hold whatever he has to say tight to my chest.

"We kept this from Sierra. I'm telling you because I know you're close, and I need you to watch out for her." He takes another long pause. "Before he went missing, we suspected Eric was on drugs."

I narrow my eyes at him. *What?*

"He wasn't," Mr. Whitaker responds quickly. "He had . . . a breakdown. He was acting erratic. Impulsive. Seeing things that weren't there. We had to admit him to Legacy Emanuel hospital for a psychiatric evaluation. We thought he was going to harm himself. Or worse, harm Sierra."

My mouth drops open, terrified for Eric. And now more worried for Sierra because she doesn't know her brother needs help.

"He stayed for seventy-two hours, until they released him for outpatient psychiatry. We knew he wasn't ready to see anyone, and with your arrest . . . we worried Eric might do something erratic. We didn't want to scare Sierra, either . . . because her mom had similar issues.

"We thought maybe with some monitoring that everything would be okay and no one would have to know. His privacy was important to us. But he ran in the middle of the night when we were sleeping. We looked for him. And finally he called to tell us he was angry. Said he couldn't trust us or the rest of the family, including Sierra. So he was going for good. That he'd be eighteen and wouldn't need us anymore."

"Why didn't you tell your other kids?" My voice is drenched with harsh judgment.

Mr. Whitaker inhales deeply. "He ran away. Said he was leaving Oregon and not to go after him. Made us promise not to tell Sierra because he knew she'd follow him. We had no choice but to keep that promise. We couldn't lose Sierra, too. We gave him some spending money. We kept telling ourselves that he would come home and we would explain things then."

"Will you ever tell her?"

"Sierra is better off not knowing, at least for now. I'm worried she might run away to find him, the way she's been acting. . . ."

I want to agree with Mr. Whitaker, but it's wrong. She deserves to know.

"One day we'll tell her, but right now things are unsteady. I hope you'll keep this between us."

I watch him get into his car with his WHITAKER 2020 sticker in the back. When he drives off, doubt grows in my chest. He left without buying any items for himself, so what was he doing here? Does this have anything to do with my dad calling about my lawyer? The dread burrowing inside my chest tells me I just accepted a buyout for my silence.

13

KILLING ME SOFTLY

March 9, 2020

All weekend I was tortured by Mr. Whitaker's secret. I get that he trusts me, but he didn't need to dump this burden for me to carry on top of everything else. That's why I almost will Sierra away as she knocks on my window. I haven't sorted out what I should do about this information.

Sierra knocks again. Her smile makes me defy my better judgment. I move fast to open my window like she's threatening to change her mind.

"You avoiding me?" Sierra chirps, climbing in.

"Course not." My chest constricts as I swallow Eric's secret for safekeeping for now. "My grandpa's been sick."

"Is it serious?" Sierra's eyebrows rise.

Lately, there's been an unsaid concern at the mention of anyone sick. Even I was tripping last night with an itchy throat, had me all jumping online researching symptoms when there's only a handful of coronavirus cases in Oregon.

"He seems better after his inhalers and some cough medicine." Mr. Whitaker and the pharmacy flood my thoughts. I wince, stalling for what to say next, but Sierra has moved on.

She roams my room as if it's an extension of her and finds her way to my desk.

"What's the password?"

"That's filed away in *things I'll never tell*." I step in front of my laptop, blocking her view as I log on.

"Another round?" She flashes that crooked smile, urging another night of videos.

For one glorious second, I imagine a do-over from the last time she was here. Having the restraint to not replay "Take My Breath Away" is a herculean effort. Sierra curls herself in the chair, and she looks like all the weight she's been carrying has been put down. My chair holds her safely in a way I don't want to disturb. And the fact is, there shouldn't be a do-over—not until truth runs between us like a breeze. Sierra would freak out if she knew what Mr. Whitaker said, and double down on her search. But I need to find Eric first.

We alternate song choices as comments flood in. Today, I play it safe, selecting old-school rap and rock ballads. After the first couple of rounds, my worries wash away and we're back to just kicking it.

"Your Wi-Fi sucks," Sierra says at our fifth attempt to go live.

"I know. Let's record and upload it. No double takes, though." I point at her. She is notorious for wanting retakes because of facial expressions she didn't like.

"Okay." She sticks her tongue out at me. "Ooh, play this one." She lights up.

"We heard that one," I say at her choice of "C.R.E.A.M." by Wu-Tang Clan. "Remember, back like three years ago."

"Play it, 'cause I don't believe you." We always argue about what songs we've heard. Some days, I do it just to annoy her. She loads up the song, but after a few chords she says, "Okay, okay, yeah, I remember now. Boogie was with us so it's not on my list."

I feel myself blush. She touches the list she left me, now taped to my desk. We give each other an awkward glance as I angle my laptop to cover it.

I'm saving that for another day—when I'm not keeping Mr. Whitaker's lie.

"You're slipping," I joke. "You used to remember everything."

"I'm rusty, I guess."

"Yeah. It's been a while." My voice grows quiet.

"I'm sorry." Sierra gives an apologetic glance. "I didn't mean to mention it."

We both know where I've been. While it's freeing to be out of MacLaren, reminders of my being gone always give me whiplash. Sometimes I'm here in the moment, then pulled back adrift like I'm stuck in the middle of the ocean.

On cue, my phone buzzes. A text from Marcus.

Marcus: I see you got a YouTube channel.

Since Marcus heard Grandpa's been sick, he's been trying to get me to engage in some back-and-forth with him. But I keep my responses brief:

Okay.

Ha!

Got it.

Good tip.

I type in a quick response.

Andre: Yip.

Before I get a text back, a frantic yell stirs me.

I jump up, running out of my room and meeting Grandpa, who is slumped in his chair, grabbing at his chest.

"What's wrong with Grandpa?" I lean down to listen to his chest. Raspy and shallow, each breath is labored.

"Call an ambulance!" I yell to Sierra, who races to the phone.

Then his body calms to a stop. Stillness. He's wearing a peaceful look that's so disturbing, it stirs me into action. I place him on the floor carefully, then press on his chest in rapid pumps, breathing life into his lungs to resuscitate him. With each breath, I am thankful for my lifeguard training, that my body somehow knows how to do this without thinking. With each breath, I will an awakening, until the EMTs finally arrive in full protective gear, wearing face masks. Grandpa's cough and the news become a reality I can't shake. And everything stops.

I PACE IN the hospital lobby while Sierra and I wait for my mom. Grandma J is somewhere in the ER with Grandpa, covering him with prayers of protection.

When Mom arrives from her floor, she rushes to us still wearing her nurse uniform.

"What happened?"

"He was having trouble breathing," I say. "But they got his heartbeat going again."

"I checked on him before I left," she says. "The medicine seemed to help."

"It happened quick. They're sending him in for tests."

Fear flashes across Mom's face.

I cluck my tongue at the back of my throat, itchy again.

"Call me when your dad's here, okay? I'll see if they'll let me work Grandpa's floor."

Mom turns to the reception desk to talk with a nurse. She takes charge and it's nice to see her in her element because if anyone will make sure Grandpa gets the best care, it's her. I missed this about her. Through my trial, it's like she was paralyzed by what would happen to me.

When I get back to my seat, Sierra's biting her nails. Her knee bounces hard and I settle my hand on hers to calm down.

"You don't have to stay, it'll be a while. We can call Brian, or your parents, to give you a ride." I want her here, with me. But then I'll be focusing on her, when all I want to do is fall apart while my parents figure this out so I can be the kid. With her here, well, I can't let go.

"No. I'm staying. I feel like they're my grandparents too. . . . I know that's weird to say."

"They're your family. Always." I squeeze her hand before letting go. She leans her head on my shoulder, closing her eyes.

I remain alert, scanning the lobby for my dad, unsure which

entrance he'll use. To the right I note the ER leads into the hospital's psychiatric ward. Eric's face flashes in front of me. This is where the Whitakers took him.

"Andre," Dad says, rushing through the lobby area toward us.

I jump up to meet him. He's shaking, jittery, and asking a million questions.

"Grandpa's in isolation, so we can't see him, but Grandma's with him and Mom's seeing if she can help."

He claps my back pridefully when he learns how I kept Grandpa breathing, but it doesn't hide that he's terrified. Shock held me together before, but the slow creep of dread is taking over.

When Mom comes back, I'm relieved, but not for long. Not when it sinks in that when I pictured my return, I expected to only feel happiness. Relief.

Not fear. Not sadness.

I look away, swallowing up how awful I feel and the heavy weight that we'll never get back to how we were before.

14

ALL THROUGH THE NIGHT

March 9, 2020

Marcus was apologetic but didn't budge as I asked for a curfew exception. I reach the front door a hair shy of nine p.m. My head on a swivel, paranoid that Jim is parked outside, but trying to play it cool so Sierra doesn't catch on.

In the kitchen I boil Top Ramen for me and Sierra.

"What you like on it?" I open up the spice cabinet to grab some hot sauce.

"Cheese."

"Cheese?" I open my mouth, horrified. "Like on the side?"

"And green onions if you have them." Sierra opens up the fridge.

This is the first thing we've said to each other since the car ride home. She's dancing around the topic of my grandpa, but he's all I can think about. I'm ripped inside with worry. I just want to hold on to Sierra and make this feeling go away.

"Thanks for hanging around."

"Of course." She meets eyes with me, soft and caring, and I can't help but let out a shy awkward smile back.

I take a bite, then pour on more hot sauce.

"How can you eat that?" Sierra curls her lip in disgust.

"How can you eat *that*?" I reply back as Sierra stirs the now-melted cheese with the noodles.

"It's like mac and cheese."

"Maybe Whitaker mac and cheese." I smirk, but it's forced. With each swallow, each word, it gets harder to hold back my fears.

"Look who's talking. You've got more hot sauce than noodles."

I lick my lips, confused. My mouth should be burning right now.

"It's probably old." I toss the hot sauce, then nibble on noodles so bland, they taste like nothing.

I was in such a rush to get inside I didn't notice I left the lights off in the family room. In the dark, the television glows in its constant state of on with the volume low 24-7.

Over the weekend, Italy enforced the most significant measures, putting a quarter of its population under lockdown, a move previously unthinkable in a Western democracy. The quarantine encircles sixteen million people.

Sierra gives me a glance as I flick the channel from CNN to local news to avoid international news that's become too terrifying.

But there's no hiding from the inevitable, the walls closing in on all of us. At the bottom of the screen, a red ticker scrolls:

BREAKING NEWS: OREGON GOVERNOR DECLARES STATE OF EMERGENCY AS CASES SURGE . . .

Sierra taps her finger near mine. "He's gonna be okay. The chances that's what it is are so slim. Like microscopic."

I turn the television off altogether, then pull my phone out, thinking about Boogie. I shoot him a text.

Andre: You feeling better?
Boogie: . . .
Boogie: I'm good. But the fam's not. They hospitalized.

I call Boogie without hesitation. "Dog."

"Hey. Been here since last night. Doctors giving us tests . . ."

I pull at my chest, it burns inside. Sierra's eyes widen, and I try to get words out.

"My grandpa's at the hospital now, he stopped breathing. He . . ." I go blank.

The fantasy I've held together that things will get better shatters into a million pieces.

—

SIERRA HAS HER blanket on the couch. Her parents were quick to say yes to staying over until we know more. The ease in their answer surprises me, but also confirms this is serious.

Although my eyes are heavy, I don't head to bed. So we sit,

together in the shadows, the same ones that haunted me my first night back. I feel it all closing in on me again.

"I'll be okay out here. I promise," Sierra says. "Go to bed."

"I'm not even sleepy," I say between yawns.

"Bed. Now." Sierra points toward my room.

"All right." I get up, then touch Sierra's arm. "Thank you, I don't think I could be alone here tonight."

Before she can respond, I walk through the dark hallway to my room, the lights from the television my guide.

I climb in bed, but it's like it's not mine anymore. The soft blanket feels scratchy against my skin. The air doesn't seem like home either. Panic races inside me that maybe I never left MacLaren and this was a long elaborate dream.

A soft tap at the door pushes those fears away.

"Come in." I sit up as Sierra enters with a blanket wrapped around her and a pillow tucked under her arm.

"Mind if you have company?"

"I mean. If you're scared." I force out a joke, but she doesn't laugh. She throws a pile of blankets on the floor and settles in.

"I can't have you on the floor."

"I've slept in worse places." Sierra shoos me away.

I shift deeper in my bed, settling in knowing I'm not alone. Minutes pass before Sierra speaks.

"Is it weird being home?"

My automatic response is to shake it off, but I let her words sit there for a while.

"When it's quiet . . . dark like this." I point like she can see my hand, but I know she can't. "When it's loud, and people are around me."

"So pretty much all the time," Sierra says with recognition in her voice.

I nod, knowing she can't see, but the ache in my throat that's threatening to break won't let me say yes.

I take in more breaths, shove out fear to leave room for courage to fill me instead.

"Not when we're together." I almost second-guess I said that out loud until she speaks.

"I used to be scared . . . like all the time. Eric and I used to share rooms because of it. Even sleep in the same bed, me on the top blanket. I thought if we were separated at night, someone would come for Eric and I'd never know until the morning. Then we'd be split apart forever." Her voice trails off.

I keep still, afraid that any movement will change our conversation. Because right now, I want to know everything Sierra's been through. The things we've never said, even though I've always felt like I know everything about her. But I realize that's not true. Her foster time, her adoption, those were things we never spoke of.

"But you got over it." I turn closer to the edge of my bed, hanging on each word in hopes she can tell me how I can stop feeling like this.

"I don't know if I can ever get over it. I haven't been okay since he's been gone. And I'm angry with him because he knows what he's doing to me. Then . . . I worry." Her voice goes almost to a whisper. "I worry all the time. Turning on the news . . . I think every story will be about him."

Silence takes over again. Guilt climbs my veins, knowing Mr. Whitaker's secret I'm not sure how to share. Each breath is a hitch in my throat soaking up everything she says.

"Maybe you can try what helped you adjust before. I mean look, you're all the way downstairs in your own room. You must've done it somehow."

"I didn't have a choice." Her voice cracks, and I imagine getting down to the floor and holding her. But I stay, waiting for her to say more.

"What does that mean?" I say after more silence kills me.

"When we first moved in, I had Luis's room, but I'd sneak into Eric's and lay on the floor . . . like this . . . until sunrise, then I'd sneak back to my room. After the first week I woke to Mrs. Whitaker freaking out. She thought . . . Ugh—he's my brother and I was like nine. Who even thinks like that?" Sierra spits out in disgust. I'm shook by the venom in her voice as she says "Mrs. Whitaker" instead of "Mom." Like there's a distinction between who her mom was back then and is now. I don't know what to make of it.

"She thought it was inappropriate. At first, she even used to keep me away from Brian and Kate. Like she was worried we were going to taint them or something. DHS had to explain it was my PTSD or whatever. . . ."

I wait for her to say more as her wall comes down, but she stops and I hang on her last words.

"Then they understood?" I'm shocked Mrs. Whitaker acted that way.

"Every home we've been in has been different. We have to learn how to live with each other. Discover what people really think about us, deal with whatever they think we are or should be . . . At the Whitakers', things were sorted out by moving me downstairs, Luis joining our family a few months later. I was so scared she'd give me that look again, I never went back in Eric's room. . . . I won't even step in it now."

"How'd you sleep down there?"

"I started staring out my window."

Her words roll through my body because that's what I did in juvie. I reach for her hand and when she finally notices, she squeezes it back. Our fingers slowly slide apart from each other, letting our fingertips linger until we separate. Chills run through me. I pause until I'm ready to ask more.

"Did Eric have a hard time, you know, adjusting?"

Sierra doesn't answer right away; my heart beats faster in worry she's icing up on me at the mention of Eric.

"He always held it in. Big laughs, showing off, you know, trying to appear like things were good . . . I feel like we lost who he was so long ago. How do you fit yourself into someone's expectations? Families that can be so different from everything you know . . ." Sierra trails off. "The only time I felt like he was himself was when we were on our old foster parents' farm. People always think we're different, didn't fit in because we had white parents. It's not the first time, most of them have been white. Our last foster home we didn't have to fit in, they fit into us. They had Black friends, even family. It wasn't this weird thing to them. My parents can barely say 'Black.' Like it's a bad word. I can survive where I'm at. For Eric, that last home was the best place for him." Sierra locks glistening eyes with me. "He'd roam for hours outside, feeding all their animals, cleaning out the stables even though at first he was terrified of horses. I miss how he was then."

I thought Eric would be on the streets, getting lost in the city. But how Sierra talks, maybe that's not where he'd end up at all.

Eric's had a dozen homes that had him constantly adapting to his environment. I never thought about this before. I knew he had a mask, that what he shared with the world was only to fit in. I never thought about what Eric was like when he could be himself. He had that, and lost it.

"You try to search for him there?"

"That's the first place I went. Paul gave me a ride. I . . . They turned me away. They could lose their other kids if it seemed like I was still trying to see them." Sierra's voice goes from floating to sadness. The image of when she left all those years ago comes back to me, when I was destroyed because I thought she'd be gone forever. But Sierra was happy to go and now I know it was because of Eric. She'd follow him anywhere. Maybe that's what Eric was worried about?

The silence crawls back, but this time it doesn't feel empty. This time it feels like it should be this way as we take in everything. Then the sound of Sierra breathing heavy begins. I whisper her name, but she's fallen asleep. I close my eyes, trying to block my mind from thinking about why they kept Eric's illness away from her, really. And I can't let go of the thought that it's got something to do with my arrest. Being set up.

15

HOLDING BACK THE YEARS

March 10, 2020

In the dark I search through Eric and Sierra's social media for any contacts from their past.

It takes a few hours, but I find a thread to pull on. A happy birthday message from last year, the one of a hundred posted on Eric's social that he actually replied to—the message is from someone named Susan Gustafson.

Susan: I'll come by!

When I click Susan Gustafson's name, I scroll through photos of a farm with horses and pictures of kids. I was too young to re-member the features of the woman who picked up Sierra all those summers ago. Just her short strawberry-blond hair and a man with olive skin. Sierra went by there already, but maybe Susan knows more about where Eric could've gone.

I make a friend request and press send on my message:

Andre: I'm neighbors with Eric and Sierra Whitaker. Eric's been missing for two months. If you've seen him, can you tell him I'm worried about him. That Sierra needs to hear from him?

Then I get lost in Eric's videos. I'm drawn to one of him at the farm where he must be like ten years old.

"I'm riding! I'm riding." Eric pushes back his helmet. The horse is barely walking, cautious with his new rider.

"What do you think, Eric?" Sierra's voice speaking from behind the camera.

"One day I'm gonna get my own farm. And I'm gonna have all the horses, except they'll live in the house and we'll live in the barn."

"What about me?" the guy says.

"You can all live in the barn too."

As Eric rides, I barely recognize him except for his smile.

I read the caption on the video post:

Seven years ago was the first time I rode a horse. I swear to God I was ready to become a cowboy. That is until I realized how much mess they be dropping you gotta clean up. But I love watching this video. It reminds me of life being simple. Feeling safe. Cleatus, I'm coming to visit you someday! I hope you remember me because I'll be honest with y'all, I'm not sure I could get on a horse by myself if I thought you'd buck me.

#CowboyEric #MeAndCleatus #INamedHimSoShutUp

THE NEXT MORNING I'm woken up by Sierra stretching her arms. "Good morning. Sleep okay?"

But I can't get up. Not because I don't want to, but because my body is literally aching, my equilibrium is off. The room spins as my head pounds.

Then Sierra sneezes. We stare back at each other.

"You okay?" she says, congested.

"I don't know." I go to shake my head, but it throbs too much, and I settle my head back on the pillow. "I feel horrible."

"What should I do?" She looks at my bedroom door, and I guess what she must be thinking: it's safer for us to stay put.

After we call for Dad, he stands in the doorway wearing a mask that he must've kept from the hospital. His eyes skitter between us. He knows too.

"I called your mom. She's finding out what we should do."

"Is it—"

"It's fine. It'll be fine."

Each time he says fine, I know it's anything but fine.

THE TESTS FOR coronavirus are limited, so they send us to a clinic a half hour away in traffic. As soon as we enter the office there are hand sanitizer stations—pumps, wipes, the works—between each seat. Every horrible zombie apocalypse movie I've seen pops into my head.

The nurse trying to keep us calm doesn't help. Not when the

news cycle repeats how badly this virus is affecting the rest of the world. Now it's finally here. With me. With my family. No comforting words can undo that reality.

The swab goes into what must be my brain, stinging.

DAYS LATER THE test results come back positive. Sierra just cries. I wrap my arms around her, my throat so swollen from holding in fears about how bad we'll be sick. About Grandpa, who's still in critical condition.

Sierra cries in my room with a pillow tucked between her legs. Her hair is in a sideways ponytail, frizzy and out of sorts. I want to tell her how beautiful she still looks, but I hold my tongue.

"I'm so mad at Eric." Her voice breaks as she leans her head on my shoulder. "He won't even know I'm sick. He won't even know if something happens to me."

I give her space to vent while I drown in secrets that, if revealed, will only be too much to handle.

I hear Dad and Grandma J whisper in the hallway.

"You should stay somewhere else. There's a good chance you've been away from us long enough to be fine," Grandma J says.

"I'm not going to leave you here," Dad says. "What if something happens to you, too? Andre won't be able to help."

"What about the bookshop?"

"Don't worry about that right now," Dad says. "We need to be very careful. There's not a cure for this, so I need you all resting."

Inside I'm scared and I just want this never-ending feeling to stop.

"Andre," Sierra says. "We're gonna be okay."

"We're gonna die," I say, unable to control myself. "This is it, this is the end."

"Stop it. Stop saying that." Sierra wraps her arms around my neck, but I want the tingling feeling to stop. I don't want her warmth. I want to hurt because my grandpa's hurting. The shock of my life falling apart builds until I move away from her. I yell out with everything I have, fall on the floor, then curl into a ball, swallowing any tears that want to escape.

THEY SAY THE virus is airborne, that it can travel up to six feet, and even infect people who wear masks. I learn these facts watching the news and scrolling through my phone. Some days I forget to speak, even with Sierra and me sharing a room. It's like my vocal cords are ripped away and I'm left in silence.

I tell myself that if I'm good enough, things will get better. But then I remember that's not how life works. That's not how any of this works.

It takes days, but I do feel better, almost normal. Dad was right; we couldn't have taken care of Grandma at all without him. The Whitakers dropped off meals for Dad to reheat, while Sierra and my symptoms were in constant motion. Each cough was a heavy ache in my chest like I'd never felt before. A fever that lingered high for days no matter how much medicine we took. All of it sent me into a tailspin as my thoughts grew darker. I'd try to get up but my legs weren't strong enough. Sleep let the days blur together until those dark thoughts were whispers.

This is the first day I have the strength to get up and leave my room. When I enter the kitchen, I'm shocked to see my dad sitting in Grandpa's chair. It's weird to say, but Grandpa's quiet presence is what I miss the most. The background noise of the television fighting against his raspy snore. The low but audible "harrumph" he makes when he disapproves of something I've said. The snap of his newspaper.

Now I'm the one that grabs the paper. I mimic reading like him, but to be honest, I feel nothing like I imagine he would. That is, until I see a headline on the governor's announcement.

ALL PUBLIC PARKS, CENTERS, AND NONESSENTIAL BUSINESSES WILL CLOSE IN A SAFETY SHUTDOWN.

I drop my head down. This means no more Albina Parks & Rec. I hover over my phone, debating who to call first, Terry or Marcus.

"How you feeling?" Marcus picks up on the second ring.

"Better. Like way better. Sierra is too."

"You've been quarantining with Sierra? Son, why aren't you giving me the important updates?" He lets out a low chuckle.

I roll my eyes, hoping he can feel it through the phone. I pause before saying, "Is it true?"

Dad glances up at me to listen to our conversation.

"About Albina Parks and Rec?" I say.

Marcus draws a long breath before saying, "Sorry, son. I thought it would work out too. I'll need to find other options. Give me a little bit of time."

"Yeah. Yeah. I was just checking. Okay, bye."

As soon as I hang up, my lungs tighten. Like my body already knew I wouldn't need the strength.

"Everything okay?" Dad's voice is scratchy. For the first time, I notice he doesn't look well.

"I'm good." I fold the paper so he doesn't see the headlines:

OREGON'S FEDERAL DELEGATION ASKS TRUMP ADMINISTRATION FOR MEDICAL EQUIPMENT, PROTECTIVE GEAR

Dad's cough pulls my attention away from the news. I place the paper down. "I'm good now, I swear. You should rest."

"Me?" Dad says. "I'm fine. I was getting your grandma some breakfast. I'll be resting soon. Promise. The bookshop can't stay open right now. Gotta figure how to pivot." Dad clears his throat again.

I have been so focused on getting better that I hadn't noticed Dad getting sick. When he was taking care of us, I told Dad we'd be okay if he just dropped off groceries and supplies at the house, but he refused. He was so damn proud. He couldn't *not* be there for Grandma. Now he's getting sick and the bookshop has to also stay closed in the shutdown. Dad's business can't survive this. And knowing this, Dad won't ever rest like he should.

"I'm way better, Dad. My fever and aches are gone. I can help with Grandma J."

"No. It's my responsibility."

"I can do it." I give him a long look. "I can handle it."

He nods reluctantly, and I get the feeling that COVID is just another thing that's helped break his belief in me.

16

ERIC, ARE YOU OKAY?

March 20, 2020

Part of my morning routine includes checking DMs and social media when Sierra's in the bathroom. I lean back when I finally get a notification from Eric and Sierra's old foster mom.

> **Susan:** I met you before, though you probably don't remember. I should mind my business, but your message worries me. Last I saw Eric was January 3rd. He was asking what to do about you actually. What happened with his situation? And your arrest?

I type and retype my message, deciding to keep it short. Keep it honest.

> **Andre:** Two months at a detention center. Now community monitoring for 6 months. I got out at the end of February. What did Eric say about me?

I go to exit messages, until three dots appear.
She's typing back.

Susan: I'm sorry about that. Eric didn't want you to get caught up in his mess. I'm still disappointed in him, he knows better. He planned to turn himself in last we talked. He was just trying to figure out the best way to save you-all.

Turning himself in was the same thing Gavin said. So maybe I should have believed him. If I knew to reach out to Susan, the Whitakers did too.

Andre: Did Mr. Whitaker know about this?
Susan: Eric wanted to stay a few more days, but we'd be in trouble with CPS. I had to call his parents. His dad picked him up. When Sierra came by asking about Eric, I assumed he was shipped off somewhere or in a juvenile detention facility and they didn't tell her. I wish I could help. I wish so many things were different for them.

I tap my knee, sorting through my thoughts. Parents keep things from their kids all the time, thinking they're protecting them. But this has gone too far. Even if they don't know where Eric is now, he could be legit hurt. So what would Mr. Whitaker gain from hiding Eric's mental health problems?

Andre: Can we talk on the phone?

Then I type in my number.

Susan: I shouldn't. All I know is Eric was going to turn himself in. I didn't tell Sierra about any of this when she visited. I don't want any trouble with the Whitakers. Please keep this between us for my other foster kids' sake.

I swallow at the idea of keeping more secrets from Sierra. Then I read her messages over and over again, before typing my next question.

Andre: I won't say anything. One more thing, did Eric seem unwell to you? Like mentally?

Susan: He was scared. You don't think he did something to himself???

Andre: I don't know. I hope not. Thank you. If you think of anything else, please reach out.

Susan: Sure thing. Please send Sierra my love and tell her I wish we could be in touch. Let me know if you find Eric.

I chew on the inside of my cheek, reading between the lines. Searching for the truth. I shut my laptop as Sierra approaches the bedroom. I'm stuck wondering what secrets I can reveal without hurting anyone.

"Um, shady." She chuckles. "You look better? Finally catching up to me?"

"Much better." I force a smile.

Each night the truth about her parents' lie has floated at the tip of my tongue. Now that she's better she'll be going home soon. And I can't imagine telling her after she's gone because she'd be too angry at all the times she cried over Eric and I didn't say something.

"Hey, Sierra." I chew on my lip.

"You okay?" She cocks her head to the side.

"What if finding Eric is actually bad for him. That him leaving was really for his own protection?"

"What are you saying?" Sierra goes rigid.

"Marcus said my case might not be over, so . . ."

"And you're thinking that's why Eric left?"

I'm ready to tell her everything. That maybe there's truth somewhere between Mr. Whitaker and Susan. That getting caught up in the system wouldn't be good for someone like Eric. Regardless of who his dad is now, he's still got a history that is hard to get past on paper. And it's more likely that Eric would get a Cowboy Jim instead of a Marcus. He'd be set up to fail. Eric could get a Measure 11 mandatory sentence if they find the rest of the stolen items. And even though Eric's wrong for what he did, there have to be other options.

"I don't care," Sierra says. "He knows we're all we got. And you know what, even when he does come back, it'll never be the same between us."

She leans her head on my shoulder. "I'm so lucky to have you, Andre. What you did for Eric—protecting him—that's what he should've done for you. He should've told me everything. If he can't trust me with the truth, well . . . maybe we're not the same people anymore. I've really thought about it. Seeing your family take care of each other when you were sick, even as worried about your grandpa . . . Eric wasn't here for me. You were."

She kisses my hand, then interlocks hers with mine.

And I feel like the worst person in the world for staying silent.

We sit a few minutes longer before Sierra drags me up from my bed. "Come on. Grandma J's at the table."

I follow, eager to drop this conversation.

"Grandma J." I hug her. "This is a good sign, I hope this means you're better."

"I'm feeling much better."

"Maybe we'll be able to visit Grandpa soon—"

"Your mom says we can't until everyone's better," Dad interrupts, "so I'm going to stay at a motel down by the hospital. Your mom will check on me and I'll be close if anything happens. You're recovered now, soon you can be free to go in public. I don't want to stop you from visiting."

"We can wait." I grab Dad's iPad so we can answer when Mom calls to talk to Grandpa.

"No. You should see him. Your mom says that more and more hospitals in Washington are locking down, that Oregon will follow soon. Don't wait for me." The way Dad speaks sounds like we're saying goodbye.

"When can he come home?" Grandma J asks this question often. When she hears the same answer, she grows quiet. Today Dad doesn't even respond to her.

Mom says Grandma J isn't quiet because she's got COVID, her quiet comes from being without Grandpa. She's heartsick. Without him here, she's lost her routine.

I try not to read the headlines as Grandpa's newspapers pile up. They're all warnings about the increased vulnerability of seniors as the death toll grows. But this article stops me and I have to read closely:

CORONAVIRUS HIGHLIGHTS RACIAL DISPARITIES

Maryland and Michigan have released race-specific COVID-19 data amid a lack of national data. An alarming trend is also found in New York City: the virus is killing Black and Latino residents at two and three times the rate of white residents. Early data on Chicago's racial demographics show that Black residents account for 72% of the city's COVID deaths, despite reports that the Black community only makes up 29% of the city's population. Densely populated areas are being blamed for the transmission rates, in addition to reports of inadequate access to hospital care and claims that patients are being turned away from clinics without testing. Such practices have routinely been blamed for the number of patients in the ER, or worse, found dead in their homes. An outcry of an old saying is growing: "When white folks catch a cold, Black folks get pneumonia."

I feel my face fall. Sierra glances my way. "What's wrong?"

I shake my head and roll up the paper, shoving it into the corner of the couch.

We gather around when the iPad rings.

Mom is covered head to toe with a shield and a mask. I brighten seeing her eyes, the crinkle in her smile I can detect under her mask. I also can't help but notice the skin around her eyes. There are new, deep wrinkles. Tired bags below them.

"Hey, family," Mom says. "Grandpa's here. He might not talk too much, but he can hear you."

Mom pans the camera to Grandpa. His typical dark brown

complexion looks gray. He's lost weight. His gown hangs on his skin, and they've wrapped him tightly in his blanket.

Grandma J's eyes water at the sight of him. She pats her lips twice and blows kisses to the screen.

Without hesitation, Grandpa shoots his arm up and with one hand catches her air kiss. We laugh, but the joy immediately turns into concern when his monitor beeps repeatedly. He takes heavy fast breaths before settling. I keep talking despite the chaos. Because if I stop, if for a moment I let him speak, I know it will break me. Then I'll see exactly why Mom's eyes have worn, why she's working round the clock.

When Grandpa's responses grow slower, we know he needs rest. Dad wraps an arm tighter around Grandma J. Her eyes dim and my throat closes as I see a piece of her fall apart without him here.

"You'll be better tomorrow, Gramps. Watch," I say when they turn the screen to me to say goodbye. He makes a fist with his fingers, showing me the universal sign of strength. A tear forms and I turn it away from my family. Sierra catches me and I can't unlock my gaze.

17

MAKE ME WANNA HOLLER

March 31, 2020

When we arrive at the hospital, I'm all nerves. Things are different from when we took Grandpa in. First off, there are people in masks and gloves everywhere, and the number of hand sanitizer stations has doubled. When we reach the reception desk, my mouth turns down as I read the sign:

NO VISITORS DURING THIS TIME

"I'm sorry. It's hospital policy," the receptionist says after we ask to see Grandpa. "We just got word an hour ago—it's to protect our high-risk patients, and with your grandmother—"

"I should be fine," Grandma J says.

Sierra holds on to my arm as we plead to see Grandpa. I can't look at Grandma. She's close to breaking down.

"I'm sorry," the attending nurse says as she joins the front desk. "There's nothing we can do. We have a visiting area through the glass, but given your grandfather's condition, we don't feel comfortable moving him."

We wait at the desk, still stunned as Mom rushes from the elevator.

"I tried to reach you," she says before giving a thankful glance at the receptionist. "I thought I could find a way for you to see him."

"I'm seeing my husband," Grandma J says. "And I'm not leaving until they make that happen. He needs me. How can he recover if I'm not there?"

Grandma J takes a seat in the lobby waiting area by Sierra while I stand with Mom at the reception desk.

"Oh Lord. This isn't good, is it?" Mom looks over at Grandma J, who rests her eyes.

"No, it's not. Is there anything you can do?"

Mom glances at the receptionist, then at me. She shakes her head. "I don't know. He can't be moved right now."

I don't ask how bad it is. From our calls over the past few days, Grandpa hasn't been breathing well enough on his own to even consider coming home.

"Sit with her. Maybe I can work something between shifts. Everyone's trying to figure out the new policy," Mom huffs. I can hear the ache behind it.

I break away to join Grandma J and Sierra.

We wait for an hour, and I feel useless, unable to control our circumstances. I check my phone repeatedly. Send a few texts back and forth with Boogie. He's going through the same thing as me, with two relatives intubated, but he's at least also recovered from his bout with the virus.

Andre: Catch you soon, man.

Boogie: Bet. When all the family's good.

I read my messages from Susan again, debate if this next move will help resolve something that's been bugging me.

"I'm going to get something to drink," I say. "Want something?"

"No. I'll go with you, though." Sierra gets up, but I wave her off.

Then I make my way to the psychiatric ward.

━

ON THE OTHER side of the hospital, I search doctors' names on the psychiatric care floor until I stop on one: Dr. Vitali. She's a friend of Mom's whom I've met a handful of times at hospital work parties.

My hands shake as I step off the elevator. I veer toward the reception desk.

"Is Dr. Vitali in?" I ask. "Danielle Jackson, my mom, is an ER nurse. My grandpa was admitted. Dr. Vitali is a friend."

The receptionist nods when I give her name. "I know your mom. Sweet lady. I'll see if Dr. Vitali's free."

Dr. Vitali comes down the hall with a hint of sadness in her eyes. We bump elbows as a greeting.

"Sorry to hear about your grandpa. What are they saying?"

I shake my head. "They've taken him to a special wing. He was having trouble breathing."

Dr. Vitali's face turns down, sympathetic. "Does your mom need something?"

The question forms in my mouth, unsure how to ask what I know she can't answer anyway.

"Actually, I need to ask you about a friend. Eric Whitaker," I begin. "He's the son of Adam Whitaker, their family lives next door to my grandparents."

"Yes, your mom has mentioned them. Five kids, right? Three boys, two girls?"

My chest loosens. She knows Eric.

"He was under observation back in the first week of January, but then he ran away. He's been gone ever since."

She twists her mouth, confused. "I'm not sure how I can help you. Does he need an evaluation?"

Dr. Vitali is beginning to look like she's got a million other things she needs to be doing besides talking with some nosy kid. But she hasn't left, so I still have a shot.

"He's missing. The whole family's worried."

"You should call the police." Her voice softens. "Did they file a missing person report for him?"

"Yes." I don't actually know. "I'm hoping you can help. Maybe someone sent him here again, or you could find out if he was in another facility?" I'm grasping at straws.

"I can't disclose medical information to you." She pauses. "If I could tell you, I would. I'm sorry about your friend."

I break down, pleading. "His life was hard. He finally has a family that takes care of him. His sister is downstairs right now, worried about my grandpa. I just want to help them. Maybe you know where I could find a runaway in his situation."

"I can give you our resource sheet for homeless teens and medical shelters." She points to the corner around the reception desk.

I follow closely, but she stops before we reach the resource desk.

"I don't want to send you on some wild-goose chase. Your mother would kill me." She pauses. "I can't tell you if I treated him. But if he had been admitted here, I would have reviewed his release paperwork. I'd have a file. I'd have remembered. And I don't."

My mouth opens. Was Eric ever treated here? "I'm sorry. I must be confused. Maybe it was somewhere else."

"They said he was treated at a hospital before he ran away?"

I nod.

"We're the only hospital in the area that would treat a minor. Maybe he had direct service, from a doctor in town?"

"Y-yeah," I stutter. "Maybe that's what it was. I'll ask them. I'll take that list of resources, though."

She offers a comforting smile. Her heels click all the way to the resource desk, where she pulls handouts and brochures. I take them carefully, trying to stop my hands from shaking. On unsteady legs, I walk to the elevator.

As soon as the doors close, I lean against the wall, whispering, *"Mr. Whitaker lied to me."*

18

LET'S STAY TOGETHER

April 5, 2020

I should be ecstatic I'm recovered, but I'm buried with sadness. Sierra's moving back home soon, and I'm dreading how lonely the house will feel. Even though she's right next door it's not the same. In the night as I toss and turn, I'll be wondering if she's thinking about me. I'll miss lying beside her at night, speaking with her until one of us falls asleep. It's easier to talk when we can't see each other. Now that's ending and I still haven't told her the truth.

"You ready for school?" Grandma J asks between sips of her tea.

"I think so," I say. "The schedule's kind of confusing." I pick up the printed papers with my A and B day schedule.

School was supposed to start last week, but after Oregon shut down, the state sent a notice instructing all schools to transition to remote learning. Portland's scrambling to figure things out. Every day there's a new email. I keep thinking about my biology teacher, how excited she'd be when I helped clean up her lab before, then set up the next class. I've been meaning to reach out to her.

At the front of the house, care packages from the Whitakers pile up. Every few days they've dropped off some new things for Sierra and me. If it wasn't food, I let it pile up by the door. I'm not interested in adding to my debt. Sierra stays silent as the stack grows.

I think she sees my resistance as a way of avoiding handouts. That's not it. It's that I keep trying to justify Mr. Whitaker's lies, and none of the excuses I craft fit. I've asked myself the same questions a hundred times. Why was he at the pharmacy? Why lie about Eric? As much as I search for answers, I come up empty. And as much as I want to confront Mr. Whitaker, I can't.

The only conclusion I come to is that her parents must know where Eric is. But I can never ask Mr. Whitaker for the truth because my freedom relies on his support. A small voice inside also says: Mr. Whitaker was there for me because he felt guilty about everything landing on me and not Eric.

After breakfast, Sierra and I head to my room. Her fancy laptop is placed near my old Dell. I only use it for surfing the net, YouTube, and writing papers.

"It's not loading," I say as I try and log on to the school site. My screen is stuck on the "in progress" page. Meanwhile Sierra clicks into her classes with ease.

She grabs my computer and toggles around. "Between the house's Wi-Fi and your laptop, you're screwed this term."

I press restart and drop my head onto the laptop until I get into class, but it just freezes. All day, Sierra uses her phone's hotspot to signal-boost while I'm kicked in and out of class. By fourth period

I don't even bother, instead planting myself on the floor and listening to Sierra's classes we share.

"This isn't going to work," I say. "I have to drop out. At least with homeschooling, I could study alone without a computer. But now I have to keep up with lessons I can't even access."

"No way. You spent four years going to school. You're graduating with me whether you like it or not." Sierra kicks at my leg.

"It's not like anyone would miss me in the graduation photos."

"I would. So would Boogie."

I shake my head. I wish this was as easy as things just going back to the way they were before I left. That's all I want.

"Why don't you email Mrs. Peters? She was totally struggling in biology today. I bet she could use your help making lab more exciting."

"Good idea." I send Mrs. Peters a message.

I've still been sticking with my plan that I'm going to college out of state. But I haven't been able to open admissions letters that have trickled in. I don't know if I can afford it, if student aid would be enough. And what I fear most, my record will somehow snatch those opportunities.

After class ends I watch Sierra pack, and a lump grows in my throat. This will be over soon. Nights that would normally seem so empty were full with her around. Even when we were terrified at being sick, we had each other.

I walk her things over to her doorstep. It's stupid really. Nothing but a strip of grass sits between our houses, but I feel like I'm losing her. I shove my hands in my pockets as we set the last of her items by the door.

"Stop it," Sierra says.

"What?" I shrug.

"That puppy-dog face. You look like you're losing your best friend." She teases, but she's the one with tears in her eyes. She flings her arms around me and I catch her, hugging her tight. After everything we've been through, I don't want to let go.

"I'm gonna miss you, too," she says.

I hold on tighter, not even cracking a joke to lighten the mood.

THE NEXT MORNING, with Sierra gone, even Grandma J floats aimlessly around the house. Now we fill our time worrying about Grandpa. I check in on Dad to make sure Mom got him breakfast before she went into work. We don't speak about not knowing when the bookshop can open, because that would remind Dad of another problem to fix he'll focus on over getting better.

Before class, the doorbell rings and I jump to reach it first. I'm expecting Sierra's smiling face, ready to eat breakfast. My mouth turns down when I see Mrs. Whitaker in her place, holding another care package. I double take—she's wearing a blinged-out face shield as part of her protective gear. Masks and excessive handwashing, and people keeping six feet apart so the virus doesn't spread, have become all too common. The latest are face shields to avoid wearing masks, which have become harder and harder to come by.

"You really don't have to do this anymore," I say. "We're all clear at the house—we can fend for ourselves."

"I just wanted to thank you for taking care of Sierra."

"We took care of each other."

She stands there holding the bag out to me and I take it, waiting for her to leave.

"Open it," she says.

I hesitate, blocking the view in our house so she can't see the pile of unopened bags. Now I wonder if Sierra told them. I open it tentatively.

"I don't even know what to say," I breathe out when I see a brand-new MacBook Pro and a hotspot. Greedily, I don't even think about school. My first thought is my YouTube channel and the better bandwidth I'll get for live recordings.

"Sierra told me about the Wi-Fi kicking you guys off, so I figured a new laptop might help with school. She wanted to bring it over, but I had to see your reaction."

"Thank you. Seriously. I never expected this."

I feel Grandma's presence, watching us from the kitchen.

Mrs. Whitaker looks past me. "Mrs. Jackson, it's good to see you. I'm so glad you're better. We're praying for Mr. Jackson and I'm sure he'll be coming home soon."

"Thank you." Grandma J steps closer but stops halfway into the family room. I still don't let Mrs. Whitaker in. And Grandma J doesn't ask me to.

"I thank you for helping my boy. But that really isn't necessary."

"You and Andre helped Sierra. I wanted to thank you for having her stay here. And I want you to know I don't blame your family for getting her sick. You know, we were worried about her spreading the virus in our house, with Brian's asthma and all."

"Mmm-hmm. I'm gonna lie down now," Grandma J says before leaving.

I want to close the door, but Mrs. Whitaker hovers like she's got something else to say.

"Well, thank you. I've got class now, so . . ."

"Yes, of course. One last thing . . . I hope you understand . . ."

I wait.

"Sierra won't be able to come over anymore. We're keeping our circle tight." She locks her fingers together. "We don't know if this virus is something you can be immune to, or if you can catch it again. I hope you understand."

My heart drops to the ocean. I grip the laptop in my hand, ready to give it back. I won't take it as a trade-off for Sierra.

I hand the laptop over. "I don't need this. Sierra and I took our classes together and it'll work out fine. I can switch into her classes and we can do that a couple more weeks until school opens. If you feel bad for me—"

"Feel bad?" She puts her hand out. "This is what we do. We take care of each other. When this is all over, you guys can spend as much time as you want together. We're doing this with all our kids, sheltering in place. Mr. Whitaker heard that cases are only going up and the state is going to keep things closed. We want to prepare for the long haul." She leans in and whispers. "There's talk school won't be in person for the rest of the year."

Closed for good? I'm dizzy at the thought of not finishing off my senior year in person. Being shut away in my house. I step back, confused.

"They can do that?"

"They'll have to." She pushes off my return. "Please accept our gift."

"Okay . . ." I pull the bag to myself. "I really appreciate it."

She gives me a warm smile and nods like she's confirming an agreement. Then she walks away across the lawn as I close the door.

Through the window, I watch her greet Mr. Whitaker on their porch.

They share words. I watch as a satisfied smile spreads across his face.

I make my way to my bedroom, setting up the laptop and hotspot before logging in to class. I turn my camera off, open up a search bar, and type the words: *Eric Whitaker Portland Oregon missing.*

19

JOY AND PAIN

April 6, 2020

Terry Jones's name flashes on my phone. With Albina Parks &
Rec closed under shelter-in-place restrictions, I've been waiting for
new service options. If I can't find a replacement, juvie could be
back on the table. I'm sure guys like Cowboy Jim would push the
state to lock up everyone in the community monitoring program
during the pandemic. I don't want to give them a reason to put
me away.

I almost send him to voice mail, but I pick up at the last
minute.

"Hey, Terry."

A long pause sits between us.

"Andre. You sound good. How you feeling?"

"Better. I got lucky." I don't want to talk about Grandpa. Or how Grandma is better, but a lot slower than she used to be. And that Dad's still recovering.

"I've been talking to Marcus about finding ways to keep you active now that you're out of quarantine."

I sit up, hope hanging on the edge of this call.

"The Parks and Rec has to stay closed . . . but I don't like leaving the building unattended. You could keep work—"

"Yes," I interrupt.

"Good. This is a big responsibility. Can you manage watching the place for me?"

"You can trust me." My muscles loosen at Terry's offer. "I promise."

"I was thinking you could get back to early workouts before your shift. Then do maintenance on the pool, check pH and chlorine levels—"

"Yes." I cut him off again. "That would be great." The thought of pool access sends me spinning with excitement.

"But if you break this trust, I promise you I won't be letting you anywhere near the building."

"Say less. I won't let you down, Terry."

We hang up, and swimming takes over my thoughts. I get a rush remembering the feeling of my toes hanging at the edge of the pool, tentatively placing my feet in the water, diving without fear.

I get down to the floor, kicking my legs out and stretching. Feeling every muscle pull and extend. Imagining myself in the water as I go through my warm-up routine.

THE NEXT MORNING, I ride my bike to Albina Parks & Rec. The weather's still cool for spring, but I like how the chill wakes me up and prepares me for an indoor swim. My routine consisted of five a.m. team trainings, in addition to extra laps I swam without telling my coach. He didn't push me hard enough, so I pushed myself, training for the city record and national competitions. Our team's season is stalled this year, but I plan to be ready for college. I smile because, until yesterday, that dream felt more than over.

Riding through the city, things look desolate. There are no kids lined up early to catch the bus, and traffic flows like a Sunday morning. I've always liked the quiet, but seeing boarded-up buildings and closed signs on storefronts fills me with dread. Especially in my neighborhood, which continues to gentrify. Businesses that have been holding on, sticking through all the change, can't afford to stay around any longer.

When I reach Albina, I wait by the door for Terry to let me in. He opens it, wide-eyed at the sight of my hospital face mask.

"You sure you should be coming in?"

"I'm good. My mom said everyone should be masked up."

Terry puts his elbow out and I tap mine to his.

"Yeah, I saw that on the news this week, that Fauci infectious disease guy is always saying we should all mask up. But you know they walked back any mandatory instructions after the president freaked out. Must've thought he might look bad."

"Think it's gonna happen? Everybody wearing masks?" I say.

"Should we, probably. Will it happen? Not in a million years." Terry belts out a heavy laugh. "Remember Annie from the Chinese exchange program? All the students that came last summer were religious about wearing masks when they got sick. Annie tried to give me one when my allergies were bad. I used it for a couple of days."

"Did it work?"

"Believe it or not. I felt a lot better when I wore it, but I couldn't take people thinking I was sick. Besides, what it look like for a big Black dude like me to be wearing a mask when I can't even wear a hoodie without a SWAT team being called? I have more to worry about than this virus to be safe."

I swallow hard because I know this is true. Riding in this morning, safety was also on my mind.

Terry outlines my responsibilities for the day. I don't even trip when I see the packed schedule. The only thing I'm thinking about is swimming.

When I finally get to the pool, I undress down to my suit all out in the open since I got the place to myself. As soon as I take off my mask, the smell of chlorine hits me in the face. I welcome the reminder of what's familiar.

I dive into the water. I'm home.

My breath catches. With each stroke, I feel more alive. I glide through the water like I'm part fish.

Pieces of me, the parts that fell apart when I was away, come back together. Some people feel confined by water because there's no place to go if you're stuck or run out of air. When I'm underwater, everything is blurry, and I can focus on intricate corrections to build my speed. Nothing else matters. When the power of my body pushes me forward, and my legs are kicking, muscles twitching, I can do anything. Underwater I'm invincible.

I stroke through the water, meticulously back and forth,

thinking about how to get back my speed. My lungs are tighter than usual. I tell myself it's because I'm out of shape so I don't have to think about the virus's lingering side effects. I push my feet at each end of the pool before lunging forward and repeat the process until I'm so exhausted that I have to stop.

When I lift myself from the water I feel a release. All the anxiety that's been clinging to my shoulders—the stress—is gone. I take in a long breath.

A survivor's breath.

I feel so good that I almost don't notice Phil, the older white guy who's on the cleaning shift today. He stares at me as I dry off. I flash a wave that's not returned, which confuses me, until I look down at my ankle monitor. I feel exposed. I hate that it feeds into some stereotype about Black boys.

I scream in my head. *Black boy! Black boy! Black boy!*

Phil keeps his distance when I pass him, sliding my mask on. Somehow, I don't think he'd change his posture even if neither the mask nor the monitor was there.

I dry myself and change in the unisex stall, rather than heading to the locker room. That's a space I can't help but associate with criminal activity. When I step out, Cowboy Jim is waiting for me by the water. I freeze.

"T-Terry said it was okay to swim before shift," I stutter out, scared he'll take this away from me.

"You disappeared from our signal. The last ping was here, so I thought I'd stop by and check on you. Phil, is it? He let me in, happy to have someone make sure everything is okay."

Phil. I narrow my eyes but don't speak, afraid what he'll say next. My electronic monitoring program won't allow me to swim.

I run my towel around my ankle like I can suck up the water that stopped it from working.

"It's back on," Marcus says, entering the pool area. It's the first time I've ever been grateful to see him. "The signal just goes weak when you're submerged. If you adjust your swim pattern so you come up closer to the top of the water, it should ping a signal every once in a while, so it doesn't send me an alert."

I nod, relieved that Marcus came with a solution and not a restriction. I also relish the fact that deep down at the bottom of the pool . . . I was invisible. I didn't have to carry the burden of deflecting the things people think of me. It was just me and the water. Free.

"Yeah, I can do that." I pause, wanting to keep the feeling I have a place to disappear, only if it doesn't draw Jim to me.

"I think it's time for you to go, Jim," Marcus says.

"If you were doing your job, maybe I wouldn't have to."

"This isn't your case. It's a violation. He has approval and he was doing exactly what I expected."

"You know what—"

"What?" Marcus cuts him short, and they face off.

"Never mind. You're not worth my time. Keep your eyes on your boy." Jim retreats. But not before shooting one last glance at me.

"Thank you." I bite my lip, figuring out what to say about Jim.

"I spoke with your lawyer," Marcus says. "We worked well together during your trial. He's taken on more pro bono cases. It's hard to find a Black attorney out here, so we now have an agreement."

"How did you know *he'd* be here?" I ask, motioning to the space Jim left behind.

"I saw your GPS disappear. It does that sometimes. I knew where you were, wasn't worried. But I had a hunch Jim'd show up here on your first day back out."

"What do I do about him?"

"You do nothing but stay out of trouble and follow the rules. I'll take care of Jim. Now that I've witnessed him bother you, I can report him for it."

"What'll happen?"

"Honestly . . . nothing. He'll get a warning and hopefully back off. He's got a thing for you because he didn't like your case moved to me through the new affinity matching process."

Marcus getting the judge to fit me with Terry was about restorative justice. Jim wanted me to do more time to learn a lesson. I'm a criminal not worth redeeming in his eyes.

I dry off, feeling better now that Marcus is here but unsure how long that'll last.

"How's your family?"

"My grandpa's . . . the same. Grandma's better. My dad's still got symptoms." I glance up. "I'm gonna help my biology teacher prep for class, had some ideas about how we can do it via Zoom. I'll be riding there after this, before class starts."

"That's real good. Stay busy, however you can. And . . . your grandpa's tough, he'll pull through."

I nod, that lump in my throat growing again.

When Marcus leaves, I finish up my work on the maintenance. My tasks aren't much different than the end-of-month closing list except for the things taken off that are no longer relevant—reviewing schedules for group lessons, processing new memberships, and wiping security tapes from the server.

I know I shouldn't go into Terry's office given my situation, but I'm desperate. Jim's not going to stop coming after me. Not with the look he gave me, and not after being checked by Marcus today. I convince myself that I have a right to break into the office. I keep telling myself that before I was taken in, I was expected to complete the monthly closeout. It makes sense for me to be here. At least that's my excuse so I don't chicken out.

Terry's office door is unlocked.

I take slow steps to his desk. Settling in his seat. Ignore the creaking of his chair. If I get caught, this could all be over for me.

I wiggle the mouse and his computer lights up. Then I take one last glance at the open door to look out for anyone nearby.

When I'm convinced there's no one close, I type the password.

With each authentication step, I hold my breath, waiting for a reset password request. But it's the same.

When I log on, I go to the security program and do a frantic search to January 1, hoping it wasn't erased at the start of the new month. I'm only searching a short window of *after* the last day I used the locker up to the moment the officers found the backpack.

Turning the tape to double speed, I watch people pass Terry's desk. I pause for anyone that might be Eric or Gavin. I make it halfway through the day's video footage, then the weighty creak of the door jolts me up.

"Andre." Terry stands in the doorway.

My mouth hangs open. The practiced lines of my excuse are stuck in my throat—caught behind the mere shock of being found.

"Hey." I stay still as Terry turns the light on.

"A little dark, don't you think?"

"Oh yeah. I was almost done with my shift. Just clearing the server from last month. I was in a rush to finish before class; I guess it's pretty dark."

I move the cursor to exit the video, without trying to make a big scene like I'm clicking out of something shady.

Terry comes around to check the screen. Now bent over, he forces eye contact.

"It's . . . been a while." I let out a heavy breath, thankful I got to the main page. "I can't remember how to do it."

"Don't worry about it. I upgraded the server."

"Really?" I sit up straighter, wiping sweat building on my forehead.

"I figured it'd come in handy for the future."

I give a puzzled look.

"The police asked for security footage after they went through your locker."

I shouldn't be surprised, but this is the first I've heard of it.

"It was cleared out the New Year's Eve shift, so they didn't find anything." The way Terry speaks makes me think he's waiting for my confession. I've been expecting this conversation.

I stand up. Terry puts his arm on my shoulder so I sit back down.

"I gotta tell you. I didn't believe you'd do something like that. I wanted to see it for myself on the tape. Prove that my gut was wrong. My gut's never wrong."

My eyes water at his disappointment in me.

"You were here, New Year's Eve, early shift. Could've been that day or any other earlier day that you stored things in your locker, that's what I keep telling myself."

I shake my head, biting my tongue. I want to say I had nothing to do with it. Tell him the truth. When I look at him, though, I'm frozen.

"I know you didn't do this by yourself. You still caught up in something?"

"No."

"Good. I can't have you here if you're getting into trouble."

"I mean, no. I didn't have anything to do with this." I collapse under the pressure. "And I get it, no one wants to hear anyone deny it. Not when evidence was found in my locker. Not when I'm paying back service hours. I do all this because I have to. But the truth is, I was searching the recordings because I want to know who framed me. I want to know if I have more to worry about."

I wait for Terry to scold me. But he doesn't do anything. I pick up my backpack, lowering my head as I walk to the exit. I stop and say, "I just had to tell you that. I'll let Marcus know I need to find another place to work off my hours."

Before I can leave, Terry speaks. "In all your time working, I've seen you carry that raggedy backpack around. I would remember if you got a new one. So whose was it really?"

I shake my head, swallow the answer, and wait for him to fire me.

"See you tomorrow, kid," Terry says. I give him a smile, thankful that he doesn't need to know more from me. He just needs to know I didn't do it.

20

LOSING MY RELIGION

April 13, 2020

Grant High's parking lot is practically empty now that Oregon schools will officially stay closed through the spring. This is my first time back in months and it hits me harder than expected. I head to the science wing. The hallway echoes with each step I take. Every classroom door is shut and most of the lights are off.

Last night, my teachers sent frantic messages before classes started today, stressed from trying to adjust to remote learning. My AP History teacher emailed to say he's retiring at the end of the year and he's like fifty-five. So when Mrs. Peters said we could work out some ideas during her office hours before class, I jumped at the chance.

"Hey, Mrs. Peters." I knock on her door, adjusting my face mask.

"Andre." She steps back and bumps into her desk. "What are you doing here?"

I do a double take. "Your office hours . . . You said I could help?"

"Oh . . . Ohhh. I meant on Zoom. I—I'm sorry. I didn't mean to be scared."

Scared?

"What were your ideas?"

I stutter out a few, but all I can keep thinking about is her reaction. *I didn't mean to be scared.* The way she said it, I can't help but keep my distance.

"Instructions without a real lab will be torture in class," I say. "You could buy a cheap computer camera online, put it in front of the lab, get some lighting. Even a lamp from home could work if you take the shade off."

She's nodding.

Stepping a bit closer, I shake off how she made me feel. I throw out thoughts about what labs she could record and how to use voice-over to give instructions. I recommend apps I use for my YouTube channel so she can edit and insert crazy fonts and sound effects.

"You're so good at this," Mrs. Peters says as we finish up the lessons for the week. "I have so many ideas now."

"Maybe we could do kits, too. I could help prepare them, so when we pick up our books and packets next week, we also have lab supplies."

"I know the school has the funds for that," she says.

The ten-minute warning bell goes off and I jump. The empty school, low lights. It's eerie. Mrs. Peters jumps too, and she gets all rigid again. I swear she stares down at my ankle.

"All right. Gotta rush home to make it to class on time," I say.

"Yes, see you in class. And Andre . . . let's do it via Zoom next time. Restrictions and all."

And how things have been going for me, I don't believe her.

I throw my hood on. "Yeah, Mrs. Peters, about that . . . I have a new job so I don't think I have time to be your lab assistant anymore, so . . . yeah. Okay."

I turn before she can see me break.

WHEN I GET home, there's a message flashing on my computer and up pops a message from Sierra.

Hey you back? Been waiting for you.

Yeah. Video call me.

I smile wearily. I don't want to talk about Mrs. Peters. I don't even want to think about school and how everything's changed. I'm just glad I'll be able to see Sierra's face. Maybe it'll feel like she's next to me again.

I answer on the second ring.

"You convince your parents to let you come over?" I say before she speaks.

"No. But I don't see a problem with meeting outside when they go to bed."

"You're going to get me in trouble, aren't you?" I think about my curfew.

"Oh, please. How can you get into trouble for standing in the grass?"

There's an awkward silence.

"What's wrong?" Sierra says. "You're not even excited."

"It's not you. . . . I won't be Mrs. Peters's lab assistant anymore."

"What? Why not?"

"I went by this morning. . . . She was weird."

"Well, the virus," Sierra says.

"It wasn't that."

"How do you know? I mean, people are freaked."

"I just know, okay. . . . Doesn't matter. School's almost over anyway. I gave her a few ideas, I think she'll try them out."

"Hey, don't do that. Don't pull away. I believe you. We hate Mrs. Peters now, okay. She's the worst."

I throw a half smile.

"That's better." Sierra scrunches her nose. "Hey, class is about to start."

We hang up, then log on to biology. Mrs. Peters is in her classroom in front of the setup we worked on.

I turn my video off so I can disappear.

Throughout class Sierra and I use our phones to talk to each other. It helps stop the weirdness of total silence in Zoom. I miss the small distractions that make school feel real. If I don't catch something important, Sierra repeats it over the phone, and I explain terms if she has trouble understanding them. It's like being in school again except this time we don't get in trouble for speaking out of turn because we're muted.

In the break between sessions, I get up.

"Look out your window," I say, carrying my laptop with me.

Sierra's head pops up. During the day, it's not as easy to see into her room. Knowing she's there still feels good.

"Now we're in class together," I tell her.

"We're already in class together!"

"No, I mean I can see you and you're not trapped in my computer screen."

"No, I'm framed by my window. This is not like class. That's why I want you to meet me tomorrow."

"What if your parents catch us?"

"Are you scared of my parents? The only one who should be scared of them is me."

I look between Sierra on the computer and her in the window. She really does sound scared and ready for battle at the same time. No longer caring. It's unsettling. I want to ask her what she means by that, but she moves on.

⸺

BY FRIDAY I think I can get used to this. Waking up and reaching for my phone to check if Sierra's sent a good morning text. Lately, we've been getting on speakerphone before class to get ready together—brushing our teeth, showering, eating breakfast. I only break away to go swimming ahead of completing my service hours for Terry. Then spend the rest of the day waiting for our secret meet-up tonight.

As soon as Sierra texts me, I creep out my window, stumbling to the grass like I have all week. I'm alert as I make my way to her backyard gate, always praying that the journey to her house won't trigger my monitor.

"That you?" she whispers over the fence.

"Yeah. Open up."

She fumbles, unlocking the fenced gate. I hear her skitter back.

"I can't see you." I enter her yard.

"Over here."

I follow the sound of her voice until I see her, shining under the moonlight. Her hair is pulled into a tiny ponytail. She wears big hoops and glossy lips. My heart beats faster. I want to rush to her, but play it cool instead.

She takes a seat on their outdoor dining table and kicks her feet back and forth. I sit across from her, checking the roof for Luis in his usual spot, smoking a cigarette. I always wanna crack down on him, but I think there's something nostalgic about smoking for him. A scent that maybe reminds him of his first family whispering empty promises they'll always be together. But tonight, there's only Sierra, just the way I like it.

"He's got an early class," Sierra says, reading my mind.

"How long you think it'll be like this?" I ask her.

"What. This virus?"

"Yeah. Being restricted."

When she talks about being on lockdown, she forgets too easily it means something entirely different for me. She complains about how hard it is to deal with everything closing, being stuck in the house. My classmates say the same thing. Our social studies class is a debrief session most of the time. Everyone says how scared they are. How disappointed we are, knowing that we won't get a prom or an in-person graduation.

What hits me harder, I'm the only one who was restricted before lockdown. And if the world reopens tomorrow, things still won't change too much for me.

What's not said, though: the fact that school is virtual through the end of year means they know things will get a lot worse before they get better. At night when I want to stay awake, I watch

BBC and Al Jazeera. What I see is scarier than the news Grandma watches. It terrifies me that half the US thinks this is like the flu or a bad cold. But almost everywhere else, it's an international crisis, with places way more locked down than we are. People are still dying.

But how I figure, America knows death all too well. Because death and loss lead to someone else's gain. And every time more news hits me, I think, what does this mean for Grandpa? Will he get better? I turn away, swallowing the thought because I can't obsess over what-ifs when it comes to him.

"I think we'll be like this for a long time," I finally say. "This is how it always starts in the movies, anyway."

"Don't say that. You know how freaked I was watching *World War Z*."

"Sorry. It's fine, it's all fine." I keep a straight face.

"I thought it was gonna be a big summer." Sierra locks eyes with me.

I sit up, feeling regret for the summer we could have had. I try to read her, to see if she's thinking about last summer too. The night before I left for the Eritrean festival with Boogie, we finally kissed. When I returned, we met up at a party, ready to begin where we left off. But by night's end, things were destroyed. I look away so my guilt doesn't show. That night is full of mistakes I don't want to revisit.

"I think we need to watch out for each other," I say.

Sierra pauses for a beat too long before saying, "You think Eric's safe?"

"Maybe." I've been thinking about Eric more and more. I

want to believe the best, and blame Gavin for it all. But the truth is clear now.

Eric is missing because he ran from trouble. His parents must know exactly where he is. He's got to be in some program to set him straight. He's not hiding to protect me. I was stupid to ever think he would.

"Why you think Eric even stole to begin with?"

"To him, it was probably just something to do." She pauses. "He was hungry for a thrill. I see the same hunger in Brian and his friends—they don't think about the bad things that can happen to them, because they've never had the lows we've seen."

"But you didn't act out."

"We all have our ways of dealing." Sierra looks away. "Anyway, me and Eric have different battles. I know this is trivial compared to what you have to go through, so I'm not saying you don't have it hard. Because you do." She points to my ankle. "But we're bombarded with this stuff sometimes in different ways. It's like a daily assault to fight the world from infecting me to think I'm less than. How many times do you see Black girls on the sidelines? All the stuff I have to deal with, comparisons of what's *good* hair, body type, looks. But we're supposed to be the strongest. Never let them see me break or I'm the angry, aggressive Black girl."

I lean in closer to touch her hair, the inside of my chest rattling.

"I've always thought you were the most beautiful girl in school." *In the world.*

It's the first time I've thought about this. My head's been in a nonstop worry on what the world thinks of me. And even though I can't remember a time I wasn't into Sierra, I never got that maybe while I was questioning if she liked me, my hesitation made us just friends. I feel a guilt inside me that I expected Boogie to keep Paul from her while I was away. Like she should be waiting on me to step it up.

I want to argue but as much as I hate to say it, I fit in with kids at school easier than she ever did, even during my most awkward stages. The beauty standard for Black girls was adjacent to whiteness. Everybody wants to be Black, but nobody wants to be Black. Just pick and choose what they want. From the Kardashians with filler lips and bodies emulating Black women. I saw it with my own eyes. I hear it every day. I've been seen as synonymous with cool, now with a record, a criminal. No in-between. At school I can count how many times white guys, even those I call my friends, mimic head nods saying *whassup* or are always *finna do somethin'*. They treat me like I'm their personal tour guide to Blackness. And I paid my Oregon Black tax entertaining that mess. See, to them it's a game. Some front—knowing they could walk away. Be whatever. I know because when my lawyer reached out to find character witnesses, friends went ghost. That's how it is when you can bounce between worlds, easily running back to your privileged life when things get hard. Gavin proved that when I spoke to him, he acted like it was out of his control, like the universe makes decisions on who gets lucky. But that's not true. Gavin stepped out of the way so everything would land on me. And somehow, I was supposed to be able to what, push someone else in front. Someone like . . . Eric?

I look at Sierra, angry what I've had to deal with. Then focused on her, how much stuff she's had to hear. To be compared to. But somehow, she didn't let that take away her shine. And it makes me feel her even harder. I want to show her she means a lot to me just being herself. That she defines the beauty standard for me.

We go back and forth in the dark talking for a few hours. I wonder what words of mine she is hanging on to. Her tinkling laugh seems harder to get to since Eric's been gone. Since I returned.

Any other time, six feet apart would feel like a million miles away, but after staring at screens all day long, sharing this space with Sierra feels intimate. I can feel the night closing in on us, and I don't want it to end.

"What would you do if this is it?" Sierra says.

"Say more."

"Like, if this was the beginning of the end."

I pull up my mask tighter before speaking. "The apocalypse?"

"Yeah."

I shrug but don't think she can see me. I don't want to think about things ending, not the way my life's been going.

"I wouldn't do anything different." Sierra answers her own question. "I'd pretend nothing has changed. That we were still us, that there was a tomorrow . . . until there wasn't."

"I like that," I say.

"Don't cop out. I want a real answer."

I blow out air. "I . . . I think it goes like it's been. The people who want to destroy things will make it worse for everyone else. Take what's not theirs. Hoard."

"You believe we're capable of changing as a society?"

I take a long pause; all answers point to no. I don't have a chance to answer because Sierra takes our conversation from topic to topic. She fills me in on all the thoughts she's been holding inside, finally getting them out. I adjust, following her, tracking the way her brain works. It's like her mind is filled with the whole world in streams, and I get a chance to catch glimpses of what's in her head. I'm just playing catch-up, chasing a trail of bread crumbs to lead me to what she wants to talk about next. Boogie says I'm wide open for her, but the truth is I'm whole.

Sierra leans back. "We should do a marathon."

I raise my eyebrows. "Is this a metaphor or an actual long-ass run?"

"We'll wear matching shirts."

Sierra goes on to ignore me and I'm side-eying her because she can't be serious.

"Short shorts, of course, with long socks. Are you in?"

"No," I laugh. "Definitely not. What are you talking about, really?"

"You've lost your touch. We used to be on the same wavelength. Do I even have to explain? I thought you could read my mind." She smirks and I just shake my head.

"Well, if I have to explain. A music marathon." She punches my arm. "We each pick your top ten songs, play them back to back. We'll have an all-nighter. Live. This time, no editing, no cutting."

Sierra has already hopped down from her seat, while my brain catches up she means right now.

"I'll hit you up online in a minute," she says.

And just like that she's gone.

I jog to my room, my laptop already ringing. I catch my breath and take a seat.

"I'm guessing you've already chosen all our songs?" I ask.

"No, the fun is you have your top five and I have my top five."

We brainstorm while we stay online. I go through the comments section, thinking of my best song like this was one of those new Verzuz battles of two artists playing their music, but one against music I've never heard of. I want songs that will either get us the best audience reactions or put us deep in our feelings.

When I'm ready, I change into a fresh tee. I put on my cross necklace and a fresh new hat. I run my fingers across my eyebrows and brush my small but noticeable mustache.

Sierra doesn't say anything, just squints at me.

"What?" I ask. "This is a battle. I gotta look good. You first."

She laughs, gliding on lip gloss with its fruity bomb scent I can practically smell from three hundred feet away.

We battle. She plays a song, and I try and pick the next one I think might top it. Before I can finish, I'm interrupted by a ping. Then another, and another. More followers and comments on our page than I've ever had before.

"You see this?" I say to Sierra. Then almost shut my screen off when I see that some of the comments come in not about music, but about us.

You two are so cute! Are you dating?

Of course they are.

No. He's like in love with her.

No. This is his page, she's totally sweating him.

I smirk at that last comment.

It's strange to be so disconnected from people physically while being more connected than ever digitally. A stadium's worth of YouTube viewers fills up my bedroom.

After three rounds, our audience is the highest it's ever been. Comments beeping, even texts from classmates. I can hear Sierra laugh here and there, wishing desperately I was next to her.

By six a.m. I'm red-eyed and sleep-deprived, only catching *zzz*s during what's usually my lap time at the pool. I rub my eyes, watching our viewers grow tenfold.

An email notification pops up and I check it. The subject reads: **YouTube premium account promotions.**

I almost delete it, thinking it's spam. But then I check anyway. The email is asking me to join the YouTube Partner program because my ad sales hit $1,000 last night.

I blink hard, double-checking I read that right. Before I went away, I signed up for AdSense. I got Grandma J to sign off on my receiving payments, convincing her the cash was for college. I never thought I'd actually make any money. Hell, I'd forgotten all about it. Until now.

I check my account and sure enough, there's a payment for $1,000.

"You think this is legit?" I ask after forwarding the message to Sierra, who's yawning more than me.

"Heck yeah, this *is* legit. You've reached that pay status. Check out all your sponsors!"

We go through the details, setting up additional revenue streams.

"How can I get your share to you?" I ask.

"My share? Nah, this is your channel. I was just moonlighting as your special guest."

She pushes back against my protests. The video intro to my channel is me, after all.

When I get off the phone with her, I call Boogie and fill him in.

"The more viewers, the more dough," Boogie repeats, then goes off on new ideas I should try.

"How you been, bruh," I say to Boogie. I haven't really spoken to him beyond text messages in weeks.

Checking in with Boogie should be easy, because we've been through the same thing being sick. But talking to him reminds me about all the bad. It's easier to keep those things locked up inside.

"All right, how's Grandpa Jackson?" Boogie takes a long breath.

I take one as well, and I'm starting to realize Boogie's been out of touch just as much as I have.

"They took him off the machine because he started to do better, but then had to put him back on."

"I'm sorry, Andre. I should've called. But I felt so bad, and didn't think you wanted to hear from me."

"I don't blame you. I don't blame anyone. I haven't been in touch with anybody since we all got sick. Mostly Sierra and school have been the things to distract me from everything that's going on."

"How's your family?"

I can fit an ocean in between Boogie's pauses.

It was automatic to call him and share the good news since

he knows how strapped my family is for cash, a debt that's always weighing on me—on my entire family. But now I feel guilty for not calling him earlier.

"My aunt passed away," Boogie says. "The funeral's next week. They say no one can go."

I suck in air. The news takes everything inside me. It's like my lungs are at the bottom of the pool and I'm racing to the top to catch my breath.

Boogie's family is dealing with this too, and I realize that this virus is spreading, skipping over people and forming a wider web until it wraps itself around us all. It is twisting and squeezing us until there's nothing left.

21

EVERY BREATH YOU TAKE

April 20, 2020

Portland is a ghost town. Riding home, the city looks like it's been hit by a bomb with its boarded-up windows, open parking spots, and the absence of cars fighting traffic. All I can think of is that Will Smith movie, *I Am Legend,* where he's the last man standing, moving around in the daylight to avoid the nightwalkers. I mean, just last week there was a report of a cougar coming down from the mountain. The message warned about animals encroaching inside city limits, and all I could think was that maybe they're taking back what's theirs.

They say in prisons, isolation morphs the brain. I wonder if we're all morphing our brains, and our six feet apart will become farther and farther. If babies born today will only know the silence, the isolation we feel now. I bite my lip, forcing these thoughts to vanish.

When I get home, Grandma J greets me, her iPad in her lap. I throw my things down and join her before class. That's when I notice that she's quiet . . . too quiet. She doesn't return my smile. Tears swell her eyes. Her shoulders are slumped. Neither she nor my mom on the other end of the video call has to say it. I brace myself for the worst.

"It won't be long." Grandma J places the iPad between us.

Mom's seated next to Grandpa at the hospital. A tube is down his throat and his skin is thin as crepe paper, more grayish brown than it's been. In the background the sounds of the machine pumping between beeps paralyzes me. Every time his chest rises I breathe a little deeper. Until Grandpa convulses. At the sight of his eyes opening and shutting, I jump, biting on my hand, which is now curled into a fist.

"What's happening?"

"His body is slowly shutting down." Mom's voice quivers. "The nurses are adjusting his pain medicine, but that will also put him deeper into a sleep. . . . It'll be harder to wake him."

Grandma J takes my hands and holds them between hers. I watch Grandpa and study every breath the machine gives him. Each time his body shakes we talk to him in case he can hear us. But each beep of the vital signs monitor in the background interrupts my thoughts as we tell him we love him.

That it'll be okay.

That the doctors are taking care of him.

That Mom is there.

When I speak it's automatic, even though I'm panicking. Inside, I want to break down and cry out why this had to happen to us. To him. But I know it will only make things worse, so I hold in all the fear and all the pain.

Mom talks to the doctor, and Grandma J and I look at each other.

"They're getting ready to take out the tubes in his throat," Grandma J whispers to me. She says it like it's been repeated to her so many times before I arrived, it's the only way she's able to tell me without falling apart herself.

"But why?" My voice breaks. "He won't be able to breathe."

"It's time, baby," she chokes out. "It's Grandpa's time."

My throat swells, tears streaming down my cheeks as I shake my head. "It's time," she repeats until I accept it. I want to speak, but nothing comes out.

"I'll call you back as soon as they're done. It can be difficult to watch . . . ," Mom says.

The video turns off.

I lean into Grandma J as words finally form. "It's not fair."

She doesn't respond, and we hold each other. I feel her heart beating fast, the wetness of her tears merging with mine. Everything hurts.

It was never supposed to be like this. To not be able to see him in person. To not hug him one more time and feel the strength and care underneath the bark in his voice. To find comfort even in the silence. Now that silence feels empty.

Thirty minutes later Mom calls, and I let out a shaky, painful breath. Grandpa is back on-screen, eyes shut and mouth closed. The room feels still behind the slowing beeps on the monitor.

"He looks . . . peaceful," Grandma J says.

"He did good, the medicine should stop the shakes, get him to relax and . . ."

"Go home," Grandma J whispers.

With blurry eyes, I study everything about Grandpa. It's surreal to see him so at peace and yet so unlike himself. I still hear him in the house, giving me advice. Telling me what I should do. I remember the way he reached for my hand at the table when we knew Dad was gonna miss dinner my first night home.

"Does Dad know?" I ask Mom.

"He does. He can't handle this right now. He was on earlier. I'll call him to see him, after . . ."

"Can we see Grandpa in person?" I say at a whisper, hoping to get one last moment.

Mom shakes her head no.

Grandma J's hands turn, wrapping around each other nervously.

Then the bedside monitor in the background takes a long beep. I wait for a break, but it doesn't change. Mom reaches for Grandpa's hand, then puts her screen down. We just hear the chaos in the background.

"You did good, Dad," Mom says. "You did so good. You held on so long."

A doctor and a few nurses say things in the background, but we can't understand. Grandma J and I just stare at the camera's view of the ceiling until Mom's face comes into sight.

"He's gone. He didn't feel any pain."

"No. no." I shake my head, my eyes welling again. I stand and grip my hair, but sit back down as my knees buckle.

"It got worse so fast." Mom's voice cracks.

I scan the room, searching for Grandpa to walk in and ask me where the TV clicker is. But no one comes.

A wail bursts from Grandma J. Her cry is strangled and painful.

I fold my tall frame around her, praying that if the two of us are together, we can make it untrue. Grandma J falls onto me as her legs give out. Her hands are folded in front of her face. My heart cracks inside. It can't be true. I look toward the iPad at Mom, feeling the weight of Dad's absence.

"Are you going to tell Dad now?" My voice cracks.

Grandma J shakes next to me as I search for answers from Mom.

"Yes. He's still not well. Your grandma and I agreed we'll delay until your dad gets better before we have a memorial service. The funeral homes are backed up, so we can wait," Mom says.

I shake my head no, no, no, no.

In the same breath she shares the news that my grandfather is gone, she also alerts me for the first time that Dad isn't as well as he's been letting on.

"Have you been seeing Dad, making sure he's okay?" Alarm rings in my voice.

"Yes. Yes. He's using an oximeter that checks his oxygen."

"Did you check him, though, really see?"

"He's moving around. I drop off food on the doorstep. I check on him. I promise. Let me talk to him first, and then I'll loop you in to the call."

Mom is gone for a while, then adds us to Dad's call.

"I'm sorry, Dad," my voice says weakly, hiding the words I want to say. Maybe if I'd never come home, this wouldn't ever have happened.

Dad's voice cuts in and out as he speaks. "He'll always be with us, Andre."

I go to speak but my breath is cut short. It feels like a boulder is on my chest and I can't get out from under it.

Dad struggles to get his words out.

"Rest, honey," Mom says to Dad. "I'll come by later. We'll take care of everything."

"I'll help too, Dad." I don't want him to worry about us or the bookshop. I'm not sure how I'll get the bookshop going again, but I will. Even if it means sacrificing my plans for college. One more dream deferred.

Grandma J gives me a weary smile as I wipe her wet cheeks. She has no words of comfort to share. She's keeping them to herself—saving them for later.

22

I'LL BE MISSING YOU

April 30, 2020

There's no wake for Grandpa. No collective mourning. Yet the house overflows with cards, flowers, and meals that leave painful reminders of loss. Each time the doorbell rings, someone scurries away, leaving more. And each time, I beg Grandma J to chase after them, tell them we don't need any more.

"I've been in their place. They want to help," she says to my questioning looks.

It's only when the house is overflowing with stacks upon stacks that Grandma J doesn't stop me from dumping things in the trash we'll never eat. I have other reasons, though. Dad's finally recovered, which means he's coming home to bury Grandpa. And all that's piled around us will be too jarring for him to take in at first.

My parents' car pulls up in the driveway. They take their time, until Dad locks eyes with me and stands taller. With my parents gone, I've been helping Grandma J with a funeral checklist that includes collecting documents, the marriage certificate for Social Security, contacting health insurance, and choosing his casket. Things I'd rather be shielded of the responsibility for.

From across the grass Sierra watches my parents' arrival. Since Grandpa's passing, I haven't stepped outside beyond going to the Parks & Rec, where I dip to the very bottom of the pool until my lungs feel like they'll explode. Then I wait even longer, so the red blip of my ankle monitor goes dark and I'm unseen by the world.

I want to hold Grandpa in this life as long as possible. But the funeral is today, and with Dad back, so is reality.

I back in so Dad doesn't catch us all staring at him at once. He knows why, even though no one will say how we feared we'd lose him, too.

There's an awkward pause, as we figure out how we'll approach social distance guidelines. "Is it okay to—"

Dad hugs me before I can finish. I feel the heaviness in every breath he takes. From being sick to reckoning with Grandpa gone. Healed yet broken.

"I'm proud of you, son," Dad whispers in my ear.

A prickle of a tear forms, stinging. I cough to let it clear from me.

Since I've been back I've felt like I wasn't good enough. His greeting now, well, it's how I wanted to feel when I returned from detention, without the loss.

Dad then wraps arms around Grandma J, and it makes her look so small next to him. There's a silence that feels charged by the long wait for this reunion. It's only broken when Grandma J takes a long breath that spins into a wail of sorrow and joy at the same time. I look away as Dad responds, "I know. I know. I know."

When we take a seat, Mom leans into Dad, leaving me with tear-filled eyes. Mom carries the weight of so much loss and responsibility from nonstop hours at the hospital. The guilt of failing piles on because I can't help ease her burdens.

After some time, our conversations shift to what we're all here for.

"Come on," Dad says. "Let's pick out something from Grandpa's closet for you to wear."

Grandpa Jackson was known for his fitted suits. There's a closet lined with them, all pressed and clean. I was planning to borrow one for prom because our measurements are close. Now it's for his funeral.

Dad pulls out a black suit and a crisp white shirt. I bring it close to me, breathing the strong, heady scent of Grandpa's aftershave, and stand there because I'm not ready for this to be real.

"We can buy a few things and borrow some of mine if you don't want to wear—"

"I'm good. I want to." Dad knows there's no time and I know there's no money. Not when the bookshop has stayed closed. I force a smile, then change in the bathroom before meeting my dad in the hallway.

"You look good, son. Grandpa'd be proud." Dad rests his hand on my shoulder.

When we're all dressed, we know it's time. We're sending Grandpa off in a way he wouldn't mind, but it devastates Grandma J that only immediate family is able to attend. She doesn't say it, but it's in everything she carries with her heavy shoulders as we pile up in our car. There're a million thing things that float to my mind to say, to break the silence, but my chest is so tight I struggle to steady my breathing.

We make it to the funeral home, joining the hearse where Grandpa lies, ready for his service. We follow as it flashes its rear lights, leading us in a funeral procession of two cars.

The cars behind us aren't for Grandpa Jackson. They know nothing of who he was to me. How he raised me by his actions, using words when it mattered. How when Grandpa spoke, everyone stopped in silence to listen. Now his memory is crowded among those dying the same day, same month. Same year. Seems like all this loss should mean something more to the world. Instead, it's only a footnote of daily counts, listing ages with notations about underlying conditions. A marker to pretend there were other reasons for their death. To pretend we shouldn't be scared because there will always be casualties.

None of this feels real. Like I'm doing all the things for a funeral, but there's no one else here with us. No one from church. No other family. None of Grandpa's military buddies. And it all feels so wrong. Makes it harder to sink in that this is real. And when I survey Grandma J, Dad, Mom, I know I'm just waiting to be punched with grief.

When we step onto the grass of the cemetery, Mom wraps her arms around me as Dad keeps a firm hold on Grandma J, who, in her grief, suddenly has difficulty walking.

The pastor, far from us, stands on ground that has been disturbed too often. When he speaks, his voice booms with conviction. It's unfit for an audience of four.

My body is outside myself, like I'm watching from above because everything is numb. Then it all just comes out in waves. Grandma J cries. I see the weight of emotion pouring out of my dad's red blotched eyes and the way Mom holds her head in her Kleenex, wiping endless tears away.

Out the corner of my blurry eyes a flowy black dress seems to float to us.

Sierra.

I know it's her even behind her black mask. Her hands are clasped tight around a small bundle of roses. She stands next to me, Grandma J throwing the funeral director a hard glance so he doesn't send her off. She's one of us.

Our fingers lock together as my dad reads from a passage in the Bible.

When Grandpa's lowered to his plot, an empty headstone stands before it, waiting to be engraved. I blink back tears until they refuse to be held. Blurry and broken, I grip my mother's hand as grief threatens to carry our collective wail of despair to the edges of the cemetery.

TWO OCCASIONS

May 13, 2020

There's a soft tap on my window that pulls me out of my darkening thoughts. Sierra squints through the cracks of my mostly closed blinds. Next my phone rings.

Sierra taps harder, then points to her phone.

I wave her away, texting.

Andre: Not right now.

Before she can respond, I shut my phone off. Then throw my covers over my head to silence the incessant knocking.

Sierra disappears. Shortly after, rapid knocks hit the front door, followed by warm greetings and soft steps down the hall.

She barges into my bedroom, then tosses my covers to the side and crashes into me.

I thought if I could shut everything out and stay in bed, that one day I'd wake up and it would all be a mistake. That the service would be just a dream.

Sierra's wet tears on my chest only tell me otherwise.

She holds on to me, prompting me to get up. To speak. But everything hurts inside.

Her lips graze my neck. I think it's a mistake, until she kisses up to my earlobe, whispering in my ear before she trails to my mouth. I'm sparked by my physical reaction, confused by this twisted feeling from having always wanted Sierra and the ever-consuming pain of my grief.

Our lips crash together, hard and fast. Heavy sobs escape from my mouth. I pull her closer, melting. No longer numb. I breathe in deep to take her in as I run my hands along her face, holding her closer and closer. Heaven to kiss her like this, a real kiss, but not when I'm filled with pain. I turn my head slightly, trying to catch my breath from how it still all hurts.

Her hand presses firm into my chest once she catches my reaction, the tears. I feel the blood drain from my body because that's not what I wanted her to do. But I'm too hot-faced and still conflicted between feelings of pain and longing.

I slide away, pulling the blanket to me and shifting back into the position I was in before she arrived. I shut my eyes to go back to my catatonic state.

"I'm sorry." Sierra gently touches my back.

I hate that I'm mad she disrupted me, when all I wanted was to be numb and sink into this pit of nothing. I'm flooded by intruding thoughts, like she never meant to kiss me. Because I do want to be with her, but I just can't focus on both loss and love. I pause for a moment, and that hesitation shifts every-thing.

A weight lifts from the bed, and I hear Sierra's footsteps back away.

"Wait," I whisper out, turning around. "I'm sorry, I didn't mean for us to stop."

She laughs an embarrassed chuckle, breathing new life into my lungs.

"It was me. I'm sorry," she says slowly and deliberately. "I know it's not the right moment for that. I guess I missed you. I hate seeing you hurt. I wanted to take that away."

Sierra sits back on the bed. "Totally harmless. Start over?"

I run my hands over my face, wishing I could place a cold cloth over my head to shock me back to myself.

She's silent, and I like the feeling. Knowing we're not totally ruined, still able to lay in my sadness with her. I feel myself com-ing back as she studies me, too.

"That was really messed up." I force a crooked smile to pretend I'm better than I look. "You totally threw yourself at me. Here I am, dead asleep, dreaming about Zendaya and Keke Palmer, and you barge in, waking me up with your tongue practically down my throat, ripping my clothes off."

"I did not." She goes to punch me in the chest, and I catch her hand. A small laugh escapes her lips.

"I mean what's a guy to do?"

"Dreaming about a threesome? Really?" She makes a gag-ging face.

"Not at the same time. I am a romantic." I say it, but there's no lift in my voice and the cover of pretending I'm fine falls.

Sierra sinks her head down at my feet, halfway lying on the edge of my bed. "I'm sorry about Grandpa Jackson."

Her words float naturally, like she was part of our family. She *is* part of our family.

"You haven't called since his service. I wanted to check on you."

"You greet Grandma J like this." I force a smirk.

She ignores my deflection. "I just wanted to see if you were okay. Give you a hug. I saw you and didn't want you to be alone."

"Say less."

"I just felt that going differently in my head."

"Oh yeah." I give a shy smile.

"Being rejected and all." Sierra jokes to lighten the mood.

"Rejection's not so bad," I say, playing it off.

"Oh yeah, why's that?"

"Builds character."

"Character, huh?"

"That's what my dad says, at least."

We sit in silence again.

"Can I help with anything?" She reaches for my hand.

"A distraction." I lift myself, suddenly more conscious of whatever funk has been building the past few days.

"You promise you're getting up?" She throws her pinkie up.

"Promise." We lock pinkies.

I try to get some dignity back, taking a long shower and putting on freshly washed clothes.

When I enter the kitchen, Sierra's making tea for Grandma J, who sits at the table eating her morning toast.

"She's a bossy one," Grandma J says. "Didn't even give me a

chance. Kicked me out of the kitchen and took my and your dad's food order."

"She is *really* invasive. No respect for boundaries," I say.

Sierra throws me a glare, but it doesn't stop me from trying to get the upper hand.

We're interrupted by a knock. I get up before anyone else, reaching for my mask. It's rare these days to have a visitor beyond mail delivery.

At the door is Marcus with a mask on. The second he sees me, his chest rises, like he's relieved.

"I thought in-person checks were suspended because of COVID?" I raise my eyebrows.

"They are . . . mostly. Your monitor broken?" He points to my ankle.

I step outside, closing the door to a sliver for some privacy. "No. Maybe swimming jacked it up." I shake my leg, half expecting water to fly out.

"I called Terry to see if you were swimming, but he said you hadn't been by today. Let me see your charger."

I go back inside, rushing down the hallway.

Panic races that Jim will have another reason to get on my case.

I drag my hand on the side of the bed to find the charger, which is dangling on the floor. I slap my head as I put two and two together at the vibrating last night. I thought it was my phone buzzing with texts. I'd reached in the dark to plug in my cell charger and must have knocked it out.

I plug it back in, but it has trouble staying in. I unplug it to show Marcus. On my way back, I give Sierra and Grandma J a forced smile before I step outside.

"Plug's loose, must've come off last night," I say as I step outside and hand it to Marcus, who surveys the bent plug. He pinches the metal closer together and returns it to me.

"You're probably gonna need to get a new one if this keeps happening."

"How much that cost?"

Marcus lets out a whistle. The wild thing about this all is if I was in MacLaren, it'd cost the state $20,000 to keep me there six months. But in the community monitoring program, I'm charged per day for the use of it, plus have to pay for the electronic monitor.

"Power cord's like sixty bucks. You got an older version, so you might need to upgrade the whole set. Eight hundred bucks." Marcus acts like it hurts him as much as it does me. "See if that works. If it keeps giving you trouble, you'll have to replace it. If the battery's dead and you were outside of your home, even within boundaries, a judge could pull you out of the program."

My mouth forms into an O.

"I'll duct-tape it to the wall if I have to."

"All right." Marcus chuckles.

I relax, but only for a moment. He might be forgiving, knowing I'm going through a hard time. But it won't stop Jim from coming after me.

"Everything good?" Marcus must pick up my mood shift. "How's your grandma holding up?"

I shake my head 'cause I don't really know. None of us do. My thoughts bounce, trying to find answers to protect myself in case Cowboy Jim shows up and brings more trouble—or worse, more charges—my way. I can't live like this. I glower over at the

Whitakers' house. The question why they lied about Eric still goes unresolved.

"Can I ask you something?" I step farther onto the porch. "Hypothetical, of course?"

"Hypothetical, huh? This like a dating-advice-type situation or—"

"No." He is relentless. "Say someone's been missing. And everybody knows it. What's the protocol?"

"You plan on running?" His face grows serious.

"Not me. Like a hypothetical friend who has been gone for months."

"Would this friend be under eighteen?"

"Yeah."

"Runaway or a kidnapping?"

"Runaway."

"Well." He rubs his chin. "They'd be in the system after the parents filed a police report. If they were brought in for an arrest, or found on a street check, there'd be updates in their file and parents contacted. Realistically, though, if they're close to eighteen, not in imminent danger, the case might as well not exist."

"Do you have access to a missing person's files?" Online there's no recent footprint of Eric. It's like everyone just accepts that Eric split.

"I could ask around. I got folks that cover youth cases. This person in trouble?"

"What would constitute imminent danger?" I come closer, still sorting out COVID safety rules.

"Someone harming someone, sex trafficking, if they were under fifteen. The younger crowd draws FBI."

"Mental health crisis?"

"Yeah. That could be dangerous. Out on the street, acting strange, police get called in to something and they look like a threat, so they stay on those cases."

I don't want to think about what could happen to a Black boy acting erratic on the street.

"You got a name?" Marcus says.

I hold my tongue.

"I'll help, if you let me."

I study the Whitakers' house again. "Eric Whitaker."

"This anything to do with your lady friend next door?"

"Sort of."

He pauses before saying, "I'll see what I can find. Can't promise anything."

"Thanks, Marcus." I share Eric's information and text Marcus a photo before he heads out.

"Everything good?" Grandma J asks.

"Yeah. My monitor didn't charge last night so he came by to check on me."

Grandma finishes up her breakfast and heads back to her room. As soon as she's out of earshot, Sierra tugs at my ankle monitor as I set it up for charging.

"Looks like we found our saving grace."

"What do you mean?"

"I mean, how long was the battery dead? All night? And he came in the morning to check on you? Might come in handy after curfew."

"Forget it." I playfully squish her head down and she ducks out from under it. "Don't event tempt me."

"Just sayin'." She throws up her hands.

I fidget with my fingers, thinking what could lead me to take that big of a risk to mess with my monitor. My only answer is if it would lead to my own freedom.

"What is it?" Sierra says.

I pause before saying, "There's a small chance I could go back to juvie."

"What are you talking about? Then no way. I was only joking."

"It's not that. Marcus warned me that they're still investigating the possibility of more robberies. If something comes of it, I could be blamed again."

"No way. Let me call Paul." She picks up her phone and I put my hand over hers.

"I know you and Paul are a thing or whatever. . . ."

"It's not like that." She turns away. "I'm sure he'd talk to you. I bet if the police were investigating robberies, he would know."

She picks up her phone again.

"Would he meet me in person?" I've got questions for Paul.

"I'll ask him."

Sierra sends Paul a text.

It pings back right away. I sit up before she shows me his response.

Paul: No way. I can't communicate with him. My dad would kill me and my attorney said not to. Sorry.

Sierra goes back and forth with him. Then puts her phone down, shaking her head. "Sorry."

"Thanks for trying." I shrug like it's no big deal when it's everything.

I cut our conversation short because I'd rather make the best of today already knowing we're breaking her parents' rules about her family's tight circle. She doesn't leave my side because we both know the second she goes home it's back to masks and being kept apart. Today, I just want one thing in my life to be normal.

Grandma gives glances wearing her mask, signaling concern, but doesn't say anything while Sierra's here. As soon as she leaves, Grandma speaks up.

"That can't happen again. You need to keep your mask on—I shouldn't have to tell you this."

"I always wear my mask, I just thought . . . Well, we both had COVID so our immunity . . ." It's a weak excuse.

"I know this is hard. You've been through so much that someone your age shouldn't. And it was nice to see you get that spark back." Grandma J touches my face. "But we just lost your grandfather. Your dad is still getting better. Every day, he's talking about getting back to the bookshop. We have to be careful, Andre. We don't know how this virus works. And I know her parents wouldn't like that you're not following—"

"I got it, Grandma J." I hug her tight, reciprocating care to her that's been so hard to give back these past few days.

"I keep messing up, huh?" I turn away, ashamed. "I'm gonna head back to my room."

"Nuh-uh. Don't do that." Grandma tugs my chin so our eyes meet. "You get to feel lost. Hurt. But we not getting Grandpa back so I don't want to see you hide away in your room. Don't honor him that way. I need you. The house is too quiet and I can't be worrying about you." Her voice shakes.

"I'll take care of the shop. Every day. I promise." The knot in my throat grows as I think about Grandma J without Grandpa. Now she's thinking about Dad. I can't lose him, too. Can't let him work himself into the ground because he's fighting for how Northeast was growing up, so Grandpa Jackson can look down on him, proud.

24

IF YOU THINK YOU'RE LONELY NOW

May 25, 2020

It's now become routine to wake up early and head to the book-shop. Today I started by sorting through bills backed up over months, paying off what I can with my YouTube money. I hope Dad doesn't notice that I'm helping out. Really it's a nice distraction from school, which I'm slowly getting back to. Like today in class I turn my camera on, but leave the lights low so I'm just a shadow. I swipe across screens, moving Sierra's square box to the main page so she's always placed between me and the teacher. In third period, our history teacher, Alex Jordan, has *he/they* after their name and it causes a slow unsaid trigger of classmates add-ing their pronouns.

During fifth period Sierra smirks, thinking she's slick picking up her phone. Seconds later, my phone buzzes:

Sierra: How adventurous do you feel?

Andre: from 0-10 I'm at about a 1.

Sierra: What if it includes Paul?

Andre: When?!?! 👀

Sierra: Tonight . . . At the park by the house.

Andre: My curfew . . . Meet up earlier?

Sierra: No. 😖 He doesn't know I'm inviting you.

Andre: I want to . . . not sure how tho.

Sierra: How about that broken charger 😉

When Sierra first joked about my ankle monitor conveniently dying, I didn't take her seriously. But now it's tied to ambushing Paul. I still don't get what's going on between them. I've been too chicken to ask.

Andre: I'll think about it.

By nightfall, I cave. When the monitor battery fully drains, I crawl out my window.

We roll into the night to Albina Park, not far from home. Cold air hits my skin as I zip my jacket. There's something about stepping outside and being free in the open that restores me. When I look at Sierra, I want to say let's forget it and just meet behind the gate like we did all those other nights. But a fire is lit in her eyes that I won't dim. The truth is, I want to talk to Paul. So, each step I take, I tell myself I can turn around at any moment.

But Sierra is the one that pulled me out of that haze—my grief. So I find myself saying yes, when inside I'm screaming no.

The park is quiet.

Eerie.

I'm struck by the freedom it now provides to white kids whose parents shared cautionary tales five and ten years ago.

Before the neighborhood changed, I knew how to navigate Albina Park because everyone looked like me. We all knew the rules, even as kids. When it was safe to play, what colors to avoid wearing. For all that was bad here, there was also a lot of good. This was our space, the only place where *we* created our own rules.

All that's disappeared now, including the community that raised me. Back when neighbors watched out for each other. From the Fullers, who'd coach my sports teams, to the Fowlers, who'd make sure no kid went hungry. Mr. Green, as big as a linebacker, would stand outside watching out for us so we had no problems early mornings or after school cutting through the park, dangerously close to hours we should be away. He also made sure we didn't stray from our route to and from home, because if we did, he had our parents on speed dial.

There was an agreement here. But what used to be a refuge is now a white space that will quickly oust me if they don't think I belong.

My old community is now gone. And what's worse, we're all so tangled in our own trauma from the place we lost, we can't connect to the place we live now because we knew what community looked and felt like. Just like how I keep coming back to my grandparents'. Because for us, living anywhere else but this neighborhood is only temporary.

This is what plagues Black Portland. Stories passed down from generations about what the small enclave of neighborhoods of Albina used to be like. Being able to say you had a cousin who went to Jefferson High or a relative still lives in the neighborhood was like claiming you're still there.

This park is haunted with the memories of everyone who left.

Behind the shadows of the park, Paul huddles with Brian, Kate, and Luis.

My stomach turns. I'm not sure what I wanna do first: punch Paul in the face or pull him aside to talk.

I tighten my mask, clenching my fist in my hoodie at the sight of him.

Paul sweeps Sierra up in a hug before he even recognizes me. I catch Sierra wincing. I can't tell if it's another bruise or an apology for my being here. My jaw tenses as swirling emotions hit me.

"You need to get out of the house more." Paul drops Sierra to the ground, tugging on her jeans. She resists only slightly. I find myself looking away, hurt.

"I know. I feel trapped. I can't go anywhere."

Listening to Sierra, I can't help but be jealous, like our time together was circumstantial.

"What are we doing out here?" I say, irritated.

Paul snaps in my direction, then interrogates Sierra. I think he's gonna run.

"He just came," Sierra says. "It's no big deal." Then she gives me a wink to play along.

"I'm supposed to believe you didn't plan this?" Paul says.

She speaks, but I can't hear what she says. Whatever it is, Paul creates distance between them, which upsets Sierra. I'm dizzy from a mix of emotions, spiraling in thoughts I'm fooling myself all this time that there's something more between us.

Brian lifts his hands in the air. "Fugitive! Boundaries are Albina Park."

Everyone whoops and hollers, but I'm silent. So is Paul, who seems torn on whether to stay.

"You in, or what?" Brian inspects me.

I bite the inside of my cheek before finally agreeing.

Brian goes over the rules to a game called Fugitive. The fugitive hides, but if the fugitive catches you, then you join their team as a believer. But nobody else knows that you've turned. So you're playing in a team but can only truly trust yourself.

I hate the idea of basically playing Cops and Robbers, especially since the movie *The Fugitive* was all about being innocent. It's just a game to them. Something they can taste for a second before they run back to their reality. But this very moment I'm risking being thrown back into detention or worse.

"Who wants to be fugitive?" Brian scans us.

I speak first. "I'm using my Black card. No way y'all chasing me around like a criminal. And definitely not in *my* park."

"Okay," Brian says. "Black reasons I will never understand but must accept to not be called racist."

"Funny." Sierra punches his arm.

"Ouch." He exaggerates rubbing his arm. "I said I accept reasons which I don't need to fully understand."

"I'll help choose," I cut in. Time is running short to when I need to get home. "I'm thinking of a number between one and a hundred. Whoever is closest is the fugitive."

"I don't trust you," Brian says. "Put it in your phone and show us when we're done."

I type in a number in my notes, and then they take turns picking numbers.

I smile when it's Brian's turn. "Twenty-seven."

I pick up my phone and show him. "Twenty-seven, lucky guy."

"Hell no," Brian says. "You cheated. Let me see that."

I hand him my phone and show the proof.

"Damn," Brian says.

"You always pick your football jersey number, asshole." I slap at his hat playfully.

"Ugh. I'm an idiot." His face mask unhooks from his ear.

"Yip." Kate laughs hard. "I feel like you've fallen for this before."

"He has." Sierra bends over laughing with everything she has.

I grin, a smile crawling back to me. "Shut your eyes and count out loud to a hundred."

They all huddle, eyes shut, and plan the first move. Mine is simple: follow Paul wherever he goes and keep my eyes open to watch where Brian hides.

"I'm climbing a tree," Luis says. "I'll see him for sure."

"You and trees," I say. "Be careful. The last thing we need is you breaking your leg."

He's gone before I finish, always finding a reason to pull away.

This park is new grounds for them, but I know each crevice like the back of my hand. Even with the cleanup and new play structures: I've memorized the way the trees block sight lines, and I know the shadows to hide in.

I take off, searching for Brian and Paul. I angle my way up the play structure, weaving between play areas toward the top of the slide. I watch from the top, catching sight of Brian running behind the edge of the park by a cluster of trees.

I follow, hood up and in the shadows. But then let him catch me.

"Gotcha." Brian grins. He takes a long breath as he pulls his mask down, wearing it like it's a chin strap. "I can't wait until we can say hindsight is twenty-twenty. Nostradamus was right."

"That wasn't Nostradamus." I chuckle.

"Well, whoever said that tried to warn us. I'm tired of being locked up in the house. This has been the worst two months ever. I can't wait until summer, when this is over."

"Over?" My face squinches up. He's so out of touch. No idea what loss has done to our family. The stories my mom shares of what she's seen at the hospital. All he sees are inconveniences. The city shut down, businesses closed, supplies running out. We might be living through the same thing, but our lives are so different.

I hear a squeal that's clearly Sierra and I can't help smiling at a pleasing distraction.

"Still crushing on my sister?"

I turn so he doesn't study my reaction.

"Don't worry, it probably won't last with her and Paul. He was around while you were gone, probably feeling guilty his party busted up the scheme. He tried to make it seem like a real robbery and not y'all, but it didn't work."

I look up at him, startled, but pull my face together.

"Why would Paul even do that?" I lean in closer, not caring about keeping distance. If Paul was involved, staging a robbery at his house would clear him as a suspect.

Brian scans the park, still playing the game. "You know Paul would do anything to get with Sierra. Gavin thought Paul tried to save his ass, but I know better. He realized it was a dick move and Sierra wouldn't forgive him if he didn't try and fix it."

I scan the park, searching for the two of them. Wondering if Paul would go as far as to set me up, and swallowing suspicions that Sierra isn't telling me everything.

The more I'm surprised by new information, the more I believe everyone was looking out for themselves and nobody cared what happened to me. Including Sierra.

"You think Eric's coming back?" I say.

Brian turns to me, waiting for me to say more.

I let the awkward silence force him to speak.

"Eric was always messing up. If it's not one thing, it's another. He never liked to follow the rules. I'm not surprised he ran."

"You don't care he's gone?" I make a face.

"Dude. You look like you're bugging. Eric made his own choices. He never listened to my parents."

"What about me?"

"It's cold how it went down, but I appreciate you not dragging our family into it. Sierra told me what you did. Not a lot of people would've taken the heat for it all."

I keep my face calm, but my mind is racing.

"We should split up," Brian says.

I want to ask Brian more about what he knows. But he's all into the game once we catch a figure hiding in the bushes at the east entrance of the park.

"I'm going for them." Brian is gone before I can speak.

Once Brian darts between the trees, I take off running, hiding in the shadows. I crouch, waiting for some movement from behind the bushes. After a few minutes Paul's face catches light from the moon and I cut him off before he weaves toward the benches near Luis.

I reach over and grab his shoulder. He gives me a murderous stare before relaxing.

"Dang. Thought you were Brian."

"Yeah, haven't seen him, but I just came from that way." I point in Brian's direction to throw him off. Paul pulls his mask down, stepping back to catch air.

"So you tried to make it look like a break-in," I say.

Paul shrugs. "Thought it might stop the chatter around all the other robberies. No use getting a bunch of people in trouble."

"Except me."

"That wasn't on me. My dad was pissed I had a party, and when things were missing, he started contacting parents. Then kids from school started admitting they were there, things taken from them. I tried to cover it up, but it got too big. But it worked out, I guess."

"It worked out?" I step closer. *This dude is really serious.*

"I didn't mean that. I just meant . . ."

"What?"

"You took a plea. Nothing else was found. If I was called in to testify, I would've let them know you didn't do anything."

"You seemed to not have any problem protecting Gavin and Eric." Paul's in their circle. It's possible he was in on it with Gavin and Eric and set up his own party. I study him, wonder what his real intentions are with Sierra. If he's really into her or if he's covering his tracks because he has something to do with Eric being gone. Paul is too perfect, had everything handed down to him. Something like a scandal in his family would be worth covering up, and for him, maybe worth killing for. I shudder at my own thought that Eric isn't just missing but gone for good. My stomach tightens at putting that thought into the universe.

"Hey, I'm sorry this happened to you, man." He slumps his shoulders. "What was I supposed to do? Make it bigger than what they knew? I wasn't gonna do that."

"Was dumping the backpack in my locker also part of your cleanup plan?"

"What are you talking about?"

"Me getting framed with stolen goods in my locker." I keep pushing, hoping he thinks I know more than I do.

"Wait, that wasn't yours?" Paul's face is genuinely shocked. "Had to be Eric."

"Why, though? When he could've just dumped it and we'd all be better off." I'm reading his face, and it seems real. But maybe he's just good at fooling everybody.

"I seriously don't know. I wasn't a part of all that. I thought you were." Paul studies me. I don't break eye contact, only wishing I could see behind his mask and catch his mouth twitching at any lies.

"Why won't your dad let me talk to you?"

"He doesn't want me getting caught in this. My future—"

"Your future? What about my future?"

"Listen. I can't help you. I seriously have no beef with you." He puts his hands out, and I mull over what he's saying.

"When was the last time you talked to Eric?"

"He bounced. Gavin was looking for him. We thought he got picked up and was gonna turn Gavin in to save you."

Gavin and Susan told me Eric was going to turn himself in. I study Paul again. How does he know this? Through Gavin, or Eric? And why would Eric tell Paul unless Paul was involved? Unless both him and Gavin are in on this. My head swims with suspicion and I don't know where it should land.

"Did Gavin do something to Eric?" My body tenses as I watch his response.

"No way." He puts his hands out. "Even when you came home, Gavin was asking if Eric was coming back now that everything was quiet. They were boys, too, you know. It was Eric who split. He left Sierra with no word and now that's all she can talk about."

His words rock me. Paul is convinced Gavin is just as clueless about Eric as he is. And with nothing more to go on, I can't help but believe him.

Sierra flashes past us, closing in on the play structure before veering to the other side. I wave off Paul. I'm done with this conversation.

I don't go toward her, but I stay in her line of sight, hoping Paul hasn't seen her yet.

The squeals and shouts of our game escape through the park, much clearer when I'm not moving. But before long, Marcus takes over my mind. *What are you doing out here, son?* And worse, what if Cowboy Jim's waiting at my house?

I duck, the brisk cold now attacking my skin as I run from tree to tree in search of Sierra. A long shadow dances across the park.

Sierra's tinkling laugh catches my attention and I follow. Before I can sneak up to her, moonlight lands on Paul's pale skin.

Paul catches sight of me, watching, then pulls Sierra toward him as she puts her finger on her lips. Hushing him to stay quiet.

I'm carried away by disappointment and jealousy. I can't watch them together because I don't want to see that maybe Sierra doesn't feel the same way I do. I search for Brian to let him know I'm making my exit.

A tug at my arm pulls me behind a row of tire swings.

Kate crouches to the ground and waves for me to copy her.

I kneel, whispering, "I'm out."

She shakes her head, drawing me closer by trapping me with her hands around my neck. I pull back but can't get her fingers to unlock. Kate is being . . . well, Kate.

"Come." She keeps her voice low. "Let's hide in the neighborhood. They'll never know we're gone."

There are things I hold tight inside because if I release them, the guilt will pull me under. This isn't the first time Kate's acted this way with me.

Last summer, after I returned from California with Boogie, I'd been partying so hard I found myself experiment drinking. Liquor is just as nasty as coffee to me, but I was limitless that summer. The road trip had freed me in a way I hadn't experienced before. I was sixteen, had a driver's license, and rode with Kidane, taking in everything he told Boogie and me about college.

That's when I first starting hanging with Gavin. I came back and he was Eric's new best friend after some golf club tournament their dads played in tied them tight together.

Paul had a party. Gavin had an endless supply of booze. And

I was happy to test the theory of how much I could drink. Which was really about how much to drink before I got the courage to flirt with Sierra. We'd kissed right before I left on my trip and I was hoping to close the deal, moving from friends to something serious.

We drank on the deck, close as two people could get without kissing. Each liquid shot of courage sank me deeper into a haze. Eric watched us with weary eyes.

It was Sierra's idea to find a room to lock ourselves in at Paul's ginormous house. She left first, giving me directions where to find her. I gave it five minutes for it to look like we had gone our separate ways.

I went upstairs. My legs were heavy as I passed blurred people, reaching for unlocked doors. Stopping at the first that opened without any shouts or screams, I went in. It was dark. My head was spinning, so I rested on the bed.

I fell on it, hard, hearing a door open and close quickly as soft steps approached me. I swear I called for Sierra, that her name escaped my lips.

And then her lips were on mine. I was numb and drowsy, until I realized it was Kate. I resisted at first, but I let my drunken self go and kissed her back. I only stopped when my brain cleared a little from the haze. All I'd wanted was to be with Sierra. Hookups like these happen all the time at parties, but I wasn't looking for that. My eyes were always searching for Sierra. So now every time I'm close to Sierra, I make excuses that things never worked out because she didn't want it. But I know it's really my fault. I kept secrets of shame because I didn't want to admit to Sierra that Kate forced herself on me. I couldn't take saying that to anyone.

I left the party without telling Sierra I was gone. I was ashamed that I didn't stop it sooner.

I'd never thought of Kate that way before. I've clawed at that memory to become clearer so I could pretend it didn't happen like that. But when I put it together, it leaves a puzzle both jumbled and so very clear. I was afraid to confront Kate, tell her she had no right to force herself on me. But I kept silent because somehow it's part of this toxic culture to assume I should be fine with it. But I wasn't, and if the tables were turned, I'd have no problem understanding how wrong it was. How bad it could've gotten.

I've never spoken about it with anyone. Not Boogie. Never again with Kate. And *never* Sierra.

That night, things changed.

Sierra avoided me like she knew. I didn't know if I should bring it up, what it would do to her and Kate. What she would think of me, and if she would believe I'd lost control because I was so out of it. But if I did tell her, then even if Kate was in the wrong, Sierra would still look at me different.

They say the truth shall set you free, but that truth could end me and Sierra before we even had a chance.

Kate hangs her arms around my neck. I smell alcohol on her breath even through her mask. Losing Sierra last summer messed me up, and now seeing her with Paul, I don't know what I deserve to feel, other than raw. But I still feel numb, empty from Kate's advances. I uncurl her fingers.

"Stop. This isn't going to happen."

"Come on, I was just—"

"No. Not now. And you know what, Kate? Not before, either."

My anger rushes out. She was supposed to be my friend. She knew how I felt about Sierra. Her sister. "It's not okay."

"I didn't mean anything by this." She points between us. "I was just trying to have some fun."

This conversation scares me, but I don't want to carry this unsaid thing between us. She used the fact that my obvious interest in Sierra would keep me silent. She'd been right. Until now.

"You need to stop this," I say firmly. "She's your sister, and what you did to me was really messed up."

"It's not a big deal. We're cool, right?"

"If the tables were turned, could anyone who just wanted to have fun do that to you?"

"I . . . no . . . we're friends. We . . ." Kate is frozen, her voice cracking. I see a flicker of reflection, from some time before that has nothing to do with me.

"I'm sorry. I'm . . . I didn't think of it like that. I'm sorry." She puts her hand out. I deflect, watching it sink in that whatever excuses she's told herself don't make it better for me. She shifts from expecting me to be cool about it to even more shock, maybe shame. It feels good to call her out, to say I'm actually not cool with it. Every time I've been around Kate since, I've braced myself for what she'll do, what that might signal to Sierra. I want that to be done with.

My face goes hard. I don't want to be around her.

"Keep away from me," I get the courage to finally say.

Before she can respond, I'm stirred by the sound of a police car, coming close with lights flashing through the park. I back up, not saying another word, just watching her face drain as I dip into more shadows.

I feel a phantom buzzing vibration on my ankle, even though it's dead. I don't know if they're here for me, but I'm not taking my chances.

I don't wait for the police to find me or draw us all in and warn us about being out so late. That's a problem for the rest of them to solve. I won't be waiting to get caught.

I run to the park's edges, dancing between shadows of the trees, hearing Kate repeat *I'm sorry* over and over again as I flee. I don't stop until I reach my house, climb back in through the window, and collapse on my bedroom floor.

25

STARIN' THROUGH MY REAR VIEW

May 25, 2020

As soon as I get home I charge my monitor. The rapid *thump thump* inside my chest doesn't relax until the steady red blinking light stops. Then I shoot Marcus a text:

Andre: Charger died again. Fixed it.

An hour later the sound of a car pulling up draws me to the window. I move the blinds a sliver and see Paul drop off the Whitaker crew. Jealousy swirls in my belly.

I want to wash the whole family from my mind and get to bed, but the sight of Paul walking Sierra to the front door paralyzes me.

Paul reaches for Sierra's hand. A rush of hope climbs through my veins when she tugs her hand back, creating distance between them. He says something to her, like pleading desperation, and she shakes her head.

They go back and forth, and just as I'm about to step away, Sierra leaves Paul in the dust. He stands there in shock, covering his face with his hands. *Did she end things?* As soon as I think it, Paul turns toward my window.

I drop to the ground.

Then my phone buzzes.

Sierra: I didn't know you left. My phone died, I tried to find you.

I rub my chin, not knowing what to say or think. Rather than respond, I save it for tomorrow so I can put myself to sleep believing I witnessed an epic breakup.

In the morning, when I reach for my phone, there's a text from Marcus.

Marcus: Got it. Proud of you for being responsible. Charge that thing!

I hate how this makes me feel. Scars healing over fresh wounds, making it hard to know where the good and the bad end.

Marcus: I looked into that missing person situation you asked about. No police report filed . . .

My mouth drops. *Seriously?*

Then I read Sierra's text again and again before writing a long response about how I really feel about her, hoping Paul's out of the picture. But I can't focus because Marcus's text hits me like a sledgehammer. I'm jammed between loneliness from last night and rage about the Whitakers' lie. Which makes me second-guess if Sierra's hiding things about Eric from me . . . but I don't want that to be true. I want Sierra to be on my team too.

I erase my text and keep it short. Who wants to pour their heart out in a text thread?

Andre: I can't risk being out. Probation. Pandemic . . .

Then I text Boogie so my thoughts don't live inside me.

Andre: Been a long time.
Boogie: Can I come thru?
Andre: If we stay outside.
Boogie: Bet.
Andre: Masks.
Boogie: Always.

Boogie arrives and I'm hoping that we're at least one thing in my life that stays the same.

"What's up, man?" We tap elbows.

"Bored." Boogie's double masked as he takes a seat on the steps near my porch swing.

I've wanted to fill him in on what he's missed. Not just about the Whitakers and the missing police report, but everything else. And I want to be *just us* again—to be in the moment, talking about whatever. Anything to melt away the awkward silence that seems to radiate when we're on video. Because when I'm on my phone, I'm forced to say something. When most of the time, I've got nothing to say, at least nothing important. Before, we could just be, hang out at each other's houses, ride around town. Be dead silent, not say a word, and it'd be all right. Big talks, or random comments. No pressure on a time clock. I guess I just wanna be.

"I miss hanging out like this," I say.

"You going soft on me?" Boogie halfway jokes.

"You stupid, man. Whatever." I wash the emotions from my face, but he knows I could go in on the side move he pulls when we're watching something sad and he doesn't want me to see his eyes watering. His go-to move is dabbing his collar to soak up his tears.

Boogie's voice lowers. "I'm not trying to be funny, but this is the longest zombie apocalypse ever."

"Right, like we know it's coming to that but we gotta get through act one."

We both laugh.

"For real, though, I don't know how much I can take of this. Check my hands." Boogie shows me his crusted-up hands.

"Hand sanitizer?"

"Yeah," Boogie says. "You know how many times I wash my hands now?"

"Don't get me started on scrubbing down every grocery item coming in the house."

"I hope our whole summer's not gonna be like this."

If anyone else was listening in our conversation, they wouldn't know how much we've lost. But that's the thing: Boogie and I don't have to explain all that to each other. In fact, I'd rather not. We both know this won't end by summer, but that's not what's worst about all this. Worst is thinking about all of next year, because while other people get tired of it and roll the dice with this virus, I know what it's like to lose something from it. To be sick from it. To watch my dad with fear that what happened to my grandpa might happen to him. So I'll be stuck in my bedroom waiting on a scientist. Praying we get this dumpster-fire president out of office because I know my life means nothing to him.

As soon as the data about the virus hitting communities of color harder came out, concern about safety started falling apart. Now the president's pushing for us to open back up as a country. Not wanting to sign relief packages for people unable to work. We're somehow supposed to go back to normal, since part of the country realized the virus might not be as bad for them. This is the American way.

Boogie kicks at the ground. "I'm finna go to any school that's got their doors open. Even if it means I can't go to MIT. Even if I gotta be locked up in the dorms. It would be better than this."

I agree. But I'm lost in thought about my own postgrad plans. College seems even further away. Before the arrest, I was thinking about HBCUs, with Morehouse at the top of my list. Now I don't know what I want. I never even opened up my decision emails, and now it's too late. My future doesn't rely on what I want; it's about if I can even afford to go anywhere. I might be stuck here. I rub my forehead, getting a headache thinking about the future.

"Wherever you go, don't be forgetting about me," I joke, even though I'm dead serious.

"Friends for life. Wherever we're at," Boogie confirms. We pretend-dap from a distance. "But I know you don't have me out here to talk about college. What's up?"

I take a heavy breath, then unload.

Boogie pulls his mask up higher. I know I shouldn't expect him to have answers right away, but I'm disappointed when he doesn't. He's about as confused as I am.

"When I spoke to the doctor at the hospital, I knew something was wrong. So I kept looking."

"Yeah, white people just giving out random gifts and acting nice by sharing secrets with you that they don't even tell their own kids . . ." Boogie shakes his head. "It's shady, bruh."

I'm glad to see it's not just me being paranoid. The laptop. Paying for things at the pharmacy . . . Now I'm convinced I'm not safe until I know exactly what's behind it all. I could end up in the same situation if I'm set up again.

"Not to sound like a jerk, but why'd it take so long to realize Eric might've been the one to set you up?" Boogie says.

"I didn't know for sure."

"No. You didn't want to say it." Boogie pushes. "Who else could it be? Even if he didn't physically frame you, he helped whoever did. And his parents not filing a missing person report would be totally negligent. I don't see them doing that. They know where he is."

That's no lie. There was a reason I was pinned. Whether it was Paul, Gavin, or Eric—they all knew the truth.

"I keep thinking, why me? Why did I have to be the one?"

"Someone had to go down before it caught up to Eric or Gavin. Maybe they thought you were an easy sell."

Boogie's right. I was an outsider—a poor kid, a Black kid—on paper that was enough.

"I know you're after an explanation, but you were the only one left that could take the fall," Boogie says. "I hate to say it, but that's how it is. That's how it's always gone for *us*."

"I may have taken the fall, but everyone at school should've known it was a lie and been character witnesses. Made the police actually do their job."

"When has that ever mattered? People believe what makes them feel better."

I want to say, *Take it back, Boogie.* Because I want to believe that truth lives deep inside us all, and it's the pursuit of truth that will help me in the end. Instead, I nod in agreement.

From the porch I hear the news turn up and Grandma J says, "Oh my God, not again."

We step closer to the doorway. Breaking news flashes on-screen. The video I've been avoiding on my social media assaults me in my home. I look away because I can't handle seeing another Black man being murdered by police. I don't want to learn another name.

"Yeah, that's crazy, right," Boogie says.

"I couldn't watch." I take a seat back on the porch steps.

"I get that. It's been retweeted everywhere, crazy how the news now comes from social media first."

I nod.

"Still thinking about Eric?" Boogie steps out to the grass and takes his mask off, breathing deeply from the air outside. I do too, not wanting to take this breath for granted.

"Why wouldn't Eric come back after my sentencing, though?

And after last night, I've been thinking about Paul. He's in on the reason I got set up. He might be behind it all."

"Maybe." Boogie doesn't sound convinced.

"What, you don't think so?"

"I think you want him to be involved." Boogie stalks Sierra's house. "Besides, I still feel like Mr. Whitaker probably shipped Eric off to some boarding school to keep the Whitaker name clean. He'll come back after the city commissioner election. Watch."

"True. Maybe Mr. Whitaker found out and said he'd ship Eric off but take care of Sierra if he stayed away. I gotta find Eric and ask him."

"You don't, though." Boogie points his finger at me. "You need to watch out for yourself. Because nobody else is. Who knows what would stir up if Eric came back."

I nod again, but inside, a little voice tells me Eric would never leave Sierra. There was only one thing that was important to him, and that was taking care of Sierra.

26

PUT YOUR HANDS WHERE
MY EYES COULD SEE

May 27, 2020

My toes grip the edge of the pool before I dive to the bottom, holding myself underwater to erase the image of George Floyd from my mind. His murder has looped on every news channel and social media. I avoided it for as long as I could, but now it's everywhere. So I went to the only place I could to get away. Let my electronic monitor be silenced. And no longer policed. To vanish.

The pressure builds inside until I explode to the top, gasping for air. But I still can't shake the visual of his head shoved onto the concrete, the police boot, the knee on his neck. George Floyd is a name I shouldn't know. Like so many names I shouldn't know.

I avoid watching live lynchings at all costs. That's all this is— a viral viewing of Black folks' humanity being ripped away. Then us having to justify our lives, over and over again. What I hate the most is it took eight minutes and forty-six seconds of brutality to slam collective consciousness into people who have always been silent. People who believe things went too far, and change will finally happen. This fills me with rage.

Our life only seems to matter when we can't breathe? When it's too late.

We've been expected to repeat this cycle of denial—believe that police supply justice. But when they don't, we're supposed to ignore that this is systemic.

I want to believe the way I'm thinking is messed up. But I know all too well that I'm right. It's as real as the ankle monitor tracking my every movement. It's as real as my grandpa's passing. Maybe what I need to come to terms with is for *us* to realize: to win, you have to know the rules. And the rules are, *we* already lost.

⌇

BY MY FIFTH plunge into the water, Terry's moved from the office to the pool deck. He doesn't interrupt, just watches my cycle of screaming underwater, letting silent bubbles mirror my existence. I only rest for a moment before doing my routine of laps, until my legs feel as heavy as tree trunks.

I finish, then prepare for storage closet duties. But when I check the clipboard my name's crossed off and I've been added to gym equipment check. I look up at Terry to thank him, but his head is back down in his work. In less than an hour, I'm done, and breathing just a little bit easier.

I almost reach home when I catch Sierra on my lawn, peering into my bedroom window.

"What're you doing?" I roll up behind her.

Sierra jumps, and my first laugh of the day escapes. She's decked out in all black, face mask down to her shoes. Out on the grass Brian and Kate rock homemade Black Lives Matter shirts, and Luis wears an Abolish ICE sweatshirt. Kate takes a few steps back to be behind Brian.

They are buzzing with energy, which zaps what I've just got back.

They have this level of enthusiasm. Of fight. Hope. Willing to risk safety if it'll make change.

And I . . . well, I am just tired.

"Come with us." Sierra's words are soft and tempting. "Brian and Kate are only coming to get out of the house because they've never protested before. You gotta come with me."

"Your parents okay with you leaving your home pod?"

"I don't care. They don't think it's my fight since they *gave me so much* I shouldn't worry about this stuff."

It's like the video of George Floyd just snapped her into action. She's realizing her *don't see color* family isn't reality. And she's known that, but now she wants to do something about it. Because outside her house, she's just another Black girl.

I'd go anywhere with her right now to escape the madness. But alone, not with a swarm of protesters. Not during a pandemic surrounded by people just seeing how bad it's always been for Black folks, even without the footage.

"I'm good." I shove my hands in my pockets, kicking my foot up so they can all see the shackle that proves that I'm not brand-new to this fight. That I have already felt loss. Have already been judged as another lost cause in Portland.

"They're not gonna get away with this." Brian puts his fist into the air.

Under my mask, my mouth twists in anger. I can't help it. The only thing tethering me in place is Sierra. If she wasn't here, I'd yell at the top of my lungs. *My grandfather is gone! My dad's still recovering from COVID!* Brian's part of the problem if he just thinks it's about George Floyd. It's about all of us. Whether it's prison. Police. Poverty. Education. Health care. It's all systemic, and I don't know if he can ever get that deep to understand what's at the root, untended. I'm also not sure this moment will have that kind of attention span to become a movement. Not when people seem to be chasing new things to be outraged over.

When I look at them, I don't feel hopeful. I feel hopeless.

"I'm gonna take a nap," I say.

Brian's eyebrows rise.

"I'll catch up with you guys." Sierra waves her siblings away, concern in her eyes. She turns back to me. "How you doing?"

I can't speak. Because if I do, everything bottled in my chest will burst.

I wait for her to leave, but she barrels into me.

I wrap my arms around her tight. Inside I'm aching, and hugging her is the only thing that makes the pain stop. I hold on like she's gonna disappear too. Eventually I let go, grinding my jaw to keep my exterior expressionless.

"I'll call you later." Sierra takes a step back.

I force a smile, turning back to my house before I crack.

—

OVER THE NEXT few days things ramp up on the news. Out my window, the Whitaker kids leave the house as if the pandemic was over, but it's Sierra who stays dressed in gear only suited for a protest.

There is desperation on every channel as people cry out for answers, for social justice. For this to stop.

Like Ahmaud Arbery, going on a run like anybody else. Except Black people can't just do that, not even in their own neighborhood. I can't pull myself away, watching these victims back to back. All imperfectly perfect.

The video goes viral even though it's been out for weeks. Each time I watch, I want to see Ahmaud get away from that white truck. It's like a horror flick I'm wishing had a different ending, except this movie is called *America 2020.* Not to be confused with *America 1920,* or *1820, 1720,* or *1620.*

Those white men couldn't even understand they were the real threat. They chased him down like he was a wild animal running loose on the street. The only difference is that if he was an animal, they would've taken more care of his life—it would have mattered. And because he wouldn't stop, they felt it was their job to make him.

Like Breonna Taylor. In her home, a no-knock warrant serving as a good enough reason for the police to kill her while she was in bed. As if someone breaking into your home, not announcing who they were, wouldn't terrify anyone. Her death hits harder knowing we're supposed to be sheltering in place. It's a sober reminder we're not all safe in our homes.

We're not safe anywhere.

The news eats me up until I feel myself building remnants of hope, that seed growing, because the protests last longer than I expect. Crowds grow all over the country, not stopped by the pandemic. People are out in the streets—night after night. And not just Black people. People of color. White folks. And I keep asking myself, *What you gonna do, Andre?*

I want to be everywhere, and nowhere.

I want to do something, and nothing.

I want to wake up and it's 2021 and have all of this be over. Each time I think that, I want to slap myself for fooling myself into believing that things will change next year, when we've been on this running clock since the very beginning.

After hours of watching news, I head outside because I'm restless and need to clear my head. I've been feeling more alone as Sierra goes back to the world to fight when it feels like no one's fighting for me. The real me.

It's almost too dark, but for some reason it feels safer to be out as the sun is setting. With a hoodie to keep me warm, I feel protected. Like I never left my bed.

The corner market light flashes "open." It carries organic groceries, making it an essential business. If it was Gary's corner store, they would've probably shut it down. Inside, I grab a pack of gum, an Izze drink, and a Snickers.

Before I pay, the owner says, "It's on me."

I raise my eyebrows, confused, as I thrust my money at him. But he doesn't accept it.

"Black Lives Matter, right!"

I stare at this white man telling me Black Lives Matter in the same store that used to be owned by a Black man until he was pushed out. It used to be the only store for a mile before this became a block known as a foodie hub.

I stumble out. Honestly dazed, like the world has turned upside down and I'm living in a simulation.

I'm walking, not paying attention, turning down a street too late, and I have to backtrack down the block because it doesn't cut over to the next street.

My phone buzzes and I answer, checking the time.

"Cutting it close to curfew," Dad says.

"I went to the corner market. I'll be home soon."

"Hurry up, now. I'll be waiting by the door."

Dad hangs up right before I see red and blue flashing, raising my instincts to flee.

Run. Don't think. Just go.

But I don't. I'm frozen, waiting to see if they're here for me or headed to the protests downtown.

A police car slows to a stop, and the first officer jumps out. Followed by another. He is locked and loaded.

I regret all decisions to leave my house, to not flee. Because I've seen it go down both ways—staying and getting shot, running and getting shot. Both executions. I stay because I don't want the story of me running in my ankle monitor to be my headline.

"Hands out of your pocket," the officer says.

I freeze. Unsure what to do.

The other officer bellows out conflicting directions.

Get down.

Hands up.

Drop it.

And I'm looking at them, knowing what they see when they look at me. If I move, even pull my hands out, I could be dead.

"Get on the ground."

"Hands out of your pockets," the officer repeats.

How do I pull my hands out of my pockets without making them think I'm carrying?

How do I get on the ground without taking my hands out of my pockets?

All I can think is I want my dad.

I want him up and healthy.

I want him storming down the street to get me because he knew something was wrong.

I want Grandpa Jackson to be alive, following Dad. Fearless as he gives the officers a piece of his mind like someone who's been through this a thousand times.

But my grandpa's gone . . . and my dad, he's . . . he's . . .

"Get on the ground."

Tears trail my face and I can't stop crying.

"It's a cell phone, Officer." I don't move my hand. "I'm gonna drop it on the ground, then put my hands up."

"Get on the ground! Get on the ground!"

"I live down the street, Officer, 555279 Ainsworth Street. My grandfather is Robert Jackson. My grandmother is Sara Jackson. My father owns Malcolm's Bookshop."

I go through my history, naming off every person I know on the street. I don't listen to a word they're saying because I pray my story of *place* in this neighborhood means something to them. That some name recognition saves my life.

But they just keep on yelling.

So I drop the phone.

Raise my hands slowly.

Then I get down on my knees, without using my hands, for fear they'll react. It crushes my knees, but not as hard as what follows.

They tackle me to the concrete. My head slapped to the ground.

Hand on neck.

Knee in my back.

The copper taste of blood runs across my tongue.

Black Lives Matter.

Black Lives Matter.

Is the running mantra in my head, until I realize I've been saying it out loud.

Somehow, this does two things: a knee digs deeper into the small of my back, forcing my skin onto the concrete. But another hand slowly releases its grip on my neck as tears trickle to the ground.

They check my hoodie and pockets.

"It's a candy bar. Some gum," one officer says.

I feel something wet and find blood trickling down the concrete.

At first, I think I'm dying, but then I hear, "Careful, it's a broken bottle."

"My soda," I gasp.

They lift me from the ground, to my knees as they unzip and remove my hoodie, leaving me in my T-shirt. I wait for them to trail down to my ankles. Knowing exactly what'll be next.

I search for help, expecting not to see any. But neighbors are stepping outside their houses, watching. Shame crawls over me, like I'm in a zoo on display, begging for someone to know me.

Flashes of light shine on us from this rising audience. Phones record. A buzz grows.

A voice calls to the cops, asking why they're being so rough on me. Asking what I've done.

"He's just a kid," someone says.

And it's like their words have cleared the lens through which the cops were analyzing me.

An officer lifts me to my feet, gently brushing off the glass and dirt. He wipes my face clean, making me look . . . presentable? Someone calls my name and fresh tears roll down my face because someone knows me.

My eyes dart until I spot the voice. Marcus is parked across the street.

"What's happening here?" Marcus's gaze shifts between me and the officers.

My eyes beg him to believe I didn't do anything.

When the cops finally give me a chance to speak for myself, I explain what happened. That's when an officer tells me that a neighbor called about a suspicious man scoping the neighborhood.

"I live the next block over, I passed it and thought I could cut over, but it's a dead end. I wasn't doing anything. I swear. My family's been sick. I was just getting fresh air, picking up some snacks."

Marcus covers for me, calling me his nephew. Tears prickle in my eyes at how close this could've gone down a whole different way. The thought terrifies me that I'm a block away from Grandma J and Dad, who I know are pacing, waiting for me to arrive.

I'm still in shock, having a hard time moving, so Marcus takes me gently by the arm and puts me in his car. Any other time I would've begged him to let me walk. But this isn't any other time.

As soon as I get in his car I shield my face with my hoodie in my hands like it's Kleenex.

When we get home, he walks me to my door and I hug him.

Because I wanna get out this fear before Grandma J or my dad sees me breaking down. I don't want to add to what they've already got to deal with.

I hug Marcus like he's my father. And Marcus hugs me like I'm his son. And when he leaves me at the door, he walks to his car without saying a word.

Marcus doesn't ask what happened. He knows what this was, and what it could've been.

DREAM ON

May 28, 2020

The next day I flip through news channels, witnessing a miracle of powerful voices being raised. The kind of thing that makes the call for justice louder, harder to ignore. Major companies. Famous people who're usually silent. Colin Kaepernick must be shell-shocked after losing everything for taking a knee just to get them to think about BLM. On top of all this, every state across the country is protesting in the name of Black Lives Matter. The shock stays; so does the outrage.

Honestly, I'm stunned it's kept growing and people in class have been talking about it. Even teachers today in Thursday advisory stopped class to talk about how we feel. There are little things happening in companies, too. I just hope their commitment includes hiring more diverse staff so they don't misstep for decades in the first place.

I thought this wouldn't last, but it looks like it's growing. Like the pandemic forced everyone inside their homes to stop long enough to pay attention and give a damn. Which let *our* truth slap them with a glimpse of being Black in America.

Now more people are beginning to recognize saying you're not racist isn't enough—you need to be antiracist. I just hope it'll catch on long enough for change to sustain. Real abolition. The liberation of Black people. We need this to be a marathon everyone is willing to be in. Not just *us*.

These thoughts race through my mind. Let's be clear, inside my house. I haven't been out since last night to test the theory that things have fully changed. Not after my own neighborhood called the cops on me for walking on the sidewalk. I hope whoever called the cops on me is haunted by what they did. Because their need to feel safe could've brought death upon me or a permanent path to incarceration.

After a few more hours of news, I gently tap Grandma, who's adding to her pile of face masks she's making for church members. She stirs from the couch in the same trance she's been in since Grandpa's funeral.

"Where's Dad?" I say.

"At the bookshop."

"What?" He should be resting. Dad no longer tests positive for COVID, but his body is weak, with lingering pains he can't explain. He runs out of breath just by standing up.

"You know your father. He's more worried about making sure he's got something to leave you than his own life." Grandma J's tone is harsher than I'm used to.

I'd much rather have my dad here than be left with a

bookshop to run myself—a constant reminder of what I cost him.

"I'm gonna meet him. How long he been there?"

"Since this morning. There's a wave to support Black bookshops across the country."

I slide my hoodie on before dipping out with my mask.

Outside air startles me. I stop only to study the new Black Lives Matter flag waving on the porch of the Whitakers. Campaign stakes are also firmly planted in the ground on both our lawns: WHITAKER WINS—WE ALL WIN.

On my bike, I kick our sign down until it has an unchangeable gangsta lean.

As I navigate my block, I'm flushed with confusion. Pride and pain. Black Lives Matter signs flood my neighborhood. What kills me is store windows with fancy designed BLM posters to match the store aesthetics.

Simultaneously I feel seen and erased.

I hop off my bike to walk and bear witness, daring anyone with a wary eye to challenge their claims that Black Lives Matter.

Mrs. Glendale walks her dog. I swivel for the best route to avoid her but she's locked on me.

"Good afternoon, Andre."

I have to pause to make sure I heard her right.

I wave, but my voice still catches in my throat. "Afternoon."

I check back at our yard just to make sure she didn't leave a gift for me to clean up later.

Walking through the streets, stopping at each sign, I take in this strange place. Through windows, smiling faces greet me.

Mr. Carlson lived in the blue house three houses down. He used to yell at me as a kid, an old Black man who used to have a job on the shipping ports. He's gone. The Kings, the Harpers, the Fowlers, even Ms. Margarett.

Gone.

Gone.

Gone.

All replaced by nice white families and Black Lives Matter signs. My throat aches from seeing the city with more Black Lives Matter signs than Black people. A city where I don't belong.

⌐

A TYPICAL LINE passes in front of Malcolm's Bookshop, but I do a double take when it's not for the Salt and Straw or the coffee shop still closed for sheltering in place. On the side of the shop, where the names of Vanport residents are marked, Dad manages a desk.

He handwrites orders and explains how curbside works. Even with his mask I can tell he's smiling.

"What's happening?" I say.

Dad gestures to the bookshop. "We're back in business."

When I enter, the bookshop mirrors the house right before Grandpa's funeral, except instead of food, it's book orders. Books from floor to nearly ceiling, stacked on the tables, and lining the hallways. Ready to be shipped out or picked up curbside.

"You see all this?" Tom appears in the hallway. "More business than we've had in a year. Two years!"

"You're back." I smile at Dad being able to afford rehiring Tom.

The phone interrupts us.

I jump in to help as Tom takes an order. After an hour the phone still hasn't stopped. I'm slammed, shoving books in boxes and double-checking addresses. Newly released books go out of stock. Tom and I switch so he can get a break.

"Malcolm's Bookshop," I say.

"Yes, I'd like to have mailed *The New Jim Crow, Me and White Supremacy,* and *White Fragility,*" a woman says.

I cover the phone and ask Tom if they're in stock.

"We have *The New Jim Crow* but the others are back-ordered. We can ship them to you still," I say.

"How long will that take?" she huffs, annoyed.

"Five days Media Mail for the books in stock, might be another week or two depending on how quickly the publisher fills out-of-stock orders."

"Weeks? This is ridiculous. Can't you at least ship Michelle Alexander's book by tomorrow? I really want to read ahead of my book club."

"If you pay for express."

"Wow. You know, I can get this elsewhere to ship in two days with no added cost."

What part of *Indie Black bookstore in a pandemic* makes them think we can ship same day at no cost? Tom gives me a knowing look.

"Yes, ma'am. As an independent Black bookstore that's received little support from the community, we can't compete with the big-box stores, but we always of course appreciate your business."

"Oh. Yes, I guess I can get them on my e-reader, then wait for the books. I want them in my home. . . ." The lady goes on trying to engage me in all things Black Lives Matter as I take her information before hanging up.

The phone rings again and I beg Tom to save me, but he just keeps prepping books with the piled-up order slips.

"Malcolm's Bookshop."

"Hello! I'm interested in a book I saw on the news, but I can't remember the title. It had a Black man on the cover."

What! My patience is all the way gone. "We're a Black bookstore—we have a lot of those. Can you narrow it to nonfiction or fiction?"

"Nonfiction."

"Ahh, do you remember the subject?"

"Policing . . . racism."

I hold back a frustrated chuckle and scan the room, naming off about five titles that don't ring a bell.

"I'm sorry. There's so many. Would you like our mass incarceration starter pack?"

"How much does that cost?"

"One hundred dollars plus shipping, and fees of course for selection."

"Oh yes, ship them, here's my information."

I take down the payment and delivery information. When I hang up, Tom is leaning on the counter. "What's the mass incarceration starter pack?"

"I'm thinking whatever books are in stock for about a hundred dollars."

Tom shakes his head. "Your dad's going to kill you."

"She's not gonna read them. Besides, she asked for a book with a Black man on the cover about policing. She didn't even know what it was about, she's got a lot to catch up on."

Tom lifts *Policing the Black Man*. "This was probably it."

"Perfect." I snicker. "She'll be thrilled."

"You are something else."

"What?" I throw out my hand. "It's performative. Modern-day Sambo dolls for their bookshelves, except this time it's PC because it's not a negative stereotype of a Black man. Until I know they're reading this stuff, that's the only way I'll see it."

"You might be right for some, but at least it'll be a reminder in their home." He scratches his chin. "But you do have something here."

"You're not going to sell dolls, are you?"

"No. Kid, I forgot how wild you can be. Themed starter packs. Antiracism. Policing. Poetry. Love stories. Black voices. I'll tell your dad—I know he'll have a field day with this. But first, we gotta take care of our regulars, and all these books piling up for pickup."

I didn't get it at first why he was saying we're sold out with some of these books sitting here, but he must be saving special orders for our regular customers. We can't afford to lose them. So I pile up a stack of orders in my dad's car for home deliveries.

Before I step out, Tom grumbles about more delays.

"Rotate them," I say. "Keep a stack of books ordered here, but don't pack them until they show up. Especially for the ones that've been sitting here. As the back orders arrive you can catch up."

"What if they come in?" Tom says.

"Replace them with another order." I point to the rows of books that are waiting for people to come in. "This way we keep all the customers happy. And the best part, our inventory is prepaid."

"You're good at this. I can already see it." Tom runs his hand up high from left to right. "Malcolm and Andre's Bookshop."

I roll my eyes, only stopping because the front entrance rings.

"Karabuni." I fix my mask while greeting. Relief settles me when it's Dad. Maybe now he'll take a break.

"There's gotta be a better way," I say. "We have to set up a website for online orders. You can't stand out there for hours."

"That's exactly what I told him." Mr. Whitaker comes into view behind my dad. He stands on a spacing guide to keep socially distanced six feet apart. "It'll be up in a few hours. I partnered with a site for the infrastructure. It should help manage these orders and get them shipped out quicker."

"We can't afford that." I state the obvious, waiting for agreement from my dad, who passed his frugal genes down to me. But he doesn't look my way. Dad staggers to a seat, catching his breath and wincing when he's settled.

"You okay?" I rush to him, resting my hand on his back.

"He hasn't stopped all morning," Tom says. "You even eat today, Malcolm?"

An untouched lunch sack on the counter with Dad's name on it tells me he hasn't.

"You still sick? Should you be—" Mr. Whitaker begins.

"I'm clear. Doctors say it's trending months to full recovery." Dad doesn't say side effects could linger for life.

I wait for Dad to explain how he'll pay Mr. Whitaker back, but he doesn't.

"Why are you helping?" I ask Mr. Whitaker.

"I saw the news. People want to help all over the country. I've been offering to take your store off your father's hands for years."

"You sold the bookshop?" My mouth drops open.

"No." They answer in unison.

"It's just a little help." Dad doesn't make eye contact. He's never liked handouts. I see his pride hollowed out in desperation. While Mr. Whitaker's chest's all puffed out.

"This neighborhood needs the bookshop. Something to retain Albina history as new stores come in. A way to always remember."

I watch Mr. Whitaker speak. He says it like he can see dollar signs in having a Black-owned business in the continuously whitening Albina. With Black Lives Matter signs replacing people, it makes everyone feel better to have a Black store like my dad's where they can pick up culture. Improved, of course, probably with a shiny new paint job to erase the Vanport memorial.

Skepticism marks my face, even with a mask on.

Dad studies me, tentative in his response.

"Just a little loan. I'll pay back Mr. Whitaker in full."

"No need to worry about that," Mr. Whitaker says. "This is a small investment in the community. The least I could do."

"What if sales stop?" I say. "There's enough orders to pay this month's bills. But what about next month, next year?"

"We can answer those questions later. We've got a lot to do." Dad ends the conversation.

I step aside to get out of the way.

"You should be proud of your dad." Mr. Whitaker corners me.

"I am."

"A lot of men would have sold a long time ago. But not your dad. That's the kind of determination we need in this community."

I wonder where this is going. When I don't answer, Mr. Whitaker jingles his keys. "Got work to do. There's a meeting today. There's a call to establish a fund for Black relief."

"Is this your bill?" Reparations? I shake my head, not believing this'll pass.

"No. It's being proposed by another group, but it has traction. I plan to endorse it. Sixty-two million dollars for Black-owned businesses and community organizations."

I give him a skeptical side eye, which I guess I'm throwing around for free today.

"We should be doing everything we can. I want to make a better world for Sierra."

"And Eric," I add.

"Excuse me?" His face twists.

"And Eric, a better world for him, too." I watch for a reaction.

He gives me a slow smile. "Of course. For Eric." Mr. Whitaker nods, empty. Like he's long given up on Eric.

"If you find him, hear from him again, tell him Dr. Vitale is a family friend," I say.

"Who?" Mr. Whitaker blinks.

"Dr. Vitale. She's the head of the hospital youth intake. She's who must have treated Eric."

"Dr. Vitale, yes. Oh yes."

"*If* you hear from him, that is."

"Yes, I hope we do."

The jingling keys slip through Mr. Whitaker's fingers to the floor and I pick them up. He takes them quickly, leaving before I can say goodbye.

28

CREEP

May 29, 2020

Since Sierra's been out protesting with her siblings, I've seen more of Mrs. Whitaker pacing in the windows or overwatering her roses in the front of the house. This evening she stares out whenever a loud car passes down our street. I notice because I been doing the same damn thing.

"Andre." She calls me over from her front door as she slides her mask on.

I lift up my mask, weary. Before I get close, she heads inside, leaving the door open.

I glance at the empty parking spot that's usually taken up by Brian's car. I've barely seen the Whitaker kids since they protested the other night.

"Um . . . Mrs. Whitaker?" I wait in the entryway.

"In here," she calls from Mr. Whitaker's office.

When I step in, she swirls a glass of wine before pulling her mask down and taking a sip.

"Are they gone?" I ask, still lingering at the study door, keeping my distance.

"Yes, they're out." She drains her glass in one long drink. "You meeting them later?"

"No," I say without hesitation. "I guess . . . tell them I said hi."

"Stay." Her words slur. "It's so quiet without them. I'm used to them sheltering here, arguing, laughing. Now they're out in the streets. . . ." She looks off into the distance.

I get how she feels. A few weeks ago I couldn't even spend time with them because Mrs. Whitaker was worried about her safety bubble. Now all that doesn't matter because there's something worth fighting for.

Worth dying for.

I turn away, thinking of Grandpa.

"Come in. Please. You'd be doing me a favor, really."

I walk in, tentatively since I've never been in the study without Mr. Whitaker, well, except when Eric would plop in his dad's chair and rummage through drawers when they were out.

Mrs. Whitaker has her feet up on his desk like she's possessed with Eric's energy.

"Shhhhhh." She laughs at her rebellion. "Don't tell."

I stand awkwardly. Deciding if I should sit, stay put, or move closer.

"Why aren't you with them?" she says.

I shrug, knowing I don't owe her my reasons.

"Fight the power, right?" She puts her fist up.

I give her a half smile, holding back from rolling my eyes.

"Mr. Whitaker's supporting the funds act as part of his platform."

"The Black relief act. I heard." If this passes, Dad won't need to borrow their family's money.

"That was good, right? He's always been kind to you. He'll be a good commissioner."

"Yeah, I guess."

"I couldn't tell by the comments online. People are bullying him to end his campaign so someone Black can run. Even with supporting the Black relief fund!" She perches up, all righteous. Like *we* should be grateful he agreed to do the right thing when it's basic as hell. "We care about this neighborhood. I've been to every meeting for the community, started our beautification group. Fundraisers. But all the talk is how we're part of the problem. We're nice people, aren't we?"

She wants to say nice *white* people. She's drinking herself into a sad white girl pity party I want nothing to do with.

"I mean, we do have Black children, for God's sake. And Luis, he's Mexican. If we hadn't adopted him, God knows what kind of life he'd have. His parents," she whispers, "didn't even have papers."

I shift on my feet in the long pause that follows as she leans in closer. "Illegals."

My stomach sours. She goes on and on about all that she's done, how terrible things are for her, and I can't take it any longer.

"At least they're just letters. Not like they're death threats that'll happen."

She waits for me to explain myself, but I don't.

"Andre, that's not what I mean. We've given a lot to serve this area. To make it better."

"You don't get to pick and choose what's good for the community. What we should be grateful for. You're not saving anybody."

"I didn't say that." She sits up, pouring herself another drink. "I just contributed where I could. We all do. A community. I didn't do anything people didn't want."

"But you did." I twist my mouth. "What people are you talking about exactly?"

"The community."

"Whose community? You moved here and started a beautification committee. You voted to move the community garden."

"To a bigger lot."

"But it was Mrs. Dover who started that garden. Now she has to walk three blocks to get there." I repeat the words Mom shared over dinner. Then I had nothing to say about it. Now it burns inside me.

"I didn't know."

I blink hard, making sure I correctly heard what she just said. "You didn't *listen*."

"We voted. It wasn't like I made some . . . arbitrary decision. It works better for everyone."

"No, it doesn't." I shake my head.

"I don't think you understand. I'm trying to make the community better."

"For whom? With every *enhancement* suited for the kind of neighbors you really want, we're priced out of our own neighborhood. Black Lives Matter isn't just about not getting killed by police. It's about being able to exist. To thrive. To stop having to be slices of ourselves where it's acceptable. Having the same chance. Loans, jobs, raises, schools. And yeah, a community garden that's for us. If you're going to live in our neighborhood, be a part of it, don't change it for yourself.

"You know in my own neighborhood the police were called on me. Someone had to speak on my behalf and vouch that I lived here. I could have been like Trayvon Martin with a neighborhood watch group. I was like George when they had their knee in my back." I unleash on her.

This was built up from the second I stepped in the door. Maybe because I've always had to be thankful for getting something I shouldn't have had to fight for in the first place.

"Let me ask you another question." I wave my finger around, high on letting everything I've been thinking about go to someone. "Did you even really care about what's happening out there, or is it all just to begin Mr. Whitaker's political career?"

"I . . ." Her face is beet red.

"Seems like if you were trying to fix things, you'd focus on your own family. Why you're making Brian stay at home when you can afford it. Why Kate's too scared to tell you she didn't get into Brown." I pause, taking a breath for what I really wanted to say. "If you love all your kids the same, why you never filed a missing person report for Eric, who's been gone for over three months now?"

I realize I've gone too far. Her eyes look like they're popping out of her head, and her anger is rushing toward being sober. I can't tell what's running through her mind. If I scared her to death. If she's thinking about me being some dangerous Black kid with a record.

And I'm alone, in this white woman's house.

"I should go to bed. I think I've had a little too much to drink.

You're still in shock about your grandfather's passing. Let's just call it a night, okay? Lock up on your way out." Mrs. Whitaker stands, then fumbles walking the stairs, missing every few steps she takes.

I hope she forgets this night as much as I want to.

I stare out the window at the empty streets. All the cars still gone.

Then I act like what they all think I am—a criminal—and go through Mr. Whitaker's desk.

U CAN'T TOUCH THIS

May 29, 2020

Eric used to get into Mr. Whitaker's desk with a set of hidden keys. And I had no business being around when he did it. But that's what always gets me in trouble. Minding my business, but not leaving, either.

Eric would scavenge through the desk for something important, then imitate his dad reading files out loud.

I flip my fingers through the right-hand drawer, which is now filled with Mr. Whitaker's campaign files. I stop at a file labeled *Application 12/15/2019.*

I tug it out. Typed and certified with the application date Mr. Whitaker filed to run for the off-cycle election. I slump back in Mr. Whitaker's chair. He lied to me. He didn't decide to run for office after I was arrested; he'd already filed and was only waiting for the right time to make an announcement.

When I've let it sink in, I search through Mr. Whitaker's desk for any sign Eric's been sent away or any plans Mr. Whitaker might have for my dad's shop.

I break into a satisfied grin when I spot a folder labeled *Jackson*.

"I knew it." I whistle through my teeth as I open it.

What's inside isn't about Malcolm Jackson and the bookshop, though; it's a file about me.

I line up Mr. Whitaker's papers on the desk. The file is filled with notes about the guys who were brought in for questioning from school. When I see Gavin's name, I whistle again. It's several pages long, including a printed email from Gavin's dad. I stop at a highlighted note.

If Eric is a problem for my son, then you've got more things to be concerned about than an election.

I skim down to Mr. Whitaker's reply.

Eric won't be turning himself in. There's no need to panic.

Mr. Whitaker helped my family get a lawyer the very next day. Probably the only way he could convince Eric to keep his mouth shut.

At the time we were grateful. No, we were desperate.

Never questioning if it was a mistake to take his offer. I just didn't want to be stuck with a court-appointed attorney. Not after seeing everyone lined up in the hallway to courtroom seven, waiting to meet their attorney for the first time. After getting my lawyer, I watched court-appointed attorneys with a stack of files enter the hallway, calling a rotation of names every ten minutes—I was thankful that wasn't gonna be me.

I felt important. Hell, I felt lucky to have my lawyer. Even celebrated getting community monitoring. How stupid was I? The game was already rigged.

Combing through the files, I learn more about my case than I did at my own trial. Eric was brought in for questioning before they picked me up. He looked out at me all innocent standing in front of his house.

But he let me take the fall.

I search the rest of the files, finding an unlabeled folder filled with brochures and pamphlets of boarding schools for boys. An application dated January second.

Resisting taking everything with me, I snap photos. My gratitude is replaced with rage.

Carefully I file everything back in order, then lock the drawer just like I found it.

When I leave the study, the front door is only steps away, but the stairs to Eric's room call me.

The stairs hardly creak, but it's tiptoeing slowly down the hall that terrifies me. Because even though I've walked the house a thousand times, I've never been upstairs to the Whitakers' knowledge. Only Eric has brought me to his room a few times.

I pass a room, unsure if it's Brian's or Kate's.

Across the way I know it's Luis's room because I see him climb out his window to get to the roof.

I open Eric's bedroom door, halfway expecting him to be sitting on his bed, waiting to ask me what the hell I'm doing there, before laughing his head off at how he scared me. But there's nothing. I mean nothing of Eric's.

His bed is made, but his posters are down, desk cleared. Even his rug is gone. Spotless, like a room for rent left undisturbed. There's no way Eric would've left with everything of his, not without being noticed.

In the dark I sit on his bed, running my hands over my face. *What the hell is going on? Where are you, Eric?*

My thoughts are filled with Mr. Whitaker's lies. Eric was a problem for Mr. Whitaker's political aspirations. I was a solution.

I get up to leave, then lock my eyes on Eric's closet. When I open it, I expect all his things to be stacked inside, but it's just as empty as his room. I flick the light on and fold the closet door wide open, studying the ceiling. Looking for the crack that opens up a tile where Eric hid a secret stash of his things. I reach up, expecting it to be empty too. But I touch a shoe box. I stretch my fingers to pull it closer to me until I can grab it.

Inside is Eric's mother's necklace, one she gave him, along with a small journal filled with his chicken-scratch handwriting, photos of his biological parents, and the first foster family that Eric thought was planning to adopt him and Sierra before the Whitakers. Susan Gustafson.

Eric wouldn't have left his most precious things behind if he ran away. Everything about Eric's room is wrong. The material things vanished, like he packed up and took them with him. But the things he cared about, the things he's kept with him for years, are still here.

I reach back to the ceiling, pushing my hand farther until it touches some files. Just like the ones in Mr. Whitaker's desk. Before I open them, I stop dead in my tracks.

Footsteps.

A voice.

I close the closet door and flick off the light just as the bedroom door creaks open.

The bedroom light turns on.

LIVIN' ON A PRAYER

May 29, 2020

Mr. Whitaker stands at the door. His eyes dart from corner to corner. He searches, but for what, I don't know.

I press my hands against the wall for something to grab on to, but there's no way to defend myself. As far as he's concerned, I'm the intruder.

Slow breaths help me think—revealing myself will only make my situation worse. If I can avoid being caught altogether, I won't have to explain why I'm here.

My breath brings air to my brain but does nothing for my rattling chest, which feels like it's vibrating against the closet door.

Waiting to get caught.

Quietly, Mr. Whitaker sits on the bed, hunched over with his hands on his head. Cradling himself in deep thought.

My palms prickle with sweat as it feels like I'm being pressed closer to the closet door slats. I widen my eyes to get used to the dimly lit area.

In between the door slats I search for answers, studying Mr. Whitaker.

As soon as I settle, he whips his face in my direction. I almost jump in this tomb as he gets up, heading my way.

A half inch of a folding closet door stands between us. I swear he can feel my breath coming through the slats of the door, passing from me to him. He rests his hand on the knob, while I swallow the urge to shout out like I'm in battle. The kind of action that, if it was in a movie, Boogie and I would shake our heads at. We'd yell at the screen about how stupid you gotta be to break into somebody's office, then go upstairs and corner yourself in a closet.

But this isn't a movie—it's me at the edges of my life. There's not one good thing that can happen by me waiting for him to open the door.

I almost give up in defeat.

Then, like a miracle, Mr. Whitaker's phone rings. He backs away and closes the door behind him.

A full hour passes before I even consider moving. The thought of everything almost crashing down on me envelops me in total fear. Each part of my body is rigid and tight. Even though Mr. Whitaker probably went to bed long ago, it's the threat of discovery that's kept me inside the closet.

He came into Eric's room for a reason. As much as I rack my brain to remember if I left the door open a crack, I can't recall.

My paranoia about being caught lingers, but my exhaustion wins out—that, and a desperate need to piss. I settle on coincidence. That maybe I just witnessed a nightly routine of Mr. Whitaker's. This empty room is meant to erase Eric's presence, but maybe it still haunts the Whitakers.

If I was smart, I'd leave everything just as I found it. But I'm not. I take a few of Eric's things, holding them tightly in my hand. Leaving the rest for a time I can return.

Not looking back as I tiptoe to the stairs, practicing lines about what I'm doing here. I repeat excuses in my head in case I'm caught.

When I make my way outside, I keep myself together, speed-walking to my grandparents'. I swear I can feel eyes burrowing into my back, watching me. It's only when I'm inside that I take a breath, resting my back against the door and locking it. Then make a beeline straight to my bedroom before Grandma J can stop me.

I spread out the contents of the file folder and find a copy of my arrest record. In Eric's handwriting is a list of parties hit since summer and the items stolen, with receipts for things traded. If this ever reached the police, it would be the end of Eric, and of me. This is why Mr. Whitaker didn't want Eric turning himself in.

I scan through the photos I took, thinking on a strategy to call the boarding schools without alerting the Whitakers. I thought Eric was like me and his only choice was to run. For a moment he planned to turn himself in. But somehow his dad must have convinced him not to. But why isn't Eric back, then?

I'm the guy that should've rolled. My biggest crime was being too poor to have my own car. Hanging with the wrong people, mostly for free rides. And being so desperate to see Sierra that I'd go wherever with her.

I was collateral damage to them.

One of us was gonna go down in this equation. Eric chose to save himself. That's the difference between him and me.

I tried to play by the same rules I grew up with, but I refused to see Eric wasn't the same. Maybe it's me that was the fool for even thinking those were rules I should live by.

I flick through the pages in Eric's small journal filled with notes and reminders. I stop at the page that includes his Parks & Rec locker code and mine. A sick laugh creeps out of me at Eric's poor attempt to remember the easy code I made up for him. I shared my code in case he ever needed something from my locker. But he didn't even write it down correctly—he swapped his locker number, 136, for mine, 139. In person, he knew which locker was which, so it wasn't a big deal. Until it was. . . .

A glimmer of hope had wormed itself inside me that maybe Eric left a thread of trust to latch on to. Something I could find among his things to prove that maybe he didn't mean to set me up. But all my weak excuses about how evidence landed in my locker have since evaporated. And maybe I just got lucky that what was put in there was right below the minimum amount that could've got me the mandatory sentence.

I scan the pages, squinting to decipher his writing. My stomach flips when I discover that Eric's passwords are now at my fingertips. Nothing left to lose, I attempt to log in to his email on my laptop.

Boom. I'm in.

His inbox is mostly spam, but I find emails from Sierra, Kate,

Luis, and Gavin. The thing is, they're all unread. With each click I brace for this violation to strike against me, but it doesn't. All the messages are pretty much the same. *Reach out. Where are you? We're worried.* The worst part, there's no indication Eric ever responded or has even touched his email since his disappearance.

I move on to social media. Eric was constantly on his phone so I check his DMs. But nothing. All's there is the same content I've been over.

When I get to the last password it's for a digital artwork site. Dope pictures of regular people living in Portland. But the way it's depicted, it's like a color explosion on the online canvas. I click the *learn more* button. My mouth drops when I see it's a video of Eric, explaining his piece. This is all his work. The most recent piece is dated December 24, called *Blessings*. An old Black man eats from a to-go container on a bench downtown wearing a fancy suit jacket, but his pants and shoes are worn and ripped. Behind him is a homeless cart full of his belongings. To the side of him is the shelter Grandma J took me to early in the morning with the Whitakers to prep food for a special holiday dinner. Afterward we all went to the movies, well, everyone but Eric. He said he had somewhere to be. I thought he was ditching us to hang with Gavin. I press play on the video.

My art is about bringing the hidden into focus. Seeing more than what appears before us. Blessings *is about a man whose life was fulfilled at one point. His parents came from Tulsa after everything was destroyed in the Race Massacre in 1921. They moved to Portland to restart but could never catch a break. A few steps forward and too many back. He reminded me of what struggles my birth parents might have been through before they had us. Before they lost us.*

His voice trails off, then the video ends. I click on the next button, which says *enter bid*.

Eight hundred dollars is what I'd need to start at if I was going to buy it. My hands shake as I check all the illustrations with bids. The site was launched in December, but he hasn't closed out to cash in any of the current bids. His bids were a couple hundred dollars after he posted, but now he's a Black artist people are supporting. Totaling it all up, it's $37,500. Enough to start a new life. Enough to start over.

31

EX-FACTOR

May 29, 2020

If we keep things the way they've been, they'll never change. That's what I repeat as I tap on Sierra's window twenty minutes after she crept back home from a night of protesting. I've kept her in the dark too long about Eric and everything I've learned. Now it's time to face her. To join our efforts.

The glass shakes as I tap lightly. A light flicks on, and a shadow passes by. I send Sierra an apologetic glance when she draws up her shade. There's a certain kind of pain to be so close, yet so far away from each other.

She pulls her window up, glancing over her shoulder before whispering, "What are you doing here?"

I hoist my body up, then heave over the windowsill with an audible thump and crash to the ground. Sierra freezes, whipping her head in the direction of her door.

I lay still.

"How graceful," Sierra jokes when the fear passes.

"It's not that easy." I signal at my masked-up face so she can put hers on.

I swallow hard to get the courage to tell her everything, including that this is the second time I've been in her house today.

"No kidding." She winks.

Even with her mouth covered, I can tell by the way her eyes are crinkled that she's smiling. My heart mends back together.

"There were so many people," Sierra says, still mesmerized from the protest. "You should come next time, they're getting bigger."

I shake my head. "I can't be out there like that." I pull up my mask tighter just thinking about all the people swarming around her.

"Most people wear masks. They say being outside is safe."

"It's not for me."

"Not for you? Of course it is. This is your time to fight back."

I focus on my ankle. She doesn't get it.

"Do you even care about this? Do you not see what's happening out there? That could've been you."

"That could've been me?" Anger blazes through my body. "That *is* me. You think I don't care because I'm not out there. Maybe the problem is *you* haven't been out there all along. You live in your big house, getting whatever you want. You've been protected. And now you get a flash of my life from the news? The thing I've been living with every day? And you're what, better than me." I spit venom, still reeling from learning Eric might be hiding safely in a boarding school. Questioning now how easily I thought his nonresponse to messages meant he was hurt, or worse. He's sitting on a stack of cash waiting for the right moment to get his.

"What are you talking about? I never said that. You act like fighting for justice doesn't matter. It matters, Andre. You think being in the foster system, on top of being Black, was easy for me or for Eric? So yeah, it matters."

I'm an asshole. I realize it the second she speaks.

I'm looking for a fight. Damn near begging for it so I can get out of telling her what I'm really doing here.

"I know it matters," I say. "I'm sick of people telling me how I should act about this all. Look at my temporary living situation. My last home was in some two-bedroom apartment built to get people like me outta this neighborhood. My grandpa passed. My dad is barely recovered, killing himself at the bookshop because he has no choice. My mom's been working nonstop, not even staying here because she's an essential worker and terrified she'll get us sick again because we don't know how this virus works. And a few days ago I was pulled down to the ground by cops in my own damn neighborhood because somebody, who probably now has a Black Lives Matter sign on their lawn, thought I looked suspicious."

"Andre—"

"I am the *definition* of what this is all about. I'm protecting my life by not going out there." I point at my ankle.

"Forget you, Andre." Sierra shoots up. "Don't try to play Oppression Olympics with me. You don't know what I've been through. What Eric and I have been through."

I swallow hard, mad I lost control. I fight the urge to leave and tell myself I tried. I turn my back, contemplating my next move.

"What are you here for?" Sierra says.

I take in a long breath to calm the rapid thumping in my chest. We stand in silence until I finally speak.

"I needed to show you this in person." I pull out Eric's necklace, letting it dangle from my fingers.

"Where did you get that?" Her voice chokes up as she reaches for it. "Did he leave it with you?"

"No," I say. "I found it in his room."

She raises a brow and blinks hard. I explain what led me there.

"Why would my dad have those files, and why would Eric hide more?"

I don't answer, treading lightly. We haven't made up from our argument yet. Then I fill her in on his digital art site, which she had no clue about.

"What did your parents tell you about Eric's disappearance?"

"Nothing. Just that he was gone." Sadness clouds her face as she pauses. "That he called to say he wasn't coming back . . . That we should forget about him."

"Even you?"

Sierra circles her fingers around her hair before speaking. "Every time I bring it up, it starts an argument. There's another reason why I didn't go to your trial. . . . It wasn't just about my parents hiding your letters."

I twist my mouth, confused.

"When you were out at MacLaren, I was pissed at you because I thought you knew where Eric was. He'd left and I thought you had something to do with it. When I found out you were writing me and asking about how Eric was doing, I realized you didn't know. And Paul was around 'cause he felt bad about Eric. We kinda started hanging out. . . ." She makes eye contact and my insides twist and turn. "It wasn't serious. That's why I didn't want you to know."

I grab a piece of my hair, pulling a section, trying to focus without getting lost in all things Paul and Sierra.

"What did the police ever say?" I ask tentatively. I already know they didn't file a missing person report. But does she?

"About your arrest?"

"No." I pause. "About Eric being missing."

"My parents filed a report, but they said the police likely wouldn't look into it since he's closer to eighteen. See how the police don't even care about a Black boy going missing? Like he doesn't matter."

I'm silent. *Sierra didn't even get to talk to the police.*

"What?" she asks. "Why are you looking at me like that?"

"What happened the time Brian didn't come home on prom night?"

"The police said it was too early to start a search, especially prom night. My dad said it's the same thing with Eric."

"They still came by your house. Your dad pulled strings and made them listen." I remember how they came by early in the morning the day after prom. Brian rolled up by noon. Eric's been gone for months.

Sierra shakes her head.

"Did you talk to anyone about Eric being missing?" I say. "Social workers, adoption agency, counselor, anyone?"

"Only my parents." Sierra's voice cracks. As it does, it's like it's shattered the thin layer holding up her parents' story. I look into her eyes and brace myself as I tell her Marcus learned her parents never reported Eric missing.

Sierra is frozen as the pieces come together. Then the tears spill. I catch them with my sleeve before they wet her mask.

"Your dad told me Eric was having some mental health issues." I recount what Mr. Whitaker said, repeating words when Sierra doesn't understand.

"Eric was fine," Sierra asserts. "Except for arguing with our parents more. They kept saying he was ungrateful and that was the reason he was acting out, hanging out at parties. That he was on drugs. But he wasn't," she says a little too loudly. "He wasn't doing drugs," she repeats, quieter.

I pause before sharing the most important detail. The one that might bring Eric home but could also be the trigger for a pending investigation to continue.

"When I was going through your dad's files, I found a stack of applications for boarding schools. Some military, some for troubled kids." I pull out my phone and show her the one with a finished application and deposit receipt.

"You're kidding. He wouldn't . . . That makes no sense. They can't keep him there forever. I'm gonna talk to Dad." Sierra gets up. I touch her arm.

"Ouch." Sierra pulls away.

"What's going on with you?" I hover. "You can tell me if someone's hurting you."

"Forget it, that doesn't matter." A long pause follows.

She doesn't answer my question, but I won't let it go. No more secrets between us. Gently, I touch her hand, searching for how to ask again who did this, because I don't think it's Paul anymore, but when I look her in the eyes, I know she won't answer.

Something inside tells me I already know.

I ask what I refused to see. "How long has this been happening?"

I wait, giving her space until she's ready.

"I don't want to talk about it. The less you know, the better for you and for me."

"Then tell me a little. How long?"

Sierra pauses with a shaky breath. "Since Eric left. He used to . . . be the one that shielded me. If I did something, he'd do something worse. At first, I didn't know that was what he was doing, until Luis pointed it out. Now it's like Luis is trying to take Eric's place with—"

"Rebelling."

"Yeah." She sniffles. "I push buttons now, just to see how far it can go. I'm so filled with hate now I don't care how angry I make my parents."

"Don't make excuses for it. It's abuse."

"I don't know." She diverts her gaze. "I thought maybe if I got into trouble, I'd have a reason to leave. To be with Eric. It's stupid, I know. . . . If I do what he says, it stops."

"It's not okay."

"I know. . . . It wasn't always like this. Things just are getting more tense, all being at home. That toxic stuff gets bottled up with nowhere else to go. Before, we had an escape with school, activities, he had work. I had Eric to get me to chill out and keep things level. With Eric gone, there is no level."

"Maybe Eric saw it coming and that's why he left, and he didn't think you'd go."

"I'd go," Sierra snaps, then whispers again. "I'd go. I'd never leave without Eric."

"So what did you do when Eric was gone and things got hard?"

"Paul would pick me up. I would've gone to you, but you were . . . away. Paul tried to cover to get his dad to drop charges if things were returned. That's how we started hanging out. If he's over, everyone has to be on their best behavior."

I was wrong about so much. I thought she was leaving at night to be with Paul, but it was more than that—she was leaving to search for Eric.

I ache at her being filled with so many secrets I never knew about.

"What are they both really like?" I want to unpack this mystery. Mr. Whitaker harming her and what her mom thinks about this?

"My dad . . ." Sierra hesitates like it's revolting to claim him as Dad. "He pretends like nothing happened. And Mom, I think when she realized we couldn't fill that big a hole, she never really wanted us anymore. She just tolerates us. Since Eric left, she can barely look at me. When people come by, she just puts her fake happy mask on. In the daytime, she works on her roses in the garden and pops pills to numb herself. At night she drinks until my dad comes home. And we all put up faces pretending things are fine to feed the lie. My siblings are better at that than me."

Behind the walls of the Whitaker house, Sierra's held so many secrets. I can't help but wonder: Which ones does Eric keep?

Sierra doesn't speak. Lost in thought.

She touches her finger below her eyes, wiping away more tears.

"He's not coming back, is he?" she asks again.

Now I don't answer.

"He would've called, right? He would've found a way."

"Maybe. I'm out early. He might not have heard yet."

"We have to find him. Will you send me photos of the boarding school brochures? I can call, pretending I'm my mom. Say we got double-billed or something."

Sierra rattles off ideas and I touch her hand. "I know you want to confront your dad, but for now, it's better not to say anything about what I shared. He's been hiding Eric this long—he might try harder. As far as we know, there's a really good reason . . . for Eric, that is. Marcus said my first juvie court counselor is still trying to go after me and more robberies," I say to make her feel better. But I don't know if I even believe it.

"Do you think Eric will come back in summer?" Sierra's eyes hollow. She's broken from saying this out loud. I try to make sense of it but I'm still not sure I have all the pieces.

Sometimes our deepest secrets are ones we don't let make it to the surface, so we can keep them from others *and* ourselves. The thought keeps coming back to me. I didn't want to see the Whitakers for who they really were because I wanted to believe they were perfect. I wanted to believe Paul was hurting Sierra so I could make up ways to protect her and get her back. But really, the people she needed protection from are in her home. People I'm powerless to combat.

32

YOU GOT ME

May 31, 2020

Early in the morning, I take my swim like usual. Only this time I don't change in the gender-neutral stall, I head to the locker room. Last night, there was one hunch I kept from Sierra that I need to check out on my own.

Inside it's quiet, no showers going off or the chatter of people that I'm used to. I pass empty lockers, and the ones with belongings left behind when things shut down.

I hold my breath as I approach my locker, checking over my shoulder to make sure I'm alone.

I wait.

Heart pounding.

Nothing.

Then I squat to get close, touching the cold handle. The

locker I've used for years is now marred with jagged marks from bolt cutters.

I open locker number 139, letting the door swing.

It's empty, but I can still imagine my goggles and one lonely backpack greeting officers. Eric had my code. I can't deny it any longer: he set me up and tipped off the cops.

I take a seat on the bench, really letting the betrayal sink in. I rub my hands over my face as the smell of chlorine consumes me.

After a few minutes I fixate on Eric's locker next to mine. A lock still snugly keeping number 136 safe. *What if* . . .

I turn over the lock. *EW* carved on the back.

I know Eric's code because I'm the one who helped him come up with it, 42-6-24. Jackie Robinson and Kobe Bryant's later jersey numbers, with 6 (4 plus 2) in the middle. An idiot-proof locker code.

With shaky hands I grip the lock, accidentally skip past 42.

I reset, then flick the dial, letting out a long breath before starting over. This time I inch slowly to stop exactly on each number. An almost-silent clicking sound shoots relief down to my toes when I pull the lock and unhook the hinge.

The locker swings open with ease.

Inside, I see something so dizzying I can't trust my eyes.

Eric's black backpack is nestled on the bottom of the locker. His signature blue-and-white embroidered patch with the number 42 on the side confirms it's his.

When the police report came in about the bag in my gym locker, they said it was black. I'd assumed it was the one Eric used. I was dead wrong.

Inside are rolled-up stacks of money the size of fists. Jewelry. The entire stash that Gavin told me Eric ran off with. The kind of cash that would keep him off the street for a while until he could find a job. Specific lockers are only assigned to employees, so they must've never known this was Eric's.

The swing of the locker room door rushes me into a panic. I slam the locker closed, with my own backpack inside.

Terry turns the corner just as I swing Eric's bag onto my shoulder. I try to keep a poker face, but inside I'm screaming in fear he'll notice.

"Thought you left?"

"No. Decided to stop avoiding the locker room. The showers are way better in here." I point to the showers, then quickly drop my hands because the floor's bone-dry.

He watches me, but I don't move. I gesture with my hand for him to go ahead as I follow, clutching the strap of Eric's backpack.

AT THE END of my shift I grab the backpack I dumped behind a desk and race out of the Parks & Rec, untangling my bike and frantically surveilling the area before heading home.

I wish the streets were packed, so I could zip by unnoticed. But the city is quiet. People working in their homes. Schools now remote. Stores closed. All leaving me out in the open as someone to scrutinize.

On my ride home, I run through memorized prayers from Grandma J. If I get caught with a bag like this, my whole life will change forever. No mercy, I'll be sent straight to MacLaren until I turn twenty-five, then finish the rest of my sentence in adult prison.

Each second, I regret taking the backpack. If anyone catches me, I'll be blamed for everything. Terry will think all this time I've been back to my "old ways." And Jim, well, let's just say he'll make sure I do my full sentence and more.

What drew me to the locker room was retracing what happened to me. The things that might explain where Eric is. Now the only thing I'm certain of is that Eric didn't run anywhere at all. And if his dad sent him away, he would've got to it first, wouldn't he? Leaving it there, without telling anyone to remove it, would be disastrous for him.

By what seems to be the grace of God, I make it to my grand-parents' house. I dump my bike in my yard, heading inside before anyone catches the 42 marked on the backpack.

When I'm safe, I shut my bedroom door and turn the blinds down.

I pull on the plastic gloves Grandma J's given me to use at the grocery store and count the first bundle of rolled money. I whistle when I count one grand, meaning there must be at least five thousand in cash. This kind of dough isn't something you just leave in your locker. Eric knew he could leave this untouched until he returned. Mr. Whitaker can't hide him forever, and when he comes, he'll have to deal with me.

33

CAN WE TALK

May 31, 2020

There's only one person I can trust to keep things real with me.

Boogie.

Boogie has a way of unpacking the truth, confronting things for what they are—not what I want them to be.

He picks up on the third ring.

"Yo. Where you been?"

I don't speak right away, still forming what to say.

"What's wrong? Your dad, is he all right?"

"Yeah. Yeah. Everyone's okay." I chew on my lip before speaking. "I found the real stash in Eric's locker at the Parks and Rec."

"The *stash*!" Boogie's voice rises before he lowers it. "Like from the parties?"

"Tons of cash. Things they jacked. They sold everything

they could just like Gavin said." I explain what else I found in Eric's room.

"So you think Mr. Whitaker has him locked away in some boarding school?"

"Yeah. I'm thinking maybe he'll come back after I'm done with the community monitoring program. He can't stay hidden forever. Sierra's almost eighteen, he'll be eighteen next year. They can't hold him forever."

I run my hands around my neck, thinking through all the possibilities.

"Well, you got his stash. Just gotta wait till he gets back. And this time I'm not letting you punk out in a phone conversation like you did with Gavin."

I let out a forced chuckle, because while I'm thinking about me, I'm also thinking about Sierra and Mr. Whitaker.

"What aren't you saying?" Boogie says. "There's something else, isn't there?"

That's all I need to tell Boogie about the bruises I saw on Sierra. And how I thought it was Paul hurting her, until last night.

"How bad is it?" Boogie asks.

"I don't know. I could only see bruises on her arm. But to be honest, I don't know if Sierra would tell me if there were more."

We stay silent.

I lean back against my bed. "What if I blackmail Mr. Whitaker?"

"How?"

"Tell him I know he's hurting her, that I know about his lies, that I'll tell unless he stops."

Boogie shakes his head. "If you did that, it'd backfire on you anyway. Who's gonna believe you? And trust me on this, Sierra'd hate you for it. Nah, you gotta find another way or convince her to say something."

"Isn't it required, though? Like see something, say something."

"If you're, like, a teacher. But this is the kind of thing you can't take back. And if you don't do it right the first time, and Sierra backpedals, you lose her and make it worse for both of you. Then nobody believes anything you have to say."

I think about my mom because I should be going to her about this. But Boogie is right. I have more to lose and should stay out of it. I'd hate myself if something happened to Sierra. And I can't see her risking saying something until she knows exactly where Eric is and Mr. Whitaker can't threaten to harm him, too. Eric's return means a lot to her. It means a lot to my life as well. My own safety from being charged again for the things that Eric did.

I have to get Mr. Whitaker to admit he had something to do with Eric being gone, then get him home. Sierra would speak up then. But I'm a kid, and even I've seen how Mr. Whitaker wields power. Like at his holiday party each year, inviting lawyers, judges, community leaders for fundraisers. Grandpa Jackson used to call him a politician before Mr. Whitaker even ran.

"I gotta watch myself around Mr. Whitaker."

"No shit," Boogie says. "Or you might conveniently get into trouble again."

"You right," I say. My thoughts have been on Jim, but there'd be no Jim if I wasn't set up. Maybe Eric and Mr. Whitaker had everything to do with it, not just Eric.

Boogie makes things clear and messy at the same time. His words twist through my gut, leaving me more confused than when I started. If I can sift through it all, I know there's truth waiting to be revealed. But there's too much to carry, and I can't take the responsibility of trusting I know the answers. Because I don't. What I do know, I need to get on the right path. I need to know what part's important and what to let go.

I RIDE OUT to the apartment my mom's been staying at with a co-worker. It's a flat square building slathered with a mosslike color, except for the tagged side of the building in the alley that's been rolled over with white paint.

Coming here was automatic, but now that I'm at Mom's door, my courage vanishes. I pace, taking my time until I'm ready to knock.

Mom answers, smoothing back her hair. With her mask on it forces me to study the heaviness that gathers under her eyes. It kills me to not see her full face, so that at least there's a moment I can let her smile tell me everything will be all right.

"Child, what are you doing out here?"

"I . . . well . . ."

"Don't go acting bashful, now. I heard you making all that noise out here." She opens the door wider for me, and I slide my mask on before entering.

"I just wanted to see you."

"Well, it's good to see you, too." She pauses. We both hold back from hugging and take a seat on the mismatched furniture. "You being safe? Wearing your mask?"

"Yeah, Mom, I'm being safe." Our safe talk now has a totally different context.

"How many miles are you out?" Mom points at my ankle.

I slap my head, trying to guess before just calling Marcus, who picks up on the second ring.

"I'm visiting my mom. That okay? She's staying closer to the hospital. . . ."

"Yeah, thanks for checking, though."

"Okay, cool." I get ready to hang up.

"You doing good?" Marcus asks.

"Yeah, I'm good."

"All right, thanks for calling."

I wait for him to hang up, but he doesn't.

"How's that girl? You take my advice?"

"Okay, I gotta go."

"That bad, huh?"

"No. I just . . . gotta go."

"Flowers."

"What?"

"Flowers will make up for it. A little love mixtape."

"Love tape? Okay, you really bugging."

"My day you make a girl a mix CD or cassette, it was on. But I guess a playlist will do."

"I'm not making her a playlist, and I have no problems. I gotta go, though. My mom's right here."

Mom snickers in the background. I hang up, cutting off Marcus as he adds to his list of ideas.

"So you've got girl trouble and had to see your mom, huh?"

"No. That's not why I'm here, Marcus just be like that some-times." I pause. "But I did want to talk to you about Sierra."

"You two are something else. I have no advice for you, just say you're sorry."

"I—" I cut myself off. This could be a mistake. Mom could stop me from finding out the truth. And what hurts more, I worry she won't believe me. The little trust left might be so broken by this I could never patch up the pieces. All this doubt floods me, taking my words away.

"What is it?" Mom says.

I study her eyes and reach for a lifeline, blurting everything out. Well, everything that won't get me grounded. I can't tell her about the backpack. I was already feeling like my parents said they believed me but had their doubts. I also don't say a word about using a key to get into Mr. Whitaker's locked drawers, just talk around it by saying I saw my name in an open file. I keep my visit to Eric's bedroom to myself and focus on the big lie—Eric being taken into the hospital and Dr. Vitale not even knowing him.

"You are in way over your head!" Mom's voice rises as she stands up. "I'm out here doing everything I can to keep it to-gether. To keep everyone safe, alone, with no one to cry to when it feels like I can't go on. And you're out here risking your freedom." Mom flips all the way out, a frazzled look in her eye.

My mouth hangs open. I fumble over my words as she paces, rubbing her hands on her temples.

"I . . . had to find out."

"That was dangerous. You don't know what you're getting into." Mom is shaking. Her voice breaks and with each catch of it a lump forms in my throat. She's terrified. Her unveiling it in front of me is a mirror of the jagged fear that's ripped itself inside me but has had nowhere to go. Then I can't hold it in any longer, and I drop my head down to my knees. I'm straight-up sobbing.

All the problems run through my mind. I'm unsure how to solve them. Eric. Mr. Whitaker. Sierra. Cowboy Jim.

"Shhh. I'm glad you came to me. I'm sorry I flipped." Mom drapes herself over me, forgetting all the safety protocols she's been hammering into us. "It's been so stressful. Then to know you've been putting yourself in danger this whole time. That's a lot for you to be holding. I'm sorry I lost it, but it's been hard for me, too, and the one thing keeping me together was that you were safe. And God, Andre. You've been in danger this whole time." She kisses my forehead and holds my head next to hers.

Her fast anger slows, and I let out what drew me here in the first place.

"There's more."

Mom takes a long breath when I tell her about Sierra's bruises.

"What do I do?" I choke out.

"We . . . we don't do anything . . . for now. Other than work on Sierra to learn more and get her to come forward."

My mouth drops. I came to Mom expecting her to drag me to the police station or call Child Protective Services.

And she just wants me to be quiet about it.

"Sierra won't. She only said something because I called her out."

"You need to know more. Be sure when you make these accusations."

I feel myself completely walling off from ever asking for help. Mom cares for people for a living every day. She's supposed to have some ethical code that if she recognized harm in a patient, she would act.

"This could be dangerous for you. For us."

I study Mom, realizing that while she'd follow the blueprint for work—something so close to home is different. There's more to consider because of how much my life is intertwined with the Whitakers. But if we don't protect Sierra, who will? And if we do, who will be there for me?

"I know you disagree, but you're going to have to trust me. Mr. Whitaker's not the kind of guy you can just go and make claims about without a lot of evidence."

"We have Sierra." My voice threatens to break. "She still has bruises, and I only saw what was on her arms."

Mom blows out a long breath and tugs at her mask so it stays over her nose.

"I'm gonna tell you something. You can't speak to anyone. Not even Sierra. We don't know what kind of trauma this could bring about."

I sink into my seat, the heaviness of her words drawing me into silence.

"When you were twelve, Mrs. Whitaker was taken by ambulance to the hospital with Luis, Eric, and Sierra. The nurse on duty and doctor called it in to social welfare as a precaution for a family welfare check. Once Mr. Whitaker got there, they lawyered up and no one could test Mrs. Whitaker or interview the kids. He approached me, made me feel like if I didn't help him, I'd regret it."

"Did he threaten you?"

"I know people like that, baby. He doesn't have to say it. You don't mess with someone like that. Do you see why I'm uncomfortable saying something? Unless we know exactly what we're dealing with?"

That summer is seared in my mind for so many reasons. Mostly because Sierra and Eric left. I'd always thought it was because she was moving on to a new home. Never wondering about the reason that might have caused her to leave in the first place.

"They left for a few months right after. And when the kids returned, the Whitakers immediately finished the adoption paperwork." Mom goes quiet, a tortured look on her face. One that reads like she wished she could've done something. But also, she knows more.

"What aren't you saying?"

"Before the accident, Mrs. Whitaker told me she wasn't keeping Eric, Luis, and Sierra. Adoption wasn't what she thought it would be like. Then the *incident* happened, and everything was fast-tracked. The previous foster parents tried to fight it, even came to the house. I heard them arguing outside."

My mouth drops at this revelation.

"Mr. Whitaker accused them of abusing the kids. Then they left. But the way he said it—"

"You think he was lying to keep them quiet," I say. "To stop them from pushing an investigation of what really happened."

If Mr. Whitaker could threaten the previous foster parents, and a hospital didn't have power to investigate, what's to say my making a report wouldn't be silenced as well? And I'd lose Sierra in the process.

"I never liked you going over there. No matter how much they acted like things were better. Your father said to let it be, that you were smart and could handle yourself."

All this time I thought Mom wanted me away because the Whitakers had things that we didn't.

"I don't know what happened, but it never made me feel good. We have to be careful, Andre." She holds my face, keeping it steady so I listen. "If Mr. Whitaker lied about Eric being away for a psychological evaluation, then he did it because he's worried about you. And I don't think it's a coincidence that he's all buddy-buddy with your father now."

"Should we tell Dad?"

Mom hesitates before answering, "Not yet. Your father thinks I'm always paranoid. He won't see the truth because he's trying to find a way to keep the shop open. This will only push him to work harder than he already is."

Dad would give all his money back. But if the money from the Black relief fund finally gets to him, then it doesn't matter what Mr. Whitaker does with his money. And we won't owe Mr. Whitaker. With my YouTube channel growing, I could pay Mr. Whitaker back for my lawyer. We'd be free from that debt.

I don't bring the backpack up. I can't do anything with it yet. At least not until I'm certain it won't be used against me.

We talk longer. I'm finally convinced to take Mom's lead and keep quiet, for now.

My phone buzzes with a text from Sierra.

Sierra: Eric isn't at any of those boarding schools.

I put my phone in my pocket. "It's Marcus. I better head home."

I know I don't have to lie, but it's just easier. I give Mom a hug because I don't know when I'll be able to do it again. When I'm out the door she calls to me.

"Pull that mask down." She gestures. "Let me see your face before you go."

I do what she says and can't help but release a smile. "Love you."

"Be safe, now. Don't do anything before talking to me first, Andre. I mean it."

I nod before riding off.

Once I'm around the corner I immediately dial Sierra. She answers on the second ring.

"What did they say?"

"I called all of them." She sniffles. "I just got off the phone with the school on the filled-out application. I said we were billed wrong. I gave them Eric's name, Social, everything. They confirmed he was registered." Sierra sounds far away, like she's outside. I realize she's at a protest, with all the chanting and talking in the background.

I step back, relieved we've got a trail. But then her voice doesn't sound right.

"Well, what's wrong? This is a good lead."

"They confirmed sending a letter that cancellations would lose their deposits. I asked when the cancellation came in, they said January sixth."

"Maybe they knew you weren't your mom."

"No. They helped me look for billing. He's not there. My

parents planned for him to be there, then didn't even file a police report when he went missing. He's gone."

When she says *gone,* I know what she's insinuating.

"I found the backpack," I finally say. "I checked his locker next to mine—all the money was still there. If he'd split, he would've taken it with him." It hurts me to say it.

Sierra sobs harder. Between spurts she speaks. "My dad did this. He hurt him. He . . . That's why he can't reach me."

"Let's talk about this. Come by my house. Make a plan."

I only hear the click of her phone. I call back, but it goes straight to voice mail.

My head spins because we might not be searching for Eric, we might be searching for his body. Eric could've easily grabbed the money and dumped the bag. I try and tell myself that Eric's alive somewhere, hitchhiking, too broke to come back, maybe sick in a hospital. But the voices inside my head get louder.

Eric didn't come back, because Eric couldn't come back.

DON'T STOP BELIEVIN'

June 2, 2020

A few days pass and Sierra is impossible to get ahold of. She's spending all her energy dipping in and out of the house to protest. I decide I'll catch her on the way home, no matter what time it is.

Grandma J sits next to Grandpa's empty chair, plugged into the news. I wave at Dad, who's in the kitchen, on the phone with Mom. So far, Mom's kept her promise to keep Sierra's secret between us.

"What's this?" I point at the television, watching crowds face off as antiprotesters are now in the mix.

"You see these Proud Boys in Portland? They came from all over trying to stir up trouble downtown, protesting the protesters."

I watch a group of people without masks, yelling, cursing, and threatening to hurt people protesting. The wild part, it's mostly white people yelling "Black Lives Matter!" against a group of white people yelling "All Lives Matter!"

"The math's not math-ing here," I chuckle out. But it's kinda nice to see battles being fought on our behalf.

"These antiprotesters think they have the right to act this way and nobody else."

"Including their one Black friend joining in. He does realize he's a member of a group that wouldn't care if he dropped dead tomorrow." I point at a racially ambiguous guy donning the black and yellow with a big American flag.

"You know how it is, they're trying to differentiate from Nazis and the Klan by saying they're not racist because they have non-white people in the group." Grandma tsks. "I've watched enough, you can turn it off."

"Nah. I wanna see."

The news makes Portland look like the entire city is under siege, but it's not even like that, the news is making it worse by turning the conversation away from why the protest is happening in the first place. The only good part about this whole thing is maybe it'll scare people away from moving to Portland, pushing us out of our neighborhoods.

I'm about to get up, until a picture of a boy hugging an older white man stops me.

"That looks like Luis." I pause the TV, then let it play when Grandma leans in to put on her glasses.

Luis holds a sign.

The still shot from the photographer captures a tear that stops midcheek. I'm mesmerized by it, even as the news goes on talking about the protest.

I'm caught up in how media picks up the image of Luis hugging that man with a crowd behind them, cheering and clapping. There's something iconic about it.

But that's not what fixates me. The image is . . . haunting.

My stomach whirls because I'm left feeling the opposite of hope. What I see isn't what the news is showing, that we can heal from this massive reckoning of race in America. What I see is a deep sorrow.

Luis is afraid.

He's clinging to this man not because he's dreaming of racial justice but because he's looking for safety.

I stand up, studying Luis's eyes on the screen. Wondering if it's just me who sees it this way. He looks terrified, like he's been betrayed so many times. And he has. His life before adoption wasn't easy. His parents were picked up and sent across the border without a second thought. He lived on the streets, hiding from police, until he was taken into Child Protective Services and finally adopted. And I don't even know what secrets he's had to shield in order to have a roof over his head. He's the one who first brought up the comment about being shipped off to school.

There's nothing joyous about this image. It should bring everyone to tears that a fourteen-year-old boy is out on the street having to carry signs that say BLACK LIVES MATTER and PEOPLE SHOULDN'T BE IN CAGES.

We keep watching, stuck on the video, which is now on loop as the newscasters talk about the protest.

"Maybe Eric will see this and come home for good, at least for a day again. He has to be ready to stop this foolishness," Grandma J says.

Then it hits me, something Grandma J said when we were eating pie outside. She saw Eric come back *after* being gone.

"When Eric came home again, was anyone else with him?"

Grandma J raises an eyebrow.

I'd taken everyone's word that they hadn't spoken to Eric since he split. But secrets encircle the Whitaker family in a web so thick I'm not convinced it's true.

"Well, I don't know. It was late. Mrs. Whitaker was the only one home. Then a few hours later I saw Mr. Whitaker arrive that Friday night?" Her statement sounds like a question.

"Did you see him again?"

"No. I went to bed. Wait, I did hear something outside when I was getting a glass of water, and Mr. Whitaker was driving Eric's car."

"Was Eric with him?" That was January third, the day his foster parent Susan called Mr. Whitaker.

"I'm assuming so. Well . . ." Grandma J focuses. "No, come to think of it, it was just Mr. Whitaker."

After my arrest it was days before they transported me to MacLaren on January sixth. By the following Friday, Mr. Whitaker sent a lawyer for me. A whole week had gone by since Eric was last seen. But all that time Mr. Whitaker didn't mention that Eric did come home, that it wasn't just a phone call.

I swipe through my phone calendar, trying to figure out where all the Whitaker kids would've been when Eric came home. Then I see the ping on my calendar. It was a concert in Seattle. I was invited to go but never made it, with my arrest. The Whitaker kids would've come home Saturday, without ever knowing Eric had been there earlier.

I stand, biting at my nails.

The news pulls away from the image, moving to live footage.

"We've found the young man from the photo. He is the son of a candidate for Portland city commissioner."

"Whoa," Dad says, entering the room. "That the Whitakers?"

A Whitaker family photo takes over the screen, then the camera goes live to them on the steps of a building downtown. Mr. Whitaker's hands are around Luis and Sierra, circled by the rest of the family.

Mr. Whitaker speaks. "If my family can live in harmony, so can the world. We can treat each other with kindness. That's how I want to serve in this city, by ending the criminalization of Black, Indigenous, and people of color. And that's why I support the Oregon Black relief fund. We need to take action, no more rhetoric. I live in the Albina community and it needs revitalization, to keep us all safe."

He goes on, acting like he's the white Cory Booker.

When Dad goes back to his room to rest, I leave the television on so Grandma J can hear if she wants to, then I step outside to pay the Whitakers another visit.

THEIR SPARE KEY is hidden inside a fake rock by the steps. There's no sound as I open the door, but the air feels alive like the house knows I'm there. The squeak of my shoes makes me pause before walking toward the study.

When I get there, I swivel the chair slowly.

It creaks, and I brace myself for someone on the other side.

Once I know I'm alone, I settle down.

With shaking hands, I take the small key on a ring hidden in the top desk drawer, jamming it in the lock and sliding it open. I sort through the files to the *J*s for the Jackson folder. Only this time, it's visibly thinner. There are referrals for my lawyer. The rest . . . gone.

Worse, the boarding school folders are missing.

Like they were never here.

My fingers tingle as I frantically search each folder in case I misplaced them. But nothing is left.

I bite the inside of my cheek, wishing I'd done this earlier with Sierra.

Maybe Sierra confronted Mr. Whitaker, so he got rid of the files. Then I think back to our last conversation. She called all the boarding schools and found no trace of Eric. She must've come back for more clues.

With nothing left for me here, I back up, locking the drawer with my sweaty hands. Then I run up to Eric's room, no longer caring about staying quiet. I lunge at the closet, frantically reaching for the box in the ceiling for what I didn't take. But that's gone too.

I pull my phone out to text Sierra, then hesitate. Last time I was here I was already inside, invited in by Mrs. Whitaker. But how do I explain that this time I grabbed a key and broke into her house? Rifled through private documents.

I text Sierra anyway.

Andre: Did you take the rest of Eric's things? Your dad's files as well?

I'm ready to leave, until Luis's haunting face takes over my better judgment. I make my way to what I'm pretty sure is his room.

Luis's space is cold and empty. There's nothing personal here, except for his skateboard, which is shoved in the corner. I search through his closet, clothing piled on the floor, only dress clothes hung up. Like those were gifts he wouldn't mind leaving behind. Or maybe that's just how they've always been. All these years, I've only seen what Mr. and Mrs. Whitaker curated for me.

I lean against the closet door, my gaze landing on the window that Luis climbs out of.

I step outside. Then grip the roof to keep my balance as I sit over the edge like Luis. From here I see the backyard, across my house, and down the street. The view is calming once I get used to being at the edge.

The puzzle swirls. Uncertainty about what happened to the files fills my mind. All I have is prayers that Sierra's got them somewhere safe. I move to go inside, until a grinding sound shakes my body. Skin prickles into goose bumps.

The garage door.

Frozen, I let the voices confirm who is home.

Everyone.

I frantically glance at the open window and my house, debating a quick escape to Eric's closet until everyone's asleep. The voices get closer, floating through the house and up to the window.

I shimmy down to the edge, jump off the roof, and crash to the ground.

READY OR NOT

June 2, 2020

I keep an eye on the Whitakers' house, searching for Sierra. She's the only one missing and still hasn't texted me back.

When Luis climbs out his bedroom window, I slip out of my house again.

I cup my hands and whisper-yell, "Luis!"

Luis signals for me to come inside. I tuck my hands in my pockets, refusing to move, so Luis flings himself off the roof more gracefully than I did.

"What's up?"

"You talk to Sierra?" My teeth chatter, still coming down from the jump. Still worried I scared Sierra into protecting the only family she has left.

"I was just with her. She wanted to stay at the rally tonight. There's a bridge demonstration."

I kick the ground, gathering my courage by reminding myself that Luis was always the peacekeeper.

"You know I'd help you if you ever needed it."

"Why would I need it?" Luis steps back. I'm halfway expecting him to scale up to the roof, but he doesn't.

"What do you think really happened to Eric?"

"We already talked about this." Luis narrows his eyes suspiciously at me. "You looking for him?"

"Kind of. For Sierra."

"He got out," Luis says, flat.

He has no affect. This isn't the Luis I knew before I left, and it hurts to see. But what I'm also beginning to accept is that they all wear their own invisible mask. The wall I was climbing with Sierra was always there. Luis is no different—he just maneuvers it by keeping distant.

"What do you mean, *he got out*?"

"He's better off."

"What about Sierra?" I ask.

"You'd have to ask her."

I bite my cheek, trying to keep my reaction cool. I hope to God I'm wrong about Eric, but if I am, Luis is lying if he thinks Eric is better off.

No one cares about boys like him.

Like me.

"What really happened?"

"I told you. He split."

"Why?" I edge closer.

"This why Sierra's acting strange? You pressed her on Eric

too?" Luis points to the roof of his room, which sits above Sierra's. Always watching.

I take a long pause, debating if I should go deeper. His face is still expressionless, but his eyes search mine.

"My mom told me the accident you had as kids was serious. The one from the summer you left." I brace myself for his reaction.

"You bring that up to Sierra?" He steps closer, like he'd fight me if he could. He doesn't back down, even though he knows I could clock him.

"I haven't had the chance. What happened?"

Luis looks away. His voice at a whisper. "That's ancient history."

"Is Eric going missing ancient history too? Because Sierra doesn't think so."

"We don't need you to save us. You're only making it worse. Bringing back old memories we've shoved away."

His words sting. I'm not trying to save her, more like be there for her. But Luis said what she'd say too. I can't help but question maybe I'm doing this more for me than her. I fight the thought. Because here's the thing: this is about me, too. I was put in the middle when Mr. Whitaker set this whole thing in motion with lies about Eric being hospitalized.

"Okay. I'm doing it for me, but I think you want to help. I think you want to help yourself." I flip it on him.

"Why the hell would you say that?" Luis sounds grown, and I have to keep reminding myself he's a ninth grader. He should be playing video games rather than watching people from his roof.

"Your photo's really taking off, hugging that man—kumbaya and all." Like I said before, I'm an asshole sometimes.

"Spur of the moment." He glances away, fidgeting with his fingers. Itching for a cigarette. And there's nothing sadder to me.

"I don't think it was. I think you were begging for help." I look him in the eye. "But nobody saw it. Nobody but me, at least."

"Sounds like you're talking to yourself." He points down to my ankle.

I flinch but don't take the bait.

"Do they hurt you, too? I can help." I'm searching for more ways to get Luis to back Sierra's story, so it won't only be me against Mr. Whitaker.

"No," Luis says. "You're trying too hard, thinking maybe Sierra will get with you. There's nothing going on here more than anywhere else."

"Most people don't have bruises."

"That's Sierra, she's been angry since Eric ran off. She might've got her arm pulled or slapped, but she and Dad have always been oil and water."

I don't know what to say in response to more excuses for an adult.

"You don't have to worry about her searching for Eric. She's all into protesting now. Fight the power. Down with the man. The fire that pushed her to find him is focused downtown now. And I hugged that guy because he was the first person who asked me if I was okay." Luis chokes. "I want everything to go back to normal. We're like every other family. Our mom was sick. Messed up. But we're all messed up, Andre. We don't have your perfect life."

"My life is hardly perfect," I spit out.

"But you act like it, don't you? You're out here, thinking you're fixing things because you don't want to see how you messed up."

"What? The only mistake I made was not ratting on Eric." I throw my hands up. "Anyway, I'm dealing with it. What about you?"

"Leave it alone. My mom was depressed and my dad thought taking on a *project* would help her, so he agreed to take us in. Maybe she got tired of the project." His voice sounds hurt. "She was ready to let us move on to another foster home because it was too much. Her running the car while we were in the garage was to get Dad's attention before it got out of control. It was a big wake-up call that actually pulled our family together. It went too far, but she's better. She went to a counselor, promised she would never do that again, and has taken care of us ever since."

I'm trying to catch up with what happened—it wasn't an accident. I held hope that maybe Mom was wrong, but carbon monoxide poisoning from the car in the garage?

Some things are so painful, responding with *I'm sorry* feels empty. I study Luis, know it's one of those times a glance can say it, without saying it.

Mrs. Whitaker knew what she was doing. Playing emotional chess with them like they were pieces on her board. Luis would've been nine then, Sierra twelve; it would be easy to mold those memories of what happened before. "What about you?" I ask softly. "Did they send *you* to a counselor?" The blank look on Luis's face tells me they didn't.

"The past is the past. You live with it or you die from it."

Shivers run down my spine. Maybe I'm not the only one that thinks Eric's dead.

"Leave my brother alone." Kate comes out from the shadows. "You think you're helping, but you're not."

Kate puts her arm around Luis, now his protective older

sibling. "We should've talked about this long ago, about the garage. About you all having to leave after."

Luis was holding his own, but soon as she says those words he breaks down. Looking like the kid I've always known him to be as he hugs Kate.

"Mom wasn't trying to get attention from Dad," Kate says to me. "I found her in the garage. She let me watch a movie while she said she was doing something. The way she said goodbye . . . it felt like she was running away with you all. I was jealous after our parents told us they'd be fostering."

That memory flashes across Kate's face, and her eyes well. I still recoil at being around her, but I can't deny her trauma from growing up in a dysfunctional house that paints a perfect picture. One where her own mother tried to die by suicide and kill her now-adopted siblings. The Whitaker parents always got their way. Maybe that's all that Kate knows.

"You helped?" Luis says. "They never told me that part."

"We weren't allowed to talk about it. . . ." Her voice trails off. "When I opened the door, the garage was closed and everyone was . . . dozing. I hit the garage door opener, screaming until you all woke up, because the car doors were locked. It didn't seem right. Then Mom stirred, got into action, and pulled you out. The ambulance finally came after I called." She chokes, crying, holding on to Luis.

"Mom would've let you all die," she goes on. "Let herself die. She didn't stop it like she and Dad pretended. They just told everyone you were on a long car trip and napping, that she didn't want to wake you all up."

"Are you in danger?" I ask.

"That was a long time ago." Kate and Luis trade knowing glances. "But they'd do anything to protect their secrets. And whatever happened with Eric changed things. Sierra got tired of pretending, of Mom treating her differently. Trying to stop her from bringing up Eric. She's being reckless, looking for a fight in the house. She wants the quiet to go loud, and she makes sure we hear it. That we stop hiding. That's why we go out with her to the protests, to make sure she doesn't take things too far."

"She's gonna get seriously hurt," I say.

"I know," Kate replies. "She's following in Eric's footsteps, hoping to bring them down by getting in trouble at the protests, and then maybe Eric will come back."

"Eric's not coming back," I whisper.

They both turn to me, waiting for me to say more. Kate gestures for me to go inside. I hesitate because I swore I'd avoid her from now on.

Instead, I follow.

36

EVERYBODY WANTS TO RULE
THE WORLD

June 2, 2020

On my way down the hall, I pass the study, glancing through a sliver of the door that's never been able to close all the way. Mr. Whitaker is propped in front of his computer with a ring light set up, like he's prepping for an interview. While Kate and Luis head down to the basement, I make an excuse to use the bathroom first.

With Mr. Whitaker's back to me, I pry the door open another inch. When I see the CNN news anchor on his screen, I realize he's got some big-time interview, so I wait.

"Portland, Oregon, has become the epicenter of a massive face-off between the police and the community. We're here today to talk to the father of the young man whose image went viral."

They flash to Luis's photo.

"Fourteen-year-old Luis Whitaker isn't new to tragedy. He

lived on the streets with his family before his parents were deported. Born in the United States, he found himself in the foster care system. Now his adopted father, a successful investment banker, is running for Portland city commissioner. Mr. Whitaker, good to see you."

Mr. Whitaker's dressed sharp for the camera. I slow my breath to catch everything he says.

"Good to be here, but I wish it were under better circumstances."

"What exactly do you see happening in Portland? How does the community feel? And what has law enforcement's response been?"

"Portland is a war zone."

What the . . . ? That's dramatic. I scrunch my eyebrows, pissed at him dragging our city.

"More and more people are demonstrating every day. After the teargassing occurred, we are seeing people come out that you typically wouldn't. I think the protest situation is being poorly managed by the mayor and the governor. If they would respond appropriately, we wouldn't have to have so many people congregating during a pandemic."

"But you were out there—your kids, even."

"Yes, I was present to support my kids. I believe in protest, freedom of speech—values that our nation was founded on. But now that we have the world's attention, we don't need to be in the streets. Especially at night. I want my kids to go to bed before curfew and wake up in the morning thinking about school, going to college. We're now seeing people out and about in the pandemic because it's been normalized, but there's still a deadly virus out there. Our mayor, our governor, should be aggressively resolving these issues."

"Sounds like you have higher political aspirations." The news anchor chuckles.

"What I'm trying to say is, this isn't easy. No one could have predicted a pandemic. The racial divide. Let's hope the city stays whole through all of this. I don't want my kids to have to live through another cycle of these protests. What's happening in Oregon is a test for the country. And what happened after the protesters were roughed up and the Wall of Moms came to shield them, it's just atrocious that they've had to go out there. My own wife is out there too, fighting for her kids. The points have been made. We now know Black Lives Matter. Let's not put anyone else at risk."

We now know?

They flash an image of Mrs. Whitaker holding a sign that says BLACK LIVES MATTER and a line of white moms blocking officers, which has grown in number over the past few days. I can't tell if it's just me, but it seems more like Mr. Whitaker's mad the issues aren't just left for Black and brown people to deal with. And now that they're not, it's a big-ass inconvenience.

He's mixed up in everything that's been angering me. All those feelings I've had of betrayal by a country that's supposed to protect me. A country that doesn't love me as much as I love it.

If Black folks aren't dying in the streets, we're left at the mercy of managing a global crisis on our own and failing miserably. It's every man for themselves, and what gets at me the most is a lot of these people are so-called Christians. But not willing to extend recognition that our lives are intertwined. Every day is survival, and in a pandemic, people like my family are dumped by the wayside. You can see it in the news, how no one cares about essential workers—who are more likely to be Black, brown, poor, and women.

People like Mr. Whitaker are the reason we haven't changed as a country. Like so many people being willing to pretend this pandemic isn't real because it's inconvenient. 'Cause for them, it's okay for people to die as we get businesses opened back up. It's okay if every state is scrambling to find masks, ventilators, and hand sanitizer. Hell, toilet paper. Flashes of my grandpa in those last moments shoot pain to my chest because I know what the aftermath of loss feels like. The fear it'll happen to my dad. The fear of my mom being at risk every single day as more places open up—more people getting sick, more people filling hospitals.

The interview ends and Mr. Whitaker jumps on another call. When I see the video, my mouth drops open. I know this face.

"I said not to contact me," Mr. Whitaker says. "I gave you a tip. I can't be involved in this case."

"Video calls are better than me making a phone call. Besides, I think you'll be interested in what I got to say," Cowboy Jim says.

I shake my head, clutching the wall to keep from falling, from yelling. I hold my breath, bracing myself for what's next.

"Downtown, at the rally, protesters are planning on doing a mass demonstration on the bridge. Well, there's an underground group who'll be wearing all black with yellow ribbons attached to backpacks. But some of the federal officers patrolling know about this. And they don't plan on stopping them."

I suck in a breath. The connections between my old probation officer and Mr. Whitaker tighten in on me. I'm ready to call him out, but I know it'd only backfire. I'm also caught up in what he's saying about tonight's protest. The last thing Portland needs is people fanning the flames of our city. The president's been waving political threats against the protest, saying he'll bring in the National Guard and federal officers to stop protesters. Even despite the resistance from the governor and mayor. It's raising tensions, creating an inevitable divide within our country. It's against everything we say we believe in. This is freedom of speech.

"Why are they stirring up trouble?" Mr. Whitaker says.

"Change the narrative of Black Lives Matter and turn them into a terrorist group. I know some guys did this in Philly with antifa. All you need is a few decoys strategically placed in front of some cameras with masks and hoodies. They'll blend in and boom, the narrative will spin online and in the media."

My throat constricts. What's happening? Is he seriously supporting this underground group starting a riot and blaming it on Black Lives Matter protesters or antifa? That's what's been pumping all over conservative news lately. That everyone out there is a protester or an anarchist. Then I feel my face go hot. I already knew Jim didn't see me for me. He'd give a white kid a chance in a heartbeat, but he felt he had me all figured out because he had his own beliefs. Of course he's no different. He's just like the antiprotesters, wanting to keep a foot on our necks. Keep us down because it was their rules they wanted to live by, the rules that put them on top.

"What about the federal officers? You think they'll just let this happen?" Mr. Whitaker says.

"The attorney general is following the president's orders. Lock 'em up. Take folks off the street. Protests across the country will end in a few days if governors are forced to make them shut down because they don't want violence coming to their cities. What do you want to do about this?"

"Nothing. I'm going to let it happen," Mr. Whitaker says.

I blink hard, repeating his words in my head.

"This'll push a recall for the governor. Mayor of Portland as well. Special election could give me my opening. I won't need to wait for 2024."

"Just don't forget about me when you get elected. I want a seat on the commissioner's board focused on criminal justice. Maybe a promotion—the director of Oregon Youth Authority is in over her head with her views on youth development. These are delinquents. Lost causes. They need someone like me who knows what works. They're too loose."

"Of course. You just keep your end of the deal and make sure you keep an eye on that kid."

I suck in a breath at him confirming he's the one who had Jim watch me.

"Your kids out there tonight?" Jim says.

I sigh, at least relieved that he'll bring Sierra home, then we can talk and figure this all out.

"Yeah. I'll get them home. One of them won't listen, though."

"I bet I know which one that is," Jim says gruffly.

I cover my mouth, fighting my urge to say something about leaving Sierra out of this. I should've been recording them. Sierra's looking for a fight, and she put herself in the middle of danger for a cause.

Shuffling footsteps down the stairs make me jump. I accidentally hit the door. There's no way to escape. I can't leave, and if I head to the basement, Mr. Whitaker could come out any second and know I was listening. So I hide in the darkness of the kitchen.

Mrs. Whitaker tightens her robe, coming toward me.

I hold my breath, wincing in preparation for the light to flick on. But she stops, steps away, and enters Mr. Whitaker's office.

I get ready to bounce, until a pair of eyes meets mine in the kitchen.

My eyes adjust.

It's Brian. His face stone cold.

How long has he been watching me?

I was so focused on listening I wasn't paying attention to my surroundings. But if he had come from the basement stairs, I would've seen him. Which means he's been watching me in the kitchen this whole time.

He doesn't speak, just bumps my shoulder as he approaches the study door. I swivel my head for an exit. The only one is through Brian or down in the basement, but I want out of this house.

But Brian doesn't enter his dad's study.

He leans his ear by the door, taking my position.

Even from the kitchen I can hear their conversation.

I tiptoe closer. *Is he really gonna let me do this?*

With each step, I wait for Brian to glare. To enter the office, but he doesn't. He listens.

Mr. Whitaker tells Mrs. Whitaker about Cowboy Jim's news.

"Call the kids for me. Get them home and safe. I can't have

them out there when I make a play for the recklessness of leadership. Heads are gonna roll if this blows up downtown like he said."

"I'll call them, but you know who won't listen," Mrs. Whitaker says.

"Figure it out. And control yourself," Mr. Whitaker says. "You catch more flies with honey. Get Sierra home, make up a reason. Tell her she can go out tomorrow."

Brian jerks his head and I flinch, heart thrumming through my ears.

A beat later I realize they're on their way out of the study.

This time I don't hesitate.

I open the front door and don't look back.

Ignoring the clicking sound in my head that feels as loud as a ticking time bomb.

37

ONLY GOD CAN JUDGE ME

June 2, 2020

I have no choice but to believe Brian won't out me. That's why I stay on the porch, pacing in the darkness until my pulse slows. This gives me time to replay everything. Those little prickles on the back of my neck are finally making sense. The ones I ignored because I wanted the shiny exterior of the Whitakers to be just as clean on the inside.

My thoughts are sluggish on what to do. I should call the cops. But the truth is, I'd need Brian to corroborate my story. I doubt Brian's put the stakes together. He wouldn't know who Jim was to me. As far as he knows, I'm just nosy. I repeat this until I believe it. I have to. I also have to hope Brian didn't put his foot in it and confront his parents, tell them I was there too.

The Whitakers' front door creaks open and I'm ready to break away down the street. But it's Luis and Kate who run swiftly toward me. Brian watches at the door, closing it just as they reach me.

"What's going on?" Luis says. "Brian is freaking out. He said to come find you, something about our parents?"

"It's really bad." I form how to approach this. I'm interrupted by Kate's phone ringing.

She flicks it up and seems relieved. "It's my mom."

I have an urge to rush her phone and throw it. Instead, I pinch my finger to my lips and say, "Don't say anything about me."

"Hey, Mom," Kate answers on speakerphone, fingers shaking.

"Hey, honey. I'm going to need you to come home. It's serious, no playing around tonight." Kate looks at Luis, and Luis looks at me.

I mouth for her to ask *Why?*

"Why?" Kate says.

"Your father heard . . . there's been some COVID exposures. Are you downtown?"

"No . . ." Kate stalls and my breath hitches as I wait on her response. "With Luis."

"Oh, good. Both of you get home right away."

"What about Sierra?"

I nod, encouraging this angle.

"She with you?"

"No, she's downtown." Kate takes a long breath. "Protesting."

"Don't worry about it. I'll call her next. Brian's home already."

"I hope everything is okay." Kate's clueless. As soon as she gets off the phone, I tell them about the video call in the study. They don't interrupt until I'm finished.

"Why would he do that?" Kate nervously brushes her hair back.

"He's wanting to . . . I don't know . . . profit over things falling apart downtown. Sounds like he's making a future political play."

"And he was talking with your old probation officer? What's that all about?" Luis jumps in. "Could it be a coincidence?"

"He'd been harassing me at home and dropping in un-announced at the Parks and Rec. My dad asked yours for advice—that's gotta be how they connected. We should've never trusted your dad." My words come out bitter and I want to swallow them back at the surprise on Kate's face. I don't fully trust her with this either.

"We don't know if that's true," Kate says. "My dad could be keeping this guy close so he'll leave you alone. This Jim guy could be trying to take advantage of my dad's connection?"

I shake my head. "He told Jim to watch me closely."

Kate chews on her lip, conceding.

"What are you gonna do?" Luis steps closer.

"I don't know." I huff out. "Let's make sure Sierra comes home. Then get word to the organizers. We'll deal with my situation later." I glance quickly at the Whitaker house, watching for movements. So far, the door stays closed. Just how I want it.

"I just don't believe my dad would be okay with this happening." Kate's trembling. I wish Brian had just sent Luis over.

"Don't act like you haven't heard him before." Luis calls Kate out. "He's for building a wall. And he had no sympathy when they showed all those families being stripped away from each other by ICE."

"That's politics," Kate says. "It's not like he controls what happens. He's just distant from the emotion of it. If it was your family, he would totally care."

"That's the problem, Kate," Luis says. "People who think like that aren't thinking about me and my family."

"He wouldn't let that happen," Kate says. "And can they actually get away with pretending to be in support of the protests and starting a riot? That seems a stretch—that there are people willing to hurt innocent people."

"Kids in cages," I say. "Very nice people. We've been numbed to this. There is no line someone won't cross for power. This is the same playbook the government did with Malcolm X. Martin. Fred Hampton. The Black Panther Party. All the progress around people supporting Black Lives Matter. Whoever was in power or against progress found a way to end things. Whether by assassination of leaders or vilifying them."

Kate looks feverish, blown away by her world crumbling from what she knows.

My phone buzzes and I hope it's Sierra and not Marcus.

It's Brian.

Brian: Sierra's not answering.

Immediately I call Sierra. Her phone goes straight to voice mail. I send her a text to call me.

I tell Luis and Kate, then text Brian back:

Andre: She's not picking up for me either.

"What should we do?" Luis says.

"I don't know," Kate says. "Find Sierra for now. Tell her whatever and get her to safety."

"And warn everyone else," I say firmly.

"How do we do that?" Luis says.

I don't answer because I don't even know.

I'm also stuck in place. Being around a crowd, all the people. I tug at my mask, making it tight over my face. Thinking how I can get past the fear that's already bringing back memories of what I've lost. I survey my ankle, my tether to reality.

"I'll go downtown," Kate says. "You coming?"

I hesitate. There're so many reasons why it's better for me to stay inside. Away from crowds. Police.

"You . . . you don't have to go." Luis turns to me, knowing. "You can call local news, tell them what you know."

I'm grateful I don't have to say it.

"Sorry," Kate says. "Is there something you can do to have your curfew changed? Like they realize they should make this exception so you can protest?"

"That won't happen." I chew on my lip, thinking how to make it work. "I'll keep calling Sierra. Maybe she'll finally answer."

"We'll try too," Luis says. "But she's usually out of touch at these things."

I text Brian.

Andre: They're going downtown to find her.

Brian: I'll stay here . . . Keep watch.

Kate and Luis head downtown, but I know Sierra will want to hear what I have to say. We have something in common—being willing to take Mr. Whitaker down on behalf of Eric. But if I help, it won't just take him down. I'll go down too; my ankle monitor will make certain of that. I need to make sure if I get caught up there's someone else who can help. So I pick up the phone and call the only person I can trust if things go south.

38

2 LEGIT 2 QUIT

June 2, 2020

I'm pacing in circles around my bedroom after my failed attempt at alerting the news. They left me to some intern who I'm not even sure believed me. I barely even believe myself. Now that an hour has gone by with no word from Luis, I move closer to risking it all and going to find Sierra myself.

My thumb hovers over my phone, waiting to send another text, until it finally lights up. It's Sierra.

"Where are you?" I say. "We've been trying to reach you."

"I'm downtown by Voodoo Doughnut." Sierra's voice shakes.

"You okay? Tell me you're okay."

"I'm fine." She sniffles. "My phone was off, just turned it on and got all the messages. I called to let you know I'm staying."

"You don't understand—"

"I do. I'm taking my dad down the only way I know how. In public, so he can't punish me."

"What are you talking about?" The phone sounds like it clicks and I yell out, "Are you there? Sierra!"

Sierra's crying in the background.

"He's gone, Andre. You helped me figure it out. I checked the ceiling of my closet, just like you did in Eric's room. He left me letters. He said if anything happened to him, to save you. He confessed to everything."

The air pulls from my lungs, then my heartbeat picks up and the loud drumming is all I hear. It's too surreal to believe.

"I can't . . . Slow down. Tell me exactly what he said." I reach for water and gulp it down, hoping it helps me settle.

"He'd threatened my dad and left me a suicide letter my mom wrote years ago when we were kids. She tried to kill us. She never wanted us. They took us from our foster mom who did. I don't know what my dad would do if he found out Eric had this."

"What should we do?" I continue to pace, head swirling as a panic to do something grows inside me. The Whitaker parents' relationship circling tighter around me.

"I'm going to read Eric's letters at the protest in front of all the cameras when they interview me about Luis and my dad running for city commissioner. I'll call you when it's done."

"Wait. Sierra. *Sierra*."

She hangs up. I redial but it goes straight to voice mail like before.

I fumble calling Luis. "I just talked to her. She's gonna do something dangerous. She wouldn't listen."

"Where is she?"

"She said downtown, by Voodoo. You gotta find her. She's gonna get caught up in all of this. She's not thinking right now, she just wants your dad to pay. She's scared what your dad might have done to keep Eric quiet."

"What do you think he did?"

I don't answer, and Luis doesn't ask again.

"Should we stop her or warn people about what's going on at the protest?" Luis says.

I'm not credible with the police. The news didn't listen. And as much as I want Mom's help, she'd tell me to mind my business.

"Do you know people she joins up with?" I say.

"She follows some people on social media that post rally points. I'll reach out to them." Luis hangs up.

Within these walls I'd finally been feeling safer. Now all I want to do is bust out into danger.

I walk circles in my room, the outside calling me until I have to answer.

Fuck it. I'm going.

Too much is at stake.

I count down the time between beeps until the red light flickers and my ankle monitor goes dead.

It's a hair over an hour to my curfew. So I take my chances, swallowing hard and praying that Marcus will check the last place the monitor pinged and assume I'm home with a broken charger.

Sierra has evidence that can clear my name. I need her, and it, safe. If she gets arrested, who knows what'll happen. Besides, she's not thinking. If she lashes out, she could get hurt. I could never forgive myself.

I reach for my hoodie and double-mask up, grab hand sanitizer, and bounce.

Outside, someone's waiting on me by the side of the house. My breath cuts short that Jim is here to stop me. But it's not him.

Boogie steps into the light with a big smirk on his face.

"You look like you're about to do something stupid," he says.

"You here to stop me?"

"Only if you don't let me back you up."

A smile takes over my face.

He was my call after the Whitaker house. And I told him everything—so there'd be one more person to tell my truth. Boogie told me to keep my probation ass home and let Kate and Luis break it down to Sierra.

"You don't have to do this." I step tentatively closer. "It could be dangerous."

"Yeah, no guts, no glory, though. Besides, I'm your best friend. Stupid shit is what I'm supposed to do. I'm not gonna miss being there for you again. I wasn't there New Year's Eve. If I was, I could've been your alibi."

"Or ended up in trouble with me."

"It woulda been worth it."

"You sure you wanna do this?"

"You're my best friend. I gotchu, whatever you need."

"Even for best friends that are horrible at calling?"

"Especially those dumb mothafuckas." Boogie elbows me. "Come on. I'm giving you one hour to search for her, then you need to get back home and charge that thing before your PO shows up. . . . You sure her family can't handle this? I got you whichever way, but just think about it."

"Sierra has evidence that I'm innocent."

"Let's go."

We fist-bump, then ride.

My legs are pumping hard as showers drizzle on me. I weave around traffic, passing Black Lives Matter signs. The whole time praying we won't be stopped.

I feel a phantom vibration on my leg, warning me to turn around. Even though I know it's just in my head, there's a tiny piece of me that believes there's always a way to track me.

"You sure you wanna take the K there?" Boogie calls back to me. Martin Luther King Boulevard is the safest way to navigate. Taking a side street will only increase the chance a neighbor calls the cops on two "suspicious" kids riding bikes. I nod, confirming it's the right move.

Finally in the distance I spot the mass of protesters lining up, chanting with signs.

"Let's walk," I say. "So we don't pass her."

At first, I think it'll be easy to spot Black and brown faces in a sea of mostly white, but I'm lost with all the masks, hats, and hoods that are ready for the sky to open up and pour down on us.

Sierra could be anywhere.

I repeatedly call out her name, hoping to hear an answer, but my voice is drowned out by chants. "No justice, no peace" and "This is what democracy looks like."

After twenty minutes of searching, it's like a light shines down on her black-and-red Trailblazers jacket. Relief sets in.

As I get closer I catch why she's stopped. She's flanked by Kate and Luis. Sierra shakes her head at them. Then Luis tugs on her arm, but she shrugs him off.

I jump off my bike so I can weave in and out through the protesters. Sierra's face is ghastly. I'm not even sure where to begin. She's so desperate to do something meaningful with Eric missing that she's not willing to listen to reason.

As I approach her, a white guy pumps his fist in the air. He's got a ribbon tied around his backpack, yellow and black. Just like Jim said. He's infiltrating the crowd to start up a riot.

"We gotta get outta here," I plead when I reach them, but they don't move.

"She won't leave," Luis says.

"This doesn't make any sense," Kate says. "But we should go home anyway."

I glance at Boogie, making sure he knows to keep an eye on Kate. He nods.

"I'm not leaving," Sierra says. "This is about a fight for justice. They want to scare us, but we can't give up."

"They're gonna blame Black Lives Matter organizers and say we destroyed the city." I try and reason with her, but her eyes glaze over. Nothing will stop her.

My phone rings, but I ignore it at first until I see it's Marcus.

"Damn," I say.

I scowl at my ankle monitor like it betrayed me.

"Answer it," Boogie urges. "He doesn't know where you are. Just that it's dead."

I pull the phone away and shout out to them, "I gotta get out of here!"

"Who's calling?" Sierra steps closer, worry filling her face. She knows what it could mean if I violate my terms.

I put my finger to my lips, then ride until I find an empty street corner to take his call.

"Hello." I fake like I'm asleep as I cup the phone to block outside noise.

"Wake up and charge your monitor."

"Must be broke." I block the phone as chants from a distance begin again. "I'll charge it and call you if I have problems."

"What's that noise?"

"Watching the protest on the news." I shut my eyes, hoping he'll believe me. "I'll check on it and charge up."

"Nah. It'll be a house check."

"What?" My throat tightens. "Now?"

Boogie approaches closer, his eyes widen. If he's at my door, Grandma J will answer and head up to an empty room.

"Jim Adkins is on his way to your house. I'm out of town, I asked for someone to cover my caseload, but he got it. I'm still tracking. Thought you'd want a heads-up he's approved to be by your house. I'm sure he's headed there now, with your monitor off."

"I'm not at home. I'm with . . . Terry. Helping out and watching news," I blurt out. "But I'll be home by curfew." I hang up, knowing I'm already busted.

"What do I do?" I look at Boogie after telling him the latest.

"Damn. You'd better go. We found Sierra, but it's up to her if she chooses to leave," Boogie says. "I'll watch out for her."

"I can't be at two places at one time." I run my hands over my face.

"Then call Terry, and maybe he'll cover for you?"

"You serious?" That's a terrible idea. But it's also the only one I have, so I dial up Terry's phone with nothing to lose.

"So, Terry . . . about making sure I'm not in trouble, how far away from downtown are you?"

"Have you lost it? This isn't like you—what are you doing?" Terry yells, and I start explaining Eric's confession letter and what I'm doing out here. Terry cuts me off.

"Well, you have ten minutes to get here and tell me all about it or I swear to God I'm calling Marcus right now."

I pull my mask down so he can hear me clearly.

"Mr. Whitaker got me a lawyer because he wanted to control the charges so they wouldn't expose Eric. He was the one who dumped the backpack in my locker." At least I think he was. The more I think about the real stash in Eric's locker, it doesn't ring true. I tell Terry about what I overheard. Not because I want to, but because I got no other choice. If I stay, I'll be caught up in whatever is about to happen downtown. But if I go, Sierra is in danger. So is everyone else here. When I hear myself talking to Terry, whose BS radar is always on point, I know I sound hella nuts.

"You can't be a hero, Andre. She got people who can watch out for her. You're walking a thin line. Microscopic, in fact." He believes me. But he doesn't care. His patience is running out, and to be honest, I don't blame him.

"I think it's my fault that Eric is gone."

"Even more reason for you to stay away from her and her family."

"I can't."

"You're a good kid, Andre. Don't be stupid."

"What am I supposed to do? They're gonna start a riot and who knows what'll happen. People could be hurt. Arrested. And it just makes it seem like we need more police involvement. It undermines what everyone's fighting for."

"There's no way they would deploy federal officers downtown, not out here. I don't think the cops would just let it slide like that. Not the mayor, and definitely not the governor."

If there's anything I've learned this year, it's that anything is possible.

"I heard it with my own ears. Maybe the authorities can warn people."

"Even if you're right, it won't stop you from getting in serious trouble. Another year of probation, my friend. You sure you're willing to risk it?"

It's not even a choice I feel like I have. It's either worse or worser.

Sierra stands with her family, unmoved. They're hopeful in a way that makes no sense. It's foolish. And yet it feels right.

Finally, Terry speaks again. "I'll pick you up in forty-five minutes, on the corner by Burgerville. If you're there, we ride home together. If you get caught, don't bring my name into anything."

"I swear. I'll be there."

"Don't make me chase you down, because I will. . . ."

"Wait," I say before Terry hangs up. "Can you do something else for me?"

"You sure are asking a lot of favors." He doesn't say no, so I ask.

"Can you search the Rec card swipe records through January second?"

"What am I looking for?" Terry's voice rises like he just might do it.

"If I can combine Eric's confession with an entry at the Parks and Rec, I could prove my innocence. The last day I was in the gym was the thirty-first. The warrant for my locker was the second, and Paul's family filed a police report New Year's Day. It had to be the first or the second when the backpack was dumped in my locker."

"What names am I looking for?"

"Eric. Mr. Whitaker. Paul Chase. Gavin Davis."

"All right. I'll do it. Meet you at the Burgerville on the other side of the bridge. Don't be late."

I hang up. Then Boogie and I ride toward the Whitaker kids, Boogie following close.

"Let's hope Terry's love for data pays off," Boogie says.

I nod as we approach the Whitaker kids.

"Terry from Parks and Rec said he'd give me time. If I don't meet him in forty-five minutes, I'm screwed."

My phone goes off, Dad calling. Then he texts.

Dad: Where are you? That probation officer is here. Your monitor dead?

My heart feels like it drops to my feet. This is all getting out of control. I quickly reply.

Andre: I'm with Terry finishing up some inventory. I told Marcus.

Then I shove my phone in my pocket.

"I was hoping you were gonna say you're wrong," Kate says as soon as I look up.

"I know what I heard," I say.

"But federal agents . . . undercover racists pretending to be BLM protesters?"

"Of course it's possible," Luis says. "Isn't that exactly what they say about antifa? That they're just out to cause chaos as paid protesters."

I look to Luis, then Kate, realizing these are debates they've had before.

"Why would the cops let them carry weapons?"

"It's never been about Blue Lives Matter. It's been about anti-Blackness. Did you see anything happen to those white men in Michigan out on the state capitol with guns and no repercussions? Let a protester say BLM and they're met with gas, batons, and beatdowns. Called un-American. When they see white boys with guns, they see themselves. Not a threat."

Sierra steps closer to me. "Go home, Andre. You don't need to be here. I'll be all right."

"I bought a little time with Terry, but come with me."

"I'm not leaving. I need to do this for Eric. Fighting out here for what's right. I need to fight for something," Sierra chokes out.

I squeeze her shoulders and pull her close, whispering, "Then I'm staying too. I need to fight." I survey the protest, intoxicated by hope. The energy around possibly making a difference makes me want to stay. Not just because of Sierra. For me.

"I'll give you the letters," Sierra says. "I'll take a photo of them and read from that. Just go home now."

Her eyes are desperate, but her voice lacks the confidence I need to leave her.

"If it's true about Eric, then your dad might be willing to hurt you, too. Something that won't just fade away after a few days."

Speaking about the inner workings of her home only causes her to bristle.

"Go home, Andre," Sierra says. "I got your warning. I'll tell the organizers what you heard. But I'm staying and I don't need you here with me."

I hold my hands to her cheeks, wanting to pull her mask down and kiss her before saying goodbye. But then I spot a white guy in his midtwenties wearing a camo hoodie floating through the crowd like he's part of it. He doesn't fit in, not in the camo. He's also got a yellow-and-black-striped ribbon tagged to his shirt.

I hop on my bike and trail behind him. Sierra calls after me, but I wave her away.

"I'll be back."

The man stops to talk to someone and I catch his words: "What we need to do is burn down the city."

"No, this is peaceful, man," one of the protesters says, his face horrified. "We're making sure they hear us. We don't need to burn anything down. Get outta here."

The same guy floats through the crowd, talking to people, raising his fist up. Working to get them riled.

People pass me, holding signs on their way to the rallying point for the bridge demonstration. Every few minutes, I catch a person with yellow and black stripes.

Turning down a blocked-off road, I see a black SUV parking.

Out comes a carload of men in black that act like military. I ride closer, passing a van near a corner. This time the men have on riot gear with tape over their names on their chests, masks and helmets on. The two groups meet in the dark of the alley.

There's no turning back now.

SET IT OFF

June 2, 2020

Boogie and I push through an endless line of protesters to find the Whitakers again. The agitators spread disruption that for now is just smoldering. But I know it's only a matter of time before the spark ignites.

I felt alone when I was arrested and throughout my trial. The world didn't care about me. All ready to throw me away as some statistic—even though my crime was their creation.

But today, as I look out, people are locked together. Risking so much to be out here in a pandemic. I refuse to let this be sabotaged. Moments like these build movements that forever change the course of history. And that's enough for me to stay and fight. So even if the protests stop tomorrow, I can't deny the impact already made. It reverberates through my body as the chants reach the sky.

My hope that any of this mattered was extinguished before, but by my being here, from the ashes a flicker came to life inside me.

"We need to disperse the crowd," I suggest as I reach the Whitaker crew. "Make it hard to corner people, so they can safely make it to the bridge without a riot."

"But if we separate—" Luis says.

"We have to. There're too many people. Boogie and I can ride down the blocks, marking off where they are, then you try and divert the crowd so they don't follow their lead."

"How?" Kate says.

"Change the route. Maybe we can find a split between roads and get the word out."

"But they already know we're headed to the bridge for the demonstration," Sierra says.

"Then we'll split up crowds," I say. "Lead them down different routes so it's harder to gather everyone in one location before we reach the mouth of the bridge."

I put my earbuds in and call everyone as Boogie and I ride.

On Fremont, before the Burnside Bridge, a white guy drags a bat on the ground, his head swiveling, looking for trouble. The same ribbon tagged to his backpack. I snap a photo with my phone.

"Do you think you can split off the first group?" I say on the group call. "Up ahead there's a guy with a bat. Warn people."

"Maybe up North Vancouver Avenue," Sierra says to Luis.

"It's not gonna work," Kate huffs. "We can't get all these people to listen to us."

"Then we need to out them," Sierra says.

I'm about to speak when a black SUV with no plates drives

slowly behind the guy in the bat. A sick feeling blooms in my stomach. They're waiting for him to set it off.

Overwhelmed by the crowd of people, we can't stop this fast enough.

"I've got an idea. Take photos and get them to the organizers so they can spread the word. Maybe we can flush them out, scare them from being outed."

The Whitaker family spreads on different corners, snapping photos, so I hang up and go onto my YouTube channel to record live. I log on to my account and press record, using the Wi-Fi from the buildings downtown.

"Usually I'm about music, but today I'm out here in downtown Portland because there's something going on you need to know. There are people posing as protesters, and they're ready to stir up a riot."

I flash my phone up, catching one guy with the same stripe I've seen, then ride up closer to an undercover agent following the guy with the bat. All I hear are chants.

My viewer numbers rise, but not as high as I hope. There's no telling any are even at the protest. But I keep recording, making sure to keep my camera on people's feet, not wanting to show faces of protesters, only agitators.

The black SUV slows. I stall, hiding behind a parked car as I speak to my YouTube audience.

"I can't tell if these are the agents, but—"

A booming crash jolts me from behind. I swing my cell around, catching the guy with the bat smashing the window of a store.

I narrate for my channel as people try to stop him. He ignores them while looting. Then I realize he's just picking stuff up and calling the crowd of people to join him. The black SUV appears and military-dressed men get out, wearing gear like they're fighting in a war. Four men move, military style, quietly behind the guy with a bat and the few people he's egging on. Crowds of people pass by, yelling at the guy to stop. A young Asian kid about my age tries to confront the guy, but before he can say anything the guys in military gear snatch him and his friend, who was just standing there waiting for him. The two are thrown into the agents' van.

"No vandalism," the guy in military gear says to the kid, whose face is terrified.

My channel grows, and a text pops up from Sierra.

Sierra: ?????? What the hell happened????
Me: Share my channel and warn organizers.

I ignore comments flying in and keep recording as the van peels off. People stand around confused, mumbling about the guy snatched away because he was "looting." Only, that's not what happened. He was taken while the real guy who escalated things was checking for his next move down the street.

"An unmarked car with military-dressed men just took a citizen off the street," I say to my channel. "There are vans like this up and down the streets. The guys roaming the street are dressed in black with ribbons on their clothing that are black with a yellow stripe. They're not here for BLM but to start a riot."

I repeat for my new viewers just logging on.

A text pops up from Boogie:

Boogie: Dafuq? We're spreading your channel for people to watch.

I watch my page views rise. I get back on my bike to follow protesters still marching, but now with phones in their hands. I scope alleys until I spot another black SUV. Then film, focusing in on anyone wearing the black-and-yellow ribbon. They become easier to spot because they have a vibe I've long known to avoid for my own survival.

Boogie catches up to me.

"What now?"

"We gotta cut them off, spread people out," I say. "Warn them not to join in on any vandalism."

Still live, Boogie gets the attention of a few people, then convinces them to play back my live recording on YouTube.

I slow, whistling at the crowd. People turn, few by few, following Boogie's direction. The murmurs of chatter spread through the streets as warnings now reach the masses. People begin confronting the lone guys in crowds.

The chatter doesn't stop the protest. It grows, spreading out with chanting echoes across what feels like the entire city. I ride some more, stopping when I see a suspicious guy yelling "Black Lives Matter!" with a gun raised in the air. He grabs a guy who looks terrified. Another van pulls up and snatches the terrified guy off the street, letting the actual one with a weapon walk past them. The van speeds off.

Prickles run up my spine, warning me to flee, but I stay on to narrate to my channel. Then text Sierra.

Andre: Are you showing the footage?

Sierra: Gave your YouTube page to organizers. They sent off group texts. Splitting people up and warning them.

"Good." I sigh, relieved.

Andre: Meet me at the corner of North Vancouver Avenue.
Sierra: I'm going to the bridge.
Andre: What? Let's get out of here, the organizers know what's going on now. Word's getting out.
Sierra: I wanna do the demonstration. I'm not stopping. Hurry up and get out of here before Terry or your PO comes looking for you.

Luis was right: Sierra has a death wish. I'm frightened by her being on such a high for danger. It's not enough to try and get the crowd apart. Destruction will come either way, and the people ready for a riot welcome the chaos.

Andre: I'm not going anywhere then. If you're going, so am I.
Sierra: Andre, stop looking out for me. Just go. I'll catch up with you.
Andre: I need to cross the bridge to meet Terry anyway. Wait for me.

My notifications go off on my channel with people commenting on the video, which makes me realize I can use this moment.

I flag Boogie, pulling up to ride next to him.

"Get home, Boogie. You don't need to be out here."

"I'm not leaving without you either, man. Don't throw your life away. You did what you needed to do. I'll be out here every night protesting in your name, but you gotta get home. This is a marathon, Dre. Let me take this leg."

"I'll go, but first I'm gonna try something."

I just hope this works.

40

DON'T BELIEVE THE HYPE

June 2, 2020

Sierra is wrapped in her coat, shaking, near the entrance to the bridge with her siblings. She stands, hesitant but ready to join. People march onto Burnside Bridge in clusters that grow. When I get closer, she opens her mouth as if to speak. The way it forms I already know she's gonna tell me to go home again.

"Before you say anything, I've got one thing I gotta do and then I'm out of here." I walk my bike to Luis.

The weather shifts from sprinkles to rain. Sierra blows into her fingers to keep them warm.

My phone rings, Dad again.

I send him to voice mail and search for an app to help me trap Mr. Whitaker. Then I go live on YouTube as I video call him. I take a breath of relief when he answers, then firm up my face. He's going to pay for everything he did to me. To Eric. To Sierra. To this city.

"Andre? Everything okay? It's loud. Where are you?" Mr. Whitaker's background is his bookshelves. All perfectly placed and camera-ready. I want all of it to crumble.

"Why'd you do it?" I say.

"What are you—"

"You allowed an infiltration of the protest to happen so federal agents could take over the city for your own political gain. You're supposed to represent us. That's what you said on the news. When really you don't have our backs. You make deals to push your own political agenda."

"You don't know what you're talking about," Mr. Whitaker says. "Where did you hear this? Why don't you come over so we can talk?"

"Is that what you and Eric did? Talk?" I push to get him angry so he says something I can use against him.

"You're out of line. This the thanks I get?"

"Thanks? Eric wanted to turn himself in. He wasn't okay with me being set up. Then what, you shut him up for good when he threatened your political aspirations?"

Sierra's face contorts, a mix between confusion and hurt. She wants to jump in on this, but I can't risk him hurting her because he thinks she was involved. I put my finger up, begging her with my eyes to let me finish.

"Maybe our talk can start with how one minute you're on CNN saying Black Lives Matter, and the next you're scheming to stir up a riot in Portland so you can run for a higher political office. You want to dilute the cause by adding violence. All while your kids are out there protesting. All while you're working with a probation officer to set me up."

There's a long pause between us.

His face twists when he realizes Luis and Kate didn't listen to Mrs. Whitaker but went to join Sierra instead.

"That's ludicrous," he finally says.

"Is it? Because I recorded your entire conversation tonight in your office." I lie, hoping my words make it real enough to him. "And I'm ready to let people know who you really are. Let them know you worked against me, even had a corrupt probation officer in your pocket. I'm going to expose you, and this time you won't get away with it."

I look away so I don't get distracted by Sierra clutching her phone watching my YouTube channel. Around me is silence, people crowded together watching us, watching their phones. There's a hush, except the feet of people marching, quieting down from their shouts for justice to listen in.

Mr. Whitaker growls, "How much would it take for you to keep this quiet?"

"You can't pay me off. That what you did to Eric?"

I watch Mr. Whitaker's face flinch, then go hard.

"I'm not worried about what Eric has to say," he replies.

I hesitate. His reaction goes cold.

"Everyone has a price. What about your dad's bookshop? You like being in debt? I could take that from him."

For a split second, I pause, thinking about the impact this will have. And then shake it away.

"Admit what you did."

Sierra's mouth twists, but she keeps silent, looking at her phone. Kate's and Luis's faces are stricken with disgust.

"Come to the house and let's talk about this," Mr. Whitaker says, rushed, running his hands through his hair before pulling out an envelope from his drawer. "Don't tell anyone and I can get more. Your dad's debt is wiped."

"First, you have to admit what you did, setting me up, letting the protest be sabotaged, all of it. I want to hear you say it."

"Forget it." He pauses. "Who's going to believe some dumb kid with a record? I bet your old parole officer would love to hear about this the next time I talk to him."

My chest tightens at him bringing up Jim again. *The next time . . .*

The crowd around me stays dead silent. It's as if everyone knows my story and is just waiting to see what happens.

"I was so scared that I wouldn't be able to make a difference. So scared to join this crowd, but that's what people like you want us to be. You want us to be silent. That's how you win. I'll never let that happen again."

Boogie throws up his fist and yells, "You're on CNN!"

Unmarked cars back up and drive away. A car door opens and a couple of kids jump out, including the one who they'd snatched earlier for claims of looting.

I let out a cunning smile so Mr. Whitaker knows I got him. He just hasn't figured out how—that is, until I see Mrs. Whitaker run behind Mr. Whitaker. He shoos her away. Until she shoves her phone at him, showing he's exposed.

The video call clicks.

"I think you did it," Sierra says, crying, when she reaches me.

Inside I crack. I did this for her. For me. But it might be the very thing that breaks us.

"I just hope it's enough. Call him out for who—" I'm blubbering and she shushes me, crashing into my chest, sobbing.

Sierra finally calms enough to speak, but the crowd surges with a new energy. Their chants feel like they're ricocheting across the city. An organizer who's been on the news calls me over as a camera operator makes his way to me, shoving a microphone in my face. I shield Sierra, holding on to her and searching for what to say.

I take a long breath before speaking. "I was terrified to leave my house because I was blamed for something I didn't do. Brainwashed to believe that it didn't matter what the truth was. I didn't want to come out here tonight, but I heard what was going to happen. Then I saw other people fighting with their voices, and I couldn't let that be ruined. Then nothing else mattered. Not federal agents sent here or even who the president is. My voice, your voice, our voice . . . matter."

Someone yells out, "Justice for George!" and I yell back at the crowd, "Justice for George. For Breonna. For Ahmaud." *For me.*

The crowd rushes with an energy that's intoxicating. That empty hole in my chest fills with hope and conviction. Cameras come closer, reporters asking me questions about Mr. Whitaker.

"Hear the truth from his daughter," I say, touching Sierra's pocket where she's kept the letters.

Sierra's body is rigid as she steps closer, pulling out what must be Eric's letter. She unfolds it before speaking.

"My brother wrote this letter in case something happened to him. In case . . ." Sierra's voice chokes.

I mouth, *You got this.*

Then she begins reading.

" 'If you're reading this, things turned out badly for me. I'm sorry. I promised myself I was gonna do right no matter what happens. I guess I failed, but I still want to fix things. Make sure you get this out to the police, tell them everything. Tell them about the abuse, the punishments. Tell them . . .' " Sierra sobs as she reads Eric's letter, choking between words. And the truth is, so do I, because Eric's voice rips through his letters as she speaks.

" 'Tell them how Mom locked us in the car for a silent death by carbon monoxide and we're only alive by chance. That Dad threatened the Gustafsons if they tried to fight for us. But most of all, tell them Andre wasn't behind the robberies. I, Eric Whitaker, have been going to parties and stealing whatever I could find because I was so desperate to get enough cash to start my own life. I tried to do it the right way, by selling my art, but who am I? I'm a nobody. So here's my confession. I'm going to hide all the money so I can take it to the police station to turn myself in. My parents are dangerous, no matter how much they try to hide it. I know what they're capable of.' "

The letter goes on, but I'm stuck on the knowledge that even when Eric wrote this desperate letter, he stayed loyal to me and Gavin as well.

Sierra's hands clutch the letter as cameras flash. She shields her eyes to block them. Then steps back when she's done. Tucking all the evidence away as she answers question after question. CNN has a field day because they just had her dad on as a guest.

March organizers pull Sierra aside to talk with her. Then they speak with the media, answering questions about the allegations that there have been infiltrators. The boy taken by agents steps up to tell his story.

Sierra is now steady and calm. Then I scan for Luis and Kate. They're silent, huddled together.

"I'm proud of you," I say, wrapping my arms around Sierra.

"What should we do now?" she says.

"We do what you wanted to do. The bridge."

Sierra wipes her face and lets go of me. Then she opens her arms to Luis, who crashes into her.

"Is it over?" Luis's voice shakes.

She touches his face. "I need you to do something important. Call this number. He's a lawyer. I got it from the organizers. Then take everything to him, tell him our story, and give him Mom's suicide letter."

"Shouldn't we take it to the police?"

Sierra shakes her head emphatically. "I can't hold this with me now. You gotta take this to him. Just in case."

I wince at her words. She's still in danger. I look over at Boogie, don't even have to tell him to make sure the package is delivered.

"Got you," Boogie says.

"Where are you going?" Kate says.

"I'm going with Andre." Sierra turns to me. "We can still make it to meet Terry." She points. "We're crossing the bridge. Go with Luis, make sure he's okay."

My phone pings with notifications, including news media commenting on my page, wanting to talk to me and ask questions about what happened.

"So you're an activist now?" Sierra says.

"I don't think that's what I am. But I showed up. I get it. What about you? You okay?"

"The truth is all out there, and it feels good . . . even if that means . . ." She doesn't finish. We know what it means for Eric.

I'm taken up by the chants, which seem stronger than before. We blend in with the crowd, still keeping a watchful eye. *Justice, justice, justice.*

For George.

Justice.

For George.

"I can't go home," Sierra says halfway across the bridge.

"I know." I put my arm around her as we walk.

I'm flooded with emotion about what Eric's letter also means for him. We've been searching for him and haven't caught a clue to where he's at. And everything points to Eric being gone for good. Sierra and I catch glances. Her eyes tell me she's thinking the same thing. I know I'm in shock, but I also feel like I've been building to this. That I knew this was where we'd end up. The reality of all that punches me hard.

"What about Eric?"

"Not now," Sierra says. "I just want to get you home. Then make sure my parents pay for what they did. I'll think about Eric later. . . ."

Her voice trails off.

"You think they'll clear your name?" she asks. "Then you won't get in trouble for coming here tonight?"

Everything has gone against me, no matter what I did. When I thought I was doing the right thing, things got worse. Part of me believes I took this risk because I was already on the path to being locked up. A path that was set before I was born a Black boy, with a one-in-three chance of being jailed in my lifetime. But that's not destiny. It doesn't have to be that way if we all fight against this.

"I don't know," I say. "What are you gonna do?"

"I don't know where I go from here, but I know I can't go back. I don't ever want to go back to before. But, Andre . . . I wasn't ready to have my life blown up like this. There will be so many questions." Sierra touches her arm, where underneath her sweatshirt bruises carry stories I'll never know.

I pull her hood up to stop the rain from pouring down on her.

"I'm sorry. I don't even know what'll happen. But what I do know is you don't deserve that. No one does. And taking it on alone, by yourself, it wasn't okay."

"I don't know either," Sierra whispers. "I don't know how to feel. There's relief. I've wanted to leave for so long, and I stayed because of Eric. But then he left without me. I was hanging on for him. Whatever it took. And now Eric might be . . ."

"We don't know for sure. Let's keep hope," I say to comfort her.

I hold her tight. Then she gazes up at me. "Let's finish the moment of silence for the bridge demonstration. Then figure it out after."

"Bear witness."

"Bear witness," she repeats.

IN THE AIR TONIGHT

June 2, 2020

A crowd of a thousand covers the bridge. There was a buzz of noise just minutes ago, and now their voices are a hush.

"Eight minutes and forty-six seconds for George Floyd," an organizer yells out. Sierra gets down first. The cement's cold and wet pressed on my body, but it feels solid, like it's holding me up.

The second I focus on the demonstration, I think about all the Georges, the lives taken away. I blink hard to stop the tears at the instances that felt too close to me, to the people I know. Then my thoughts go back to George. I think about how long that time must've felt to him while people watched helplessly as his breath was stolen from him.

The rain dumps on us, testing our commitment. The only sounds are trucks lining the exits from the bridge so we're forced to exit away from downtown. I reach for Sierra's hand. When we're linked, I let go of the fear.

I can feel her pulse through my fingers as I rub her trembling cold hand. Then I listen to my heart pound as I think about my own life. When I felt so alone on trial, like no one cared. Not school. Friends. Teachers. I'd given up on trying. I just wanted to survive in a world that was prepared to hate me so much. But for the first time in my life I don't feel alone in the world. I feel a part of it as much as I can breathe this fresh air, this crisp night as the rain baptizes us. A rush of possibilities takes over. That maybe my fight doesn't have to be alone. I turn to Sierra, her eyes blinking bright at me, wild frizzy hair peeking out from under her beanie. We take it all in. And for a moment I forget about the repercussions of my decisions.

When the time is up, an eerie silence takes over as a rush of hope floats across people on the ground. Taken with emotion, but also taken with the community in the making.

"Will you be in my bubble?" I whisper to her.

Her eyes crinkle and she lets out her sweet laugh. "Does that include a lot of kissing?"

I strip my mask off, then move toward her. She leans in closer, letting me remove her mask.

I cup her ears with my hands. My feelings caught up in my throat before kissing her.

The earth shatters.

It's like I'm clipped from all the times I've dreamed about kissing her, now hitting me all at once. Without any of the guilt lingering on Grandpa, on Eric, or even Kate. And it's more than I can describe. Everything is cold except her lips, which are warm and soft.

Sierra fills every empty feeling that's been burying me. By the way her body trembles, she never wants me to let her go. Nothing else matters as I take her in kisses, which carry me through the fear of what might be on the other side of tonight. There's no going back for us. All my feelings out on the table.

A crowd of people around us whoop and holler. Someone yells, "It's that YouTube kid and his crush, Sierra Sierra."

Sierra pulls away, laughing. "We should go. Let's get you home before I lose you. We've got things we need to sort out, but I need you here with me to do it. No more missed moments."

The unspeakable threat of Jim coming for me shakes me into reality. We slip our masks on, joining the crowd, which is now walking at a quick pace as more officers with riot gear and gas masks line up.

"Andre, they're making everyone get off the bridge." Sierra points.

"Let's hurry. Stay close." I take her hand, leading her to the other side of the bridge, dodging people. I don't want this night to end in tragedy.

The pit of my stomach tightens as people close in, frantic.

Sierra tenses too, making it harder to move forward. I can see that her fear is taking over. As she freezes I flounder on how to help her. Then I get an idea.

"Put your earbuds in," I say.

I put mine in and she hesitates, confused.

"Let's play a song, live." I pull out my phone.

"Right now?" She shivers, eyes tearing.

I flick through song choices, rushing to get her out of her anxiety, which could stop her from moving. I pick Phil Collins's "In the Air Tonight."

"Just think about the music," I say.

When the music drops, slapping that intro, Sierra's eyes relax. Her mood lifting as I drown out the fear with music. Hoping that's what will carry us out of here.

Her eyes crinkle and her face goes back to normal.

"We're getting out of here safely tonight," I say to my channel.

My numbers have grown to a million followers as notifications go off that I'm live again, the viewers tuning in.

The music slaps, beat after beat.

I check out people putting in their earbuds, tuning into my channel. But this time I don't have a reaction to the song, this time it's the soundtrack to what's happing tonight. The moment to be with Sierra, the moment to be free, unafraid.

We weave through the crowd as the music continues. When the mouth of the bridge opens up, we run at the throwing of tear gas, batons shoving people in different directions. Sierra screams and I tug her closer so I take the brunt of bumping into the people.

"We can't get there from here," Sierra says, pointing to the direction of our meet-up with Terry.

I see twinkling lights flickering in the distance like a road map to our way out.

"There."

Then things clear. It's like the earth is on our side, because while the tear gas spreads, the rain pours down harder, dousing the gas so it's ineffective. The wind floating the gas back on the officers and agents.

I turn up the music to drown out the screams and shouting as we run through the streets, weaving and bobbing. When we reach a clearing, I jump on top of a car.

"What are you doing?" Sierra asks.

"I want everyone to remember tonight. Remember we weren't afraid."

My comments fly up, filling my screen as the music plays.

I record people as they run, but not forever. They'll be back tomorrow. And the next day. But tonight, we retreat, because we still won. We let the world know we're stronger.

42

THA CROSSROADS

June 2, 2020

We reach a quiet side street under construction. I search for the closest street number. When I see 1369, I go left for the numbers to get higher, leading us to the entrance of a lit-up walkway built like a tunnel for workers to pass through the building site safely. Countless twinkling lights lead us to the exit.

"Through there," I say. "Then we cut over two more blocks."

"How do you know?"

I don't answer, because I just know. When we reach the end of the block, across the street sits Terry in his car. He whips the car around when he sees us.

The ride is filled with Terry asking questions, but he quiets when we get closer to my home. I place my arm protectively over Sierra's shoulder when we turn onto our street. She glances at her house, shaky at all the lights being off.

But it's Cowboy Jim on my porch that makes me tremble. When Terry parks, he doesn't let me out even as my curfew passes.

"You're within a hundred feet of home. Just wait," Terry says. The longest five minutes of my life passes before he speaks. "Let's go."

Kate pulls up with Luis and Boogie. But she parks behind us instead of at her house. Then we get out.

"Did you—" Sierra runs to Luis.

"I called him, and we dropped off the letters," Luis says.

"What is going on?" Grandma J cinches her robe. My parents step outside. Dread builds as I realize it's so bad that Dad called Mom at work.

"I can explain."

"I'd love to hear it." Jim steps closer, gripping the backpack I should've tossed.

"No," I can't help but say. I tug my hair, breathing heavy as my throat closes. *I can't go back to MacLaren.*

I study my dad, then look back at Terry. I want to stutter out an excuse, but they've seen the news. And none of it matters, not even with the backpack. Not even with Eric's confession letter.

Headlights flash over us. I shield my eyes from the glare of a car pulling up. Seconds later, I recognize Marcus.

"Glad you finally made it." Jim lifts the backpack up with a cocky grin. "You know what your boy has in this—a whole lot more evidence of robberies."

I can't hold myself up any longer. I fall to my knees, automatic. My life flashes in front of me. This might be the last time I see them all, with me free, for a long time.

"You got a warrant for that?" Marcus asks.

"It's not his," Terry says.

Marcus and Terry give each other a knowing look. I stand when Terry signals for me to get up.

"I got the info you needed," Terry tells me. "I've watched all the video footage. The backpack found when he was arrested wasn't his."

I'm stuck with what to say to him. Does any of that even matter if the other backpack was in my house? I can already see officers building an elaborate story with the district attorney.

"I don't need a warrant," Jim says. "I'm allowed to do visits, especially after a dead ankle monitor."

"He trashed your room and found that under your bed." Dad's voice is icy, but I don't know if it's for me or for Jim. Probably both.

"I can explain," I say again.

Marcus approaches Jim.

"He's going away for a long time," Jim says.

"For the backpack you planted?" Marcus says. "Because that's what I'm going to tell them." Marcus turns toward us. I flick my head between Marcus and Terry.

"You see, after hearing about your call with Mr. Whitaker, I did some digging on you," Marcus says. "You entered yourself as my replacement without supervisor approval."

I put two and two together: Marcus believes me. Then I step closer, ready to twist this back on Jim.

"I heard your call earlier today," I say. "And there's a lot of dirt I'm sure Mr. Whitaker will say about you. Who do you think's more at risk, you or him? Because it's clear you've had a thing for me a long time, and I bet you helped him set me up."

Jim gets flustered, cursing, but I can tell his heart isn't in it.

He's scared. He gawks at the Whitaker house like there's rescue there, but all lights are off and Mr. Whitaker's car is gone.

"I think you should go," Marcus says to Jim. "And why don't you leave that with me."

Jim glares, twisting his mouth. "I don't think so."

"Okay, then explain what role you had in the altercations downtown."

"I had nothing to do with that."

"Bet Mr. Whitaker won't say that," I threaten. "You don't think he'll roll everything back on you?"

Jim reluctantly hands the backpack to Marcus and gets into his car and drives away.

"Thanks, Marcus." My shoulders relax.

"It's not over. There's still some explaining you need to do," Dad says.

Mom cuts him off by going in to hug me first, then gives them an abbreviated rundown of events.

"I knew it." Grandma J shakes her head.

"What were you thinking, going live?" Dad says. "That'll be used against you for breaking curfew. It's things like this that make it hard to believe you when you say you had nothing to do with that backpack."

"I can help with that," Marcus says. "You'll have to trust me, though."

The way he says "trust" definitely makes me not trust him.

Terry speaks. "Andre asked me to go by my office to check the card swipe system for who visited the gym New Year's Day."

"What did you find?" I hold my breath, hoping he came through.

"Neither Gavin, Eric, Paul, nor Mr. Whitaker stopped by. But

I did get a lot of guest passes with everyone starting their resolutions." Terry lets silence hang.

"And?" I say.

I hear Brian's voice behind me, coming from the Whitaker house.

"It wasn't Eric who put the backpack in your locker," Brian says. "It was me."

"No. No. No," Sierra slowly repeats, pulling in closer to Luis, who flinches at Brian's words.

I jump up, ready to lunge at Brian, but Terry pulls me back.

"This isn't how we're gonna do this," Terry says.

"I swear I thought I was helping." Brian doesn't even acknowledge me. He's explaining to his siblings.

"Why would you do that?" Kate says.

"Dad said Eric was in big trouble. That he could do ten years. He said he knew how to fix it, that he tried to reason with Eric to turn himself in. But he wouldn't. Dad said I could help to reduce the sentence. When he gave me the code, I didn't know it was your locker. I did what he said. I thought Eric could beat it with Dad getting him a good lawyer."

My throat is raw. The only thing that stops me from taking Brian down is Terry's hold.

"Then why'd they arrest me?"

"Dad must've called a tip in and said it was yours. I didn't want to believe it, and I couldn't say anything or else I'd be caught up in it too. But after that call, the way he's been acting lately, I knew he lied to me." Brian's voice lowers in shame.

"What'd Eric say about this?" Sierra's voice shakes. "He was okay with this plan?"

"He was. . . . Well, I mean, Dad said he was. I thought that was the reason Eric didn't come back. All this time I swear I thought you knew, that any day now Eric would come home in his bright yellow car because Dad fixed everything."

"I went through Eric's locker," I say. "It had all the stolen stuff there. Eric didn't know about your plan, because if he did, the first thing he would've done is have you empty his locker."

The conversation stops, everyone thinking through reasons. I began to doubt Eric's loyalty when Mr. Whitaker started getting in my head, but I knew deep down that he wouldn't betray me. That's why I protected him. Eric tried to protect me, too. And it might've cost him his life.

"Eric isn't coming back." Sierra begins crying. Her siblings look confused. They just haven't pieced it together.

They start to argue about what they think happened to Eric. Brian is the only one convinced Eric is in boarding school.

I study Luis, always the tiebreaker, the one put in the middle to make the split.

He shakes, tears coming down his face.

"Luis. It's gonna be all right. We'll figure this out," Brian says.

"You can't stay with your family. Stay with us," I say. I don't know if that's true, but I look at Dad and Grandma J, hoping one of them agrees. They have to.

"Eric isn't coming back," Luis squeaks out so quietly I can barely hear him. "I got home and the house was quiet, except the banister was broken. They didn't know I ditched you guys when you went to the concert in Seattle."

This admission sucks the air from us.

"Why didn't you say anything?" Sierra says.

"I . . . I didn't know what was going on. You know how things get, so I went straight to my room."

You can hear a pin drop, it's so quiet.

"What did you see?" Sierra says.

From the ghastly look on Luis's face, I know what he's going to say.

Sierra looks at me, then back to Luis.

"They were arguing. I could hear them in my room. Then all of a sudden, it was silent. Dead silent. I was too scared of what that meant, so I climbed out my window onto the roof. Dad came out to the backyard, piling all of Eric's things and Mom's robe in a metal trash can. Then he set it on fire in the backyard. All I saw was a tarp, but I couldn't see what was under."

There's a collective gasp. When I watch Sierra's siblings, there's sadness, but not shock. Not like how I feel, not like how my family looks. This isn't a surprise to them. This is something they know their parents are capable of.

"Please. No," Brian says, then sits next to Kate, holding her hand.

All of us hang on Luis's words.

"I was worried they'd see me, so I snuck back in my room. Then Mom came in, shocked I was home. I heard them whispering behind my door."

"What did you do?" Sierra says.

"Nothing. I was scared and pretended to be asleep. I threw my headphones on and stayed as still as I could."

"Did you hear Eric?" I ask.

He shakes his head. No.

"Did they leave?" Sierra asks.

"No. They were outside. Then they went to bed. When I woke up, Mom was sitting in my chair, watching me. She was shaking, saying she didn't know I was home. She told me Eric left. That he wouldn't be coming back."

"Why didn't you say anything?" Kate says.

"People leaving is all I know." Luis looks at Sierra. "You know how it is growing up in foster care. People always leave, gone for good. You never see them again. Even siblings . . . I just wanted to believe Eric did the same."

I can see why Luis wanted to believe that. He's fourteen, a kid—like all of us. But you can't explain why they'd burn Eric's things. Why they'd act like he took everything when they knew there was a chance he'd come back for Sierra. No, he would certainly come back for her. And the reason he didn't is because he couldn't.

"This is enough to help. Then the police will investigate and find Eric. Make your dad pay for all the abuse." I turn to Sierra, then to my mom.

I expect someone to say something, agree with me. But the Whitaker kids are silent, hollow.

And I finally realize I was wrong all along. It wasn't Mr. Whitaker.

"Your mom," I whisper.

Sierra cries. I wait for somebody to say I'm wrong. Nobody corrects me. "All this time I thought it was your dad who was . . . abusing you." My voice cracks.

"He just covers it up," Brian says. "He's the fixer. Thinks he can solve everything."

Mr. Whitaker covered up the incident in the garage. Got the

hospital to stop investigating. Threatened their former foster parents and pushed through an adoption to keep the secret within the family. Then there's me, a lawyer, and a story about Eric to go with it. All to keep the image going.

"Maybe he did pay off Eric," I say desperately, now realizing maybe Mr. Whitaker isn't capable of murder and Eric will come home soon.

"My mom didn't call Sierra," Brian says. "She told Dad she'd call us to come home the night of the protest on the bridge. She told me to stay home and called Kate, who was with Luis. But she didn't call Sierra—I watched her. I checked her phone."

"She called you, right?" Kate turns to Sierra.

Sierra shakes her head.

"What are you saying, Brian?" Kate says. "She probably thought we called her already."

Luis steps in closer. "The night Eric was home, it was just Eric and Mom in his room. They were arguing. I heard a thud and then it was silent. And a few hours later Dad came home and Mom and him were arguing outside. I think she hurt Eric. . . ."

"And your dad covered it up." I think the unspeakable—Mrs. Whitaker killed Eric.

"We need to involve the police," Marcus says. "Let them investigate this along with the rest of what was discovered tonight. We need to act quickly, though, before Jim covers his tracks and gets to Mr. Whitaker."

"What about my son?" Dad says.

I glance up at Marcus, hopeful.

"Remember how I said you gotta trust me," Marcus says to me.

I back up until I run into Terry, who is rock-solid, not moving.

"I need to take you in," Marcus says.

"What? No!" I yell out.

Everyone speaks up, and Mom starts crying.

"You broke perimeter and monitor-charging rules. I can't deny that. It's protocol." Marcus pulls out a plastic zip tie. "I'm sorry I have to do this."

Marcus gently takes my wrist, but it's worse than officers doing it. It's betrayal, after everything we've heard.

"Do you really have to do this?" Dad says.

"Jim will make claims about why he was here. He'll try to place blame. My word can't go against him if I don't follow protocol. I gotta bring you in. Have a hearing with a judge where I can give my recommendations. That's how the juvenile court handles it with mediation decisions. I promise you, this is the worst part about my job. I don't want to do this."

"Don't take me back, you can't. Marcus, please. Please. No," I sob, snot coming out of my nose. I can feel my eyes reddening.

Then Marcus takes me to his car like the cop he pretends not to be.

LIKE A PRAYER

June 4, 2020

I'm furious at Marcus, but my anger slowly wears off two days later. It's still there, but I'm at least talking to him again. Mainly because I knew the risk of my actions and went through with them anyway. The whole ride, I expected Marcus to be taking me to MacLaren until a courtroom visit. Neither happened. After Marcus filed paperwork at his office to send to the Youth Authority, they let me go back home because of COVID restrictions.

Marcus has stayed in contact ever since, and I've been begrudgingly accepting his coaching help. Along with my lawyer. My new lawyer, that is. Even though I trusted my previous lawyer, I couldn't take the chance Mr. Whitaker didn't have influence on him.

I sit in a conference room in front of a computer screen, my dad and my lawyer by my side. When we log on, the first person I see is Marcus, dressed up in a black suit and purple tie. I tighten up when the title *Director of Oregon Youth Authority* pops up on the black screen. But I let out a long hopeful breath when I see she's Black and maybe, just maybe, I'll catch a break.

My lawyer promised this isn't a court session but an evaluation by the judge of my situation based on new evidence. That they could end, add to, or reassess my community monitoring agreement.

Dad gives me a look that says this could be a good sign. I'll have a shot to tell my story.

When the judge comes on-screen, it doesn't feel like court. I'm relieved all they're doing is providing written statements. I repeat in my head my memorized statement, hoping it's enough.

"Is this statement accurate?" the judge says to me.

"Yes, ma'am. I mean, Your Honor."

Then the judge speaks to the director, who oversees state placements. "Do you concur with the recommendation?"

"I concur. This looks like it's still Multnomah County jurisdiction. With the pending investigation about the other party, we would recommend maintaining the current monitoring plan under Marcus Smith's care until we learn more about the claims concerning Eric Whitaker."

I squeeze Dad's hand, trying to keep my face calm.

"I agree," the judge says. "We will need a new monitor to avoid the charging issue. And, Mr. Smith, no more evening approvals during a pandemic . . . or downtown during a protest."

"The situation unfolded quickly," Marcus says. "I believe his actions were stress-related because of the family's recent recovery from coronavirus, Andre learning of the circumstances that led to his ultimate detention, and, of course, the uprising on these issues that deeply affect him. I'm confident that with the support of his parents and myself, things will be resolved even before this six-month window."

"Absolutely, Your Honor," I say. "The circumstances, I didn't realize they would . . . uh . . . get out of hand."

The judge shuffles papers and takes a long breath before speaking. "Well, it's settled. Young man, I hope the next time I see you, this will be all cleared up. But until then, let's stay out of trouble."

"Yes, Your Honor."

Then the Zoom ends. I relax my face only after I'm certain it's over.

"That's it, right?" I study my lawyer.

"For now. I'll be working with the prosecutor on appealing your situation with this new evidence. I'm hoping we can handle this quickly."

I bow. Like, literally bow, because we can't shake hands.

He chuckles, but I don't care.

Part of me believes the judge knew Marcus was lying about approving my evening involvements, but the news has me painted like a hero, uncovering corruption and scandal, so I'm the least of their worries.

As we head to the car, Marcus texts me.

Marcus: 👊

Marcus: I know you mad, but I had to follow protocol.

Andre: Ok.

Marcus: Nah. You gonna give me more than that. Hit me up with a fist.

Marcus: Come on.

Marcus: I'm waiting.

Marcus: I could go on like this all day.

Andre: 👊

Marcus: There you go. Give me some.

Marcus: 😄

Dad drives me home, and it's like, I'm traveling with him, but in a fog. Unsure if it's safe for me to relax. Safe for me to believe that this could soon be all over.

We approach my grandparents' street, which is blocked off.

Dad pulls to the side and parks.

"Let's walk," he says.

Hesitantly, I unbuckle my seat belt.

"It's not for you, son." Dad grips my arm and gives it a reassuring squeeze. "I didn't want to tell you before your hearing, needed to see it myself to believe it."

Dad points to the Whitakers' house, which has been taped off. We walk closer to an officer, and Dad shows his ID, which gets us past the tape near police officers and media.

A solemn crowd gathers down and around my block. My live recordings going viral not only amplified what was going on in Portland but put a laser focus on Mr. Whitaker. Each day some investigative reporter has called, but I've mostly ignored it, since I wanted to have the judge's decision over.

Luis's iconic picture became a story about Mrs. Whitaker and the day she stayed in the garage with Eric, Sierra, and Luis.

The rumors are that she's behind Eric's disappearance as well. There was another report about social welfare never interfering and allowing the Whitakers to adopt Sierra and Luis after the garage incident. Through all of this, the Whitaker kids have watched news reporters camp out on their lawn, the kids packed tight like sardines in my grandparents' house until the state can decide what to do with Luis, since Sierra, Kate, and Brian are all now over eighteen. What I've been waiting for is the cops to show up and drag Mr. and Mrs. Whitaker away like they dragged me. They drove to the police station but made bail the same day because all the police really have is suspicions and a phone call where Mr. Whitaker had information but didn't act. They cooped themselves up in their house.

So I watched. And I waited.

All these years I looked across the way at the Whitakers like they had everything. I was jealous too many times. Envious the kids didn't have packed bags like me that rotated between my parents' apartment and grandparents' home. And now everything's come tumbling down after years of hiding behind climbing roses and walls filled with secrets.

On my lawn, Mom and Grandma J huddle with the Whitaker kids. On the other side, behind the tape, where Sierra and I used to meet late evenings, are the Whitaker parents. Free, but I'm hoping not for long.

I join Sierra, shoulder to shoulder, as the police search the house and survey the garage and backyard.

"They issued a warrant finally," Sierra says. "They've been here for hours trying to find any clue about Eric."

An officer stands on the roof, scanning the yard like Luis. He seems to be doing the last observation, because nothing's been found.

Mr. and Mrs. Whitaker stand by, watching the inside of their house be tossed, boxes of files from the study removed, all while their kids watch too.

"What happens now?" Sierra chokes out, and I take her hand.

We've been preparing for the worst. Mixed emotions ricochet through us all. Part of me feels sick thinking that they did something to Eric, but there's no other way to explain his sudden disappearance. I study Luis, who now looks so much younger than when I saw him climbing on the roof.

He saw something. I just don't think his brain will let him put together the pieces.

I let go of Sierra and walk over to an officer to make sure they're not giving up. But when I approach, I freeze. I'm struck with fear, stuck on piercing eyes I'll never forget. It's the same officer who pulled me down onto the street the night Marcus had to save me. He doesn't seem to recognize me, but I flash back to that night and retreat like a wounded animal. I move so quick I trip, landing hard on the ground. And then it's like I'm back to a few months ago, being taken away by more officers. That night flashes in my mind, being dragged by an officer and fixated on the Whitaker house with Eric standing by. I shot Eric a look like I'd protect him.

Except this time when I look across the way, it isn't Eric. It's the Whitakers' front porch I see.

I know I'm tripping, but something scratches at the back of my mind, wanting to reveal itself. It was dark that night, and now in broad daylight there are people surrounding the house, the chaos of shovels, officers, a digging truck. But something is off. It's like the same feeling I had when I came home for the first time with Marcus and noticed the view from my bedroom window had changed. I thought it was just the mark of a continuously changing city. But it was more than that. I didn't know how to sift through it all. Until now.

I pull out my phone and go to my channel, watch the live recording of my arrest from my laptop positioned in front of the window just to catch better Wi-Fi at the time.

Sierra and Luis circle around me as I stay on the ground, holding my phone out in front of me so I can compare the video to the Whitaker house.

I play the video, focusing on the image that's not sitting well with me. I study how my head passes by the window. Then I freeze the image.

Long after I'm gone and in the police car, the video records Eric standing in the shadows, watching the officer drive away. He's just a small sliver, barely noticeable before the computer was closed by my grandpa. But it's what I needed to unlock the memory of that night, and so many nights when I watched Sierra run to my window.

Eric had stood in front of his house. I'd turned off the video before I was out of view, after the officers threw me in the car and drove away. But this time I let the camera roll and watch Eric pace back and forth. Things flash back at me, the way I gazed out of the police car as Eric watched with desperate eyes. That moment haunted me for so long. It was my last image of home, leaving my block. But it seared a picture in my mind that doesn't match what I see now.

I get up off the ground and push past mostly masked officers to talk to the one who seems in charge. He's waving at everyone to pack it up and go.

"Excuse me," I say.

Following my line of sight, I blink like I did that night, picturing where Eric last was. But instead of Eric standing there, there are rows of roses, tall and rich in color, climbing up a trellis by the porch. To the right stand the Whitakers, clutched in each other's arms, relieved that the officers are leaving. Then I think about Mrs. Whitaker's daily gardening, her pacing when the kids were out, her chaotic energy in the study. Like she was possessed with guilt.

I run toward the trellis, ignoring officers who yell for me to stop.

"There! He's there—under the roses!" I yell.

I look toward Luis, then Sierra.

"The roses. The roses," I say as officers tackle me. My head pushes into the dirt, but I don't stop moving around, yelling, "They buried him!"

Within seconds, Sierra is running toward me, screaming at the top of her lungs. She grabs at the ground and starts digging with her hands around the roots of the rosebushes.

Mrs. Whitaker runs to her, ripping at her arms to pull her away. Sierra backs up, retreating, clawing at the ground, blaring out Eric's name.

The officers let go of me to help Sierra. I follow after, dropping to my knees when I reach her. Cuts slash her arms from jumping into the rosebushes.

"The roses—when did they come?" I size up Sierra's siblings.

Luis comes closer, whispering, "The next day. There was a tarp in the back, then it was gone, the hole filled and then the roses planted."

An officer looks at Luis, and Sierra crumples to the ground.

The Whitakers are furious. But behind that fury I recognize another look. Fear.

The officer whistles. "Get me a shovel."

A police van is opened and out come supplies for digging. Before they plunge into the ground, I yell, "Wait! Be careful. The roses. If he's there, she'll want to keep them." I point to Sierra.

The officer nods, and Sierra drops the clump of dirt from her hands. I help her up, wrapping my arms around her and kissing the top of her head as we back up to give them space. Her siblings act as a shield as we watch. But my eyes glance between Sierra and the Whitakers. The look in Mrs. Whitaker's eyes is a fury of anger and disbelief. She looks up at Mr. Whitaker and he looks like he's already thinking of a plan for how to handle this.

Halfway through digging, the soil is suddenly too easy to pull up. I watch the frantic digging of one man slow and become more careful. You can feel something happening. The camera crews move in closer, panning between us and the ground.

I look past them, trying to remain strong.

I hope to find Eric so he can be at peace, but at the same time, I hope I'm wrong. That he pulls up to the house any minute. But each time I blink, I see Eric, standing where the roses were.

One officer signals to another, who then pulls out the crime tape and says, "We got something."

KISS FROM A ROSE

July 6, 2020

The Whitakers haven't said a word since their arrest. They lawyered up and are awaiting a trial date, which includes bail consideration. So far, they're denying any involvement. Saying it's a setup. That someone else was involved, knew Mrs. Whitaker would be planting roses and placed Eric there. It's a shaky story that no one believes.

Since the cops finally finished collecting evidence, their house is free for the kids to move back to. The Whitakers gave Brian the house, but the kids banned the parents from ever coming home. Even with that, they've yet to stay there. Brian filed for guardianship of Luis. I don't know how this is going to work for the Whitakers. The state agreed to drop any charges Brian would face for putting the backpack in my locker if he testified against his parents. They thought giving him the house would help. It didn't.

Every morning I wake up thinking about Eric being found, and I can't help but feel there's more I can do. To bring closure, because the way it's going, I don't know if the Whitaker parents will ever admit what happened that night.

Sierra fits her body snugly in her favorite chair in my room, giving me flicks of her brown eyes.

"You know I'll go with you," I say.

"I can't go inside. Never again."

"I gotchu." I kiss her lips, then take her key and head to her house.

You'd think after breaking in multiple times I'd feel more comfortable walking in with a key and permission, but I don't. A cold rush prickles my neck each time I go up the stairs, and each time, I expect something to pop up and surprise me.

On Eric's door is police caution tape. We've avoided his room, but today, I'm drawn to face my fears.

I step cautiously, darting my eyes around. Last time I was here, I was after clues to where Eric went. This time, what happened to him.

The room is still emptied out like before. I almost turn back, but then I think about Mr. Whitaker. His holding his hands to his head, glancing down to the floor. I mimic him, his exact posture. *What were you thinking about?*

My eyes draw up to Eric's cabinet in front of me. Off-center, but nothing that would tell me if it was like that before.

I plant my feet firmly on the floor.

Perfectly shiny wood floors. But the finish is duller at the edges of his room. Like it'd been scrubbed more than the rest.

Then I know. It happened here.

An accident.

An attack.

Something violent.

Something that caused them to remove Eric's gray shaggy rug.

Then I make a call to the lead investigator on Eric's case.

―

MOM'S REPLANTING ROSES alongside the Whitaker house. Sierra smiles as she places a rose on a small pile on the ground by the bushes.

"You're late."

"You started without me." I kiss her. Then give my mom and Grandma J a hug.

"She didn't want to wait any longer," Mom says.

A car pulls up and Sierra runs toward her last foster parents, the Gustafsons. She's been staying on their farm a lot lately. I think in some way, she feels like she's honoring Eric. They gave her a home to always be able to run to, but she plans to find her way on her own. Part of it's about the option to choose her family however she wants to define it.

The Gustafsons join us. There will be a service soon, but Sierra wanted to do something special. Cleanse the house by bringing friends to say goodbye to Eric.

Grandma J says a prayer as she burns sage. We replant the

rosebushes that were uprooted last month. There was conflict among the Whitaker kids about whether to keep them, but this time Sierra was the decision-maker. Part of Eric was in that earth that grew those roses. They had to stay.

The Whitaker kids take turns covering the roots with dirt, then stand back as Sierra pours water over the bushes.

I stand shoulder to shoulder in a circle with the Whitaker kids. Silently waiting for everyone to arrive. Boogie, then Gavin, and finally Paul. Each time, they slowly approach, testing if it's okay to be here.

We share stories about Eric and make promises to him about how we'll live our lives.

"I promise to take care of my siblings. Watch out for Sierra. Be better in knowing my privilege, even if it's hard for me to get," Brian says.

"You were the best big brother to me. I promise to watch out for the family and never forget about you. I'm gonna make you proud," Luis says, chewing gum to curb the nicotine cravings.

Kate takes a long pause and shares, and we go in a circle. I'm close with the family, more than ever, but things between me and Kate are broken. But we can't be cool to each other. It's now an understanding between us: we work together for Sierra, Luis, and Brian. I'm good. When Marcus took me home after Cowboy Jim threatened me, Grandma J handed me a sealed envelope from Kate. It was a long accountability letter filled with apologies, but I haven't read it yet. Don't know if I ever will. I heard she's going through therapy for all the family dysfunction she wants to unpack. I'm thinking about it too, for everything I've been through.

For the things I ignored—how it felt to be accused and pulled away from my family for those months. For losing Eric. For Grandpa.

Each time we go around for Eric, I pass, mustering up the perfect words to say. Sierra passes too, smiling through the tears in every round.

Finally, I'm ready to speak to Eric's memory.

"I'm sorry I couldn't see past my own experience to know something was wrong with your parents. There are so many things I wish I could say to you. I've replayed all the times that maybe you wanted to tell me what was going on, every time I should've noticed your pain, or the ways you acted out because of wanting to get away from your parents. I wish I'd known how to help, so you wouldn't feel like you needed to do it all by yourself. Face your parents. But I promise to remember you. I promise to be a good friend to the people around me. To be there like a brother to Luis for you. To watch out for Sierra. To speak up when I know it's needed."

I choke up at the tears that are streaming now as I think about Eric. Each word confirms he's gone, but I won't allow it to swipe my memories of him. "Every time I go into a corner market, I'm gonna think of you. The way you liked to get to know the workers, so they'd remember your face. How you always dropped coins in the donation tub, even when you were broke. How you complained about my YouTube music channel but made sure to comment on every single video. I promise not to forget any of that. I promise to tell people about you. I'll say you were a great teammate, even though you sucked at basketball. How you always rode with me, no matter what. Even if you knew it'd risk your own safety." My voice trails off because I have so much to say. I'll save it for another day.

Gavin waits the longest to speak.

"I should've been there for you," he says. "It hurts me to say it, but I knew you had more to lose than me each time we went to parties. I egged you on, knowing deep down it wouldn't be the same for us if we got caught. You were my best friend, and I wish I was a better one to you. I wish I'd known how to help." Gavin goes on, sharing old stories about all the good times that somehow bring us back into a place filled with more good than bad.

When it gets dark and everyone is gone, Sierra and I remain.

EPILOGUE

August 2020

Dad parks in front of the house before he plans to head back to the bookshop, which is in a much better place. We've touched up the mural and given the carved wooden door a fresh stain. The Black relief fund helped bridge us out of debt. Business is steady and Dad's been renovating by adding a new coffee corner and stage area ready for talks when this is all over. For now, we let Black organizers use the space for free.

The summer still unhinges me. School's over, a time to heal. But the aftermath is such a tidal wave I've barely scratched the surface. Because, well, there's still a pandemic. There's still a news cycle that any moment things can turn with this virus. There's still a fight for equality as the country reckons with race. On top of that, Oregon wildfires waft heavy smoke expected to drift our way and keep us in our homes as thousands of acres burn.

All of that wraps itself around me and has become a condition of my life. But whatever I do, I'll never accept that I can't strip away those layers for my own liberation. All that I'm dealing with has pieces of me, but I won't let it take all of me.

So I take it slow. Day by day.

"You sure you want to stay for college?" Dad says, leaving the car running as Sierra waits on my porch for me. "The shop is doing great. You have the money now for school."

"I'm sure. It'll be remote for a while—I can't be locked up in a dorm somewhere doing online classes. This way, I can go to Portland Community College and stay home, earn money."

Dad thinks I'm still worried about his health, and I get it. After all I've been through, you think I'd be the first one to leave this place. Just be happy that the Whitakers are going to pay for what they did to Eric, to me, to Sierra. But my story here isn't done, even if Morehouse College offered me a full ride.

If you asked me a year ago what I'd do if I was headed to an all-Black male college with Spelman women right next door, I'd be on the first plane out of Portland. Especially now that I can fly without the tight pull of an ankle monitor tethering me in place. But Atlanta is so far away right now. After losing my grandpa, I'm not ready to leave my family, not during a pandemic. The possibility I could be stuck because of restrictions suffocates me. I'm free now, physically and psychologically, mostly. And I want to keep it that way. So if staying close by gives me the illusion of freedom, then I'll take it. I'm holding it down here, to be ready for whatever happens next.

"Promise this isn't because Sierra will be going to University of Oregon?" Dad looks over at Sierra.

Since she moved out to stay with the Gustafsons until she starts school, her visits include staying with me at my grandparents' home, where my parents and I have moved permanently. We're no longer looking to find a new home in Northeast. We're planting ourselves where we've always belonged. Sierra almost couldn't afford to go to college after what happened. Word got out that Eric had an art website and bids went hella high, but Sierra could never sell his art. So a GoFundMe page was created that covered four years' tuition and room and board.

"No. I promise. Things are still going to be remote and masked, and I'd rather experience college the way I imagined it to be. Morehouse said I could transfer anytime. I just want a year to be present. Make sure I'm whole when I go to college."

Dad leans in for a hug and I wriggle out, but not before letting him know I really don't mind the attention.

"I'm proud of you. Terry's new program will make a difference here."

Since my record's been expunged, Terry asked me to help him start a diversion and community program for Black and brown kids. These options are limited when you get referred to juvenile authority, which is why the Cowboy Jims of the world so easily divert white kids into resourced programs and send kids like me to detention. They haven't seen us do well in alternative places because those weren't made for us. Marcus got a grant to work with Terry on this new program, which will have a counselor, a social worker, a college program, job corps options, and classes. It will also have an advocacy program to combat the profiling that happens in the schools. But I also told Terry we need a place to gather, so that those who're looking for that community can still find it in Northeast. All that is worth staying for.

Dad pulls away and Sierra waves for me to meet her in the backyard. This time I'm not on curfew, this time it's a celebration. I'm officially ankle-monitor-free with a record cleared up showing my innocence.

"You good?" Sierra says as she lays a blanket on the ground.

"Never been better."

We lie back. The trees near our houses are filled with lights I've strung up.

We lay on the grass, kissing and catching up. On all my youth advocacy work in the community with Terry and Marcus, and Sierra shares what she thinks college life will be like in the pandemic. It's all a lot we're dealing with.

But when we're here, with each other, everything releases. Feeling chained up, monitored, erased, it all disappears. And I have love. Joy. Hope. Just filling myself up at every moment I can. Because here, in the night, it's just me and her, staring up at the roses, watching them as if they are dancing across the stars in the sky. Bright and seen and never forgotten.

ANDRE'S PLAYLIST

Don't Speak — No Doubt

I Can't Go for That (No Can Do) — Daryl Hall and John Oates

I Belong to You (Every Time I See Your Face) — Rome

Sweet Dreams (Are Made of This) — Eurythmics (Annie Lennox and Dave Stewart)

Juicy (Don't Let 'Em Hold You Down) — The Notorious B.I.G.

It Was a Good Day — Ice Cube

Lost in Emotion — Lisa Lisa & Cult Jam

Poison — Bell Biv DeVoe

Still D.R.E. — Dr. Dre

With or Without You — U2

When Doves Cry — Prince and the Revolution

A Change Is Gonna Come — Sam Cooke

Killing Me Softly — Fugees

All Through the Night — Cyndi Lauper

Holding Back the Years — Simply Red

Smooth Criminal — Michael Jackson

Inner City Blues (Make Me Wanna Holler) — Marvin Gaye

Let's Stay Together — Al Green

Joy and Pain — Rob Base & D.J. E-Z Rock

Losing My Religion — R.E.M.

Every Breath You Take — The Police

I'll Be Missing You — Puff Daddy (featuring Faith Evans & 112)

Two Occasions — The Deele

If You Think You're Lonely Now — K-Ci Hailey (of Jodeci)

Starin' Through My Rear View — 2Pac (featuring Outlawz)

Put Your Hands Where My Eyes Could See — Busta Rhymes

Dream On — Aerosmith

Creep — Radiohead

U Can't Touch This — MC Hammer

Livin' on a Prayer — Bon Jovi

Ex-Factor — Lauryn Hill

You Got Me — The Roots (featuring Erykah Badu)

Can We Talk — Tevin Campbell

Don't Stop Believin' — Journey

Ready or Not — Fugees

Everybody Wants to Rule the World — Tears for Fears

Only God Can Judge Me — 2Pac (featuring Rappin' 4-Tay)

2 Legit 2 Quit — MC Hammer

Set It Off — Strafe

Don't Believe the Hype — Public Enemy

In the Air Tonight — Phil Collins

Tha Crossroads — Bone Thugs-n-Harmony

Like a Prayer — Madonna

Kiss from a Rose — Seal

AUTHOR'S NOTE

In the midst of a scary political time and a worldwide pandemic, often the last thing on a writer's or reader's mind is bearing witness while they are going through what can only be described as collective trauma. In the early months of the COVID-19 pandemic, so much of my writer head was telling me to find something joyful or escapist, but I kept thinking about the need to mark this time while it occurred. To give space to everyone who needed to process what we were going through, what others might have experienced in real time. Because every day I meet young people who want to understand and be seen.

The pandemic was (is) terrifying. It has at times felt like the end of the world. Like we're in a war with our morality, our humanity. The delayed response to the pandemic and the politicization of vaccines and masks have caused countless deaths. As I spent eighteen months working at home remotely because of the pandemic and watching my kids go through early elementary and finishing middle school, their own processing of this experience was largely silent. I needed to write to the experience of Black and brown people, to shine a light on the people who were disproportionately impacted physically and psychologically. During the pandemic, these communities not only faced COVID; we also shared the loss of some of the most traditional moments of our lives—graduations, dances, weddings, and, yes, funerals. All of this while witnessing this country's racial reckoning.

I needed to write to the Andres of the world. The readers whose lives funneled through the prison pipeline. Who regularly faced prejudice and injustice and didn't want to protest, just wanted to fix the things happening in their lives at that moment. I wanted to show that kind of bravery and how beauty can be found in our darkest moments. The effects are here and now as I write this, and if my book can help spark some understanding, advocacy, or change, then I've done my job.

As I am writing this note in late 2022, over a million people have died from COVID-19 in the United States, and nearly 100 million people have been infected, and counting. After more than two years, with schools and universities across the country physically closing, so many people have experienced loss, stress, and challenges in managing their lives and the obligations and realities that come with them. We received some relief with the creation of vaccines and the slow rollouts that followed. But the world still makes this political; our recovery will be decades in the making. Generations will suffer grievous damage. And the global pandemic rages on with new variants as the virus continues to spread.

This book touches on history, and the past is still very present.

We carry our histories with us, and we're as much a product of our predecessors as our communities are. Portland, Oregon, is the whitest city in America. The city's racial makeup is intentional, crafted in state legislation written in the books as Black exclusion laws.

The story of the dam bursting in Vanport, flooding the homes of and killing Black and poor residents, is true. The story of the Black movement to the Northeast is also true. The themes I've written about are like a time capsule of Portland, of the country, of my experiences and observations. I've taken much of my story from the headlines, starting with the failure to prepare the country for COVID. The images I've depicted of Luis and his transracial adoption capture the essence of the story of Devonte Hart, whose photo went viral in the first iteration of BLM protests in 2014 when he hugged an officer. In 2018, he and his five adopted siblings were presumed dead after their parents intentionally plunged their SUV off a hundred-foot cliff. On several occasions the siblings had gone to neighbors asking for rescue from abuse. Sadly, all bodies have been recovered except for Devonte's. We can't know our future if we don't know our past.

Those affected by these events in Vanport still live in Oregon. My husband's grandparents came to Oregon in the 1940s from Louisiana to work on the railroads. They settled on the only property Blacks were allowed to live on—the outskirts of town in Eugene. His grandmother now has sixteen great-grandchildren and three great-great-grandchildren, many of whom still live in Oregon. Our generations are still very much a part of those histories shared throughout Oregon.

This book, much like my novel *This Is My America,* has many central themes—with wide-reaching commentary and thus an even wider resource and reading list to prepare. I write complicated stories with interwoven themes that can't be neatly resolved in reality or adequately covered in a book. But I believe that's the beauty of fiction modeled on reality. The students I know aren't perfect packages of a few things happening in their lives. They are complex and should be shown as such. I touch on transracial adoption—done poorly and well—and poverty, gentrification, multigenerational homes, racism, the juvenile justice system, mental health, depression, consent. On top of family, love, hope, and forgiveness. May this book be a conversation starter, sparking talk about a multitude of topics and experiences.

This book is fictional, but the people I write about can be found everywhere.

With love and gratitude,

Kim Johnson

RESOURCES

Oregon Racial History

Alana Semuels. "The Racist History of Portland, the Whitest City
in America." *Atlantic,* July 22, 2016. theatlantic.com/business/
archive/2016/07/racist-history-portland/492035.

University of Oregon Research Guides: Anti-racism: Race in
Oregon. researchguides.uoregon.edu/antiracism/oregon.

Youth Incarceration

We'll Fly Away by Bryan Bliss

We Were Here by Matt de la Peña

Monster by Walter Dean Myers

Just Mercy: A Story of Justice and Redemption by Bryan Stevenson

Dear Justyce by Nic Stone

Punching the Air by Ibi Zoboi and Yusef Salaam

Juvenile Youth Advocacy

Juvenile Law Center. Youth Advocacy. jlc.org/youth-advocacy.

Gentrification

Evicted: Poverty and Profit in the American City by Matthew
    Desmond
Take Back the Block by Chrystal D. Giles
The Education of Margot Sanchez by Lilliam Rivera
*The Color of Law: A Forgotten History of How Our Government
    Segregated America* by Richard Rothstein
*Race for Profit: How Banks and the Real Estate Industry Undermined
    Black Homeownership* by Keeanga-Yamahtta Taylor
This Side of Home by Renée Watson

Transracial Adoption

Adoptee Reading. Books Written and Recommended by Adoptees.
    adopteereading.com.
All You Can Ever Know: A Memoir by Nicole Chung
*What White Parents Should Know About Transracial Adoption:
    An Adoptee's Perspective on Its History, Nuances, and Practices*
    by Melissa Guida-Richards

ACKNOWLEDGMENTS

The pandemic began to change our lives in 2020 in ways we may never fully account for, on top of a tumultuous political and social upheaval and reckoning with race. I captured what I could process at the time to bear witness. Through fear, loss, and achievements, this book was there for it all.

Thank you, God, for watching over me and continuing to guide me in my purpose and my calling. I have so many people to thank:

My heart, Kevin, Westley, Joelle: Thank you for your love and for being there through all my involvements and writing. My mom and sisters/cousin, who share their love and support in everything I do, Mom/Annie, Kalizya, Kawezya, Kanyanta; my dad, I'm still heartbroken that the pandemic delayed my regular visits until your unexpected passing at ninety years young. I never imagined, writing in this novel about Grandpa

Jackson, that I would experience saying goodbye virtually in the same way.

To my extended family, and friends who are like family. My nieces, nephews, baby cousins, all destined for greatness. Cousin Sue Hutchinson for those homemade dinners. My cousins Nikki and Ethan Thrower, our conversations and your love of the Northeast Portland community you grew up in shined so much light in the story I wanted to tell.

My incredible Penguin Random House family, you make everything possible, especially Barbara Marcus, Michelle Nagler, Lisa McClatchy, Natalie Capogrossi, Kristin Schulz, Emily DuVal, Adrienne Waintraub, Caitlin Whalen, Jenn Inzetta, and Barbara Bakowski.

My amazing design and cover team, Ray Shappell and Michelle Crowe. Chuck Styles, for giving me two of the best illustrated covers out there (I said what I said!).

My publicist, Kathy Dunn, who is an amazing person and champion.

My copy editor, Barbara Perris.

My editor, Caroline Abbey, for all your advocacy and your ability to ensure that my story shines through in the way I intended it to be told. Thank you for taking a leap with me in shifting my would-have-been-next novel into the future and letting me embark on the pandemic book that was on my heart and my mind! I'm so grateful to be able to work with you. Sara Sargent, your added guidance and support ensured that my book was carefully carried through the entire process—it was seamless, so thank you. Lois Evans, I am so thankful for your powerful eye, notes, and conversations that let me unpeel all the layers, especially as I worked to add more nuance to my story. What a gift to have had the chance to work with you.

My film and TV agent, Mary Pender, I am honored to have my work represented by you because you see my stories for so much more.

My literary agent, Jennifer March Soloway, you are so supportive of my work and my writing, always cheering me on and having my back! There is nothing I can't share with you. Thank you to everyone at Andrea Brown Literary Agency, who I know is right there with me, always.

My field experts, Nakeia Daniels and Andre Lockett from Oregon Youth Authority. Thank you for providing me more context and understanding of a complicated system. Our community is lucky to have Black change makers like you in the system. Andre—I can't believe my luck in finding the real Marcus Smith in my community.

My amazing writer friends—there are too many to count, but especially to Namina Forna, Christina Hammonds Reed, Kelly McWilliams. Your stories and friendship mean so much to me. Nic Stone, for your wisdom and support. Yas M. for your keen eye. To Jennie Komp, our journey began with our love of the CW's *Supernatural* and writing. Thank you for all your assistance and support this past year! You have been gracious and kind, and a dear friend. All the many writers, readers, bloggers, booklovers, teachers, librarians who show love and support.

My work family, Oregon 6, senior leadership team, Hiroe and Ellen. My students, my mentees, and my sorority sisters in service.

To TwinsthenewTrend, your epic excitement listening for the first time to Phil Collins's "In the Air Tonight" brought me pure happiness from your Black boy joy. The scene on Burnside Bridge with music playing flashed through my mind and *Invisible Son* was born.

To all those touched by my work, whether because it showed pieces of you or moved you in some way, I see you, thank you!

ABOUT THE AUTHOR

KIM JOHNSON held leadership positions in social justice organizations as a teen. She is the author of *This Is My America,* which won the Malka Penn Award for Human Rights in Children's Literature and the Pacific Northwest Book Award. She is a vice provost dedicated to transformational experiences for the next generation of leaders. She holds degrees from the University of Oregon and the University of Maryland, College Park.

kcjohnsonwrites.com